Author Elizabeth Gowans has led an extraordinary life. A Londoner, she has an honours degree in Psychology and speaks several languages including Japanese.

She has lived throughout Asia, South America and the USA earning her living as (amongst other things) a teacher, a court interpreter, a legal adviser and a Buddhist nun.

Since starting full-time writing in 1978, she has seen much of her work produced, including radio plays for the BBC, plays for the fringe theatre, an award-winning television play and a television mini series which screened worldwide.

By the same author

A Woman of Good Character

ELIZABETH GOWANS

Where Two Roads Cross

This edition published 1994 by
Diamond Books
77–85 Fulham Palace Road
Hammersmith, London W6 8JB

A Grafton Paperback Original 1988
Copyright © Elizabeth Gowans 1988

The Author asserts the moral right to be identified
as the author of this work

Printed and bound in Great Britain

Set in Sabon

To Philip Carlson

Part One

Chapter 1

In the weeks following Ceci's return to Hexham she made strenuous efforts to overcome feelings of shyness towards Ginger. That he had grown into a fine man, stronger and more in control of his life than when she had first known him, she could see. That much self-examination had gone into his pursuit of her and that he was aware of the great demands their coming together had created was equally clear. Given their years separated by a chain of mountains, was it surprising there should be gaps between them? Gradually, though, the familiarity of the old house and surrounding landscape together with the presence of the nearby village of Moke combined to produce within Ceci a sense of inevitability, of having come home. In bed now in the house, Hexham, she marvelled at the tremendous arc she had travelled since meeting Ginger and realized with a jolt that it had been her own pride in the first instance which had forced their lives to grow in different directions despite always pulling back towards each other.

She remembered now the day she had stepped ashore in New Zealand, a lonely immigrant, little more than a child. What a disappointment it had been to be allocated to Reg Bowen and transported to the remote High Country! She had hoped the situation of waiting on him, his aged father and simpleton brother would be temporary, but events there had come to dominate her life. Ginger had spoken to her as they passed through Moke on the way up, she recalled. He had even said Reg was 'all right': not the word she would have used for a man who had gone on to rape then abandon her. How different things might have been had she had the courage to speak up about her circumstances to Ginger then! It was shame that had led her to marry Reg's father, Old Bowen, and that was the truth. Shame and convenience. Pregnant and spoken for she had watched Ginger fall into an arranged marriage with a local girl, Maureen, and as the years passed, however distant, had known she was a magnet dragging at their marriage until, after an extraordinary occurrence, the unfortunate woman had taken her own life. Now, turning to Ginger and seeing the love break in his eyes, she decided to set the record straight.

'You once asked how I could marry a man like Old Bowen . . .'

'You said you could marry whom you liked,' Ginger reminded her.

'It took some effort – Reg had raped me. He felt I'd stay with him because no one else would have me – '

'Reg Bowen raped you?'

'I said I'd tell the buyer he was selling off diseased sheep – '

'Your daughter – Olwen – is Reg Bowen's child?'

'You didn't think she was Old Bowen's?'

Ginger got up. 'You could have told me anytime between then and now . . .'

Ceci shook her head. '*You* could have guessed when you found me crying at the boundary fence!'

Ginger stood by the window. It had taken them half a lifetime to come together and he wasn't getting bogged in the past now. But if he had known! It had been his obsession with Ceci that had forced her to flee to hardship on the West Coast rather than countenance his infidelity. And it had been his dismay at not knowing her whereabouts which had caused the breakdown of his vulnerable wife.

10

Coming to stand next to him Ceci leaned on his shoulder.

'I thank God for you . . .' Ginger told her.

'And I you,' she replied, her eyes drifting to the fences of their sheep station, stretching beyond them to the horizon. As Ginger went downstairs Ceci raised the window to let in the air and sounds. How often with joy, as dawn crept over this very sill, had she lain listening to Ginger's family awakening round her? A door would close as Faith, the eldest of his daughters now that Lizabeth had gone, left her room. At fifteen Faith was a single-minded girl. In fact the more Ceci watched her moving about the house the more she became aware of her striking physical resemblance to her mother, the dead Maureen. But there the likeness ended for while Maureen had been unstable, Faith had such a hard shell the best Ceci could sense beneath it was a coolness and indifference. Presumably girls of Faith's age liked their privacy, yet the feeling no one was close to Faith and that she knew nothing of her persisted. Lizabeth had been noted for being the eldest, Michael and Kevin as twins and Myra as youngest. But coming between the twins and Myra, Faith had slipped notice. Indeed the only image Ceci could recall of her as a child was when she had shouted: 'You're not in charge!' and snatched a tin of sweets from Lizabeth. And there was a question! Like all Moke Ceci knew Lizabeth had 'run off with a man' and the fact that Ginger had not gone looking for her made folk wonder if there were more to it . . . But though she would love to have known, Ceci had not pushed the matter.

Descending the great stairway to the hall her fingers glanced on a set of initials carved into the banister. It was a far cry from the days when *she* had been mistress of Hexham. How the floor had shone and the silver gleamed! How the beautiful old Imari china had stared back at her

11

and the Bokhara and Kashmir rugs had known their exact dimensions and lain there, never a hair out of place or visitor to tread on them! Despite the dejection of those days the abuse the house had suffered in recent happier times saddened her. Though he had bought Hexham for her, Moke's Protestants did not regard Ginger as owning it. Rather they saw the house as having 'fallen to Catholics', a breed they considered had a marked disregard for material belongings.

Even after her years of absence she knew people regarded *her* as the mistress of Hexham, conveniently having forgotten her own rise from absolute poverty to become the wife of Calvin Laird, Hexham's one-time owner. That he had scarce bothered to enjoy her none had known and she had felt herself fortunate as a young widow to find such a situation. Yet it had been hard: and all the time there was Ginger on the outskirts – multiplying. One thing was for sure, she thought, remembering those days: Calvin's mother would turn in her grave at the idea of either she or Ginger owning Hexham. It would have given Calvin a nasty lurch to even *think* of Catholics in the house, for the situation between Catholics and Protestants then, as now, at times resembled a muted civil war. The communities did not mix or marry. They chose different names for their children and even at a distance of yards could tell by their clothes or carriages their differing allegiances. Irish, of course, like Ginger, were presumed to be Catholics – and she, being English, a Protestant of some sort.

As she passed the open front door she looked out on Calvin's lawn, awash with weeds but still recognizable as a lawn. It had been his greatest achievement; an amazing sight and reminder of refinement in this wilderness. But with finality Ginger's horde had trampled his garden, run amok amongst his formal borders and the imported English roses he had tended so carefully. His mother's currant bushes had gone the way of all things but her annuals came up as remembrances of her.

Entering the kitchen Ceci found Ginger walking with his breakfast in one hand.

'Get those boys organized today,' he promised. 'Get things moving.'

Ceci smiled. Had he been talking about horses it might have been different but at sixteen twins Kevin and Michael were interested in neither girls nor working the land. It was odd Ginger had not noticed.

Stepping out for Moke's store she saw Theresa making for her across the field and, though she knew the conversation would turn quickly to the topic which fascinated Moke, she stood waiting.

'How old are you now?' Theresa enquired.

'Thirty-four.'

'John the Baptist's mother was fifty-seven when she had him!' Theresa encouraged.

'I know you find it remarkable I haven't already conceived but – '

'You say no whenever you feel like it,' counselled Theresa. 'Doesn't do them one bit of harm.' She waited. 'Too many women afraid to say no and that's the God's truth! In case they get thrown out. And their men only do it to get back at them!'

'Nice talk for a Catholic,' Ceci teased. 'Last week you said I'd be better off raising pigs!'

'You're a hard woman!'

'I haven't any secret if that's your meaning – '

'Well *there's* the way to end up with a string of them!'

'I didn't say we were trying – '

'You make up your mind before getting into bed,' Theresa admonished. 'Unless he's made it up for you.'

13

'How do you mean?'

'See these beads,' Theresa said, holding out her rosary. 'Here now . . .' She began spreading the beads on the back of her hand.

'If you start *here*, the first day of your bleeding, even in the dark you could tell when to be careful.' She slid her fingers over the beads. 'Now if he's wanting a child, *these* are the days he'll be having you.'

'And I thought you used them for praying!'

'No harm in asking! And no harm in knowing when to say no!'

'Maybe he doesn't know about the special days –'

'Depend upon it he does!'

On the way home Ceci thought. There had been days when Ginger had 'avoided' her but she had not given the matter much thought; much less noted which the days were. That he might privately be using some chemistry to prevent a child cast a shadow over their open friendship. Until now she had been happy with his family; happy that her own child, Olwen, was starting out well in the North Island. The possibility that he could have taken a decision without consulting her was ludicrous but she would certainly give the beads a try.

As she closed the last boundary gate on their land she saw Tommy Houlihan skipping towards her.

'Yev a carriage at your place! Yev visitors!'

'Are you sure, Tommy? I didn't see the trap –'

'From the trunk route!' Tommy shouted.

Because it was unusual for a hired carriage to turn off the route between Christchurch and Otago Ceci hurried on. People tended to rely on smaller conveyances to transport them beyond the main road so this meant either an important visitor, a face from the past, or, more likely, that Tommy was mistaken.

Entering the gates of Hexham and seeing the way in

14

which the gravel had been scudded she realized Tommy was right. Clearly a four-wheeled conveyance had arrived which implied several persons or a person with baggage.

'Olwen?' she cried, running into the hall.

'Sssh!' Myra motioned, finger to her lips, ear pressed to the drawing room door. 'It's Lizabeth – Father's furious.'

Ceci reached for the door handle but Myra stayed her hand.

'So your home is here now, is it?' Ginger was demanding.

'It's my life and I shall do as I please!'

Ceci blanched. At eighteen, exactly the age of her own daughter Olwen, she could hardly argue with that.

'You might take an interest in them!' Lizabeth accused.

'Those children will be fostered out.'

Ceci gaped.

'Little twins,' Myra whispered.

'I have a right to come back and stay or leave as I choose!' shouted Lizabeth. 'And the right to bring my children with me and take them away again!'

There was a brief silence then a muttered word from Ginger that sounded like 'bastards!'.

'Such a welcome!'

As Ceci and Myra looked at each other Ginger opened the door on them. 'I don't want either of you speaking to her,' he said, striding past them.

'We have to!'

'Nobody is to speak to Lizabeth,' Ginger repeated. 'While she's here Faith will take her food and attend to her. In the room at the back. Whatever she needs – washing water, anything you have to buy her . . . I don't want Moke knowing she's here.'

'Too late for that!' Ceci said sharply. 'They've seen the carriage.'

15

'It isn't fair him keeping us apart like this,' Myra protested as Ginger frogmarched Lizabeth up the stairs, her mites struggling in her arms.

'Give me a chance,' Ceci whispered.

'It won't make any difference,' Kevin assured her. 'You don't know how angry Father is about Lizabeth.'

'His favourite,' Faith said drily.

'Mind you, he won't learn anything Lizabeth doesn't want to tell him,' Michael grinned.

When Ginger came down Ceci tried. 'You must let me talk to her.'

'You know nothing about this.'

'It was she who welcomed me when I came to your house that first time. If it weren't for her I would never have gone in.'

Ginger frowned.

'And I think you've forgotten how good she was to you,' Ceci went on. 'Who was it looked after you all when Maureen died? Who raised Myra? Who gave you the courage to come seeking me? Who never criticized *your* morals – '

'Stay out of this, Ceci,' Ginger pleaded.

'I'm going to her now.'

As she stepped from the room Ceci almost heard a door close between them and as each stair passed under her feet she felt the distance grow greater as the gap between herself and Lizabeth's room narrowed. But as her hand touched the doorknob and turned it she felt the rush of one human being eclipsing another.

'Lizabeth!'

The girl ran forward. 'He's very angry. We'll have to leave!'

'Let me look at you!' Holding her at arm's length Ceci noticed her stomach was bulging anew.

The girl twisted an old wedding ring on her finger and,

in a gesture which took in the infant twins wedged on the bed, patted her distended stomach and said shyly: 'Frank doesn't waste time.'

'Can I come in?' called Myra.

Ceci nodded and in the next moment the boys stepped quickly, closing the door. Despite their excitement all were very aware of Ginger passing on the landing. Conversation abruptly stopped then re-started.

'That one looks like Frank,' Kevin said, meaning the larger twin, her colouring on the dark side.

'You know this Frank?' Ceci asked.

'Seen him about . . .'

'How old are they?' Myra demanded.

'Nearly a year.'

Conversation stopped again as Ginger re-passed the door.

'The other one looks like you though,' Kevin grinned.

'I think she looks like Ginger,' Ceci said, touching the shorter plumper twin with chestnut hair. At that moment they heard Ginger on the stairs.

'I could get them some milk,' Myra said. 'But I'm afraid to go downstairs because of Father – '

Suddenly a door below banged.

'Now we've done it,' Michael groaned, walking towards the window.

'We'll go downstairs together,' Ceci said lightly, 'And continue in the drawing room.'

As the day wore on Ceci realized she had underestimated Ginger. It was as if a million years lay between them. Before leaving the house he had removed his belongings from their bedroom and installed them in a spare room. What's more, he had not come back.

'This house has a knack of driving people to sleep apart,' she told herself, trying to make light of it, but it was embarrassing, especially in front of the children at the age

17

where their ideas on men and women were developing. It was not good that they should see a grown man sulking or two adults unable to resolve their differences.

'You should all stop talking to Lizabeth,' Faith advised. 'That would do it.'

Sinking her hands into her pockets Ceci felt them close around Theresa's beads. Ginger would not come to her for a few days now: that was for sure! Maybe the Catholics were right in that God worked in strange ways but surely He did not have to provoke an entire domestic upheaval to achieve His ends?

Angry to the pit of his stomach Ginger walked the grounds of Hexham. He had hoped that if Lizabeth came back he could handle it better but his anger had overmastered him. The sight of her bulging stomach had made him even angrier than the fact of the twins or her original disobedience. He could not even say the man's name without wanting to crash a fist into his face. Much as he'd like to have been seen as 'right' in Ceci's eyes the sense of hurt would not go. That Lizabeth had gone with Frank he had known. He should have realized they would indulge themselves – Lizabeth as much as Frank – and naturally there would be no precautions. There was no solution. The children could not be fostered out for Lizabeth would not allow it. Ceci would not ignore Lizabeth's presence in the house and would lead the children against him. If she had only stood by and helped him to save face things would have been different.

Approaching the back door he heard voices go quiet in the kitchen. Now they feared him. Abruptly he turned away towards the woodpile, got out his block and despite the quantity of logs already stacked, began to splice and re-splice them.

'He does that when he's angry,' Michael explained.

'He'll go right on chopping until he feels better, then he'll come in.'

'This time we might run out of wood.'

Late into the night Ginger chopped.

'Don't listen,' Lizabeth told Myra. 'He's doing it to make us feel guilty.'

When Ginger finally came in his hands were blistered and swollen. He did not lift the cloth from the supper Ceci had left for him nor take water from the kettle where it stood warming on the stove. Deliberately treading mud and dropping sawdust he moved up the great staircase and into the small room where the listening house heard the door close. Ceci sat up in bed. She would not go to him. She would not set Faith or Myra or Lizabeth the example of climbing down when they had done no wrong, nor would she teach Kevin or Michael to expect they could get around women by sulking. With deliberate effort she lay down in the large bed, alone for the first time since their marriage, and carefully stilled her breathing till sleep came.

Ginger rubbed at his eyes: the sawdust made them itch. His hair was sticky and matted with wood dust. He had dirtied the sheets and in the morning would feel silly. Worst of all he would have to wake up alone. Somehow, he realized, he must work things out and return his household to an even keel. It was he, not them, who had been unreasonable. It was *he* who must change. With a prayer of regret on his lips he fell suddenly asleep.

Chapter 2

In the following days, Ceci observed Ginger trying to mend fences with Lizabeth. She would catch him observing the twins, wanting to be offered them but Lizabeth, it seemed, was in no hurry to reconcile. She treated Ginger coolly and volunteered the household no further information about her husband. Other than that his name was Frank, Ceci was in the dark. Nor did she feel it right to question the other children or press Ginger on the matter. Whoever he was, Frank clearly was not about to visit Hexham. Perhaps he did not even know Lizabeth was there.

As time passed and the house settled into a routine Ginger managed to sit next to Lizabeth more often, lift a child from her lap and hold it, and Lizabeth returned to caring for Myra, watchful that the girl did not get jealous of her twins. There was, Ceci noticed, a slight anger on Faith's part – presumably because she was no longer in a position to boss Myra. She did not seem to resent Lizabeth's presence in the house; rather it fired in her a disdain for all Lizabeth stood for: for her casual motherhood, her ability to fly in the face of society where her impulses were concerned, her unfair 'right' to the unquestioned affections of both their father whom she had disappointed and their younger sister to whom she was such a bad example . . . Ceci sensed Faith's disapproval even of Lizabeth's handling of her twins – her casual confidence about them.

'Take them for an airing!' she would shout at Michael and Kevin as they set off for Moke. 'Ride into town with a girl on your horse!'

As Lizabeth's stomach grew larger the fact of it happening in their family and before their eyes only made them feel the coming child would belong to them and was nothing to do with Frank. Even Ginger in his way seemed protective of Lizabeth now that there was no other man there . . .

From the kitchen Ceci watched with pleasure as the family, bar herself and the infant twins, set off, according to Ginger, to 'inspect fences'. No fences, she was confident, would get looked at other than from the safe distance of the shade of a tree under which they would be sheltering from the sun! Crossing to open the drawing room windows she stared at the haze shimmering at the end of the lawn. The day was impossibly hot. It magnified even the smallest sounds. Leaving by the back door she stepped towards the ice house Ginger had dug in a shaded spot and lined with stones and thatch. She would chip some ice off and make cold drinks for their return. Picking up a chisel she drove at the ice with it. Clunk! A slab dropped. She did not like being in the ice house alone for it gave her the shivers and she had always been afraid of being shut in there. Grasping the slab in her arms she stumbled up the stairs towards the light and pushed at the door with a foot. It clacked to behind her, then, in the silence, she heard a sound which was not an echo. Spinning, she looked around the court-yard. No one. Clasping the ice she crossed to the kitchen and was about to push the door when again she heard another sound – this time like a pebble kicked or a dropped key clattering. She stood looking cautiously around, the ice block slithering in her arms. Then came a fresh sound: a scrunching on the gravel. Quickly she ran into the kitchen and slammed the bolt on the door.

Someone was out there. She was sure. They had not called out though in these parts no one approached a house or even a work party without first hailing them. She stood listening. There came a careful knock on their front door. Taking the poker from the kitchen range she moved quickly through the hallway and, catching sight of her image in the mirror, tried to adjust it to look less frightened. Concealing the poker in the folds of her skirt she opened the door a crack to discover a powerful man not much older than she, with dark complexion but kindly eyes which fell with amusement to the handle of the poker protruding from her skirt.

'Oh!' Ceci murmured, removing it, leaning it on the wall as if it was the result of absent-mindedness. The man frowned. Now she could see it was not his eyes but the lines around them that were kindly. His eyes were, in fact, commanding and tinged with anger, or was it hurt?

'I'm a friend of the family,' he said, as if not expecting to be believed.

Ceci looked up at him earnestly.

'How are you?' he demanded.

'We – we're all fine – '

'All?'

Was she being interrogated? Although she felt drawn to the man, her sixth sense cautioned her to adopt a more formal tack.

'As we have no previous acquaintance – ' she began.

The man stepped past her into the hall and stood listening. 'Are they out?'

'You had better wait in the drawing room until my husband returns,' Ceci advised, aware – now that the man was in – she could not physically eject him from the house. 'I'll make you some tea.'

In the kitchen Ceci chipped at the ice while the kettle boiled. A glance across the courtyard told her the man had no horse. In other words he had come on foot – which could be read many ways. Even tinkers had horses. Yet, she told herself, there had been a certain quality to the man which would hardly have justified her keeping him on

22

the porch even had he been prepared to stand there . . .
She poured water into the teapot. He was a good-looking
man. That he had walked from Moke in this heat seemed
unlikely for he would have streamed with sweat. Nor,
surely, could he be roaming the countryside given that he
was clean-shaven and his hands no dirtier than Ginger's
on an average day. Had he perhaps left his horse tethered
in a sheltered spot to graze as it would? Those clinking
sounds could indicate that he had been taking a quick
splash in their water butt. There was a gravity in him to
which she was drawn. Stirring his tea she was tempted to
go in and sit with him but at the same time something told
her to stay clear away.

Opening the door she caught him standing by the
window, lost in thought. As his hands closed around the
saucer Ceci sensed a possibility of violence in them and for
a chilling moment felt he wished evil on their house.
Closing the door she hurried upstairs to check on the twins
who were still sleeping. Without asking herself why, she
felt suddenly relieved.

In the garden she set about picking flowers to arrange in
the hall to give the appearance of coolness. Whoever the
man was he would probably eat with them. She had never
come to terms with the local custom of serving hot mutton,
swimming in grease, regardless of the weather and, though
her neighbours might consider her uppity, she intended to
go on preparing such delicacies as she could remember
being served in Lord K's house when she was a child. They
took very little work, she told herself, crossing to the
vegetable plot and bending to seek a healthy lettuce.
Although on the West Coast she would have given her
right arm for a decent lump of mutton, winter *or* summer
– those days were well gone, thank God! A jug of iced
lemonade and a crisp salad was just the ticket! At a loud
shout she looked up and there, coming in at the gate, was

23

Ginger, his children bunched around him like an invading army about to trample the lawn. Lizabeth was far too pregnant to be on a horse, Ceci thought, straightening up, shaking earth from the lettuce. She crossed to pull tomatoes from the vine with one eye on Ginger as he helped Lizabeth dismount, his affection for her visible even at this distance. They could not see her amongst the vegetables yet, watching, the sight of them together was a relief to her. Deliberately she let them continue on alone and enter the house via, as usual, the kitchen door, Ginger opening it for Lizabeth, Myra trailing behind and Faith ordering the boys to 'take care of the horses'. In a minute no doubt she would hear a high-pitched: 'Iced lemonade!' from Myra, then the boys would let go the horses and dive through the door.

She was aware of silence. Quickly she hurried forward. There, in the doorway leading from the kitchen to the hall, stood the visitor, the eyes of the room on him. Ceci's hand flew to her mouth. He was talking to Lizabeth.

'I've come for you.'

Her face didn't move.

'Get the kids. We're going.'

Lizabeth sat and folded her arms.

'I want to speak to her alone,' Frank informed the staring family.

'It's *me* you'll be speaking to alone!' Ginger barked.

'I've come for my wife and children!' Frank shouted. 'You've no right to keep them here.'

'Lizabeth came of her own free will,' Faith stated.

'Shut up, you,' Frank turned on her, betraying, Ceci feared, either his true nature or the degree of stress he was suffering.

In a minute Ginger's hands were round his throat, the lemonade pitcher in pieces on the floor, slivers of glass indistinguishable from the ice. Ceci caught a fleeting look

24

of derision on Faith's face as if disgusted at Frank for being what he was; at Lizabeth for loving him and at her father for fighting.

Before anyone should notice, Lizabeth hurried upstairs. She did not want Frank putting on acts of bravado for her, nor her father getting beaten up.

'Tell them to stop!' Myra pleaded, running after her.

'They'll feel better after it,' Lizabeth said. 'But don't you watch.' She crossed to the landing. By now the men were brawling on the lawn.

'Your man will kill my husband,' Ceci said, arriving by the window.

'My *husband*. Not my man!'

Below Ginger struggled to his feet, having fallen and struck his head on a bird bath.

'You seemed to forget him soon enough after you arrived – '

'I can't stand much more of this!' Lizabeth screamed. 'I *had* to leave him!'

'He hardly gets on with your father – '

'Father can't stand the fact they're the same age! It's his fault for making me used to older men – from when I used to look after him.'

Below on the lawn Frank gave Ginger a mighty crack which sent him flying.

'I hope he doesn't hit you too,' Ceci murmured.

Lizabeth shook her head. 'But I don't know what to do . . .' she confided. 'Maybe I should have stayed and not walked out . . .'

'Do you love him?'

Lizabeth nodded.

'He must love you a lot to fight for you.'

'Frank is – brave.' Lizabeth said carefully.

By now the men were going at each other like beggars, biting and kicking. Lizabeth passed a hand across her face.

25

'Please, please stop!' shrilled Myra, running across the lawn to the men.

Instantly they got to their feet. Slowly Frank turned his head to stare at Lizabeth at the upper window. She did not wave. Ceci saw him thrust his hands into his pockets and, still looking at Lizabeth, fling a handful of change on the lawn before Ginger. She heard Lizabeth draw in her breath beside her, sensed her sway slightly as Frank turned from Ginger and walked away towards the stables.

Behind the house Frank dipped his face in the water butt, scooped water into his mouth and spat it out. Without glancing back he headed off at an angle towards the hills.

Ginger remained shaking on the lawn.

'How could you?' Lizabeth demanded, as he poured himself a Scotch.

'Got rid of him!'

Ceci bit her lip.

'You don't think that because he comes howling around here like a tom cat you have to go to him?'

'That was my husband!'

As if sensing Frank's retreat, upstairs the twins began to cry.

'How do you think *they* feel,' Lizabeth shouted, pointing at the ceiling.

'He left because I beat him,' Ginger boasted. 'You saw.'

Lizabeth clenched her fists.

'Even threw some money on the grass towards your keep.'

'Would anyone care for tea?' Faith asked, with a detachment which suggested she was pleased at the disharmony around her. Lizabeth walked to the door.

'I don't understand your attitude, Faith,' Ceci began gently.

'Me? I can't stand to see persons throw themselves after rubbish, that's all.' Faith replied in surprise.

'Your father may have well-founded reasons for disliking Frank but surely you will allow that Lizabeth may have seen a more winning side of him?'

'He's a degenerate and wanton.'

'Faith knows nothing about Frank,' Ginger stated.

'He's a drinker!'

'I never thought to hear that word in this house after Calvin's death,' Ceci murmured.

'You ask in Moke and see what kind of faces people pull!' Faith went on.

'People have no right pulling faces if they don't know the facts,' Ginger informed her.

'Are you Temperance, Faith?' Ceci enquired. 'Using words like "degenerate" and "wanton" for human enjoyments – '

'The fact I'm not Temperance doesn't mean I agree with slovenly – '

'I forbid you to argue with Ceci!' Ginger shouted.

Faith snorted.

'I'm the one who asked the question,' Ceci said quietly, realizing she was in the midst of a family row and that, when he thought about it, Ginger would probably not thank her for taking Frank's part earlier. 'You're both right. I don't know Frank. But I found the man had a certain dignity – '

'And if you'd met him in other circumstances – ' Faith began snidely.

'That's enough, Faith.'

Smiling, Faith left the room.

'It doesn't do to talk to grown girls like that, Ginger,' Ceci said quietly. 'It doesn't work.'

Ginger walked to the door. 'Fetch Lizabeth down here. I want a word with her!' he shouted.

27

'And Ceci would you wait outside?'

As Ceci stepped into the corridor she saw Lizabeth coming down the stairs, not as a child who had been sent for but as a person with a definite opinion to express.

'Come in too, Ceci,' Lizabeth whispered. 'I'd like you to hear this.'

'Your father asked me to wait out here.'

Giving her a disappointed look Lizabeth passed through into the drawing room.

'Don't you think, Ceci, it serves Lizabeth right?' Faith queried, leaning on the banister.

'Don't you feel any affection for her at all?'

'Affection?' Faith frowned. 'I would help her if she needed me . . .'

Briefly it occurred to Ceci that Faith felt affection for no one because no one needed her.

'Listen to them now!' Faith shrugged. 'They're so ridiculous!'

In a pitch of frustration Ginger stared at Lizabeth. She was not listening, would not accept what he was saying. His insistence that he was acting in her best interests was proving as successful as in any household. Constantly she returned to the theme that she was a married woman and answerable only to her husband. And the more excited he became, the more she distanced herself until, with a coolness which hurt more than any amount of shouting, she simply left the room.

Because she did not come down for tea Ceci took it up to her on a tray. 'This is a fine situation,' she said, buttering some bread and passing it to Lizabeth.

'I gave as good as I got.'

'He's hurt.'

'I didn't intend to upset anyone . . .'

'Tell your father you wanted to punish Frank, to teach him a lesson.'

28

'Father thinks he knows all about Frank,' Lizabeth said. 'He doesn't. And I won't tell him things he can't understand.'

'Did you expect Frank to come after you?'

'Yes. And I thought we'd leave together! But Father had to be here!'

'You are married?'

'How many times do I have to get married before people will believe me? If I could leave the twins here for a while . . .'

'Frank wouldn't thank you for it.'

'Ceci, if you were me – '

'I'd do what I felt was right.'

'He *was* awful to me. Just the once. But I feel empty . . .'

'Forgive him the once?'

Entering the bedroom, feeling the day had ended on a brighter note, Ceci found Ginger rubbing witch hazel into his knuckles.

'I can't understand your disregard for the fact of Lizabeth and Frank's marriage – '

'Well, don't talk about things you can't understand.'

'We've to be an example – '

'I hope to be. And I shall see she doesn't go after him, I assure you.'

'People must get on with their lives, Ginger.'

'What did you say?'

'I said we don't do right to interfere. Now that she's married, what point is there in Lizabeth hanging around Hexham? Those are my feelings. I good as told her so.'

'You *what*?'

'Lizabeth has chosen Frank. She married him. He may be a perfectly terrible man but I have enough confidence in her judgement to assume he isn't.'

'I must ask you not to give Lizabeth advice independently of me!' Ginger urged.

'Do you want me to exist separately from your children? Like a – a – sort of horse you own?' Ceci asked. 'I am not shutting myself off and saying that because they are your children I am not concerned with them.'

'Don't make me choose – ' Ginger said tiredly.

'You already have chosen, Ginger. You married me and you're also their father. It's *you* who has to come to terms with that. Not me.'

For a while they sat in silence, upset by the fact they'd disagreed.

'You're right,' Ginger finally shrugged. 'And she's not even my child. Perhaps that's why I love her the more.'

Ceci looked at the swelling appearing on Ginger's head.

'By the time you were Lizabeth's age you'd already had Olwen. Maureen had had Lizabeth from God knows who – and our twins were on the way. Maybe she hasn't made such a bad beginning. But at the back of my mind I can't help hoping . . .' He stopped. 'Just give me time, Ceci,' he said, turning back the covers.

Ceci glanced at Theresa's rosary beads lying on the bedside table. It looked as if they would be a permanent fixture if Ginger's children were going to regularly disrupt them.

'What have you got these for?' Ginger asked.

'Nothing special,' Ceci smiled.

'Did Theresa tell you they were some kind of ornament we wear?'

Settling down beside Ceci Ginger reminded himself that again he had played an entire hand of cards very badly and achieved the exact results he did not want. 'You're going to have to give me more help with these girls,' he admitted, drawing Ceci closer. 'And I don't want Lizabeth leaving until we've cleared something up with her.'

'In the morning, we'll have a go at Lizabeth together.'

But in the morning Myra came running with the news

that Lizabeth had left and hurrying to her room Ceci picked up and quickly crumpled the note thanking her for the advice which had helped her to reach a decision. Knowing that Ginger would not be happy until he had farewelled Lizabeth properly, meaning on *his* terms, Ceci was saddened. The girl's return had made them all a deal too outspoken and her situation remained largely unresolved. Had she done wrong to advise the girl? Once married a woman should stay with her husband, surely? People disagreed and their reasons were private, but had it not been right to respect the privacy of Lizabeth's marriage? The possibility that there was something she did not know that Ginger did nagged at her, and caused her to fear her actions were not as blameless as she'd believed. Carefully closing the door to Lizabeth's room she reminded herself that the girl's visit had not ended entirely brilliantly.

Chapter 3

It gave Olwen pleasure to think of her mother happily settled in Hexham, for she prided herself deeply on her part in having brought Ginger and Ceci together again. Indeed, had she not forcibly removed her mother from Grevillton or, more to the point, taken the trouble to track down her renegade father, Reg, and investigate his old piece of land, who was to say where they would both have ended up? Still, that was the past and to Olwen the present mattered more.

True to her intention to start a new life for herself in nothing more than the clothes she stood up in, with a small sum which Ginger had advanced her, she had abandoned the South Island totally and gone north. Neither Ceci, Ginger, Reg, nor anyone she knew had been to the North Island. Nor did South Islanders refer to it in conversation. For all they knew it might not have existed and the reason for this was now very clear to Olwen. Compared with the oppressive, stodgy, church-going population of the South Island, the petty squabbles of its large landholders, the provincial concerns of its towns and the overwhelming mudslinging conservatism of its villages, it could fairly be said that the North Island knocked the South Island into a cocked hat. At least Wellington did. Set in hills like San Francisco the city was vibrant and spread in all directions, boasting busy docks, a commercial section, courthouses, government buildings, gardens, parks and numerous hotels. It even, Olwen discovered, had a notorious district where opium was smoked, a woman could lose and find herself and murders were efficiently carried out. She was quite sure Christchurch had not been similarly endowed, for the idea of anything untoward, anything with the slightest hint of savour occurring there was ludicrous in the extreme. Whether or not Wellington had a sense of propriety she had yet to discover but clearly it was in no way a mealy-mouthed town. As the seat of government it drew to itself not only the legitimate interests of Empire but a host of motley men who stood on corners shifting from foot to foot watched by scratching dogs with an eye for the next bone. It was a place where questionable types from home, literate men – no questions asked, men with pedigrees who fascinated and repelled, rubbed shoulders with those abandoning the South Island for private reasons and heading north to dig kauri gum; men who chose to be unafraid of the large Maori communities they would encounter on the way ...

As Olwen's eyes glanced from Jervois Quay up Hunter Street she sensed it was a place where a glamorous woman could become powerful. Clearly the wild and dangerous Cook Strait separated more than two islands and, by the look of it, Wellington was certainly a match for her.

She felt the money belt pressed to her body in which Ginger's allowance remained virtually untouched. Of course there had been the ticket from the South Island port of Lyttelton but again she had good reason to be pleased with herself for remembering, before boarding the vessel, to stop in at the storage yards and pick up the trunk she had abandoned there before setting off on that wild-goose chase through the mining towns of the West Coast in search of her mother. She was mightily thankful not only that no one had thrown it out, but that Ginger's allowance had enabled her to pay the dues and that the trunk's original good manufacture had protected its contents from the damp. How fortunate it was that she had been so impecunious as to be obliged to leave it in storage!

33

Unpacking it again in Wellington, the sight of the robes and dresses, bonnets and shoes delighted her and stirred memories. There lay the formal gowns designed and made especially for her by that Indian seamstress during her brief sojourn in India as the wife of Edmund. Running the gossamer through her hands brought back painful memories of the little Indian woman carefully packing her belongings for her in tissue but unable to meet her eye since she had fallen foul of the master ... She had had robes for every kind of occasion from afternoon parties on the lawn at the Governor's mansion to dinners at the Officer's Club, not to mention dresses of a more intimate nature which she had unwisely worn in the days when things had begun to go wrong and were now better not thought of. These dresses, though all that she owned, were surely worth a fortune in fashion-hungry Wellington. Was it not a fact that not a boat could put in from home without people finding an excuse to 'take a turn' along the quay and glance with impertinent scrutiny at the arrivals? The slightest adjustment in the position of a button, the number of pins in a hat or slides in a coif were instantly noticed.

Poring over the contents of her trunk in a small room in a boarding house for women run by a Mrs Griffin an idea occurred to Olwen. She would wear one of the dresses to the Star and Garter and just take it from there. No one could accuse her in a dress of that quality of soliciting. In fact there would probably be a stampede to open doors for her! The only question which really preoccupied her now was whether the Star and Garter, or Alzdorf's, or the Oriental would be the better venue, for while it was said that Alzdorf's was *the* place for conversation, the three-storeyed Oriental definitely had more style. With its popular 'shilling luncheons' it drew crowds which would make it difficult for a person to assess whether she were alone or accompanied and the presence of its two retiring rooms for ladies would provide an absolute guarantee of character for any sole lady who happened to be there. Consequently the next day saw her make a dignified entry there, her precious 'black' trailing behind her.

Although the place was unbearably crowded with some three theatrical companies, a visiting boat race team and a number of bookmakers staying, hardly had Olwen sat down than she was aware of an expensive-looking woman across the way observing her and nudging her husband. The woman leaned forward and whispered something. The man shook his head. Obviously he had been asked to come across and put a question to Olwen but in the silly way men had, was refusing to do so because it would draw attention to him. Olwen grinned infectiously at the frustrated woman. The man came over.

'If you will forgive the impertinence,' he began, 'my wife wants to know where you got that dress . . .'

Instantly the lie came: 'I made it.'

The man returned across the room with his morsel only to be sent straight back.

'And how much, if I might ask, would you charge to undertake such another?'

Olwen paused. 'You must appreciate the cloth is not readily available,' she began, wondering how much could be charged.

'I am connected with a firm importing cloth,' the man informed her.

Olwen blinked casually. 'Are you offering me a special concessionary rate?' she enquired.

'I am merely saying that I can obtain the cloth for my wife should you be prepared to undertake the dress for her,' he replied as if irritated by her attitude.

Olwen watched him return to his table.

In a second the woman had bounded over. 'When may I come for a fitting?' she demanded.

'Next Tuesday,' Olwen replied calmly. 'If your husband can obtain the cloth.'

The woman shrugged petulantly. 'Surely you can measure me at least so that we may be ready to begin when you are able!'

Olwen shook her head.

Arriving home Olwen took off and examined the dress in minute detail. She set about unpicking and measuring it, noticing little notches that matched up, chalk spots which, owing to its newness, had not been removed. In fact, on closer scrutiny the seams were so poorly finished that the Indian dressmaker must have been certain the owner would never inspect them. She laid the pieces of the dress on paper and reproduced the pattern, marvelling at how easily, with the addition of a flare or button, a style could be made different. Why, she could even remove bits from her own clothes and add them to it as 'modifications of style'. Looking at the dress in pieces on the table before her she became suddenly aware that styles catered to nuances, emphasized, flattered or disguised. Basically, then, dressmaking was a political act. Although she was far from confident that she could make such a dress (or any dress) for the woman, she did believe she could put this one back together again to her ultimate satisfaction. Further, were she to acquire a sewing machine and really put her mind to it, on the basis of the contents of her trunk she could probably come up with enough original modes to set herself in the forefront of Wellington as a couturièr or fashion designer for the better off. In the meantime more appropriate premises were imperative even if it meant a trip to the money lenders, for if one thing was clear in her mind, it was that she was coming in at the top end of the market. If it was true there was plenty of room at the bottom, there was room also at the top and it was there that Olwen was setting her cap.

In her quest for more suitable accommodation it did not take Olwen long to settle on an exclusive newly burgeoning suburb, Khandallah, on the outskirts of Wellington. A deciding factor had been that it was on the railway line, the station of Khandallah being named for the original homestead, a fine-looking building standing slightly off the track and set about with trees. In the recent past the area had consisted of country estates interrupted by the occasional dairy farm. Since sections had been put up for sale the response had been slow but now in the '90s it was 'picking up', for, distant from the trams and horse buses of Wellington as it was, Khandallah could keep a certain type of person at bay. Nor could it be said that those who could afford to live there were hard done by for, not only did the more influential Wellington stores send a man out by train to take their orders, but perspicacious Italian and Chinese vendors trekked out with horse and cart, or fruit and vegetables slung in panniers from their shoulders. Back of the suburb brooded Mount Misery, named by the sentries who had done look-out duty there in the days before the rail when the route had been used as a northbound corridor from Wellington by the military, by travellers and even by Wellingtonians escaping the Maori massacre at Wairau.

As Olwen stood on the balcony of her new home, one hand resting on her trunk, she congratulated herself that she had chosen Khandallah for not only was the mix of history and deference right but the suburb was at the same time the epitome of normality: in a word, 'respectable'. That she was in fact caretaking the house she had moved into there was no reason for anyone to know.

Peeping through their nets, while they may not have

37

approached her, Olwen's neighbours had noticed the haughty young woman who lived alone. They had also noticed the slightly older, well-heeled and somewhat impetuous Wellington lady who arrived by private carriage twice a week. At times they would see Olwen return in the carriage with her, the two women seeming to be quite friendly. What precisely went on in Olwen's house when her 'friend' visited and they vanished to the back of the premises they would love to have known but though they sought hard for ways of ascertaining the truth, as introductions had not been acquired, experience counselled patience. Meanwhile, in a spacious room overlooking a luxuriant gorge Olwen and the 'lady' passed the time as the creation for which the lady longed gradually came together.

Gwen, as Olwen was invited to address her client, was powerfully connected, for her husband Venables belonged to a group jokingly known as the 'Notables': men who, by their stranglehold on influence, indirectly controlled most aspects of the Wellington economy. Though clearly, despite a studied fussiness, she was a person to be taken seriously, it amused Olwen to see her consumed with curiosity and frustration because she was not allowed to try on even a piece of the creation that lay in maddening bits on the floor around her. Olwen had two reasons for this. Firstly she had made such a mess of the material Gwen's husband had provided that it was plain she would have to modify her own dress and present that as the finished product. She could only be thankful the cloth was so perfect a match it could have come from the same roll! To let the woman handle any of the pieces at this stage, especially those cut against the grain, would give the show away. Thus the charade continued, Olwen pinning up a section of skirt, chattering knowingly about the difference it made to fashion now that the bustle had gone out and the attention had shifted to a woman's bodice. It could truly be said, Gwen obliged by observing, that they had the medical men to thank for restoring the female shape to something nearer its God-given form. No wonder people had been constantly fainting, she added, what with the unnatural constrictions of their waists and pads on their rears! Now look at the recent fashion of blown-out upper sleeves which made women's arms resemble legs of mutton, she protested. Why, it was a wonder that women remained able to participate in sports such as tennis and cycling.

'Do you play tennis or cycle?' Olwen enquired.

Gwen shook her head. That would be going too far. It occurred to Olwen as she silently measured and pinned that she could design dresses that would reflect her customers' aspirations, their changed places in society, the fact that they had been given the vote and longed to take part in many of the things they were now permitted to . . . Such a slightly more racy line, if she could push it, might well take Wellington by storm.

'I don't usually make clothes for people,' Olwen said. 'I design them.'

This scandalized Gwen. 'Not to imply that you would need to – but with your gift – you should approach your bank to put up the finance to set you up in business,' she advised. 'You could hire girls, machinery . . .'

Olwen nodded, pins in her mouth. She could certainly use someone to cut and sew for her! It would even save her the trouble of learning to work a sewing machine.

'Now when will my dress be ready?' Gwen demanded.

Though Olwen knew it did the woman good to wait and the longer she waited the more excited she would become when she saw it, she knew there was a limit to her patience. She had yet, however, to settle on some minute way in which to change her own dress so that on the one hand the woman would not recognize it and on the other, it would have that touch that would in some way speak to the woman's soul or proclaim her inner yearnings.

No sooner had Gwen departed than it came to her. She would reflect her hankering for the forbidden joy of bicycle riding! Taking a looped bow from the front she quickly remade it as two garters of the sort men wore to fix their pantaloons above their knees when attempting the bicycle. Trying them for position, she finally attached them to the right hip, bunch of grapes fashion, and waited with confident interest to see the result. Though she liked Gwen and would love to have told her the truth about herself, she knew, were she to do so, it would cost her her future, for it was the fact that she had not actually been a seamstress that had paved the way for their friendship. Indeed it had occurred to Olwen that there might be some percentage in not charging Gwen for the work at all but simply using the situation to allow Gwen to manipulate her husband into setting her up, almost unwillingly, in a boutique.

As she awaited Gwen's arrival to pick up the finished item, Olwen found herself speculating on the progress she had made since coming to Khandallah. Because she had been deeply conscious that in the New World you are what is known about you – and how much is known is largely up to you, she had deliberately not represented herself as an individual fettered by the restraints of a previous marriage. All that was known about her was what she had deliberately let slip to Gwen, namely that she had grown up on a large sheep station in the South Island. She had had the satisfaction of hearing Gwen state that the surname she used, 'Laird', had been recognized by one of her husband's banking colleagues who had come from Christchurch to Wellington on business. This would quite have authenticated her status, it being widely known in the

Christchurch banking community that the sheep station, Hexham, had been in the hands of the Lairds ... To enhance the good, Olwen had occasionally given Gwen letters to take into Wellington to mail for her, confident that she would notice, as she was intended to, that they were addressed to Hexham.

'But I thought your mother's name was Laird?' Gwen queried.

'My mother remarried,' Olwen replied, smiling, delighted at the chance to clear that one up. 'As a result of the death of her husband.'

How true that was! It had created quite the right impression. Indeed she had been unable to resist adorning it with the addition that she had been sent 'home' to be educated – which went down very well, as did her bearing which she knew suggested gentry. All that remained now, provided the dress went over smoothly, was to allow Gwen to cajole her into a full-time situation, ideally embedded in the very fabric of Gwen's social existence and the contacts and colleagues of her well-placed, influential but tedious husband.

First should come the friendships, then the languid commitment to make other gowns, as if their manufacture were the product more of a collapse of her will under their insistence than any desire on her part to receive outrageous sums. The final freedom from Gwen's set must be achieved before the contents of her trunk were exhausted. First, however, the hurdle on which all depended: the dress. Had she succeeded in understanding what Gwen was trying to say about herself through her clothes?

When the day came Olwen opened the door essaying confidence but feeling slightly nervous and produced the dress, starched to an unnatural stiffness. She had taken the care to put extra chalk marks on seams and leave an occasional pin in to scratch Gwen's thighs.

'Ouch!' screamed Gwen obligingly.

'Oh sorry,' Olwen shrugged.

The dress on, the previously tense Gwen was in tears of joy. She spun before the mirror, turned to Olwen and clasped her hands: 'Darling!' she breathed. 'Promise me one thing! Never to wear your dress at the same time I wear mine.'

Olwen gave a small gulp.

'In fact,' Gwen continued urgently, 'Could we come to an arrangement whereby you would never be seen in that dress again? With your skills you can so easily design another and I would be only too happy to procure the cloth for you.'

Chapter 4

Despite his good intentions, since Lizabeth's departure Ginger felt he had been made a fool of in his own house and had difficulty coming to terms with it. It was common knowledge that Ceci had supported Lizabeth's case, perhaps, Ginger suspected, even urging her to leave against his will . . . Now he almost felt that showing any affection would undermine his masculinity. Though he knew his pretences to be transparent, having started on a course of distancing himself he found things had become out of hand. Further, he could not think of a way to climb down.

Turning her head, Ceci eyed him. He was awake all right – just pretending not to be. With a loud sigh she flung an arm out, letting her chest follow its motion till it came to rest facing him. She was aware her upper body protruded both from her nightdress and the covers and felt Ginger turn to look; heard his breathing change. With eyes shut, she kept up the deep breaths of imagined sleep, the communicative mattress indicating he was well awake. Ceci got up, allowing the lace of her sleeve to slip across the eyes he was trying to keep closed. She crossed to the window. How long would this situation continue? Gone were the grunts and sighs, the occasional expressions of spoken love or outbursts of waking truths which came to him with clarity in phrases such as: 'I might cut the back hedge today.' Recently she had sensed the desire for intimacy hovering in his mind but remembering the small rift created between them by Lizabeth's return, he had checked it. Standing at the window now she knew he was longing to squeeze her; to return to his waking up routine which had previously embraced her.

Cautiously Ginger opened his eyes to peer at the shape outlined against the window. He wanted her. No doubt she would dress in front of him again and he would have to pretend to be asleep. Was it a coincidence that all sorts of fetching underthings had suddenly appeared; things he had never seen in Catholic laundry baskets or on any washing line in Moke? Certainly she had been to Christchurch shopping with Faith and Myra but he had not expected to see such purchases on the woman herself! How she had got them past Faith he did not know and, harmless though they probably were, he certainly hoped Myra had not been influenced. It was maddening the way she slept beyond arm's reach so that if he 'accidentally' flung out a limb during the night it fell short. Most men, he felt, would simply have 'jumped' her while she slept but this was not a good idea for she might have considered it rape and then he'd be in deeper than ever . . .

Standing by the window Ceci knew she could take the first step but doubted the wisdom of it. With Calvin Laird she had always taken the first step simply because his anger was so unrelenting that without her continual yielding he would not even have made the small progress he thankfully had made towards becoming a decent human being before fate despatched him. But Ginger would have to choose his own time. Frequently she caught him glancing at her. In fact it amused her to go some way away from him, suddenly twirl and catch him at it.

With the fascination of a child watching a cat stuck up a telegraph pole Ceci observed Ginger's discomfort and the indifference he feigned which suited him not at all. He was on the point of jumping, she was sure, and she was looking forward to it when an event occurred which made her draw her own barricades up.

Being the afternoon, Ginger and the station hands were away and, as luck would have it, even Faith and Myra, Kevin and Michael had gone over to Moke to help get the barn ready for a midsummer dance. Taking advantage of the lull, in the cool of the pantry, Ceci was getting her jars sorted for the jam making to come, counting, stacking, removing old labels and tasting offerings pushed to the back of shelves when suddenly, to her amazement, there was a disturbance at the front door. Marvelling that anyone would dare to assault it in such a fashion, Ceci ran through the hallway and opened it on an utterly filthy man whom she took to be drunk, swearing and muttering in a broad brogue and demanding to be let in and offered refreshment. Though she could not put her finger on it, there was something familiar about him. Brusquely she ordered him around to the kitchen door but he beat her there and was already standing in the kitchen when she arrived.

'How dare you come into my kitchen!' she demanded.

'Do as I like, woman, do as I like,' the man muttered. Were he not filthy to the point that his features were indistinct she would have physically ejected him from the room.

'Now where's the best silver? Let's be having you!' he called out, walking ahead of her from the kitchen into the hallway. 'There'll be not a thing of value left in this house by the time I'm done with you.'

'Get out!' Ceci gasped.

'It'll take more than you, lassy, to make me point me boots away from ye!' the man replied confidently, tucking a silver plate inside his jacket. 'And you're taking your time with that tea!'

Ceci ran to the kitchen, flung open the back door and beat loudly on the skillet to attract attention. This *would* happen in the slow time of the afternoon when the workers

45

were far away! There was no saying how much the man would take: probably all he could carry! She hurried back in to keep an eye on him but found the front door open and there he was, vanishing across the lawn, heading for their bushes.

'Damn!' she heard herself say. Angry for not having taken a broom to him she set about checking the silver. Only the plate appeared to be missing.

What galled her was that at tea that evening none would take her seriously. Faith grinned superciliously, Myra chortled and the boys looked away in embarrassment.

'That's what you call a hallucination,' Ginger explained kindly from the head of the table, making Ceci so angry she could have smacked him.

'So where's the silver plate?' she demanded.

'Where's anything? Where's the Chinese jug?' Ginger shrugged.

At that moment Ceci decided that were he even to roll to her side of the bed that night she would have nothing to do with him. Did he really think she was the sort of person who would make up such a story to impress him?

'Still thinking of that man of yours?' Ginger teased from the bed as Ceci brushed her hair. She went on brushing. 'With those nerves you'd better sleep with me tonight,' he chided. 'Know you want to.'

'If you were the last man on the face of the earth – ' Ceci began.

'So now that I want you,' Ginger said sadly, 'You don't want me. Is that it?'

Ceci paused. 'There *was* a man.'

Their relationship might still have mended, leaving the incident little more than an irritant in Ceci's mind had the man not returned on two occasions on both of which Ginger was out. Again Ceci was not believed and again her indignation seemed to arouse Ginger to the extent that he felt moved to make advances to her in bed which she heatedly rejected. That he found her frustration cute was no basis for lovemaking: in fact it incensed her.

'Do you want me to stay home and protect you?' Ginger asked.

'No!' barked Ceci, determining next time to delay the man until someone should come. However, although she knew she was being childish, as days passed without sign of him, she feared she would lose the chance to prove herself right.

Already the matter was a dead dog, she told herself, stepping into the laundry room with a clothes basket on one arm. Suddenly she saw the man standing behind the boiler. He was so close she could see the muddy hairs on the back of his wrists. Quickly he slid the bolt on the door.

'Ginger!' Ceci yelled.

'Ginger?' the man said, as if being offered spices. 'Is that what you're wanting?'

'Ginger!' Ceci screamed. 'Quick!'

The man reached up a lace pillowcase, dipped it into a bucket of water and started mopping at his filthy face with it. Seeing him occupied, Ceci scrambled on to the bench and tried to force a window, but strong arms caught her from behind.

'Let me *go*!'

'Heard ye with me own ears,' the man laughed. 'Ye wanted Ginger! And 'tis Ginger's got you!'

Spinning round, Ceci saw he spoke the truth. 'I could *kill* you!' she shouted, relief coming as anger. 'And look at the mud on these sheets!'

Ginger wrestled her to the ground.

'And I've a couple of questions,' she protested from under him. 'Now that you're finally talking!'

Ginger flicked hair from his eyes and leaned on an elbow

amongst the tea towels. 'I did this to get back in your good books. The whole business about Lizabeth . . .'

'It's easier here,' Ceci agreed, lying in the spoiled laundry.

'In the bedroom I couldn't put it right,' Ginger went on. 'I didn't tell you the truth about Frank,' he confessed. 'Problem is – he's married.'

'Married?' Ceci repeated. 'Are you sure?'

'All the older ones around here knew Frank was married.'

'Did Lizabeth know?'

'I was asking her that very question when she stormed out of the drawing room.' Ginger sighed, rubbing at the toe of his boot with the pumice.

'But how could you let – '

'We knew she had a boyfriend. We didn't know it was him.'

Ceci pulled the pumice from him. Odd that in a place the size of Moke Ginger could *not* have known.

'Frank's a stone-mason,' he explained. 'Works for the Church Board – '

'But you don't *have* a church! You use that barn – '

'We share Moke's graveyard. Lizabeth used to go there to visit her mother's grave. Out shopping – that sort of thing. Fact is,' Ginger said, scratching his neck, 'she had a free run to do as she pleased since Maureen died. And I was grateful to her.'

He looked sadly at Ceci. 'Seems it had been going on for a long time. A certain amount of work piled up in the cemetery. Frank sitting amongst the graves chiselling away. Suppose she heard the flints flying. Or maybe he looked over the hedge which separates our part and saw her praying. Must've had a lot to think about bringing up her brothers and sisters. She could have heard a sound and been distracted by it and gone to see. Maybe he heard her

48

praying or saw her slip through the hedge. How long they met, watched each other for, I don't know.'

'If he *was* married it's unlikely he would have told her,' Ceci began, but even as Ginger picked pieces from the soap and shrugged, she felt sorry that at the expense of satisfying her curiosity, he had been caused to remember. Had it been the supposition that Frank was married that had driven Lizabeth back in the first place, only to be advised by her, Ceci, to return to him if she loved him? Yet when demanding his 'wife' the man's injured attitude had not struck Ceci as that of a bigamist.

'I had wanted more for her than to be the common-law wife of a travelling man,' Ginger said sadly.

Lizabeth's presence lingered. Why, Ginger asked, did girls with everything before them frequently throw themselves into the first pit they came upon?

Probably because they mistook it for the most wonderful opportunity life could ever hold out, Ceci replied. *She* had marvelled that her own mother could not see her good fortune in being granted an assisted passage to New Zealand and had at the time wondered why every girl in England hadn't stampeded the ship! The early arrival of her own illegitimate firstborn had seemed natural. Illegitimate? Lizabeth had insisted she was married and there had been no deceit or double meaning in the way she had said it. Had the girl meant they had been through a form of ceremony together? She was loath to raise the matter but it seemed there was more to it than had been discovered. Though they had resumed the state of harmony they had enjoyed prior to Lizabeth's arrival – in fact the disagreements had drawn them closer – she would certainly keep a weather-eye open to see what she could garner.

When they held Masses at Hexham Ginger had prayed

for Lizabeth: she was sure of it. Though she did not mind to see women praying, the sight of a man with his head bowed disturbed her. There had to be something in it, she felt, for his community did leave their services in a state of heightened awareness and were more open to each other. It was strange they were not conscious of her standing at the back observing them. Particularly she found herself noticing the children, their fingers curling patiently at shoulders, caught up in hair . . . She would watch toddlers in tiny territorial battles, reaching behind their parents to the next child, sucking the edge of the chair or fidgeting with some small item they had brought. They were learning something, watching their mothers' faces in prayer. Standing following likenesses amongst families up benches and crossing to lines of cousins, as their chairs scraped back after the service it occurred to Ceci with a blinding suddenness there was nothing she would rather do than lovingly raise children.

On the West Coast, every bit as muddy as Ginger had been, Reg Bowen slowed to wait for Annie. She had caught up with him at a pub and greeted him warmly, curious to hear any news he might have of events at Ceci's old haunt in Grevillton. Reg had told her about the union and the miners' strike, the Temperance Women, the terrible disaster at the mine which had killed so many and how the town, led by Ceci, had taken the mining company to court and won, only to have recompense snatched away when the mining company appealed the decision and were smart enough to declare themselves bankrupt while the appeal was being heard.

'What happened to Ceci?' Annie asked, for she had never got over Ceci's tremendous kindness to her, for her act of befriending her when she was homeless and maligned.

'Oh,' Reg drawled, 'she done all right. Some geezer come along, helped out.'

Talk of men always interested Annie. 'Who?' she demanded. 'What?'

'Aw – handsome bloke,' Reg said modestly.

'Can't say as I saw any man in Grevillton could rightly be described as handsome,' Annie admitted, there not having been one of them whose face was not pitted with coal dust.

'Now this fellow see, he came from the other side of the mountains and had a piece of land he give to her,' Reg elaborated.

'Oh?' Annie walked for a while in silence.

'So how come you cleared out of Grevillton?' he needled. 'First time I comes, there you was pretending as you owns the pub and trying to pick up everything in trousers – '

'Made a run for it when they caught me nicking coal,' Annie interrupted. 'We was going through hard times.'

Reg nodded. That was an understatement for what had happened in Grevillton. 'I reckon as how Ceci would be liking to hear from you,' he told her.

Annie smiled. The idea that anyone was interested in her welfare quite touched her. Indeed, in Ceci she could honestly say she had found the only true friend she had ever had. 'You got her address then?'

'Might have. Then again might not.'

Well, that was something, Annie thought, remembering when Reg had first turned up at their pub and, though he had been too proud to recognize Ceci at the time, had given the distinct impression that he knew her. She too had seemed to know and be afraid of him. 'What was between you?' Annie enquired carefully.

'She'd had my kid.'

Annie gaped. This defied even her imagination.

'When she came over here as a bit of a girl it was me

51

wot picked her up from the Immigrant Barracks,' Reg stated. 'It was me she started working for. Wouldn't credit that, would you?' Annie shook her head. 'She's back over that way now,' he said. 'At Hexham, which is next to ours.'

Listening to him Annie grasped that 'ours' was not an estate of the magnitude of the fabled Hexham but a large ditch or gully formerly belonging to Reg which lay between Hexham and the next station over. 'And how do you know she's there?' Annie asked.

'Got a letter from me daughter care of General Delivery Hokitika,' Reg said proudly.

Annie frowned. All this information coming of a sudden took some grasping but didn't it go to show that other people's lives seemed to work out a deal better than hers?

'The daughter's very smart,' Reg went on boastfully. 'Knows wherever there's minerals found she's only to write to General Delivery because I'll be along there prospectin'.'

Annie made a note in her mind to write to Ceci. If she could only get hold of a permanent address for herself, a little stability in this endless searching life she was leading . . . 'Where are you going?' she asked Reg.

'South,' he replied, busy thinking of the packets of seeds he'd purchased the day he'd gone to the Immigrant Barracks at Lyttelton to fetch 'a girl'; of how they'd shouted at each other in the kitchen and how the seeds had never got planted . . .

'Funny,' said Annie. 'So am I!'

Reg grunted.

'Mind if I come along?' she asked cheerily.

'Suit yourself,' Reg shrugged. 'No skin off my nose.'

Despite his apparent indifference to her Reg was pleased to have Annie along, for she was a good companion on the rough tracks that passed as roads, could smooth their way through many a situation and with her clever tongue had an ability to beg food for 'man and wife' when they passed through towns. For her part, though Annie was not enamoured of sleeping out under the sky, Reg represented a sort of permanence to her, a friend of a friend of a friend . . . Indeed she knew that behind his taciturn manner lurked not a little fondness for her. How to turn this to her advantage was the big question. She would go two miles with any man who asked her to go a mile if he would only treat her with kindness. Indeed she would go six miles if he would put food in her mouth! How other women made men do this for them was a thing beyond her understanding.

'Like this? Is this right?' she asked Reg, trying to draw him out on the subject of gold panning.

Kneeling in a stream Reg glanced up. The woman's knuckles were bashed. She had already knocked the head off his pick axe and was generally beginning to be a bit of a nuisance. However, no harm in showing her a little kindness. He got up, his knees cracking, and made his way over to her.

'So what you got then?' he asked.

'I mean this here.' She handed him the enamel dish she had been using.

'Can't catch much in a thing like that,' Reg drawled.

'Well, I put the big ones over there,' Annie said, pointing to a handful of pebbles and stones.

Women! Was it even worth walking over there and looking? He pushed his felt hat back on his head and belched. To take it off would mean carrying it and would cast his neck in the sun but beneath its crumpled dome his thinning hair was already stuck to his scalp and rivulets of dusty sweat were escaping where the hat didn't fit right, trickling and running down the scrawny depressions in his neck.

Annie watched him standing. 'If I were a man I wouldn't spend my life paddling about in streams,' she assured him.

Reg moved off. 'Oh? And what would *you* do?' he grizzled, fiddling with one of the pebbles she had tossed aside. Even his lucky nugget had long since gone and that had turned out to be fool's gold. In fact if someone was to turn up now and try giving him another he might just tell them what to do with it . . .

Waiting patiently, Annie saw him cock his head in disbelief and begin screwing his eyes up at one of her stones. 'What's the matter?' she called over.

'I'll be jiggered!' said Reg. 'Blimey!' He'd been fooled once. Could be he was wrong again. Annie came to stand by him.

'By the heck, girl,' Reg said, pushing the battered hat back on his head. 'You got a nugget!'

For a moment there was silence.

'What do you reckon then?' asked Annie.

'I reckon we not tell anyone about this and head for the nearest bank.'

Although Annie was pleased at Reg's use of the word 'we' she was not aware of the extent of her good fortune until her beginner's luck translated itself into a considerable sum before their eyes. Reg coughed and looked down, relieved to have been right for once.

'How come you was so straight-faced about it all the time we was carrying it if you knew it was worth so much?' Annie asked boldly.

'Didn't want to give you no ideas,' Reg said. Staring away.

Suddenly it came to Annie what to do with the money. 'I reckon we should make a stake,' she said.

'Oh?'

'I reckon this kind of wandering about is no good for

man or beast, Reg,' she said. 'Seems to me, this is a chance to "become permanent".'

Reg knew she didn't mean marriage. She meant 'settled'. 'Haven't you never been "permanent" before?' he asked carefully.

Annie grinned and looked at her feet. Indeed, for all her stories about having been married and having had three children, one of whom was drowned, another variously hit by a train or killed by a falling tree – she had never had a home or children but had merely said these things because she felt they were expected of her. The fact of the matter was, she had such a humble opinion of herself she was amazed she could get by on a daily basis. That another human being, Reg, might agree to 'become permanent' with her filled her with such joy she was almost afraid to think!

'Just seems to me a bit daft to keep wandering about when you can settle,' she said carefully.

Probably the woman was inviting him, Reg thought, scratching his ear. It was unlikely she would try anything physical with him, though. Despite having a nice chest on her. Indeed he detected in her a deep shyness and respect for men. It just went to show how little people understood the so-called 'wayward' woman hopping from pub to pub. He stretched and stared skyward. He had been on the road a long time himself; his joints were becoming ugly with rheumatism and, despite bluster, he could not pretend that fossicking was a continual source of joy. Even the luckiest of strikes were far between and, should truth be told, most of the time he was still a sheep thief and scrounger. But no need to tell Annie that.

'Now listen, Reg,' Annie said, 'I reckon we should sit down right now, here on this bit of ground and figure this thing out properly.'

Reg sat down. He thought of the other men he'd tried

working with, of the dredges and sluices: it had meant sharing his tobacco and he'd much preferred the company of himself. 'If we're going to get a piece of land,' he began, 'shouldn't be this side of the Alps. Should be over the other side. Too much rain here. Can't raise nothing.'

Annie nodded. The man was probably right. It would be smarter to have a piece of land that would grow something. Her mind did not run any farther than that. Get a piece of land. Get a piece of land and become permanent. Eat roots if need be.

Reg frowned at the West Coast he would now leave. It had been rocks and mud and earth and always climbing up and down and never setting your foot on a straight piece of ground. It had been hope retreating before the eyes till finally caught up with and found to be delusion. Sure there was gold there. And rubies. People found stones and metals he didn't even know the names of. They cashed in and got drunk, had a few women then decided they preferred beer. But at the end of it all? Just another hobo who'd die in his sleep under a tree.

'You just see as how you pick us out a decent piece of land, Reg,' Annie was saying.

Reg stared at the horizon. He would pick them a good piece of land. He would make a point of picking it in the best place they could get for the price, and although he might not ever tell her, he would do his best to make a go of it for this woman who genuinely respected him. That put her in a class of her own did that, seeing as no one else respected him at all . . .

'Right girl,' he said. 'Get your sticks together.'

Annie got quickly to her feet. They were leaving the West Coast – the only place she knew and where she was known too well. At last, she asked herself, could something new actually be happening to *her*?

Chapter 5

Ceci turned into Sweetwater's store and stared at the 'NO CREDIT — A PUNCH IN THE MOUTH SOMETIMES OFFENDS' sign by the till, racking her brains for what she had come for. Suddenly it came: a stamp for a letter to Olwen. 'Do you have any mail for us?' she asked the new owner the local people had nicknamed Moribund. He glared at her. 'I just thought to save someone a trip out to the house . . .' she explained, letting her voice trail off.

Moribund dragged his drawer open, pulled out an envelope and slapped it on the counter.

Why he had not given it to her in the first place without needing to wring some speech from the situation Ceci did not know. This was exactly the man's way: he would do nothing without a private piece of information first. Determining not to say thank you, she snatched up the letter. 'Thank you,' she said.

Moribund smiled.

Returning to Hexham Ceci now knew why Ginger had insisted she remember to enquire after mail. The letter was clearly from Faith and how long Moribund had sat on it there was no telling. By now the girl might be impatient for a reply. Unconsciously she urged her horse faster, toying with the idea of riding out to Ginger and giving it to him at once. She turned the envelope. The address on the back was of Ginger's parents, now living with his sister Mairead in Dunedin. Speculating on what news it might contain she found she could no longer be sure whose idea it had originally been to send Faith to Dunedin. She looked at the handwriting. Surely the girl was old enough to address her own envelopes? But wait – the letter was not from Faith. It was from her grandparents.

Ginger took the letter with anxious hands and opened it. Something in the sight of the handwriting seemed to irritate him, but as Ceci watched his eyes trace the words of his father on the spidery paper, she saw him become so bound up in what he was reading that his anger slipped away. Without a word he passed the letter to Ceci.

'"... Despite rigid instructions on our part the girl is beyond control." They *can't* be talking about Faith!'

'Read on.'

'"... that the boy himself is of sound and upright family and that he behaved properly on the occasion he did visit here ..." He visited?'

'Read,' said Ginger.

'"But on account of his being Presbyterian we naturally forbade it. His parents too, who consider him to be scraping the bottom of the barrel, have also been unable to intervene." Well I don't know about scraping the bottom of the barrel,' Ceci retorted. Faith taking up with a young man and defying her grandparents? Hard to believe. Yet if she were to be really truthful – it was the fact of someone like Faith being capable of inspiring this degree of affection in a suitor that amazed. 'It just goes to show we were sitting on a firebrand!' she shrugged.

'I shall have to put a stop to it of course.'

'Ginger, let the girl have some fun!'

'With a Presbyterian?'

Although it was a monstrous thing to say, from her own experience with Calvin Ceci knew what he meant. 'If the girl has found a chink in his armour –'

'I shall go down there.'

'Don't you think it would be better if I went?'

Ginger scratched the back of his neck uncomfortably. 'It'd be difficult – you with my family ...'

58

'I'm thinking of saving the relationship between you and Faith. It doesn't matter how angry she gets with me – but I don't want you flying off at her like you did with Lizabeth.'

'She *has* to come back!'

'One day she won't.'

Ginger was at a loss for words.

'We'll make her an offer,' Ceci began quietly. 'We'll ask her to come back and think about it. Ask her to invite him here.'

Ginger frowned hard.

'You must at least be curious to meet him?'

The idea struck Ginger like a breath of fresh air.

'He may turn out to be quite awful. Faith may only be doing it to annoy you. In fact he may be so awful she won't bring him here. Call her bluff!'

'All right, Ceci,' Ginger said, putting the letter behind the clock. 'This time we'll do it your way. You help me with the reply and we won't send it till we've got it exactly right.'

When Faith returned she was a changed girl; brighter, brisker and with no intimation that she had the slightest intention of abandoning Dougall. She let it be known that she approved of her father and stepmother's handling of her situation but at the same time made it clear that whatever they'd said would have made no difference anyway. She was not prepared to keep quiet about it in Moke where it soon became a nine-day wonder. How a girl from a 'good Catholic family' could become involved with a Presbyterian boy, not to mention in so short a time and without parental approval, struck both Catholic and Protestant alike by the magnitude of its strangeness. It enjoined elements of rebelliousness and doctrinal dispute and, given the Catholic community's secondary status, cut across both social and economic barriers. Uncomfortably Ceci heard it agreed that a girl could find no surer way of slapping her father across the face.

After his local humiliation over Lizabeth, though he was convinced that the match would come to nothing, Ginger prepared himself to run another public gauntlet. 'We should have made secrecy a condition of the agreement,' he grumbled to Ceci. 'While they saw if they were suited.'

'While they fell out with each other, you mean,' Ceci corrected under her breath, though that did not look at all like happening. Dougall had already visited Hexham twice and for her part she could see nothing wrong with him. As Ginger was so much against the idea this worried her and the fact that it worried her, worried her even more. Faith and Dougall seemed so well suited, so businesslike, going along side by side if not together. Could her worry be nothing other than the fear that she and Ginger would take opposite sides in the matter of another of his children? She watched Ginger conduct himself with forbearance, eat humble pie in front of Dougall for the sake of sticking to his bargain of letting Faith try. She caught, she was sure, a glint of pleasure in Faith's eyes at seeing him humiliated. At least the household was spared the agony of Moke's entire Catholic community attending at Hexham for a closer view of their scandal, the weather thankfully staying fine enough for them to continue using the barn for services. Were it to rain, it occurred to Ceci, in her present frame of mind Faith might even urge her father to forbid the community to use Hexham in order that Dougall might not be embarrassed by being present with so many Catholics in the house. This was where the danger lay, Ceci sensed. This was the flashpoint. That Faith was ready to sacrifice her religion for the sake of this young man was to Ginger and the community vitally important. The girl was publicly telling them there was something in Dougall

60

which Ginger and all of them lacked, which their Church lacked, which was beckoning to her and which she was free to follow. That it was this change of allegiances which was at the root of the wrangle became clear to Ceci in three short words, proudly thrown at Ginger by Faith as she left the drawing room to go upstairs and write to Dougall.

'I'm taking instruction.'

The girl must have known in a 'mixed marriage' it was expected of her to have her partner convert to Catholicism. Even Ceci knew that was the way of it – though in her case Ginger had declined. Had this been impossible, had Faith even gone into the marriage unhappy about promising to raise their children exclusively as Catholics, had she lapsed even . . . But to not merely abandon her faith but take up another was a rejection of all Ginger had given her and doubtless the girl knew it.

He saw her draw her head back and wait, pleasure playing in her eyes as the effect of her words struck. He said nothing. He was not in a position to say anything. Anything he said might destroy the fragile bond he hoped he did not imagine still existed, which was all he could hope to preserve between them. He shot Ceci a desperate glance.

'That's very good, Faith,' she said. 'We're happy for you.'

'*Are* you?' Faith demanded from the doorway.

'Of course we are,' Ceci replied calmly. 'You're taking instruction. You'll learn a lot.'

'What about him?' Faith asked, looking at her father.

'Why shouldn't he be delighted? You've found what you wanted?'

Ginger rose. 'You may do as you like, Faith,' he said. 'It's your life.'

Now Faith looked angry. She turned and hurried up the stairs.

Ceci went to stand by Ginger and reached for his arm. 'I can't promise you she'll get tired of him but I do know we can't stop her.'

Accepting what he could not change, Ginger bore the situation and continued to be courteous to Dougall. He insisted the boys treat him as a friend and that visitors to the house, be they Catholic or Protestant, make no reference to religion, to the Church of England, more especially the Church of Scotland, or in any way create embarrassment for the young couple. The more he mastered his discomfort the more fractious Faith became, until at one stage Ceci almost believed she would throw Dougall aside because the fight had gone out of her father. How wasteful it was! If Ginger were to fall off his horse and break his neck she was sure Faith would not have looked at Dougall twice! Indeed she longed to ask Faith if she was using the young man to distance herself from her family or to pay her father back for some inadequacy, real or imagined, perhaps when the poor man had been too busy to rise to the height of her ideals. But of course – and a further indication of her solitariness – Faith talked to no one. She would not have talked to Lizabeth had she been there, nor naturally to Myra nor the boys. Somewhere in her mind it was as if she was checking off a list, organizing her future. To catch Faith and Dougall on their own eluded even Myra's door-leaning habits, for they kept quiet, knowing she would eavesdrop. Seen walking from a distance they were a sober, sombre couple, Faith seeming to ask many questions which Dougall answered in his handsome solemn way, looking down earnestly at her, sometimes moving a hand as if to illustrate a point but the hand never reaching for Faith's. As the figures vanished down the drive Ceci wondered. Once they had passed behind the tall hedge would he reach for Faith's hand?

On the few occasions when she had been alone with Dougall Ceci had to admit that he was attentive. He had drawn back her chair for her, enquired politely after her health and filled the room with a light chatter. But there was a lack of energy in his hands; a quiet acceptance or stillness. Not for him the twitches and nervous movements of a young suitor before his prospective in-laws. His eyes did not look away when he was stared at. It was almost as if he was simply tolerating them all for this short period which must be endured before he carried his bride back to Dunedin. He was, in a word, beyond the reach of Ceci's imagination.

She sensed in Ginger a growing sadness.

'What do you pray for?' she asked, as he climbed into bed after some considerable time on his knees.

'He hasn't asked me for her hand yet,' Ginger replied. 'There's still a chance they won't marry.'

'Perhaps Faith doesn't want him to ask. Perhaps she feels it's hers to give,' Ceci offered.

'He would. A man would ask.'

While they were neither of them willing to unleash the storm of criticism of their own way of life which they felt sure would be the result of asking Faith why she had chosen Dougall, Ceci felt she might risk asking Dougall himself. Cornering him one day she put the question but by the briefest movement of a finger Dougall managed to convey that her question had been gauche; the enquiry less than had been expected and that the matter was closed. Shortly after this he had simply announced that they would be marrying the following month in Dunedin.

'We haven't had our "talk" yet,' Ginger complained. 'How is he to support her?'

Angered, Ceci approached Faith. 'I *must* know for your father's sake,' she insisted.

'You don't need to know anything!' Faith replied. 'When

my parents had me – as the result of their lust – they took on the obligation to raise me. Now that I am raised, my life is my own.'

'*Lust?*'

'You have lived so long and never come across it, I suppose?' Faith asked wryly.

That night Ceci lay close with Ginger, lust far from them. The blankets wrapped them in and the house wrapped the blankets; the hills closed in on the house and the darkness pressed against it. Faith's words had winded her.

'Everyone has a cross,' Ginger said tiredly. 'Perhaps Faith is mine.'

'And Faith's?'

'A piece of wood'll come floating by,' he mused. 'She'll grab on to it, thinking it'll do her good. Next thing she'll wash up on an island with it and notice it's in the shape of a cross.'

'Are you saying it's the instinct for self-preservation which humanizes us?'

'How should I know?' Ginger shrugged. 'I've made a fine mess of raising my daughters!'

'Faith's a fine girl and just beginning to show some spirit. She'll give as good as she gets.'

'You don't follow,' Ginger said. 'She's left the Church!'

'Is there something in your religion Faith can't do without?'

'That's the truth of it.'

What being a Catholic meant to any of them Ceci did not know except that they felt the girl was stepping out into famine. There were differences between the Churches, about who received Christ in Holy Communion and who didn't, yet while both sides were aware of the indignity of the arguments, the urgency of their souls' journeys stood above all.

'Do you think ordinary people will one day discuss politics with the same fervour they now reserve for religion?' she asked, adding, 'He struck me as a nice young man.'

'You think it's the scandal or her rejection of me,' Ginger began. 'But –'

'No – I understand. It's her soul you're worried for.'

First there was the wedding to be got through and it was down to her to prepare the girl for married life – which would be difficult given Faith believed she already knew everything. It would also take considerable time before Ginger would adjust to what *could* be a very good match. But when their first child came surely he would change his mind?

'Things always look worse at night,' she counselled, stroking the side of his face. 'Never think about dark things at night.'

Ginger pulled her to him. It had been a lot worse than he had told her for, taking her advice about not interfering had started him down a particular road where he had been obliged to defend to the local community Faith's right to choose. In doing this, hardly surprisingly, he had fallen out with both Catholic and Protestant alike and though he knew it would blow over and that in time they would start talking to him again, the scars of his act would never be far below the surface. He had been forced to make much of the inviolability of *all* marriages; to insist to the Catholic priest – who nearly punched him – that it was not a question of what the Catholic Church thought but of 'what God had put together'. Having used that phrase whenever backed into a corner, he would now have to remember it. He knew some accused him of being a man who did not love his daughter enough to assure her happiness by making her conform. In their ignorance they accused him of not having taken the trouble to obtain from the bishop a dispensation for the mixed marriage or permission for the ceremony to take place in a differing church. That Dougall had got there first didn't occur to any and it was not his job to inform them. Let them think he was a hundred per cent behind the couple! He had retrieved the Baptismal Certificate Faith would need for a Christian service but it was known there had been no request from him for permission for *him* to attend the service and, in a climate where neither faith was allowed to pray in the church of the other, this amounted to a choice of two things: either Ginger was thumbing his nose at his own Church or Ginger was not intending going to the wedding.

Chapter 6

Intent on getting the best possible deal from the Notables Olwen set off for the station and stood glancing hopefully up the tracks. Given that Khandallah was still virtually in the country, its clean, sweeping hills and clear sky above made it a pleasant place to catch a last breath of quiet before boarding the Wellington train. She looked at the sun glinting off the rails which had not yet begun to hum in anticipation of the train's arrival. Although only the stop of Crofton remained before Wellington, the train had come down from Longburn, stopping at places like Paikakariki and Otaki for water and coal or to turn into sidings while its counterpart from Wellington sped by. Unlike the earlier train which hurried in to meet Wellington's work day, there was no knowing who might be on this second train. Though the run would last only twenty minutes it could be very crowded or almost empty for, except on Tuesdays, Wednesdays and the weekends, there would not be another train until late afternoon.

In her bag lay her mother's letter which she had barely had time to glance at. There would be little need to say anything about herself in reply, she decided, for Hexham was clearly taken up with the affair of Faith's marriage. Tempted to pull the letter out but preferring to keep it to savour on the train, she held on to her skirt. She had been torn between looking businesslike or indifferent for the meeting but did not want to look altogether too windswept. She watched a small white cloud lit with the brilliance of the morning sun pushing itself gainfully towards Mount Misery. Reading between the lines of her mother's letter she'd detected there had been a bit of a skirmish about the marriage in Moke. Although she was not clear on those things, nor was her mother specific, it seemed that neither the Catholic nor the Presbyterian Churches fully respected each other's ceremonies and as Faith was marrying in the Presbyterian Church, though she would be legally bound by the marriage, it was generally felt amongst the Catholics that she would be living in sin. Had she gone the whole hog in fact, and actually converted to her husband's religion, that particular sin would be wiped out. Apparently, however, she had gone no further with her 'instruction' than had been necessary to please Dougall.

Olwen pulled herself up sharply. She was supposed to be readying herself for the meeting but, as always, her mother's letters, chatty with a wealth of detail and careful character observations, had served to distract her. On paper they enjoyed a relationship of equals, Olwen at least being aware that face to face with her mother much of it could not have been said. She watched the Station Master cross the line, climb up his ladder and adjust a signal. The train would be along soon. Ceci had described Ginger taking a brave stand in the face of Moke, insisting that if the young people had overcome sectarian vicissitudes they had probably made a better start towards happiness than the majority who fell in with the ways of their forebears. Knowing Ginger, Olwen could not imagine this speech coming from him: he must surely be mouthing Ceci's sentiments! She doubted Moke would take kindly to his right about turn on the subject of religion even if it *had* been done for the sake of his daughter. That small communities did not like people to change character Olwen knew well. The way she read her mother's letter it seemed that not only had Ginger fallen out with half the community for Faith's sake but had painted himself into a corner where it would take a long time for the paint to dry. Unable to resist it a moment longer she pulled her mother's letter from her bag and continued reading:

. . . more than a little unfair for despite Calvin's peculiar attitude towards pleasure I have met many Presbyterians who, while perhaps not *fun* to be with, have impressed me by their upstanding nature. The fact that a person chooses not to drink is neither here nor there and for my part, Faith's marriage comes as a relief . . .

Olwen folded the letter and replaced it in her bag. Faith had always been a strange one. Odd that it had not occurred to Ginger that her desire to somehow discipline him by her choice reflected the extent of her feeling for him. Had she *not* cared, she would surely have felt free to make a choice without implied reference to her father's 'shortcomings'.

With a loud whistle Olwen heard the train coming and stood well back to avoid a dousing with soot. It slowed down, its smoke settling in the trees, darkening the sky and providing an arch for Olwen to walk under. She climbed into an empty carriage and sat listening to the dripping water. Drip, drip, drip! 'Crofton and Wellington!' she heard the Station Master shout. 'Crofton! Wellington!' No doors opened. Nobody wanted to get off at Khandallah. Groaning and shrieking the train began to pull out.

'Hey you! Wait! Stop!' she heard shouted. Quickly Olwen threw down her window to see a young Maori girl carrying a large pot and tripping on her skirts as she ran after the train.

'In here!' Olwen called, struggling to open her door as the train gained speed but the girl, balanced on the running board, already had one foot in the next carriage.

'Not in here, young woman!' came a peremptory male voice. 'This is a Gentlemen's Smoker.'

'Oh, you're probably lying!' shouted the girl, hanging on to the handle of the open door, swinging out wildly over the track. Amazed, Olwen saw her haul herself in and heard the door slam, followed by a great peal of laughter, the sound of coughing and a crash, probably the girl's pot landing on a Gentleman Smoker!

'Can't you read English!' came the angry male voice again, instantly covered by another great peal of laughter from the girl. '. . . good mind to pull the emergency chain!'

As the train jogged down the hill Olwen glanced out of the window. She could catch glimpses of the jagged bay below, a small boat making for Days Bay opposite, no doubt to enjoy a picnic. Children who should have been in school had come to watch the train or throw stones at it. They waved, then threw stones. Some took to running the mile and a half down the hill to get to the shore first. From the carriage next door came only the sound of the Maori girl scolding the men and laughing at them. No doubt she would be put off at Crofton, Olwen thought.

Crofton came. The girl did not get off though Olwen could hear her protesting and laughing at the men, one of whom rashly got down and hurried from the carriage, shouting, 'Station Master! Station Master!' As the Station Master was not to be seen he ran, waving angrily, towards the guard, just as the whistle went and the train took off. Leaning forward Olwen saw the Maori girl put her face to the window and give a great shout on his behalf which stopped the train and brought the guard running.

'That girl should not be in our compartment!' the frightened man was ungracious enough to complain.

'*Au-e!*' the girl shouted. 'Woe is me!'

The guard hurried up. 'This is a Gentlemen's Smoker,' he scolded.

'*E tika ana*,' the girl agreed. 'Quite true.'

'You shouldn't have got into this carriage,' the guard continued.

'You are asking for an earthquake!' the girl told him. 'The train was already moving!'

'Out!'

The girl stumbled on to the platform.

'Come in here,' Olwen called, annoyed at their rudeness.

'Take this!' the girl said, forcing the large wicker-clad pot into Olwen's hands. '*Upoko kohua*.'

'*Upoko kohua?*' Olwen repeated.

'Pot head,' the girl grinned. 'Him.' She lifted her pot on to the rack and pointed at its smooth shiny bottom, then back at the bald head of the guard hurrying from their carriage.

Now the Station Master came up to frown through the window at them.

'*Ti, he atua!*' the girl said, rolling her eyes heavenward. 'Lo, a god!'

Delighted at her irreverence Olwen saw the Station Master withdraw. She imagined the girl to be about fifteen. On closer inspection her 'pot' turned out to be a gourd and the wicker surrounding it a form of woven flax.

'I got pigeons in there,' the girl informed Olwen. 'My granny does them. She bones them and forces them in and pours hot fat on to keep the air out.'

Olwen nodded. Being sealed in dried dripping would certainly preserve anything though she had never thought to do it.

'It's a present for my other granny,' the girl went on. 'All I got is this and my bundle of clo – ' Suddenly her hand flew to her mouth. 'Au-e! I hope that Station Master at Khandallah don't make off with my clothing!'

'What were you doing at Khandallah?' Olwen asked.

'Getting on the train of course,' the girl answered. 'I not walking back to Paikakariki to get on! Where you going?'

71

'Wellington,' Olwen said, adding an 'of course' to even the score.

Leaving the station Olwen saw Gwen hurrying towards her.

'That wasn't a Maori I saw you with, was it?' Gwen demanded anxiously. 'You must be careful. They are not, how shall I say, accepted.'

Olwen smiled. Despite their differences she had done very well out of the dress she had 'made' for Gwen and now several of Gwen's friends had put pressure on their own husbands to give backing to her dressmaking venture.

'I admit they're tall and handsome, perhaps a little overweight,' Gwen chattered on, anxious not to give offence. 'But at the same time one cannot be too careful . . .'

'She sat next to me on the train.'

'It is to be hoped nothing jumped off on to your skirt,' Gwen frowned. 'We have time, dear. Will you visit my house? It is not a great distance and there are things I must tell you. Now remember, dear, although you are invited to sit in the meeting you are not expected to say anything. Unless of course you are asked.'

As they waited to cross the road, Gwen's mind once more returned to the Maori. 'Of course I know you do not have them in great numbers in the South Island and no doubt in England they are still a great curiosity . . .' Her voice trailed off as she turned her head to gauge the movement of traffic. 'They are not allowed in the hotels here or given wine, you know.'

'Who?'

'Why the half castes!' Gwen smiled, linking arms with Olwen. 'Quick, I think we can run.' Reaching the safety of the opposite pavement Gwen once again took up the subject. 'There are a great many here. A certain type of person is marrying them. But their ways are not our ways. Venables can explain.'

That occasional Europeans – whalers she supposed – should have chosen to intermarry with Maoris came as no surprise to Olwen. There must have been more than a few lonely men left to mind coastal depots, not to mention the fraternity of Australian criminals deliberately poached from penal colonies by skulking ships, who would be grateful to hide from the law or seek comfort in the heart of tribal society. The fact that the mixed offspring were so strikingly handsome would have made it even easier for a drifting man to take the welcome step. In fact, looking at the girl she had just been talking with and then looking at Gwen, Olwen was in no doubt, were she a man, who she would rather spend her last days with!

'I never heard of Maoris when I was in England,' she confessed.

'Really?' Gwen cooed. 'A party went over in '63 – I say went but really they were taken!' she giggled. 'A Wesleyan preacher, I believe – though Venables would know more about it. They spoke to Queen Victoria. Didn't get them anywhere!'

Olwen tried to imagine people like the girl she had just met trying to 'get somewhere' with Queen Victoria.

'A whole deputation went in '82 actually led by one of them, would you believe, a Member of the House of Representatives. It seems they wanted to talk to the Queen directly as they felt their agreements had been made with her, their treaty thing you know? Didn't get them anywhere!' Gwen paused outside an impressive building. 'And back they went again in '84 with their own King that time, my dear, can you believe?'

'King?'

'Well they felt to get anywhere, dear, they had to have a

King like we had a Queen. You follow? *That* didn't get them anywhere!'

'Did they see the Queen?' Olwen asked.

Gwen shook her head. 'At least they can play rugby! Excuse the word!'

'I'm surprised you know so much about Maoris – ' Olwen began.

Gwen flushed. 'I just repeat what I hear Venables saying. He can't stand them.'

Olwen felt as if she had been punched.

'Are you all right, dear?' Gwen asked. 'The men will be ready for us soon. Mustn't drag our steps! Let us just pop into the house quickly and next time you shall visit properly.'

'I appreciate your husband setting up this meeting for me,' Olwen said as they crossed the landscaped garden and mounted the steps to the porch.

'He worked hard but there *was* support,' Gwen said, turning the key. 'I would advise you most particularly to watch out for James who is Venables' colleague.' She stood back to allow Olwen to enter. 'I say colleague, but in fact you will appreciate that it is a mere kindness on James' part allowing Venables to consider him thus. The relationship truthfully is more like dog and master. In fact Venables bent over backwards to get James to agree to come this morning at all. Without James' approval the community will do nothing. That is to say, the finance will not be forthcoming.'

'I am sure I can manage this James – '

'Oh, my dear, you must *not* call him "James",' fussed Gwen, peering awkwardly around them as if afraid the maid would hear. 'And do try most particularly not to interrupt him when he speaks. Because we *need* you here, dear, do you see? To design clothes . . .'

Cynicism played on Olwen's face.

When later they left the prestigious residential area where, according to Gwen, most of the Notables lived, Gwen began to get anxious. 'I won't come in with you, dear, when we arrive if that will be all right? We'll meet at lunch.'

Olwen nodded.

'Venables appreciates you feel you should be at the meeting as it is *your* business they will be discussing,' she repeated, excusing herself as they reached Commercial Building.

Aware Gwen thought she would actually have been better to leave the whole thing to Venables, Olwen entered the building and grasped the polished wood banister firmly affixed to the wall's plaster by giant brass rings. Her objectives were clear in her mind. The people awaiting her in the upper room represented the cream of the wealth of Wellington and from them she wanted enough credit to set up shop, workroom, take on girls and bank-roll them until she was in a position to pay off the Notables and be independent. Then she would survive on her reputation as a designer and work-in-hand. She was indebted to Venables for representing her – albeit on his wife's behalf – and though she doubted a man in the room would dare cheek her lest she withhold her dressmaking favours from their wives, of a sudden she felt she had no wish to associate with any of them. There had been something about the girl in the train which was a breath of fresh air undermining and blowing away everything her plans and ambitions had stood for. Reminding herself her objective was to come out of the meeting with as much control over her own affairs as possible Olwen willed herself forward and sought the clerk of the building: 'Will you announce me,' she said crisply. 'It would not be appropriate for me to knock.'

The room came to attention as the proud young woman entered, only an older man whom Olwen took to be James failing to get to his feet. Glancing about Olwen noted the responsibility of grandeur had caused early loss of hair, a certain thickening of the stomach, and in some cases flaccidity of the skin or a yellowness akin to kidney trouble. As the faces turned towards James, who had started speaking, she could sense men disagreeing but not daring to interrupt as he reminded them that in his capacity as Director of Imports there were occasions when he did not see fit to agree with them. Their only exports, he said, were agricultural and as internal trade depended on imports *selected* . . . Olwen caught the eye of a younger man who all but winked at her. Quickly she looked at James. There was something familiar about the arrogance in his voice; hadn't she once heard it objecting or asking people if they could not read English? Sniffing the stale smell of cigars in the room Olwen wondered what this talk of agricultural exports could have to do with her? Did they not have a responsibility, James was asking, to encourage, or in some cases discourage, by means of tariffs certain items? He dusted Olwen with his eyes adding, 'which are not in the genuine interests of the economy?'

So he was trying to bargain with her already, Olwen realized! Trying to make her feel at a disadvantage!

'. . . with a view to the wise use of shipping space,' the voice went on.

His wife would not thank him for *those* sentiments, Olwen told herself, watching the wedding ring flash on James' rotund finger. She would probably be very mad to be done out of her bit of taffeta . . .

'. . . Basically, Venables, you are asking me – or should I say us – to co-finance, am I right, a private cloth business using the services of this young lady who makes dresses . . .'

'I don't make dresses. I design them,' Olwen interrupted loudly.

Venables went from bilious yellow to pink. 'Excuse me, James,' he murmured.

Teased back into speech James went on to make it clear the most 'they' were prepared to offer would be a trust — if the young lady could understand the term — whereby —

'Are you telling me,' Olwen interrupted, 'that the business would be yours?'

'Please try not to interrupt,' Venables whispered as water was drunk and throats cleared.

'The business would naturally belong to those of us who put up the capital, yes,' a colleague of James' stated.

Olwen smiled. She was beginning to remember where she had heard James' voice. 'May I know if you came down from Paikakariki?' she asked politely.

James flinched. 'It is most certainly not your business,' he replied.

Quickly Venables suggested they retire for an early lunch, leaving Olwen the distinct impression that, regardless of where he lived, or the clubs he could 'stay at' James had spent the night somewhere up the line and did not want to be reminded of it! There could not have been two voices like that and she could still hear him shouting: 'This is a Gentlemen's Smoker!'

As the chairs scraped back Olwen made a decision. She would not allow James to sweep out of the room before her with the men following and leaving her till last! At the door in a flash, she found a hand on the handle opening it for her.

'I see you like to live dangerously,' murmured the young man she had noticed biding his time in the meeting.

'I think, don't you,' she replied, 'that it is best to start off by being thoroughly outrageous.' She felt the man's gaze follow her.

Waiting in the corridor Olwen told herself she had not mistaken the look of malice, or had it been anger, on the face of James as she'd swept through the door ahead of him. He was not a big enough man to stand aside for a lady.

'I hope you are not under the impression that we were outrageous in our treatment of you?' a soft voice asked, and glancing up Olwen recognized the man who had held the door for her. 'Watch your step, though. It would be a pity to hurt old Venables.'

'And I should watch your step if I were *you*, young man,' Olwen replied sternly.

The man walked on a few paces as if fighting down a remark he longed to make, then came back to her: 'I think we all know if it weren't for Venables you wouldn't be here. You should apologize to him for creating that disturbance with James. In your own interests.'

At that moment Gwen came running to meet them. 'Is Marshall pestering you?' she enquired.

'Yes!'

Quickly Marshall left.

'He is extremely fast. I do apologize,' Gwen lamented. 'Still, business to one side – I know we can rely on you to give him short shrift.'

'Does – Marshall – work for the same firm as your husband?' Olwen asked cautiously.

'Marshall Cavanaugh? Good heavens no! They are in association, you understand, because all imports have to go through the Board – meaning James.'

'I see,' said Olwen letting her eyes follow the self-assured young man as he insinuated himself into the group.

'There is a lot of money slushing about – which Marshall doesn't have – and don't let him tell you different. The problem is he is, how shall I say, very up and coming . . .'

'Oh?'

'If he would only come to heel,' Gwen explained as if pained by his inability to compromise. 'Young as he is I think James would like one day to think of him as a successor.'

'I thought you said James worked for the Board?'

'He has his own company in addition.'

Olwen and Gwen stepped into the dining room where the wives who had been allowed to attend the luncheon in the hope of impressing themselves upon her clamoured at their husbands for introduction. Little cards had been placed neatly pairing husband and wife with husband and wife. Looking up, Olwen found she had been paired with Marshall Cavanaugh who was now pretending an indifference towards her.

James, also at the table together with his wife, looked from one of them to the other. 'I don't believe you two have met?' he said politely as if the earlier reference to Paikakariki was a thing of the board room now that his lady wife was present. 'Mr Cavanaugh would not be part of the financial package owning your business,' James went on to explain. 'He's here for the experience.'

'Do you go to Paikakariki often?' Olwen asked James' wife directly.

Not a muscle on James' face moved. 'My wife, Henrietta,' he said.

'I have my own conditions to be met before there will be any possibility of a business,' Olwen informed him. 'Although of course I hate to disappoint any of the women here – especially your wife.'

James looked away. He does not, Olwen thought, want his wife to know about his little flutter in Paikakariki. Whether he spent the night there or merely went in on the first train!

'I spent last night in Paikakariki myself,' Olwen lied. 'Measuring a client. You often see a familiar face – '

'I think we will be able to come to a suitable arrangement,' James said heavily to Olwen. 'May I pass you the salt?'

As Olwen stepped briskly across Lambton Quay a carriage stopped.

'Can I carry you home?'

Looking up, to her amazement she saw Marshall Cavanaugh. 'To Khandallah?' she replied unthinkingly.

'If you like.'

Olwen paused: 'I prefer the train. For the view.'

'The second half of the meeting went better from your point of view than the first, I thought,' Marshall observed. 'You played your cards well. James is no fool, however, and though you choose to laugh at our conventions, they grind exceeding small.'

'I find business practices here quite unethical compared with the South Island,' Olwen assured him.

'Nonetheless there are things we do and things we don't do – '

'He was patronizing *you*, I noticed.' Watching him, Olwen saw her remark sting. She tossed her head and walked away towards the station, aware of him watching her go. Let him watch! She had hounded the Notables from one set of proposals to another, wooing, bargaining, arguing, picking faults – yet always coming back to lock eyes with James.

Arriving at the station a familiar sight met her eyes – the Maori girl standing by the timetable board pestering travellers to read the timetable to her. Having delivered her large pot she was intent on returning to Khandallah for her bundle of clothing.

'Look!' said Olwen. 'The train's gone. The next one isn't for an hour and a half.'

'That's not what I'm asking,' the girl said indignantly. 'I'm looking to take the Kaiwarra line then walk up the

Khandallah road and if you've got any sense you'll do the same instead of waiting here an hour and a half.'

Olwen agreed. A walk up a hill would do a lot to blow the clutter of Wellington from her mind. Turning to board the Kaiwarra train she half thought she saw Venables parting company with James and his wife, glimpsing her with a Maori and hastily turning them around so they would not see. No doubt she was flouting another of their customs by travelling with a Maori! As the train moved out of the station she looked at the girl opposite her and the warmth and contentment in her eyes as they rested on the calm waters of the bay as if she understood nature and was a part of it.

'What's your name?' the girl asked abruptly.

'Olwen. Yours?'

'Kura. That means red colour, like your purple. It's the colour for chiefs. Everyone got a white feather except chiefs: they got a red feather. Like *kaka-kura* – or chiefly parrot. What you call an orator.'

'So you were a noble-looking baby?'

'I stared at them!'

'Maybe you just had a red face.'

'My mother calls me Hari because I'm lazy. That means happy.'

They left the train and began climbing on foot above sea level, leaving Wellington and its harbour behind them.

'Does Kaiwarra mean anything?' Olwen asked.

Happi giggled. 'It's *Kaiwharawhara*,' she chided. 'And it means to eat *wharawhara*. *Wharawhara* is a fruit of – I don't know the name – it grows in the forks of trees . . .'

Typical, Olwen thought, that her people would come along, borrow a local name they did not understand, shorten and misspell it. 'Where do you come from?' she asked Happi.

'My mother's a *hawini*.'

'*Hawini?*' Olwen repeated.

'A house servant. Because she likes to look in their drawers at their silver and things.'

'Where?'

'They good people. They all right. Picton way.' Happi knelt and with her finger drew the two islands: 'This is the fish *Maui* fished up,' she said, indicating the entire North Island of New Zealand. Olwen let that pass.

'He was standing here, see,' she said, pointing at about where Olwen had boarded the ferry from Lyttelton, 'and he threw his line and just fished it up to beat his brothers. But then they got greedy and cut it all about which is why it doesn't look right now. See here the Head of the Fish,' she said pointing at the Wellington area. 'My people all around here, and here,' she added, her finger stabbing at the top of the South Island.

'You mean you came across Cook Strait with that pot thing?' Olwen asked incredulously.

'We coming and going all the time,' Happi grinned.

'In a canoe?'

'My uncle's fishing boat.'

It seemed very odd to Olwen that a fifteen-year-old girl should leave her mother behind and travel with a pot of pressed pigeons to the North Island.

'It's all right,' Happi assured her. 'I got relatives. If I want to go and live with my aunty, okay. If my aunty want to go and get my little sister and bring her to live here, that okay too. If my mother and father want to come and live with my granny and bring all their brothers and sisters and husbands and wives and children and pigs and dogs and chickens – that okay too. My word,' she said, looking at the darkening sky, 'I think I better stay at your place tonight!'

Olwen got into bed strangely untroubled by the presence of a stranger in her house. Lying on her back she ran the day's events through her mind – especially the second half of her meeting with the Notables. In retrospect, although Venables had been afraid to speak out on her behalf she was a bit ashamed of having put him on the spot. But they *had* been aiming at a situation which would have put her in their pockets. It was all very well to offer to bank-roll the quantities of fine cloth they felt their wives would have occasion to sport; to provide capital for the purchase of sewing machines and the initial hiring expenses of girls to sew her designs but had she not been allowed to set her own prices and decide which percentage of her take to keep for the day-to-day running of her affairs and which to pay back, she might have been little more than a working girl herself. The very idea of having a 'financial overseer' to give her an 'allowance' was outrageous and a sly word for 'salary'. Even after she had fought that one down, their suggestion that she rent the premises they would secure for her rather than put higher instalments as she wished towards its ultimate purchase was downright wicked.

She had had to fight them on every front; push them like an army through the trees. All except that Marshall Cavanaugh who had kept carefully out of things. Each time they had agreed one condition they would impose another and so it had gone on. But she hadn't tired and it had surely been a combination of three factors which had enabled her to win the day. First, that she had refused to take up the business on any conditions other than her own; second that, possibly because of her mention of the word Paikakariki, James had become distinctly more amenable, and third, of course, her own bloody-mindedness which stood to get between the men and their wives' desires. Possibly there would be a skirmish with James later. Possibly even now he was falling out with the Notables for acquitting themselves less than honourably on the bargaining table. Soon she would get to know all their wives, their little secrets and problems and indirectly, of course, the hearts of these men. Each morning she would have to get the early morning train into Wellington: her life would change beyond recognition. As she fell into sleep an image lingered on the edge of her mind: it was Venables carefully steering James away so that he might not see her entering the train with a Maori girl. Let them stare at her if they liked. The papers were already signed and the chips could fall where they willed.

Chapter 7

It seemed clear to Reg and Annie that the land clerk was not intent on being helpful. He had laid a large subdivided map before them, said, 'That's it. Pick your number,' then walked away into the next room to resume his grumbles about the amalgamation of various government services into something new called the Department of Agriculture. Reg stood with his ear cocked listening. It did seem a strange idea to use the same people to check for scab disease in sheep as to test the quality of milk, seeing as sheep and cattle had nothing to do with each other.

'Concentrate, Reg,' said Annie, pointing at the papers again. But the more they stared the harder it became for there were large holdings and small holdings up for offer, the small holdings often costing a great deal more.

Reg frowned at the squiggly lines darting across the white sheet of paper. 'Got to be a river, that,' he observed. 'See, it comes up out of the middle of nowhere. Even the Department of Agriculture wouldn't be daft enough to plumb up and start building a road there. If they could have got up there in the first place!'

'Could have gone the other way,' Annie pointed out reasonably, following the river with her finger. 'Could've started it at the coast – '

'Nah!'

From the next room the voice of the clerk rose, now condemning ding-dang meddlers in the government who wanted to break up the larger land holdings so that the little man could have his chance.

'I don't see how we can go in and ask him anything with that attitude,' Annie sighed.

It seemed that the Crown was buying up and subdividing vast estates on their behalf and the owners of unprofitable land who wished to be rid of it had found a way of jumping on the bandwagon. If they disputed the government's tax valuation of their land, under present law, the government had to come in and buy it off them at the lower figure.

'Hardly our problem,' Reg muttered.

Now the recipient of the clerk's indignation raised his voice, apparently in agreement with anything favouring the little man or making more land available to him. 'Why should a piece of land carry 80,000 sheep, a handful of people – most of them working for someone else when – '

Reg strode over and shut the door on them. Whatever the government's motives it was good for them that things were looking the smallholder's way. The same bloke with the Department of Agriculture idea had apparently that year thrown out some Land Act and come up with a fairer system Reg did not understand any better than the one it had replaced, but which meant that if they lived on their land and made improvements, after seven years, if they could put up the full money, or ten years if they couldn't, or 999 years if they felt they never would be able to, they could call it their own. The word 'freehold' was so very precious to both Reg and Annie that they had wanted to spend all their money up front ('Not allowed,' the clerk had said. 'Got to save some to live on.') rather than use it to effect the improvements on the land the government would recognize as 'qualifying'. 'Either way you got to improve it,' the clerk had said unhelpfully, 'or lose it.' Quite who would own the land was difficult for them to understand: until the deeds were buried in a tin or canister on their plot neither would feel at ease.

'Don't want to be working nobody *else's* land!' Reg frowned. 'Government nor nobody's!'

He cocked his head to listen to the argument in the next room as it reached renewed heights, the door suddenly opening and the man in favour of looking kindly towards the smallholder being edged physically from the room.

'Why don't you two come back when you've made up your minds?' he said irritably. Reg glared at him.

'See here,' Annie said. 'If these are rivers like you think, Reg, then these lines squeezing them in must be steep banks. Mountains, see, because it's deep up where we crossed over. Can you read?'

Reg shook his head. He could, but he didn't want to make a fool of himself in front of the man.

'Hoh-ki-ti-ka!' Annie said, pointing triumphantly. 'Look! And over this side, see, where it's all flat – no lines? That's the plain!'

Reg screwed his eyes up at the plan and leant forward. By jiminy she was right! Even though he'd never seen a map of his country nor could point out where any of the towns were on one, that place name was definitely Hoki-tika and what's more he recognized several other names of places along the routes he'd trodden. The streams and gullies he now saw coming down out of the mountains his tired feet remembered; he could almost feel the wind biting the back of his neck as with amazement his finger traced what he now knew to be the route they had followed over the Alps and down into the lowlands!

'Would you credit it?' he asked. 'That's why those big pieces was so cheap! They was all rocks and mountains. Good job we didn't buy none of those! Better get a real small flat piece somewhere.'

Annie nodded fervently. In the corner the friend of smallholders shook his head in pitying bureaucratic amazement at the ignorance of these people he had previously championed. There were a lot of problems they would not know about. They were not married, so whose name would the land go in . . .? Although a fair bit of land did remain, the best had long since gone — except what the government was now busy buying back from the heirs of settlers or the Maoris when they would come forward. Chances were their land would have trees on it, native bush the felling of which would be arduous for a man the age and strength of this man before him. Were he to hire a bushman it could cost anything between fifteen bob and two pound an acre; there'd be another one to three pounds an acre getting rid of the felled logs, not to mention the cost of burning . . . And then they'd be left with the stumps to clear: a good seven or ten pounds an acre they wouldn't have thought of unless they could do it themselves! Probably thinking they could rush into their first ploughing for a measly pound. Probably the woman's mind didn't run any further than getting up a fence, though by the look of her she wouldn't mind mucking in.

There were no easy answers. For each question that was raised another stood in its way.

'Seems to me, Reg,' Annie began, 'we got to decide between sheep and cattle.'

'Can't without seeing the land.'

'No point going up there to see it without taking some tools – '

'No point buying bill-hooks, fern-hooks and scythes if we're going to end up needing American axes, crosscut saws and maul rings . . .'

'Isn't there nothing on this piece of paper would tell us what kind of land this is?' Annie demanded of the friend of smallholders.

'You just pick your number, dear, and it's yours!'

'No point – '

'Don't you say that, Reg Bowen!' Annie interrupted.

'And we're not walking all the way up to a dozen of these places and then back down here again to find the piece gone.'

'So pick one! Pick anything!' Reg shouted, losing his temper.

'All right!' Annie flared. 'We'll have this one.' Carefully she brought her finger down in descending spirals. Reg watched it waver like a water diviner's hazel twig before coming to light on a small plot.

'You can get over here now,' she called to the man, anticipation and fear on her face.

Slowly he ambled to the desk. 'This one, eh?' he asked.

'Yes,' Annie said firmly.

Reg cleared his throat.

'So this is the one you want, eh?'

Was Annie imagining it or were the corners of his mouth beginning to curl?

'It just goes to show,' said the man as he moved into the other room, 'Doesn't matter how much you try to help people, they have an instinct for catastrophe.'

Reg leapt after him: 'Listen you! Is that a good piece of land?'

'Good? What makes a piece of land good? It's what you do to it. Your improvements.'

On the long journey up to the backblocks, even though they had not seen their piece of land, Reg and Annie chawed on the sheep/cattle problem.

'I don't mind telling you, Reg, I favour cattle – ' Annie began.

'It's a well-known fact,' Reg intoned, 'that sheep make gentlemen of you and cows drag you down.'

Annie held her peace.

'You don't find no cow farmer with a big house,' Reg went on. 'You take your sheep farmer – 'course not like

89

my father — 'uge houses, brick chimneys, proper roofs — not a one of them without thirty rooms!'

'I've got a way with cheese,' Annie offered.

Reg looked at her. Was it possible the girl had learnt cheese making in a reformatory? 'Never see a cow cocky live in anything better than a two-room shack with a tin roof,' he said. 'Best they can do is a paling fence.'

'Cows are nice friendly creatures.'

'An' I suppose you'd milk them?'

'Save *you* the trouble!'

Well, there was something in that. 'If maybe God could see his way to sending a fowl towards us I might consider it,' said Reg and hardly were the words out of his mouth than one unwittingly wandered out of the bush.

'Here, chickie chickie . . .' he called, crouching in front of the bird. Annie watched amazed as the foolish creature approached Reg, fooled by the movement of his lanky arm, pretending to throw grain at it. 'Took took Thank you, God!' the chicken seemed to be saying as it made its way towards Reg, pecking at the bits he had not thrown. 'Took took, Thank you!' With a snap of Reg's thumb the hen was soon a bulge in his jacket and as they hurried away from the spot Annie saw shame flash in his eyes.

'That's a nice hen, Reg,' she said.

Instantly his guilt was replaced by gratitude. 'I do that once in a while,' he admitted.

After they had walked some paces Annie brought the subject up again: 'I just feel that we are cow cockies, Reg,' she explained. 'I don't see us as sheep farmers.' At the back of her reasoning was a fear that the plot she had picked would be so far distant from humanity that they would need all the company they could get and cows were better company than sheep. Further, they were not sheep people. Sheep people owned huge tracts of land; belonged to clubs in cities, enjoyed luxury and comfort and paid as much attention to their leisure activities as their work. They were people whose children went to universities or joined the government. Cow people were a step up from coal people. They did not work in a mine: they worked above ground. They did not work for another person, yet at the same time they were less likely to employ others. True, they were not to be seen without mud on their trousers; true, the cow was considered a poor joke alongside a sheep yet the people who attended cow sales, who sat on the wooden fence bars in a scenery of recently burned desolation, were their kind of people. They were not the sort who attended the sheep auctions in the established saleyards of the lowlands.

Reg wiped his neck. 'Bloomin' long way!'

'How much further, you reckon?'

'About two inches!' He grinned at her sideways, remembering what a short distance it had looked on the map. 'Leastways we ain't come upon none o' them little black boxes yet.'

Annie frowned then recalled a cluster of small black marks like boxes that she had seen on the larger survey version indicating their plot.

'I seen maps in houses all framed up like pictures with little curly Ns and Ws embroidered on the edges like samplers. Well, not embroidered,' Annie said truthfully. 'But written as a decoration. And slatted lines at the bottom.' She nodded. 'Very proud of them their owners are. Hang 'em on the walls behind glass. Faded, y'know. They showed the whole world I shouldn't wonder!'

The whole world! Reg listened as she told of a map she had once seen with the intricate wavy edges of the two islands of New Zealand, the North Island and the South Island, all drawn in. Nobody would have dared to make up a thing like that she insisted. She had seen all the bays and curves, how the mountains went down the middle and jammed up to fill the bottom of the land.

'Where d'you see a thing like that then?'

'Mine manager's office. Grevillton.'

'When you was locked in for pinching coal?'

Annie nodded sternly.

'I had me own map,' Reg shrugged, thinking of the one drawn out by his worn boots and telling him how to get from Grevillton to Hokitika. What had lain beyond or between the paths he'd trodden had remained an unquestioned blank. How he would now have liked a large map of the sort the government had, showing everywhere he'd ever been! How he'd have liked a map of the world so that he wouldn't never even have to bother going nowhere!

'What are you thinking, Reg?'

'Oh nothin' . . .' He scratched at his chest. 'That chicken had her some fleas,' he said, pushing the carcass further into his jacket and glancing up at the sky. Despite everything, after the West Coast he found the constant openness above him disconcerting; he missed the canopy of trees which had so often given him a good drenching but at least provided shield from the sun.

As the glare lessened they struck camp off the road a bit, Annie watching while Reg slunk about kicking dung and bits of kindling into a heap. It didn't do to interfere.

'Get out there and fill this billy,' he called, throwing the pot at her.

Annie shielded her eyes and glanced around the barren landscape.

'Dig, woman, dig!' Reg urged, hunger making him angry.

With a will Annie fell to the ground, stabbing at it with the toe of her shoe and alternately hammering at it with the heel. As a hole opened up she scrabbled with both hands till gradually it filled with water. Of a very dirty kind.

'Don't be fussy,' Reg said. 'That'll settle in the pot.'

Nonetheless Annie continued to dig. Suddenly her nostrils were arrested by an acrid smell and, turning, she saw Reg holding the chicken by its feet and waving it in the flames. Cautiously she came up behind him. Already most of the feathers were burned off, leaving only the blackened stumps of quills protruding from the greasy, now oozing skin. Reg changed his grip, intent on getting the best out of the heat and seemingly untroubled by the pungent smoke from the feathers shrivelling in the embers.

'It'll make a good broth, this.'

Annie returned to her waterhole and filled the pot. Reg came over, emptied it out, shoved the chicken in, head and all, and dipped it into the water again. Soon it was bubbling on the fire, giving off a grey-black froth which Reg knocked clear with a stick. Not for him the messing around with giblets, the cutting of things into little pieces and the bothering about the smell. Where were the extra pots anyway? Suddenly he pulled the hen out and snapped off its legs, setting each one of them on a stone in the embers where the skin began to crackle and dry out. Annie licked her lips.

'Make a good breakfast,' said Reg, rising and stuffing them in his jacket pocket. He lifted the billy off the fire and put it before Annie: 'You first,' he said.

Oh for a couple of enamel plates, a length of muslin and a tree to hang it in, thought Annie, seeing the beautiful chicken legs now stuck with fluff protruding from Reg's pockets!

'I hope,' said Reg. 'We don't get sour land like this.' Annie bit her lip. 'We don't want to use ourselves up for nothing.'

'I reckon, Reg, when we get up a bit higher, the land'll be good for grass.'

'Cows'll make fools out of you,' Reg warned. 'And you'd never get the butter down.'

'It'd be for us Reg. *We'd* eat it.'

The next day as they ascended trees began to appear, becoming increasingly more frequent till Reg was anxiously eyeing their girth. Gradually the land gave way to thick native forest. On and on they went without sign of habitation until, cresting a hill, they were met with the amazing sight of a broad shaved belt as far as the next ridge of hills divided into sections by sapling fences. From mud, the skeletons of burned trees forked at the sky and already here and there pale dwellings of new-cut timber were to be seen.

'How scattered they are! How far away from each other!' Annie murmured.

Had she hoped for a town, Reg wondered? The whole idea of blocks was to give people blocks to live on so of course they were fenced off; of course houses were on different blocks!

'Look!' Annie whispered.

Following her pointing finger Reg saw a group of people who looked like foreigners kneeling in prayer, peculiar little scarves on the heads of the women. An older man seemed to be leading them.

Finishing their prayers and looking up, the man saw Reg and Annie. 'Welcome!' he said, walking towards them.

Reg stepped forward. Looking at them Annie thought there was something funny about them but she could not put her finger on it.

'Looking for 442,' Reg said gruffly.

A flutter went through the community as the words 'four-forty-two' were repeated.

'It's the only bit left,' said the man, pointing towards the ridge of hills. 'You'll be in the midst of us.'

Something told Annie it would not do Reg any good to go pinching chickens here.

'Where are your horses?' the man asked.

'We were on foot – trusting in God,' Annie put in wisely.

'Pieter,' the man introduced himself, extending his hand towards Annie to squeeze hers warmly.

Unused to these kinds of carryings-on Reg cleared his throat. Already the men were coming towards him, enquiring after his tools. 'Thought we'd take a look at the place first,' he mumbled.

'You'll be too late,' put in Pieter. 'You've to be cutting down your trees so you can burn them come winter.'

'Cut 'em in winter!' Reg retorted.

Pieter shook his head. 'No, my good friend,' he insisted. 'Cut them now and you get the bracken and undergrowth with it. That way when you fire them, you get a good blaze. The leaves burn good. You cut them in winter, you won't get them afire.'

Reg stared at him evenly.

'You burn them in winter,' the man went on. 'Then on the cusp of spring when the ashes are falling on to the ground still warm, you toss in your seed. That way they'll up with the first rains. You must to get them in sharp.'

'What?'

'Your cocksfoot,' Pieter smiled in a friendly fashion.

'Cocksfoot?' Reg repeated.

'Cocksfoot grass,' Pieter nodded.

Annie frowned. Here was something called 'cocksfoot' that Reg didn't know about. She cast an anxious glance at Pieter.

'Now you know as well as me,' Pieter said kindly. 'That's the best thing you can put in after clearing out the forest.'

'You'd never get a traction engine up here,' Reg said shiftily.

Pieter laughed. 'Maybe you're right but it makes excellent pasture!'

Reg and Annie continued on up the road towards 442 in silence. Although Annie was grateful for the nearness of other humans she knew that Reg was not happy to find a community there. When the men had come forward offering to help she had sensed their women weren't too keen on having their men's tools lent out to be blunted on a latecomer's land. Although many seemed foreign – and apart from their leaders were all younger than Reg – she sensed they were men who had worked on the land of others, newly marrieds, those who had, as was said, 'come to their senses' in time. Yet something had drawn them to make a community. They had lent not only the tools but themselves to help in neighbourly fashion before winter set in. *That* was something. And she must surely find some way to repay their kindness in the future . . .

Four-forty-two turned out to be farther away than Reg had imagined, an uneven parcel of land sliding up an incline, dipping and rising with it. Taking his hat off he stared at the mighty trees which covered the land and blocked out the sun, at the tangle of veins clawing up their trunks to the light, at the undergrowth which scratched his knees and pulled at Annie's skirts and at the birds hopping loudly away, disturbed by the sound of giant falling leaves in their wilderness. There was no way they could have got those trees down on their own!

'Maybe they'll be all right, those people,' he murmured, pacing away from Annie. 'Hey!' he called sharply. 'Someone's been here!'

Mindful that they might have been slightly in the wrong place Annie hurried over to see Reg pointing with resentment at a stunted berry tree.

'That don't grow natural here!' he grumbled.

'Could have been a pip spat out,' Annie replied. 'Dropped by a bird.'

But Reg was now disgruntled. The idea that someone had lived on his piece of land, planted things, perhaps even built a shanty there was anathema.

'It's not as if you haven't trespassed a few times yourself, Reg,' Annie pointed out.

'Toh!' As far as Reg was concerned this was entirely different.

Although they were prepared to accept help clearing the land Reg drew the line at staying in the houses of the community. Proud and defiant, though he could not cut his own trees, he insisted they camp under a lean-to and in the daytime tried to impress Annie with his usefulness, though none of the community would let go of the ends of their saws or pass over an axe to him. What a joke! he thought. There he'd been in Bowens Gully – sheep, outhouses, the dwelling itself – the town of Moke not a stone's throw away and all he'd needed to do was fix a few fence posts! But oh no! He'd had to get the girl Ceci from the Immigrant Barracks, have it out with her in the kitchen, violate her without being sufficiently aware of her existence as a separate person to know he was doing it, then take off with his pittance like the Prodigal Son and spend it! Well, now he was paying the price. It was not a pretty thing for a man to have his woman watch other men do his work for him, even if they were only taking down the larger trees . . .

From a discreet position Annie watched the men. They spent some time walking from tree to tree then coming back to confer. At times she thought they were speaking another language and why they spent so long discussing and pointing when they could simply have set about

97

cutting the trees down she did not know. Drawn closer by curiosity she saw their leader had cleared a space on the ground, put twigs and earth to one side and placed marks on it like checkers on a draughts board: the men were nodding and agreeing about it. Suddenly they arose and positioned themselves more or less in a line away from her, falling to work on individual trees with vigour, their axes rising in the air, hands sliding up and down shafts as blades descended and bit into virgin wood. The sound of the splintering made the hills ring as the white chips flew faster, higher into the air till 'Hoh!' shouted their leader, and, as the men ran clear, he delivered to his giant the final crippling blow. For a moment it swayed and creaked, then with great thrashing and groaning tore its branches from amongst its neighbours and, swaying in drunken fury, began its lurching descent to the forest floor. Hardly had it begun to move than it struck the next tree, also cut at the base, causing it to plunge and screech with wild convulsions, toppling and passing the death blow to the next tree and on down the line. As the next and the next and the next tree fell – the men standing back in the rising dust – the ground shook; the noise defied belief as the crashing giants sent thick clouds up to choke in the white light searing in through the open gaps. So brilliant were these shafts, so keen their edges, Annie could not look at them. Like panes of glass they stood sideways between the trees. All around she felt things running: insects, birds. It was as if nature had been taken on, a work started which could not be abandoned.

Reg gaped with incredulity then glanced at Annie, wiping her eyes perhaps from dust, perhaps tears. He went to stand by her. 'Thanks,' he called gruffly, but already the community were leaving, their voices muffled, descending echoes. This was it. This was their home. If they could hold on to it for seven years and make improvements before their capital ran out, it would be theirs forever.

Annie coughed the dust from her throat and looked up at Reg cautiously. 'You want to sleep in the front room or the kitchen tonight?' she grinned.

Reg glanced at the sky now visible through the opening above. 'We're not borrowing from those people,' he said sternly. 'We'll have to shift fast before winter comes . . .'

Annie nodded. Now they knew what they needed. If she had to go back down and drag it all back up in a cart fixed to her teeth one thing was for sure: by the time the first rains fell they would have a meat safe; a basin, some tin plates and knives, enough pots to boil bush tea at the same time as a wild bird; and the extra tools they would need to bring the rest of the cover down. But not the cocksfoot seed. There was no point in keeping that over winter. It might spoil.

Reg stared at the undergrowth thinking of gimlets, spokeshaves, a smoothing plane for the timber for the house, grubbing hoes and, yes, garden spades for the spring. And while he was at it he would ask the price of a bullock team . . . His stomach was empty and he was hungry. Had Annie not been there, he would have turned his jacket pockets inside out to suck the grease off them, to taste the remains of the chicken. They should at least have thought to bring flour with them to make dampers!

'I don't think God will be sending many chickens towards you in a place like this,' Annie said gently.

Reg stretched. 'Be that as it may, girl,' he teased, 'them fern roots is good to eat. Now you get over there and dig some up then look about for water while I light a fire.'

Well, well, well, thought Annie. Maybe Reg did know a thing or two after all!

Chapter 8

'It's hard to lay things down when your children leave home,' Ginger admitted. He dwelled on his absent daughters, being less bothered by Lizabeth's situation than Faith's – perhaps because as it was not 'legal' he still believed in some way it could be rectified.

'You had hopes for them that weren't realized.' Ceci shrugged.

'Maybe we could have Faith and Dougall up?' he suggested. 'She may not come. She's angry with me.'

'For what reason?'

At the back of his mind, though he did not admit it to Ceci, Ginger hoped, and knew he hoped, that Faith would bring Dougall around, would convert him so that while people might say: 'Her husband is a convert . . .' at least their children would be Catholics. In his heart Ginger knew this would make him feel better about everything. Yet he felt guilty for wanting it.

'If you're worrying about Lizabeth we could try to find her,' Ceci offered.

'How?'

'Didn't you say her husband – '

'He's not her husband.'

'Well – Frank – whom she told me she'd married. Didn't you say he worked for the Church Board?'

Ginger nodded.

'They could trace him.'

'Won't get much out of them,' Ginger grumbled. 'Not after I've done falling out with everyone.'

'If the Church Board administers Moke's graveyard –

and you Catholics are allowed to use it – it must be a joint commission. It's probably a committee that churches of all denominations subscribe to which maintains a journeyman to go around repairing their buildings.'

Ginger shrugged.

'Have the boys look for the Board's office next time they're in Christchurch. I could go with them . . .' Ceci let her voice trail off. If she *did* go she'd take a look at the existing marriage registers.

Ginger squeezed her shoulder: 'You're good to me.'

Hardly that good, Ceci thought, recalling the part she had played in sending Lizabeth after Frank and prohibiting Ginger from putting his foot down with Faith. Even now he was afraid to make contact though he desperately wanted to see the girl.

'Let me write that letter to Dougall,' she said, rising.

'You're good to me,' Ginger repeated. 'I may seem taken up with my daughters, Ceci, but – you are my life.'

Ceci closed the drawing room door and sat in her French chair by the windows which looked out on to the lawn. Although summer was nearing its end and the large dry leaves from the stand of poplars Calvin had planted as a windbreak were to be found dashed into little heaps, the smell and the scent of summer lingered headily. She had never been Calvin's 'life'. He had never seen the work of his hands come to maturity, never profited from his toil or reaped joy anywhere. How like gold those leaves were – an absent man's offerings scattered on a lawn.

Crossing to her davenport Ceci drew out Olwen's latest letter to re-read. By the sound of it Khandallah was without a church of any kind – which must have been a relief for Olwen. Ceci could imagine her lying in bed of a Sunday, glad not to be forced to choose between hypocrisies. Those who felt so inclined, Olwen had written, were at liberty to walk over the hill or even take a train to satisfy their cravings. Yet for all this rarely did the rumble of a carriage disturb Khandallah's Sunday morning calm . . . Briefly Ceci thought of Reg. Olwen, who kept up with him in a vague fashion, spoke of having had her letter to him care of General Delivery Parapara returned, having been forwarded first to Taipapu on the word of some miner. All Olwen could tell Ceci of Taipapu was that it was a Maori word meaning 'sacred place' and had once been a boundary of some sort for the Maoris. It was a piece of land they had hung on to as long as they could before selling out to the *pakehas*. *Pakehas*? The first to admit she knew nothing of Maori culture, to hear her own daughter describe Europeans as *pakehas* gave Ceci a jolt. She gathered Olwen was worried there may have been friction when the land changed hands and feared Reg might have blundered into some *tapu*. Taboo? Herself she could not worry about Reg for the image of him as a young man who had frightened her persisted. The arm raised, the eyes flaring . . . The last time she had seen him his balding head had been dipped to conceal moist eyes as the carriage taking her and Olwen from Grevillton left. But perhaps Olwen was right to worry. Reg would be getting on now and if he *had* wandered from the track, his would not be the first corpse to be discovered between rocks after the snows melted . . .

'Who are you writing to?'

Ceci turned. 'I was reading Olwen's letter.'

'May I see?' Myra exclaimed with excitement.

Ceci hesitated. While she knew Myra had a pash on Olwen, regarding her as the height of glamour, there were often attitudes in Olwen's letters she felt Ginger would not appreciate Myra acquiring. In this instance there was an entire paragraph making caustic reference to some poor young man who had sent her flowers and whom she was taking delight in rebuffing, without feeling, Ceci would say. It was clear from the way Olwen wrote that she had not taken the trouble to advise the person of her conjugal status for he would certainly not be pursuing her if she had. Assurances about not intending to 'fall in love and waste herself' were some comfort, Ceci supposed, though hardly good reading for a girl Myra's age. Was it possible, given no one could handle potential suitors better than Olwen, that her remarks were simply a way of telling Ceci she remembered she was fettered by the restraints of a previous marriage and was behaving accordingly? Or could it be that she would prefer to set herself up as out of reach than be seen as an object of pity who would love to be married but was denied forever that pleasure? 'You don't want to take too much notice of everything Olwen says,' Ceci smiled, handing Myra the letter. 'It's just her way of talking. Fashionable talk.'

Myra read avidly.

Ceci took up her pen. 'I'm writing to Faith and Dougall. Would you like to add a line?'

'Tell them the boys are getting a racehorse,' Myra reminded her.

'I don't think we'd better mention that just yet,' Ceci said carefully.

'Why?'

'Your father does not necessarily – '

'Whether he agrees or not they'll get one!'

What Ceci had been about to say was, 'know about it'.

'When are Faith and Dougie coming?' Myra demanded. 'Father says you're asking them.'

Ceci smiled. With Faith and Lizabeth gone, Myra and she had become as close as she imagined possible for them. She had seen the girl flourish, loving the attention she received from all around. It took only a letter from the outside world to raise her to a state of great excitement.

103

'Why don't you write the actual invitation?' Ceci said, leaning back in her chair.

'Because I can't be bothered.'

'Don't be so lazy! I'm leaving a space for you to do the last paragraph.' That should do it, Ceci thought. That would save both her and Ginger bearing responsibility for the idea. Who could accuse them now of seeking to monitor the development of the marriage? Strange that Myra, who had always been the first in line for spying, could so openly make the overture yet conceal the intention with impetuous childish joy.

It is clear she has come as a visitor, Ceci thought, opening the door on Faith. The girl did not take one step towards her father who waited hesitantly behind Ceci, afraid to put a foot wrong, but remained immobile on the porch. Dougall came quickly forward, grasped Ceci's hands and, murmuring a greeting, stepped into the house. 'Dougall!' shouted Myra from the back of the hall. Standing on the slab beyond the door, Faith's eyes dropped to the wrought-iron bootscraper. Quickly Ceci stepped forward.

Faith entered and stood in the hallway, making no attempt to remove her coat. Nor did Dougall, presently handing his gloves to Ginger, pay her any attention.

'Let me,' Ceci began, reaching towards Faith, but with a quick movement the girl turned her back on the gathering, slipped off her gloves and almost with ill will removed her coat.

'I think I at least remember the way in,' Dougall joked, an element of chiding in his voice as he glanced back at Faith. 'Shall we?' And as if it were his house, he led the family into the drawing room.

Faith's eyes passed over the chairs and ornaments as if remembering a place from another world. She seemed almost confused by the use of language when invited by

Myra to visit her room. On the stairway her step faltered and her breathing sounded peculiar.

'Are you all right?'

'Why wouldn't I be?'

'You're – you're not –'

'Oh, nothing like that. Not yet!'

'Well he's so handsome,' Myra encouraged.

Faith smiled.

'He's not like Kevin and Michael and us though, is he?' Myra asked. 'Though I think you did very well.'

Faith's mouth tightened. 'When you leave Hexham, you may learn that the purpose of life – I don't just mean in the city – is not about getting through the day and enjoying yourself. It's about responsibility. And serious behaviour.'

Myra fiddled with the doll's bonnet she had kept on her dressing table since childhood and, as Faith talked on about duty and morality, recalled how they'd used to kneel together pretending to be in church as children, passing holy pictures to each other and taking it in turns to be priest. Particularly she remembered Faith making all the dolls go to communion against the hearth fender, bending them backwards so they'd knelt. Her sister now was a stranger to her.

'. . . marriage is a very serious institution,' Faith was saying.

Myra put the doll's bonnet in a drawer. Faith was not remotely interested in her room. She had not even commented on the pink coverlet Ceci had made for her bed nor the matching frilled skirts that had been sewn around the pink tins in which she kept candies!

As they re-entered the drawing room the sight of Dougall laughing seemed to arrest Faith and in the briefest instant Myra caught her amazement. Though she could not understand it, Faith felt cheated. Further, when her father asked how she liked Myra's room, though she managed to shrug the question off, she found she resented being spoken to. Ginger began drumming his fingers, a habit Ceci knew annoyed Faith intensely. She signed at him to stop.

'Things seem to have settled down in Moke,' Ceci began.

'Storm in a tea cup,' Faith said, regretting how it sounded as soon as it came out.

'On the contrary,' Dougall countered. 'We had no intention to cause trouble.'

'But it was their mistaken ideas,' Faith persisted. 'Wasn't it?'

Dougall remained silent.

As they moved into the dining room Ceci realized Faith did not want to eat with them. Against Dougall's show of bonhomie she looked wretched and unhappy. 'Faith,' she whispered, 'can you not manage a little kindness towards your father?'

Suddenly Faith's eyes filled with tears.

'Would you like to sit here, Dougall?' Ginger asked, indicating the head of the table. 'And Faith here,' he patted the chair to his left.

Ceci would be to Dougall's right and Ginger on his left, Faith realized and she, pinioned between her father and younger sister, separated from her new husband, now wedged between Ceci and her father like some new toy she had brought into the house for their pleasure!

'She wants to sit next to Dougall,' Myra whispered.

'How silly of me,' Ceci murmured in the same instant that Ginger vacated his place and hurried to sit by Ceci.

Myra saw Faith dart a quick glance at Dougall as if seeking reassurance but he looked down, not wanting anything to do with it.

Conversation turned to their house in Dunedin which Faith had previously described to Myra as exactly the kind of domicile a young couple would choose for themselves were they lucky enough to have a choice.

'There's certainly a lot wrong with it,' Dougall began, cutting a piece of food and careful not to look at Faith.

Myra saw her sister gape. That she would love to have cried out: 'There certainly is not!' Myra knew well for Faith had always been the first to interrupt. Indeed even *she* felt Dougall was fibbing in order to somehow deprive Faith of the opportunity of boasting about her new situation.

'What's wrong with it?' Ceci asked pleasantly.

Myra watched Dougall delineate a number of small deficiencies any able-bodied workman could put right and as the rage on Faith's face grew and Ginger fell for it, telling Dougall he only needed a couple of nails here or to climb on the roof or to make a new hole and pull a wire through, Myra sensed he was taunting her sister.

'I'll come down and take a look at it for you if you like,' Ginger said, not particularly meaning it.

Faith laid her knife by her plate.

'I'm sure Dougall can cope with all those small things,' Ceci said, a note of warning in her voice.

Dougall changed tack. 'We're very blessed with the neighbours too,' he threw out.

Faith watched the fly bobbing within reach. Surely he did not think she was so stupid as to take a gulp at that! Apart from suggesting he was a useless husband and putting himself under the father who finally had no more say over her he was now trying to somehow tempt her into dangerous waters.

'One of the neighbours,' she began in a careful voice, 'actually attacked a journeyman with an iron – '

'Don't make up stories,' Dougall smiled and this time Ceci caught the expression before Faith's eyes dived to the table. She had not expected to be contradicted nor had she

107

been exaggerating. Even if Dougall were trying to teach her not to discuss unsavoury matters at table there had been no need for him to be so abrupt.

'We are fortunate in our landlady too,' Dougall continued suavely. 'Aren't we Faith?'

Faith chose to remain silent.

Ginger fetched out some wine.

How could he be so stupid as to offer a Presbyterian wine, Myra winced, when they were all supposed to be Temperance!

'What a pleasant idea,' Dougall said firmly.

Faith raised betrayed eyes.

'May I?' Dougall continued, passing the dessert to Ceci. 'Eat your sweet, Faith. It's delicious.'

Myra saw the edges of Faith's mouth wobble.

'Perhaps we should stay the night?' he said, glancing at his watch.

'You know you have work tomorrow,' Faith said quietly.

'I told them I might be unavailable.'

For some reason, Myra did not believe this. She gazed at the wine swirling in the glass he held in his hand and took a sip of her own. Her father was observing Faith as if to say: 'How she must hate me!' She took a sip of Faith's wine and offered it to her but Faith ignored it. Her new habit of looking no one in the eye struck Myra as very odd. Still holding Faith's glass she took another sip. The wine was very good. It was a wine her father had been saving for a special occasion. He had started buying wine since marrying Ceci because it was a drink that all could share. Before that he had drunk Scotch.

Dougall stood in the hall thanking her parents for their kindness, their hospitality, for the delicious food. It seemed to Myra he was overdoing it but his comments obviously pleased Ceci and the man-to-man approach he had adopted with her father had cemented things there. Already the two men were slapping each other's backs as if they'd known one another for years. In a corner Faith waited.

'Where are the boys tonight?' Dougall quipped.

'Christchurch. At the race track probably. Thinking I don't know,' Ginger grinned.

Myra frowned. Her sister had changed beyond recognition and it had to be something to do with Dougall. Where were the attitudes Faith had spoken of in the bedroom upstairs: the righteous living, the sobriety, the avoidance of gambling and indulgence? If Dougall really thought it funny that the boys were at the race track having deceived their father, then the new words Faith had learned were mere coins he had bought her with. Indeed there was nothing in Dougall's overt behaviour to suggest he was any different from them.

'Nice boy,' sighed Ginger, closing the door. 'It goes to show how wrong the Church attitude is.'

'You were very good with both of them.'

'Why does she hate me?'

Ceci paused. There was a lot to be thought out here. 'Perhaps she doesn't,' she said honestly. 'I have no idea. It seems we were very wrong about him though. I for one put too much credence in Calvin's attitudes as being indicative of the reformed way. I should have put all that out of my mind. In fact it wasn't even him – it was Miss Robertson who insisted time spent in enjoyment was time removed from the service of God. Dougall even drank wine!'

'He didn't,' came a small voice from the stairway. 'He took up the glass in his hand but he didn't drink it.'

Ginger frowned. He could recall that some of the wine had not been finished but surely it was Faith's glass not

109

Dougall's which had remained untouched? He had certainly seen him lift the glass in toast.

Ceci cocked her ear to the driveway. Even now their carriage was rumbling away, its sense of mystery intact and the relationship between its occupants as secret as an iceberg whose tip they had seen passing at a great distance.

'She's gone, Ginger. She wanted to marry him and we didn't stop her. As far as I can see he's a fine young man. You have nothing to reproach yourself for.'

On the stairway Myra bit her thumb. It seemed to her that Someone had made their bed and Someone was going to have to lie on it.

Chapter 9

With the house almost empty now that the boys were
spending so much time in Christchurch Myra did not
bother getting up early. Soon she too would be gone,
Ginger realized. Not, he hoped, in the way Lizabeth had
gone, or Faith. Olwen? He did not worry about her for she
was not his and it seemed only natural that brave and
adventurous things should happen to her. Since she was
seven years old he had associated her with exceptional
events, with the crossing of oceans alone. As a small child
she had had that sense of independence and pride –
probably the mixture of Reg and Ceci in her. Myra?
Although impatient to be gone she was still without ideas
of her own, wavering between the lives of her sisters,
between Faith, Lizabeth and Olwen in their very different
circumstances.

He carried the tea upstairs, tapped on the door and took
a cup in to Myra. Lying in bed with the doll that she slept
with the girl still looked so childish it was impossible to
believe she would one day be gone! Almost as difficult as
it now was to believe that Faith had ever been anything to
do with them; been a child of his even, or reached up to
be placed lovingly on his knee. On that last visit she had
seemed so very mature and distant that she had ever been
anyone's child was hard to reconcile.

Propping the door open with one knee Ginger carried in
the tray to Ceci. She too had fallen back to sleep looking
even more trusting and child-like than Myra. He set the
tray on the table, sat on the bed and looked at her. She
wanted a child, he realized, reaching for the hand that lay

on the counterpane. Her wanting had started, he felt, as a belief that a child would be a natural expression of their love but this had been overtaken by a desire to give him children to replace the ones he had lost. That she would put herself through all the hard work of raising a family to stir him to life was amazing. But it wouldn't work. She was beautiful in mind and body as well as soul. Even were it not possible for humans to make children by being together, he would still have wanted her, have worked at himself so that she would have less cause to be disappointed, less need to fortify and encourage and, perhaps, even time to admire? 'What is there about me she could admire?' he shrugged, getting into bed, 'Except that I make good tea!'

Ceci opened her eyes. He was wrong about her reasons for wanting a child. They had more to do with the passing of time, flowers making a last bid before winter, the changed behaviour of birds, breezes picking up, the smell of autumn on the grass . . .

'If we don't make a definite effort towards a child, Ginger,' she began, 'we'll be too late.'

'We don't need to have one – '

'I would *like* us to – '

'You've enough on your plate.'

'I could manage.'

'I'll think about it,' Ginger said, a phrase he had found served increasingly well.

How to express her feelings to him without sounding edgy Ceci did not know. Had Calvin ever taken advantage of his position as her husband she would have baulked strongly at the idea of letting part of her own personality wander towards eternity welded to his. Indeed she would not, could not have contemplated reproduction with him other than as an act of gross betrayal to an unborn child far better left locked away in their separate bodies.

'If you have to think about it that much it can't be right,' Ginger teased as she frowned into her tea cup.

'How is it we haven't had a child, then?' Ceci asked.

He took the cup from her: 'Must be the will of God.'

Ceci flicked back the blankets and strode to the window. Will of God indeed! This was either a joke or a blatant assertion that he did not know her fertile periods for he avoided her during them. If she was up against this sort of thing, she decided, she might as well take the bull by the horns, get the day right and make sure that, drunk or sober, Ginger wanted her. Then they would see how much the will of God it was!

On the day Ceci had chosen to put the will of God to the test she heard the yard gate clack and, hurrying down, found Michael and Kevin backing a large horse into the stables.

'What an amazing creature!' she exclaimed.

'Isn't she!' Michael agreed. 'She's marvellous!'

Ceci watched the boys settling her down.

'Her name's Elke,' Kevin explained.

'Did you take my letter to the Marriage Registry?'

The boys nodded.

'And did you get a reply for me?'

After some scrabbling in a haversack the letter was produced, by its crumpled state clearly of small consequence next to the horse. 'Frank's left the Church Board,' Kevin stated. 'We asked.'

'Dad doesn't exactly know about this horse,' Michael began.

'How long will it be here?'

There was a silence. 'We bought it,' Kevin said. 'We brought it up here to show you then we're taking it back down to race.'

It would have been much wiser to have left it in

113

Christchurch, Ceci felt, wondering where they'd got the money.

'Thing is,' Michael said, rubbing his ear, 'we kind of hoped when he set his eyes on it Dad would like it –' He looked at Kevin. 'Thing is, you see,' he went on, 'we sold some of those old glass bits from the cupboard upstairs to get it.'

Ceci gaped. Those old glass bits, as Michael had so prosaically put it, were extremely valuable statuettes from Venice: Venetian glass. Vividly she remembered the bright red and deep blue of their hues.

'Well, they were only lying there wrapped up in a bit of an old duster,' Michael protested.

From a distance Ceci heard the row. No, Ginger did not care about the 'glass bits'; he did not disagree that it was a good horse as horses went: he did not doubt that they would 'get their money back on it' and yes, he was grateful to have been shown the beast. What he objected to was the fact that they had not consulted with him *first*.

'Don't be hard, Pa,' Michael argued. 'We could hardly cart the horse up here for you to look at –'

'What do you know about horses?' Ginger demanded.

'A bit,' Michael defended himself.

Yes, thought Ceci, and she knew were that bit came from. From Maureen's father, Old Nolan with his whisky in his back pocket . . . As the row grew louder and Ginger became more incensed she could see her opportunity of putting the will of God to the test that night retreating farther. Indeed, given the emotions flowing, it was unlikely she would have a chance of enjoying his favours in the next four days at all for the boys would be there for three of them and it would take Ginger at least one day to cool off after they'd gone . . . But it wasn't a bad-looking horse. Were the matter discussed, she would have to be extremely careful what she said.

Leaving the window she withdrew to her sewing room to study the letter from Christchurch. Did it never rain but it poured? Here – in black and white before her – was the evidence that Frank had married. What made it worse – or better depending on viewpoint – was the next written fact: he had divorced! Therefore when he had told Lizabeth he was free to marry her, in a sense he was. But Ginger would not see it that way any more than would the Pope himself. On the subject of divorce and remarriage as far as she understood it the Catholic Church's view was that a person could not vow to do something a second time having clearly demonstrated they could not do it the first! If his marriage to Lizabeth had been a Catholic ceremony, it went without saying that Frank would not have admitted his status to either the priest or the girl. Therefore the marriage would be invalid in the eyes of that Church. If, however, Lizabeth had married Frank in some other Church, one which accepted divorce, there may have been no element of trickery on Frank's part. He'd have said he was free to marry her and left it at that. It was the devil's choice for if Lizabeth had married Frank in a Catholic church she was – as Ginger hoped – free to leave him, for the ceremony would be considered fraudulent. If, on the other hand, a Protestant minister had married them she would have betrayed her own principles by entering into a marriage her conscience did not respect. In either case she would be legally bound to Frank. Whether Ceci would prefer Lizabeth to be legally bound to a man she was not morally married to or simply – as Ginger hoped – 'living in sin' she did not know. The fact Frank had divorced had at least raised him one notch by no longer being bigamous. But his marriage to Lizabeth had not yet found its way into the District Registry. Had it taken place? There was nothing in the letter worth telling Ginger. The fact that Frank was divorced had no meaning for

Catholics. Lizabeth would always be considered to be 'living in sin' because to them marriage was forever and divorce a poor man-made excuse which changed nothing.

She heard the hall door slam and reached the window in time to see Ginger flinging open the stable door and driving the new resident out with a firm switch across the behind which sent her scudding down the driveway in a hail of gravel. Instantly her mind was cleared. If the boys were to have a racehorse, better that they have a good one than a bad one. Better, in fact, to sell *all* Mrs Laird's finery – which was as much hers as Ginger's – and send the boys to Ireland or Australia and have them come back with a first-class racehorse the like of which Christchurch had never seen. She had stood up for Lizabeth and Faith and in fairness to the boys would stand up to Ginger on this one. As soon as he got over his humour about the horse, when he could see it in a different light, she would bring the matter up. In any case, for the time being it looked as if the things she wanted would certainly have to wait!

Even with the rush of establishing her own business Olwen had found time to notice Marshall Cavanaugh and be impressed by him. Although he treated her with courtesy and remained just beyond arm's reach she sensed he found her attractive and when occasionally they would pass in the street, or he caught sight of her as he turned to enter a building, she felt a spark being given off between them. As a subordinate of James, Marshall had been appointed to indirectly oversee the setting up of her business to the extent that certain papers had to be carried to him for approval. Rather than take them herself, Olwen sent a girl with them. It was also up to Marshall to visit the premises, note the serial numbers of the Wheeler and Wilson sewing machines, check that windows and doors locked properly and that the investment of the Notables was duly protected. It seemed to Olwen that he could have sent a man to do this, not of course that he had installed or physically delivered any of these goods himself. Always well, but conservatively, dressed, he did what he had to do then left. Olwen found herself wondering what he did at night. Was he a man who gambled or drank? She could imagine him reclining by the billiard table in a club room, looking at the cues but not taking one down. His hands were not the hands of a man given to gambling or sport. She could not imagine him grasping a fishing rod, polo hammer or cricket bat. His were well-shaped hands, sensitive, intelligent. There was no arrogance in them. He stood and walked well, having few mannerisms or affectations. If anything, Olwen would say he had been descended from a line of gentlemen, rather than jumped up from the labouring class. What had happened to his ancestors, she wondered? His voice she found particularly attractive. When he would spread his hands on the desk, suddenly raise baffled eyes from checking a list of materials she had ordered, let his mouth crack into a half smile, then ask with a mixture of dignity and awkwardness what was the difference between tulle and taffeta she could have hugged him.

Now that the business was set up he did not visit but left her alone with her two main girls, a middle-aged woman who could work from simple drawing to finished product and a young girl who needed much directing. Sitting outside the workshop and glancing towards the bay Olwen asked herself repeatedly why the older woman had never gone into business on her own account. It seemed extraordinary and very exciting to her to be spoken to with such respect by an older woman, to see her rise as she entered the room, take the designs willingly and improvise where the drawing was indistinct. Whether the woman suspected she knew little about sewing machines Olwen did not know. As long as they made good money her part-

117

time and full-time girls would stay, and as long as she treated them with respect and behaved as an employer and not one of the girls, things would go well. There were times, however, when she would love to have joked with them, shared a confidence. But the price was too high.

For his part Marshall was strongly drawn towards Olwen. He did not know where she came from. Indeed very little was known about the girl other than by Gwen, the wife of his colleague Venables, but it was no more seemly for Marshall to enquire of Venables than for Venables to repeat the gossip of Gwen. Clearly the girl's background was respectable or they would not have been involved with her. Desperately he sought about for an introduction of the sort which would permit him to meet her socially. What was needed was a situation where she would become friendly with someone in Gwen's circle who had an acquaintance who was a friend of one of his male friends. That way a group outing could be arranged or some kind of party. Unfortunately, however, the girl kept constantly to herself and as time passed and her business flourished, her work becoming better known and her dresses appearing on the best backs, it became clear to Marshall that she was not going to mix. For some reason she was above them. Yet he had sensed in her a need for others which suggested she was not a snob. Perhaps the other women had not approached her directly? Perhaps they were even jealous of her? Perhaps it would be appropriate for him to take a direct and independent step? With this in mind he began to have flowers delivered to her boutique every Wednesday, occasionally slipping in a courteous card enquiring after her health.

As Olwen saw the boy enter her workshop holding the flowers she knew at once who they were from. She saw his mouth moving as he asked the woman at the front a question, saw her nod towards the back, then carry on working. When he had gone she toyed with the card. She was married. She glanced at the women working beyond her door. No one must know this fact. Were she to take the flowers home it would be an encouragement to Marshall. That would be wrong. Yet she did want to encourage him.

'Mrs Hampton,' she called through the door. 'Would you please arrange these in the girls' workroom. They are an appreciation.'

In the following week the flowers contained a ticket for a concert.

It came as no surprise to Marshall as he waited in the foyer that Olwen was not amongst the celebrities crowding its doors. Although the visiting orchestra was of such repute that all of Wellington had queued up willingly to buy tickets long in advance, either the young lady he was pursuing was not to be tempted by bright lights or else he must interpret her habitual disdain as a desire to discontinue their slight association. Feeling extremely conscious that his contemporaries would note he was 'alone', Marshall raked the crowd with his eyes lest the girl be hovering on the outskirts. He spotted two of her designs, at least designs which people would impute to her for already her flair was becoming known, yet as the couples drifted towards the glass doors and he glanced anxiously at his watch and heard bells ring, he was forced to accept she was not coming. Everyone who was anyone in Wellington would see the empty seat beside him, the only one in the auditorium, and realize that Marshall Cavanaugh had been stood up. Damn! he thought, pacing the lobby. Perhaps it would simply be better to hand in his ticket. But he enjoyed classical music and a concert of this quality was a rare occurrence in the Antipodes.

At that moment a most extraordinary thing happened. A young man, who must have been a recent arrival in the colony, presented himself at the box office incredibly believing he could actually get a ticket! He looked to Marshall to be wearing his best clothes and possibly there simply to rub shoulders.

'Did I hear you enquire after a ticket?' he said agreeably, stepping over. 'The seat next to mine is vacant. You will find the ticket in my name,' he told the clerk. 'The ticket has not been taken up.'

The clerk reissued the ticket and the two men strode through the glass doors together as the lights dimmed.

During the interval the chap got talking and introduced himself as Brigham. He was, Marshall noticed, easily beaten to the bar when it came time to buy drinks.

'So what are you doing out here?' Marshall asked, wishing to appear deep in conversation lest his colleagues discern the slightness of their acquaintance. 'And how are you getting on with your various attempts to find work?'

'I'll try anything,' Brigham frowned. 'At home I was in trade . . .'

There was something vaguely disreputable about the man, Marshall thought, yet given a proper start, he could turn out to be as good as any of them.

'You'll do anything, you say?'

The fellow nodded.

'I could introduce you to the Inspector of Nuisances.'

'Beg pardon?'

'In the matter of hygiene. Unsanitary situations. Rats,' Marshall lowered his voice which had risen slightly owing to the drink and the crowded room. 'If, as you say, you'll try anything. There is certainly an opening there.'

The man became silent and shifted. Probably one of those who expects to find everything ready and waiting for them the minute they step off the ship, Marshall concluded, his mind returning to Olwen.

'I appreciated you giving me the seat,' Brigham was saying, offering him a card.

Marshall glanced at it. A hotel address. No doubt he would use it until he was established.

Despite everything, as they returned to their seats Marshall felt unreasonably grateful to the man for being with him. He was probably not a bad sort of tyke and, as he felt the eyes of his colleagues following them down the aisle, he realized people would think he had been entertaining a newcomer. That was always worth a few invitations in event-hungry Wellington, opportunities to either invite Olwen along, hope she had been invited, or put her out of his mind.

The following morning, selecting a pair of trousers, Marshall decided to make a direct approach. He had drunk slightly more than was usual for him after the concert, had told Brigham too much about his own insignificant commodity business, his part-time involvement with James and the importance of that income. He could even recall mentioning Olwen's name and seeing the man repeat it, linger on it. The melody of the previous night's music moved in his head. Now he could not remember the composer's name but the work had been mordant, pessimistic and dull, with such difficulty in reaching conclusions that the entire sinfonietta had been an exhibition of self-doubt. Of course, had Olwen been sitting next to him he might have felt differently ... Choosing a favourite soft cloth shirt freshly returned from the laundry he posed before the mirror.

The time had come to stop giving the girl gifts. She would have a direct visit but under what pretext? From the legal papers he knew her exact address in Khandallah. Some hours beyond it was a sporting club where the fishless rivers the colonists had learned to live with had been stocked with trout. Perhaps if he could obtain one –

for he could certainly not catch one – he could pass through Khandallah on the way back and present it to her? The situation would then seem casual and quite fair.

Abandoning work and arriving at the sporting club Marshall found his luck was in. A party of visiting fishermen had had what they called 'a good day' and fish were lying about for the taking.

'Let me give you something for it, fine fish like that!' Marshall urged.

But the proud fisherman would have nothing. 'You're very welcome,' he insisted. 'After all, only catch 'em to eat!'

He even went so far as to wrap the dead fish up in leaves and fix it with a wooden pin until it looked so good Marshall almost believed he had caught it himself.

Entering Khandallah he began to feel self-conscious. Should he say he had *bought* it or *brought* it? The word caught must be avoided for it was not true. Although the fish had been in his possession only a short time already it was beginning to smell, probably a fate all game that was not dealt with promptly suffered. About to turn in at the gate he wondered. If the girl lived alone would his visit compromise her? Already he could sense curtains across the road moving. Standing there he became aware how much the girl had drawn him on her own terms. Moving up the path he was relieved when not Olwen but a young Maori girl opened the door.

'Is – is Miss Laird receiving?' he began awkwardly.

'What?'

'Would you please take this – and place it in your larder.' Marshall frowned, by now merely wanting to be rid of the fish.

'Pooh!' said the girl, pulling off the wrapper. 'How long you had this fish?'

Aware of the indignity of being questioned from a higher step by a maid, Marshall fixed Happi with a stare.

'You want to come in?' the girl asked. 'Who this fish for again?'

'Miss Laird.'

'You got the wrong house. You better take your fish!' She thrust it back at him.

Was it just possible, Marshall wondered, that Olwen had seen him through the window and set her maid up to insult him? 'Doesn't Olwen live here?' he asked and saw with a rush a smile spread on the girl's face.

'She does.'

'Then you may say this is a gentleman's calling card.' Marshall turned and walked to the gate. If they were to end, this was a very good note to do it on.

Happi went into the kitchen with the fish.

'Whew!' Olwen cried, clutching her handkerchief to her nose.

Happi burst out laughing. 'It's for a Miss Laird!' she gasped. 'You should see the man that brought it! What a half-starved nose!'

'You should have asked him in,' Olwen grinned, used to Happi's habit of describing English people's faces as not having enough flesh on them.

'You not Miss Laird!' Happi retorted.

'Have you been poking in my cupboards?'

Happi nodded enthusiastically. 'They was good photographs, them,' she said warmly. 'Of you getting married.'

'Happi, this is a secret between you and me. No one must know.'

Surprised by her intensity Happi nodded. 'You finished with him is okay by me!' she reassured her. 'Look. I thought up a name for your boutique!'

'And?'

'*Toia mai te waka ki te urunga.*'

123

Olwen gasped. 'What on *earth* does that mean?'

'That?' Happi asked, as if amazed Olwen didn't know. 'That means "Haul up your canoe to its resting-place" which is the great greeting song chanted on the beach for Quini Wikitoria!'

The thought of dumpy Queen Victoria hauling her canoe up the beach with a good helping thwack from behind by a Maori warrior amused Olwen intensely! In Happi she had found her hunger for a true friend with whom she could be totally honest satisfied. The girl's fearless, irreverent nature, her almost childish personality, in that it seemed based on emotion or circumstance, was a complete contradiction to the sort of women Olwen spent her working hours with, all of them sodden with duplicity and serving the insatiable many-headed god of propriety and compromise: Respectability. New Zealand, to Happi, was not cluttered with settlements named after distant admirals or visiting ships that themselves had been named after admirals, but regions like 'The Place of Maru-the-Eater-of-Bread-Fruit'; or 'The Heroic Diving' – a site where the *paua* shellfish and crayfish were in such deep water a man had to be brave to get them. With the beauty of their language her people named mountain ranges 'Mackerel' for their shape or called their valleys 'Broken Backbone'; their beaches 'Red Crabs', or their shores such deeply moving names as 'Cliff of Echoes'.

'You want to be careful going by there!' Happi assured Olwen, shuddering. She was deeply superstitious and firmly believed that the echoes there were the '*reo*' or voice of a woman who had committed suicide by jumping. That the sea itself made the noises only indicated to Happi its sympathy.

'*Parikarangaranga* . . .' Olwen repeated, hearing it. 'The Cliff of Echoes.'

'*Au-e*! Talk about something else!'

124

'I think you should let that man in next time he comes,' Olwen suggested. 'He's my friend. I might go to the races with him if he asks me.'

'*Nera*? You will, eh?'

Olwen nodded.

'*Kauaka*!' Happi warned. 'Don't!'

'Why not?'

'*He aroha*!' she teased. 'It is love!'

'You and I are like lips and teeth,' said Olwen pointing at her own mouth. 'You keep quiet about my past!'

Marshall turned into his quarters. He had probably made a fool of himself and the smell of the fish was damnable. On top of everything here was a note from the Brigham person, reminding him that he had agreed to speak to the Inspector of Nuisances on his behalf! The things one offered to do when feeling let down! If he were so lacking in self-respect as to invite Olwen to another occasion without first receiving some commitment from the girl – he would certainly take care to get three tickets and offer one to Brigham in case she didn't show. It looked like that person at least would be around for a while. Was it not better to have done with Olwen, or perhaps to have done with both of them together? There was the matter of the girl's choice of maid, which would be seen as socially provocative, should she choose to entertain; not to mention her instinct to rile those in authority. These things should be considered. He too was striving to establish himself. When all was said and done, though she was the one woman in a million he wanted, was she worth it?

On her way to work Olwen paused, noticing as she did the file of prisoners wending their way. Though late she waited while they came up, their slow unwilling steps dragging them from the gaol to their place of work. Others

125

turned their heads away but Olwen found herself searching the men's eyes. For what? Could some part of her future be walking by? Pathetic, angry, their skins as yellow as their uniforms, they moved past.

Olwen crossed the street, wishing she were married to Marshall and secure. But how to approach him? In order to impress him she must maintain her independent spirit for it was surely her ability to support herself which had attracted him. She could not show weakness. Nor could she use another woman as go-between for the kind of women she serviced paid exorbitant sums for her work because they believed her to be an artist, different from themselves, indifferent to the petty considerations which ruled their lives and which they wanted denied or accentuated in her designs. They wanted her to be beyond them. To be seen now as a woman with woman's first weakness – man – would cause them to lose respect for her. Worst of all, open to their destructive facility for gossip, her trade would suffer. How was she to respond to Marshall's overtures? She did not want to let him go and was worried that Happi's treatment of him the previous night might have caused serious affront. That she should care so much surprised her, for after her experiences with Edmund, she had tried to stamp out in herself the taste for sophisticated men – or at least to see beyond it. Where before Edmund she might have wished to be seen walking with a smart man in public, now there remained only the conviction that if she had Marshall, because of his strength of character, she would be safe and never have to worry again. By the end of the year her debts to the Notables would be behind her and she would then be less dependent on the goodwill of their wives. She would need less money and could afford to lose clients by being more 'human'. If Marshall would only wait that long!

'Now what I want,' Henrietta, the wife of James, began, 'is a robe which will – which will say . . .'

Olwen nodded.

'Do we understand each other?'

'You want dignity, which is beyond age,' Olwen stated. 'You don't necessarily want a feminine or even an attractive creation. You want something that will say you no longer need to pander to man's lower sensibilities because you are above them.' Glancing up, Olwen could tell she had put her finger on it. The lady was a little embarrassed. 'At the same time there is an element of the, shall I say, "regal" in your requirements – having to do with your husband's bearing in the community. Am I right, madam?'

'Call me Hetty,' the woman said in a more humble voice. 'Were any of your designs on show at the concert?'

'I didn't go.'

'I heard Muriel Farquharson was looking quite – quite – "exceptional",' Hetty said pointedly. 'And there isn't a ship in . . .'

'Has Muriel been away?' Olwen asked facetiously.

'My meaning is she could not have received the dress as an *import*.'

Olwen shrugged.

'There are some around who would give their eye tooth to know what her precise instructions for that dress had been,' Hetty held out hopefully. 'It was – it was somewhat, may I say "intimate" for a woman of that age. Particularly one whose husband is away.'

'As I say, I did not go to the recital.'

'But what did you think of that dress?'

'Were I to see it I might have some thought,' Olwen said, deciding to terminate the conversation. 'No doubt whoever designed it was responding to some very private requirement or instruction, as am I in your case . . .' She let her voice trail off. 'Which naturally I would not repeat to anyone any more than I would breach the confidence of my profession by designing an article of wardrobe which was at variance with a person's position.' That should do it.

After a while Hetty took the subject up again: 'Odd that you have not seen that dress . . .'

'As you know, Hetty, I don't mix.'

'Why is that, I wonder?'

'Shall we say,' Olwen smiled up at her, once again thankful for her policy of avoiding private alliances with women and men alike, 'that I like my designs to be fresh and original. I would not wish them to be sullied with other people's advice and opinions.'

'We are having a party next Tuesday,' Hetty began. 'Gwen and Venables will be coming and if perhaps you could find an escort . . .'

Olwen shook her head and although Hetty would love to have asked she dared not breathe the question that was on her lips, namely who was the mystery suitor who sent flowers to her boutique addressed to *her*, and why would she never produce him in public? A spiteful little word she had once heard a maid use darted across her mind. Was it possible, could it be that Olwen, who took such interest in the measuring and clothing of ladies, was a little off-centre?

As Olwen pulled her cape about her on this crisp winter's day she felt time drawing in. Perhaps even now was too late to respond to Marshall: she had stood aloof so long. Would it not be in character to simply turn up at his apartment and knock at the door as he had done on hers? No flowers or little cakes, no sops to convention. Returning Hetty's designs to the workshop and giving instructions on them she set out. His address was known to her from the card which had accompanied his first flowers. It was an apartment on the side of a hill not far from an open park. Reaching the residence she swept in past the doorman and hurried up the carpeted stairs to the first-floor flat, the door of which bore the gold letter 'C'. Briefly she hesitated. From within came the sounds of movement. Raising a cautious hand she let it hover then brought it down firmly on the panelled wood.

Chapter 10

'Your daughter has the right idea from what I hear,' Theresa observed.

'Well, a career to think of,' Ceci found herself apologizing.

'Avoiding men and children,' Theresa went on. 'Now why would you want to climb to the top of a tree only to be pushed off?'

'Did I say –'

Theresa folded her arms: 'Are millions like us to fill the world with people so we can feel useful? My dear, if God in his goodness sees fit to send children to you –'

'Did I say I was trying to trick Ginger into one?'

'And you decide to keep them –' Theresa continued.

'Of course I'd keep them!'

' – you've to bear in mind they are on trust and each day you've to help them walk farther from you. So much as you want them, with each act you're plaiting the rope that'll hang you.'

Ceci shrugged, by now annoyed at herself for having made it clear to Theresa she wanted a child.

'Look about you,' Theresa urged, pointing towards a group of women outside Moribund's with nothing to talk about. 'Their children have gone.'

'I enjoy Ginger's children that have gone,' Ceci defended herself. 'They give me plenty to think about.'

'But they're not *yours*! Do you think they'd let you near them if they were? Your own mother's always the last to be told anything of importance. And the last, poor soul, to see all the fine manners she's troubled to teach you!'

130

Ceci sighed. As winter came on she had felt a regret in her body that pained like a tooth and though she tried to avoid the subject it would suddenly present itself as she turned back a sheet or reached up to wind the clock. She wanted children.

'Is it that you feel you are passing the age?' Theresa enquired.

Ceci shook her head.

'You're not just after a slate to write your name on?'

'That thought's not worthy of you.'

'If those pretty bundles of fluff were born aged thirty, would you want one?'

'It's just that I – I – feel Ginger is – standing in the way of things,' Ceci stammered. 'Not that he uses devices; it just works out that he avoids me at the – the time we could best use.'

'Have it out with him.'

'I'm not even sure why I want children,' Ceci confessed.

'You're drinking a sweet poison for the fear you'd be missing something if you didn't.'

'If he had *really* tried,' Ceci began, 'I could accept that it wasn't meant to happen if he had really tried.'

As the two women turned to cut back across the fields they linked arms.

'Children are seeds from mixed packets that shoot off to break their heads on different walls,' Theresa observed. She bent to gather some mushrooms. 'Have half,' she said, giving some to Ceci.

When the women parted Ceci watched Theresa retreating through the wet grass towards Moke. She was a good friend – given, despite a lack of education, a depth of thought rarely encountered in the environs. Had she been a man she could have been a politician. How often she'd felt like snapping 'Don't be unkind!' at Theresa, but the fact was, the woman was one jump ahead of her and she was lucky to have such a person to confide in without fear of ridicule or scandal. But Theresa's thoughts had a bleak quality to them which Ceci did not want to take for reality. 'I wouldn't go back five minutes' was one of the women's favourite expressions. Thinking about it Ceci concluded that, second by second, Theresa valued her life so deeply and was so conscious of its passing she could scarce bear to look back ... Like a terminal illness, despite bleak jokes, Theresa loved life.

Ceci turned in at the gate of Hexham. If it had not been children it would have been something else which would have awakened in her that sense of dissatisfaction at the fleeting nature of existence. Life was brief, she thought, stepping into the kitchen. She could neither paint it nor write about it nor express it in a symphony or sculpture. Was this then why she still wanted to have babies?

'That Theresa makes you think too much,' Ginger observed from the kitchen door.

'Do you think female artists want to have children too?' Ceci queried.

'Female artists?' Ginger repeated. 'Ask Olwen when she visits. Bound to know several "female artistes".'

Irritated by his flippancy Ceci clicked her tongue. Did he think she meant striptease girls?

'Aha,' Ginger teased. 'Broody again? Clucky?'

'Don't you ever sense the pointlessness of it all?' Ceci said quietly.

'We have enough to eat.'

'You don't understand what I am saying. When I see something very ordinary – sometimes it strikes me with such force I – I want to cry ...'

'See a doctor.'

'Exactly what Calvin said when I wanted to dance! Just when I'm trying to explain you say something like that and ...'

'Are you upset?'

'Oh I feel better now,' Ceci shrugged. 'I can always walk over and look at the insects in the water butt to get a sense of creation!'

'We'll have a child.'

Stopped in her tracks, Ceci waited.

'I can't bear to see you like this.'

Ceci looked at Ginger.

'I hadn't realized it meant so much to you.'

She felt tears on her face.

'Little streams vanishing in the grass,' he teased. 'The rain you get melancholy about.' He brushed her cheek with a thumb. 'It took a while to get over your encouraging the boys about that racehorse, I don't mind saying, but I can accept disagreement between us.'

Ceci glanced away. She hadn't even told him the news she had got about Frank from the Marriage Registry in Christchurch . . . She found Ginger eyeing her knowingly. 'You do mean it about the child, don't you?' she asked quickly.

'I'll take care of it,' Ginger nodded.

As she stood there Ginger recalled how, prior to their marriage, when she had been an exile from human comfort on the West Coast, this woman had developed an indifference to herself, a generosity towards others which had made her irresistible, had made him love her even more. Now, for the first time, she was asking for something for herself . . .

Hardly had two months passed when Ceci's yearning for children was answered in a tangible, imprecise form with the arrival of Lizabeth, her sixteen-month-old twins and a small bundle of possessions. Huge with pregnancy, now full term, she swayed on the doorstep.

'My dear!' Ceci gasped, running forward to support her.

'Get her into the house!' Ginger called, grabbing at the twins as Lizabeth went down. 'We must be careful not to drive her away this time. We musn't do anything to drive her out . . .'

'I don't think she's got long,' Ceci whispered, feeling her stomach. 'Just think of her struggling through the hills in this condition! Put the twins upstairs, Ginger. Sort out her room. I can manage here.'

Opening her eyes and focusing on Ceci, Lizabeth looked at the ceiling. 'Sorry to be a trouble.'

'You'll be no trouble.'

'Don't bank on it,' Lizabeth smiled wryly. 'The twins were born small. This is a big one.'

As they toiled on into the afternoon and night, which of them was the tiredest was hard to tell. Though Lizabeth had arrived in time she fought against the birth instead of co-operating with it, cursed Frank, called for him, showed to Ceci a part of herself that neither would forget.

Hours later when Ginger finally heard a child cry and opened the door, he caught Ceci and Lizabeth leaning on each other in exhaustion; between them a little boy. 'This is your home now,' he told Lizabeth in a rush of love.

'Frank is my home,' Lizabeth replied.

While Ceci admired her for the remark, she knew it had hurt Ginger. He withdrew.

'Where did you marry Frank?' she asked casually.

'In chapel.'

'A Catholic chapel?'

'Yes. And at the Register.'

'No ceremony in Frank's church, then?'

'Frank's a Catholic.'

Ceci held her peace.

'Father thinks he's been married before but he hasn't,' Lizabeth said firmly.

134

'Come on, Little Frank,' said Ceci, dabbing at the child's face.

'He'll look after the girls,' Lizabeth said, looking tiredly at the baby. 'When he grows up. If anything happens to me.'

'I'll prove it to her that Frank was married!' Ginger railed, his good resolutions behind him at the mere mention of Frank's name. 'She doesn't believe it, does she?'

Ceci shrugged and cradled Little Frank to her. 'We said we'd give her some peace, Ginger.'

Ginger gave Little Frank a hard look. Though he seemed used to the twin girls it struck Ceci he might give a boy a harder time.

'At least let her get over the birth. Would you like to hold him?' She offered the child.

Ginger shook his head. The truth about Frank was a lot worse than he guessed, Ceci reminded herself. It was well for Ginger to think Lizabeth was 'living in sin with Frank' and accordingly could stop at any time. The fact that Frank had married, divorced and remarried in a Catholic chapel, no less, put a completely different complexion on the matter and meant that in the eyes of the Catholic community, not only was this poor tiny child illegitimate in that its mother had gone through a meaningless ceremony with a man not free to marry her – but that Lizabeth was in the unenviable position of being legally tied to Frank in the eyes of the state and hence not free to contract a relationship with anyone else. Well, thank God Lizabeth didn't realize that! Thank God Frank *had* lied to her. And he would have done! No doubt when the priest had asked: 'Are you free to marry?' he had simply chosen to reply: 'Yes.' And Lizabeth had believed him.

Quickly the care of children took from Ceci the sense of urgency which had previously possessed her. Was to be a woman simply to be satisfied to be a part of someone else's life, someone's mother, someone's sister, someone's aunt, yet, unlike a man, never to have a life of one's own? Hadn't Theresa said that any woman who felt an urge for a child should take another woman's child into her arms and watch the urge go? And not five minutes would she give it, not even that . . .?

Gradually Ginger's resentment of Frank's existence returned to brood over the house, causing Lizabeth, despite her differences with Frank, to stand up for him and, missing him, neglect her children to the extent that the care of Little Frank and the twins fell more and more to Ceci. As Ginger watched her move out of his life, tending the twins, washing the baby, rising from sleep to quieten them, he grew irritable. That Lizabeth was losing touch with her children in a perverse way pleased him, yet he resented the fact that she would not get up in the night and help out. It was almost as if she were willing Little Frank and the twins on them . . .

'If Lizabeth goes after Frank again,' Ginger warned, 'she can no longer consider Hexham her home.'

'She doesn't.'

What sort of compromise would have satisfied Ginger was hard to tell but as the days became fraught with the voices of Lizabeth and Ginger constantly raised in anger, to her dismay Ceci found herself supporting Lizabeth against Ginger and being critical of him in his different attitudes towards his own children. It was clear to Ceci Ginger would drive Lizabeth out, that this was something he did not want, and that she was powerless to stop him. As she sided with Lizabeth in one particular row – which she realized by its fierceness would be their last, knowing that it would destroy any chance of a 'coming together' between her and Ginger in the lull which would take place following the girl's departure – each word cost dear. In her mind was the suspicion that her siding might be the final straw which would drive Ginger to the extreme of throwing her out. Painful, too, was the realization that she was unable to abandon her own principles to please her husband but must speak in favour of what she believed to be right.

Lizabeth left. She did not say goodbye. She left Little Frank and the twins in Ceci's care, kissed her, said she was going for a stroll and didn't come back. Because her bundle of possessions had gone Ceci realized the act had been intentional, that – despite their differences – the girl had gone looking for Frank and would in all probability discover what remained to be learned when she confronted him. Turning on the spot in the empty house she realized it would take Ginger some time to 'come right' . . . What she had glimpsed before Lizabeth's arrival – the ideal of her and Ginger expressing their love, their unison, in a child – was retreating before her eyes, shown up for what it was: a dream as hopelessly perfect as a Japanese porcelain; a thing to be taken out, looked at and put away again . . . Quietly she watched Ginger come into the room.

Reg watched the mist rising over the blackened tree stumps. 'Don't seem right all this being in my name,' he mused, staring over the brilliant green spikes of the cocksfoot grass cut with sunlight, lining the hollow of their clearing like an uneven dappled cloth. He watched the mist rise, past the remaining shrubs of the thicket, their packed greenery tight with the sound of bird and insect life. Already in its wake, hot needles of sun were reaching over the tree line to strike at the back of his neck, making him move to the shade. Though the ground was wet, by midday it would be dry as a bone, the grass limp before the heat. Whenever he emerged from their cabin he was struck by the brilliance of the light up here. Not that inside the cabin was darker than the next one over but, built with a view to sturdiness, its windows and doors being small and its roof tall to allow a good run-off, maybe it *was* a mite dark inside.

'I say it don't seem right this all being in my name,' he repeated in a raised voice. Where was the woman? Suddenly he heard a scream like a nightjar from the woodpile and ambled over to find her dancing about, waving her arms in the air.

'Oh Reg!' shrilled Annie. 'The ants done got me!'

Reg closed a hand round each of her upper arms and brought them down in long sweeps, scattering the ants. 'How many times I told you to look where you're putting your hands?' he murmured.

'Can't expect a body to see clear into the woodpile,' Annie grumbled. 'You think I got eyes on the end of my fingers?' She was still shaking from the ants. 'I *hate* things crawling over me!'

'Don't seem right all this being in my name,' Reg repeated.

Annie straightened up. 'I didn't want them poking about in my past, finding out where I was maybe.'

'Could set it right now,' Reg murmured, staring fixedly above the tree line.

Annie put her hands on her hips. What could be the meaning of that? 'I don't want people poking about in my past,' she repeated.

Reg shrugged. 'If it's your name you're worried about – '

'Exactly!' Annie interrupted. 'I skipped out on a sentence.'

Reg always knew she had been in gaol though he'd never asked her directly nor had she referred to it. 'There's one answer to that,' he said faintly. 'Change your name.'

Annie picked up the wood. Talk like that wouldn't get breakfast cooked.

138

Reg followed her into their cabin. 'How many times you bin married then?' he asked.

'Get your feet off that table!'

'Ain't no table, it's a box. I said, how many times you bin married?'

Annie reached up to the tin drum on the wall, one side cut open to resemble a door, and felt around for the sugar. 'Some people are very nosy this morning,' she said, keeping her back to him.

'I reckon you ain't never been married,' Reg told her. 'I reckon it's all just talk with you.'

Annie's hand found the sugar and lifted it out. There were no ants on it.

'Why'd you tell all those stories – about the one kid who drowned, the one killed by a falling tree and the rest of it? I reckon you ain't never had no kids at all!'

'Some people won't be getting any breakfast this morning,' Annie told him.

'I reckon you're what they call a virgin,' Reg said boldly.

Annie moved the sugar to one side. 'Happen I haven't been married, Reg. What would you expect a woman like me to say? I was born to the kind of life I've had – fell into it. Get me a *long* way tellin' folk I were never married! Nobody minds going with another bloke's wife!'

She was a funny woman, Reg thought, feeling she wasn't worthy of things. Behind her manner there was a humility he always sensed. 'Clever of you to miss out on having kids. Given the way you've been . . .'

Annie put her head on one side. Now Reg knew for a fact she'd wanted them. 'No point having kids you can't raise,' Annie shrugged, ''sides, I was careful.' Putting the sugar back in the cupboard she glanced at Reg. That had given him something to think about, that word 'careful'. 'Long time since you heard from your Olwen,' she went on. 'I've a mind to write to Ceci. That's what I'll do!'

Reg hadn't seemed to hear her. 'What?'

'I'll invite her up – '

Reg began to laugh. He laughed till Annie felt like hitting him.

'I don't see what's funny about that!'

'You sit down then and get out a nice piece of your scented stationery and drop her a line then,' Reg grinned. 'I'm sure she'll be right up on the next horse tram! What address you going to give? Block 442?' Annie frowned at their uneven floor. 'I expect she's had a dozen kids by now,' Reg went on. 'We'll have her up sometime though,' he said, glancing around the cabin. 'When I'm good and ready.' He rose and stretched. He intended chalking up a few notches first, though. That meant sortin' the place out, getting married to Annie proper and getting her pregnant. Stupid woman couldn't even tell she'd been proposed to three times already that morning. 'When she comes up here we'll have something to show her, Annie,' he said solemnly.

'Lying mongrel,' Annie thought. With the amount of work to be done it'd take them years to look decent. 'You're no spring chicken, Reg,' she pointed out. 'Better not wait.'

'No spring chicken yourself!' Reg retorted.

'Well, never mind arguing with me. Get over and find out how soon it's right to put cows on this cocksfoot grass and get rid of that hang-dog look when you're asking questions. There's nothing wrong in ignorance,' she assured him. 'Nothing to be ashamed of.'

Reg dragged himself to the doorway and looked out at the bright light and the green tips of the cocksfoot poking up at the sun. At the back of his mind their future was beginning to take shape. Though Annie might not know it, the biggest surprise of her life was in store.

Chapter 11

If there was one thing Ceci admired about Ginger it was that he seemed not to let the trouble with Lizabeth get him down. On the contrary, even though she was gone and had abandoned her children to them, he remained adamant that he would prove to her that her husband had been married.

'And how will you do that?' Ceci asked. It was in fact amazing he'd never thought to try the Marriage Registry himself.

'I'm not so stupid as to go looking for Frank,' he assured her. 'Leave that to Lizabeth. But I'll find his family.'

Ceci frowned.

'You can be sure people know where he comes from!'

'Does his speech give him away?'

'Frank's from the Dunedin area.'

'If by any chance you were right, what is the purpose of indicating this to Lizabeth? If the man had a family and has left it, do you think shouting at Lizabeth will make him go back to them? What is the point, if there is any truth in it, of her knowing?'

'She'll get away from him.'

Now it was Ceci's turn to scoff. Ginger didn't know much about Lizabeth!

'Someone else will marry her,' he insisted.

'Don't be ridiculous, Ginger!' Ceci said sharply. 'People around here are far too small-minded to marry a woman who has "lived in sin" as you put it and has three children by another man! They wouldn't let their sons near a woman who'd been trailing over the country after a tyke

141

like Frank! *I* think it does her credit!' Ginger glared at her. 'You don't surely think anyone in the city would marry her, do you?' Ceci went on. 'She's not bred for the city.'

'I'd marry her,' Ginger replied quietly. 'I'd get her away from him.'

'If you get her away from him she'll have to live here forever with her children. Is that what you want? When it's plain to everyone you resent them?'

'What's the alternative?' Ginger snapped.

'I suggest you find Frank and have it out with him properly. A real knock-down fight! Then leave him with Lizabeth. Why do you keep thrusting respectability on a child who wishes to be a vagabond?'

After a pause Ginger spoke again: 'I'll tell you one thing,' he assured Ceci, 'I'll find his family first. And you'll come with me and see them!'

Although tempted by the idea, it alarmed Ceci. 'And who will look after the children?'

'Myra.'

Ceci hesitated. The idea of Myra looking after the little ones bothered her and although it may not have been fair to think it she could imagine the girl standing staring from the window while behind her a child cried and cried, confident that because they were alone in the house none could criticize her.

'When the boys get back from Christchurch I'll make the arrangements,' Ginger went on.

'I don't want to leave the children with Myra,' Ceci said firmly.

'It's time she learnt a couple of things – '

'And I'm not sure she should be left with the boys either. They talk a deal too much about racing. By the sound of it it's high time there was some government intervention at that track. Do you realize your boys make as much money offering advice on placing bets as they do on racing that horse? It's a relief to talk about something other than Lizabeth but I do wish you would send them to Ireland and let them purchase a proper horse that would win more and get them away from the betting angle. If not Ireland then Australia. I know they have found their way into the best circles with their knowledge of racing and it's a credit to them, but people are only seeing them for their use.'

'When the boys come back, we'll go,' Ginger repeated. 'You're getting a sight too fond of those children.'

So that was it, Ceci told herself. The break was because she was getting too fond of the children. But they had been with her so long: Little Frank from his actual birth. Already he was trying to stand and she feared Ginger had overheard him calling her something that sounded dangerously like 'Ma'. In fact the twin girls had picked it up off him and as there was no sign of Lizabeth's return it seemed pointless to prevent them ... With gaps in their teeth which exactly matched she loved them dearly. Milk teeth of course. But Ginger was right. She was getting too fond of them.

Soon the day came for them to depart on the quest Ceci hoped would prove fruitless: the search for Frank's family. The public reason that had been given for the trip was a visit to Ginger's parents who, since Mairead and her husband had moved away, were living alone in Dunedin. Even had it not been a fact that his father's health was deteriorating the story would have been believed in Moke. It seemed, however, that Ceci was not destined to meet the old man for Ginger insisted she fill her time otherwise during their visit.

'He doesn't remember you anyway,' he'd said. 'He keeps asking about Maureen.'

Ceci nodded. Whether or not that was true there was no

point in thrusting herself on Ginger's parents. What opinion they held of her she did not know, never having met them, but she was in no hurry to play his piece of fluff on the sidelines.

'There is something you could do for me though,' Ginger began awkwardly as they reached their boarding house in Dunedin. 'Would you mind looking in on Faith while we're here?'

Relieved to be of some consequence Ceci agreed. She certainly did not want to go chasing after Frank's family and indeed it was a consolation that Ginger still trusted her in the matter of his daughters. In his request too she had sensed his fear of being turned away by Faith or rejected somehow; the prospect that the girl would be angry with him had been couched in his voice. Yet already she was missing the little ones, she realized, particularly Little Frank – always so grateful to be picked up. Her arms ached for him as she walked towards Faith's house, her steps echoing in the deserted street. Hastily she reminded herself that Little Frank was not hers and that she must steel herself against thoughts of this kind, must prevent possessive emotions or a sense of identification emerging. Lizabeth would surely be back and, if not, as soon as they were old enough to understand, the children must know who their mother was.

Remembering how charming Dougall had been she turned the corner and brightened up as the house she was seeking came into view. It wasn't a bad house, nowhere near as ramshackle as Dougall, presumably in modesty, had implied. In fact it was very much the sort of house any girl moving to the city would be pleased to live in, particularly a girl like Faith. Pushing open the front gate she noticed how tidy the garden was, its path swept clean, the earth behind the line of tiles raked to a fine tilth, bone dry and crumbling in the midday sun. There were three rose trees which had finished blooming and were cut to the knuckle, neither haw nor leaf left on them. Ceci paused. The sight of a tree so brutally pruned brought home to her the fact that she came from the country where things were allowed to grow. Here were no twigs on the ground, no seed pods, stones or bark. All was stark order. Hastily she rang the bell.

She stood on the doorstep wearing the right face for some moments then let it flag and turned to observe the houses opposite. Doubtless they were out – Dougall at work and Faith with friends – yet she was in no hurry to wander in a strange town when she could stand on their doorstep. The single-storeyed houses opposite were identical, their roofs, their windows, their curtains, their neatly swept paths, their tidy earth and cruelly pruned roses.

'What do you want?' came a sharp voice from behind her.

Ceci spun to find a woman in drab clothes covered over with a cheap house-pinafore that fastened from behind. Her hair was steel grey and wrenched back without the kindness of a curl or stray wisp to soften her glare.

'I came to see – ' she began.

'They're out,' snapped the woman, folding her arms.

Ceci paused. 'I'm Faith's – ' the word 'stepmother' suggested itself but was instantly rejected – 'mother, come from the country to visit – '

The woman stepped back abruptly and marched ahead of Ceci through the narrow hallway into the kitchen. 'I'll make you some tea.'

'That isn't necessary,' Ceci murmured, aghast at this woman, presumably the landlady, flinging open the doors of Faith's cupboards, reaching for their tea caddy, taking down cups . . .

'Look at this!' the woman tutted, glaring into a cup. She hurried outside with it and Ceci heard the sound of running water and a muttered remark about some people being too lazy to get the stains off.

'I'm going to lie down,' the woman advised when she'd poured the tea. 'You wait in the front room.'

Front room! How cheap the words sounded! Turning to look up the hallway Ceci saw the woman going into the next room. Surely she was not going to take a nap in the young couple's house while they were both out? Was she even now settling her bulk on their bed, her feet on their counterpane? Ceci finished her tea. The door opened.

'Leave that cup there, I'll wash it.' Ceci put the cup down. 'Now go into the front room,' the woman ordered.

How she would hate to be bossed around in a place she rented by a person like this, Ceci told herself! A domineering person with a mean mouth and darting eyes constantly seeking stains!

The front room, like the front garden, looked as if it belonged to no one in particular. The few pieces of furniture were heavy and dismal with the feeling that the polishing was done every day but with little joy. An unpleasant photograph of the landlady's relatives hung in a corner. That's the *first* thing I'd remove if I lived in this house, Ceci vowed. There was a piano against the wall but it was unlikely it was ever played for the array of stuffed horses' hooves, ink wells and old dusty shells balanced on top would all have had to be removed. On every surface lay a white antimacassar as if a charm to protect the item from human contagion. It was the most profoundly depressing room Ceci had ever been in. The grate was blacked, the windows cleaned and the flower vases empty yet the feeling that the landlady would burst through the door should one lay a finger on the fireguard persisted. Sitting in a wing chair with her back to the window Ceci began to doze.

Meanwhile Ginger hurried away from his parents'

house, took a local coach to a rural area then pressed his feet busily to a country track which led to a settlement little different from any other. Children came out to point at him, run back in and tell their mothers who too came to stare. He was entering the village Frank had come from: he was sure of it. People in Dunedin had remembered Frank and by dint of going from one pub to another, knocking on the occasional door and enquiring of the stone-mason by the graveyard, he had had no difficulty uncovering this truth. With mounting excitement he had asked the same casual question: 'You know where Frank is these days?' and people had pushed their hats back on their heads and smiled at him. 'Frank, eh. You a friend of his?' Ginger had nodded, his sense of pursuit making it easy to lie and do it smiling. 'Old Frank, eh? Not around these parts now. You might try his mother out at her place . . .' Their voices fading in his ears Ginger had hurried on. It annoyed him that all had spoken well of Frank. Indeed the closer he had got the more people hoped he would have news of Frank for *them*. He said he had no news. He did not tell them Frank had married his daughter, had a new family and would very soon be caught up with. The fact that people spoke well of the man irked him further.

Locating the house that had been described to him Ginger knocked on the door, everything in him becoming alert.

A tired woman, no doubt Frank's mother, appeared. 'Oh, Frank,' she said, scratching in her hair. 'What's the matter? He owe you something? You ask his wife.'

It was exactly what Ginger had been waiting for. 'Frank doesn't owe me anything,' he smiled. 'But he sent something for her.'

The woman eyed him thoughtfully: 'You want me to give it to her for you then?' There was a fear in her eyes that betrayed her deep poverty, her conviction that he would not trust her with anything; that life had used her hard and because of this, though she was honest, she no longer expected to be believed.

'I'll drop by myself,' Ginger said. 'Wouldn't want to put you out.'

'She's the other side of the tracks now,' said the woman, almost as if she disapproved. 'The tracks you know. The railway yard . . .'

Returning to Dunedin and heading for the railyards, Ginger hoped. He hoped the woman would be living alone with a lot of children in a state of destitution. He most particularly did *not* want her to have found someone else. Still less did he want her to be fast or flashy, the sort of person who might have provoked Frank's departure . . . She had to be abandoned . . . There must be children . . .

Hurrying on, worried by the idea the woman might be living in comfort, Ginger dodged between stationary engines, climbed over discarded sleepers and old rails, tripped on clinker and squeezed through a gap in a fence which a child had indicated to him and which let on to the meanest possible row of dwellings, built one against another with common walls. His heart rose. Reaching an unnumbered shack with a painted door he felt certain. It was a street where no washing hung out. No children played. At night, though, those who could afford none better would steal over the tracks and come here. He heard a child crying beyond the door, another shout at it and the crash of an enamel plate slipping from a table. In his heart he knew that the woman was destitute and that he was pleased. And he knew it was very wrong to be so . . .

Ceci slept on. At one stage she had sensed the landlady pushing a cat into the room and closing the door on it but since then fatigue had caught up with her in the darkening room. Now opening her eyes she could see nothing. Best to get to her feet and make her way to the door, she thought, leaning around the chair and turning towards the window for light. There to her amazement she saw Dougall standing, his back to her – unaware of her presence in the room. Alone and relaxed his fingers lay on the sill as he stared at the sun even now setting beyond the roofs opposite. The room door opened.

'Dougall?' Faith said softly.

Dougall did not move.

Faith stepped into the room. 'Dougall?' she repeated.

Paralyzed with embarrassment Ceci sat in the shade of the wing chair watching the street light play on the girl's face.

'Dougall!' she said a little louder, a hysterical note in her voice as if she might burst into tears. Dougall continued staring yet something in his manner, the slightest suspicion that he *had* heard Faith calling persisted.

Retreating into the farthest recesses of the chair Ceci saw Faith withdraw and after some seconds saw Dougall turn and cross to the door himself. Grossly uncomfortable, she reckoned the odds on creeping from their house and presenting herself again the following day, but, entering the hallway, her nerve failed. 'Anyone home?' she called.

The look on their faces when they saw her was of total shock.

Dougall recovered first. 'My dear Ceci,' he replied, hurrying forward and leading her into their dining room. 'Please have a chair.'

Ceci caught Faith's expression as he placed his hand in the small of her back and guided her forward. The girl was not jealous. She was shocked.

'Fay,' he said brightly, 'isn't this wonderful!'

'Fay?' Ceci repeated.

'My special name for her,' Dougall replied. Faith looked at him steadily but said nothing. In this fiercely Scottish

149

Presbyterian town an Irish Catholic name like Faith might have stood out, Ceci supposed. He was hardly likely to be trying to depersonalize the girl! By now Dougall was pulling back a chair for Faith who seemed to know it was behind her and intended for her but had difficulty bending her knees to sit on it . . .

'I must apologize for arriving at this time,' Ceci began. 'In fact I've been here quite a while. Your landlady had the kindness to let me in – '

'Isn't she marvellous?' Dougall interrupted. Faith's face remained expressionless. 'I hope she made you a cup of tea?'

Ceci nodded. 'Faith's father,' she found herself explaining to Dougall rather than Faith, 'wanted to visit his parents. There is no need to be alarmed, Faith,' she said, turning to the girl. 'He hasn't seen them for a long time. He was showing concern.'

'Of course,' said Dougall.

'I gather they have – things to discuss so I hoped you'd forgive the liberty of my dropping in. You certainly have a lovely home, Faith,' she smiled. Why had she stumbled on the word 'home' and almost said 'house'?

'We like it,' Faith said, glancing at Dougall.

'It's wonderful you could come,' Dougall repeated.

'Shall we invite her to eat?' Faith whispered.

'Oh, I must be going,' Ceci answered quickly. 'Your father will be wondering what's happened to me! We're putting up at a boarding house and have assured the proprietor we'll be there for dinner.'

'You'll find you get a very generous helping down here,' Dougall assured Ceci, as if relieved she was going. 'More than you'd reckoned on.'

As she rose Ceci sensed Faith would have liked to cook a meal for her; that in fact there was nothing the girl would have like more than for Dougall to have been out

150

so that they might have had a chat together. Given her memories of Faith it was an odd thought yet it stayed with her as she walked down the street and away from their house. They had shaken hands with her and, each in their own way, expressed the hope she would return. What would they be talking about now that their door was closed?

'How was your father?' Ceci asked Ginger as he plunged his fork into an unconscionably large piece of meat.

Ginger chewed thoughtfully.

He could have replied before putting the meat in his mouth, Ceci thought. And he looked more pleased with himself than Ceci would have expected.

'Oh, he's good.'

'Did he ask about me?'

'What?'

'Did your father ask about me?' she repeated.

'Don't think so.'

Ceci put some food in her mouth and considered. 'How's his chest?' she demanded.

Rather than reply Ginger put more food in his own mouth.

'So I take it you've started on Frank?'

Ginger shrugged: 'Might have.' He felt so pleased with the way the afternoon had gone, he hesitated to tell Ceci. He reached across the table for the paper. 'Did Faith ask after me?'

'Not that I recall.'

Ginger nodded, his mouth full.

'I see you discovered something,' Ceci said.

He nodded again. 'I'll take you and show you.'

'You certainly won't,' Ceci replied firmly. 'I'm not poking my nose into Lizabeth's business.'

Ginger went on eating, the scene of that one-roomed

151

shack so clear in his mind it made him smile. Frank's wife's language had not been pretty, nor her request for money, nor the hunger on the faces of her children. She had not known who he was. He *had* given her money but had refused her favours.

'Would you pass the salt?' Ceci asked abruptly.

'I'll send the children outside,' the woman had said.

Ginger took more meat. Now that he dared to think about it he found himself wondering what it would have been like to have her, driven as she was by desperation to satisfy her customers so that they would return and give her more money. She had not been a bad-looking woman either despite her pallor. When Ceci was picking at him like this it pleased him to recall the woman, to imagine himself forcing his way on her knowing that she was Frank's wife. But the woman's humility, her ultimate need of his money would have spoiled the thrill. He had heard it said there was no love like stolen love: the sweetest, wildest and best. He glanced across at Ceci now wiping her mouth carefully and looking angry.

'We're staying over,' he announced. 'If you don't want to come with me and see, too bad.'

'Oh Mother Mary,' Faith prayed. 'Help me not to make a noise as I get out of bed. Don't let me wake him!' Carefully she eased herself to the edge of the bed, the need to urinate denying her sleep. Earlier the landlady had been in the outside toilet and after that Dougall, who had hurried to bed with his usual haste. Had she not run into the bedroom after him, the candle would have been blown out without a word of goodnight and she would have lost the chance of trying to speak to him. His breathing changed. He was awake. Faith froze where she stood and began to count . . . thirteen, fourteen, fifteen, sixteen . . . His breathing slowed, a sure indication that he was asleep. Carefully she placed one foot after the other on the boards and crossed the room, hesitating before the door and opening it only the smallest amount so that she might squeeze through before it reached the point where it creaked. The back door was the worst, for on the instructions of the landlady Dougall made a great show of bolting it every night and the three great bolts were in place. Faith eyed a saucepan, the urge to go in her conflicting with the fear of awakening Dougall, of being caught out of bed in the middle of the night when 'normal people' did not go to the toilet. Were she to use the saucepan he might hear and come out . . . Carefully she reached for the bolt . . .

Dougall sat up in bed, placed one foot on the floor and then another. He walked into the kitchen. There, kneeling by the door clasping the bottom bolt, was Faith in a puddle of her own making.

'I – I'm trying to go to the toilet,' she explained, turning a crimson face towards him.

'Normal people don't go to the toilet in the middle of the night,' Dougall said quietly.

'Please,' Faith urged, 'keep your voice down! The landlady – '

'And you're not coming into the bedroom smelling like that,' he went on, flinging the back door open.

'I'll put my nightdress in soak – '

'And you're not taking that thing off in a room where food is prepared.'

From her knees Faith looked up at him.

'And a fine fool you made of yourself today,' he continued, in a louder voice, now leaning on their stove. 'That woman must be quite sorry for me being stuck with you.'

Faith hung her head, the wet nightdress stuck to her side, and began to cry. No one will comfort you so why cry? a voice told her. Yet the more she repeated this, the louder her wail rose till she was sure that the landlady and the people next door and the people next door to that would hear, and what's more she did not care. As her voice rose in great convulsive sobs which were more like shouts, she heard their bedroom door bang. He would not return, shake her and urge her to stop. He would let her cry and no one would come. No one would *ever* come and worst of all she must go on with this charade; this lying forever about Dougall being 'kind' in order to save face . . .

Ceci passed the toast to Ginger.

'You may not wish to discuss it,' he said. 'But I have the proof I want. Next time I get my hands on Lizabeth I shall bring her down here and *show* her Frank is married.'

'Divorced,' Ceci corrected him.

Ginger almost choked. 'You knew?'

Ceci nodded.

'Why didn't you – '

'What's the difference?'

Instead of shouting at her Ginger nodded.

'But *I* would have thought there was a difference,' Ceci continued cautiously.

'What God has joined together let no man put asunder,' Ginger replied.

'Have you forgotten the time when you wished to put your own wife aside?'

'When Maureen was in the Institute for the Criminally Insane,' Ginger warned, 'I asked you to come and live with me.'

'But you very properly didn't propose marriage.'

'There is no such thing as divorce,' Ginger stated loudly.

With a sense of having been there before Ceci watched his lips move. She could imagine him shouting the phrase, thundering it, insisting on the irrevocability of the institution of marriage. She felt a chill move over her. 'That woman you visited yesterday was divorced,' she said quietly.

'She's married to Frank. Always will be.'

'Don't you think if she or Frank had done something very terrible there might have been a possibility for them to go separate ways?'

'They can go separate ways – but they'll still be married.'

There was no doubt about it, Ceci realized, while he had been prepared to negotiate on a question of Faith's mixed marriage, when it came to divorce the barriers were firmly down. Why, hadn't the very business of clearing the way for Faith and Dougall caused him to reiterate 'What God has joined together let no man put asunder' over and again to the people of Moke, until he spat it out at the slightest provocation?

'When you've finished with your father we'd better get back to Hexham,' Ceci sighed.

'I'm done,' Ginger nodded. 'Let's not start the journey arguing.' Reaching over he kissed her.

In truth he had almost forgotten about his father. The trip had given him so much to think about, not least the disturbing fact that he had been glad at another's misfortune, that for the time being, he wanted things on an even keel. Beneath the surface, though, a sense of elation persisted.

As they boarded the coach for the long ride back and began to rise to the hills, the oppressiveness of Dunedin fell away behind them.

'At least we've one joy we can share,' Ginger said turning to Ceci. 'Even if Faith's still angry with me at least she's well settled. It could be that Dougall was just what she needed in her life.'

Ceci nodded. Faith had always been, well, difficult, she agreed, and Dougall was a pleasant boy – but whether what a woman old enough to be his mother found 'pleasant' meant anything to a girl Faith's age she could not say. Frank's type seemed more the ideal or perhaps the glamorous foxy men Olwen spoke of in Wellington. 'You know that smart card Olwen said she went to the races with? I hope he doesn't turn out to be a bad hat,' she confided. 'And I hope the Wellington races don't have the same reputation as those in Christchurch!'

Ginger shrugged. 'Who knows anything about the North Island? They say we're so quiet down here we complain about the grass growing. I'll never go north. I know in my bones I won't.'

'I feel I will,' Ceci replied. 'But let us put Dunedin out of our minds for the time being, shall we?'

As the Moke trap turned in at their gates instantly Ceci sensed something was wrong.

In the doorway stood Myra: 'They've gone. Lizabeth came for them.'

'Did you ask her to come?' Ceci demanded.

Myra shook her head. 'The boys knew she was coming. They watched the track to be sure you were away.'

'Me?' Ceci burst out, unable to believe it.

Myra shook her head. 'Father.'

Ceci heard Ginger draw in breath. While he had been in Dunedin trying to destroy Lizabeth's life, she had simply come, taken her children and gone! The irony caught in his throat as did the memory of his malicious lusting towards Frank's wife . . .

'I didn't say goodbye to Little Frank,' Ceci sobbed, turning to him. 'I didn't tell Lizabeth which toys he liked!'

'I showed her everything,' Myra said coolly.

That night in bed Ginger held Ceci silently. He stroked her head and murmured her name, guilt making him uncomfortable, as he willed his attention away from what he saw as his just punishment which had landed on her. He sensed she missed the children intolerably and the fact

156

that they were not hers added a sense of uselessness to it as if she had no right to her tears.

'I just wish I could have said goodbye properly!'

'We've plans of our own,' he said. 'Had you forgotten?'

But it was Little Frank she wanted back.

Ginger kissed her eyes. 'Maybe I haven't been the greatest thing in your life but we're still together. Say we're friends.'

She squeezed him. When strangers spoke hard words, the warmth of one's mate was ointment on bruises. Often, when she had lost her grip, Ginger had climbed up to secure her. He was comforting her now while doubtless unhappy himself.

As she fell asleep he moved away. His thoughts were of the two photos he had bought from the woman – the one taken probably some four years before Frank had 'divorced' her – for the children in it ranged from absolute infancy to five years. She had willingly handed over the photographs, that woman. Probably thought he had come with 'the intention', lost his courage and tried to save face by giving her money and taking some trifle for it. Probably thought it was the frames he was after. Her youngest child would now be seven or eight, the oldest perhaps eleven. The crying baby she must have been minding for coppers – and the other gaping mouths would have been neighbours' children. In the morning he would wrap that photo and lay it in a drawer. But as for the other one, he would take especial care of that – for it had been taken outside what looked like Frank's mother's house and was of Frank and the woman on their wedding day.

Chapter 12

Faith hurried out of the butcher's shop and ran after Dougall. 'Why did you leave me in there?' she cried, catching up with him as he crossed the road. Coming towards them, bound for the shops, their landlady paused on the opposite side, her basket on her arm, and stared.

'She heard you last night.'

'Why did you leave me in the butcher's shop?'

'You're embarrassing to shop with,' Dougall said, now walking so fast Faith had to run to keep up with him. 'You don't ask butchers to turn over meat!'

'I asked him to turn it over so I could see how much fat was underneath,' Faith protested.

'And then you asked how much a pound it was!' Dougall scolded. 'That's as good as accusing him of being a liar.'

'We're not beholden to the butcher,' Faith cried. 'You should support me in public.'

'You don't know how to behave in public.'

'Then let me shop alone.'

'You'd buy the wrong foods.'

At that Faith nearly laughed aloud. What a man from the city could teach a country girl about buying meat you could put in your eye! 'You grovel in shops, Dougall,' she accused.

'Be quiet.'

'You wanted Moss Cough Drops and she tried to sell you those other things. The Moss Cough Drops were right there on the shelf behind her and when I pointed them out – '

'She could see how rude you were – ' Dougall interrupted.

'Look!' Faith said, grasping his sleeve and almost bringing them to a stop in the street. 'You said "A quarter of Moss Lollies" and she said "Try these other ones" – '

'You were shouting at her.'

'I may have raised my voice. When two women are disputing it's fatal for the husband to come down on the other woman's side. And then you walked out!'

'I'm not staying in a shop when you're behaving like that. Remember it.'

'People go into shops and ask questions!' Faith burst out. 'They say, "Do you have this? How much a pound is that? Where did this come from?" Why do you always burst into smiles at shop assistants as if you can't wait to agree with them? Roll your eyes at the ceiling when I ask questions! I never thought I'd have a use for the word, but you're fawning! That's what you are!'

Dougall was not looking at her now but his pace had quickened. It was only in public that she could argue with him, her tone becoming more strident than she would have wished, for once inside their door, cut off from the world, the situation changed.

Dougall walked ahead of her and opened the front door of the house Faith now dreaded entering. There was nothing to indicate that she was with him. His manner was of a person alone. He passed through the hallway into the kitchen, pausing to bend and stroke his cat. There was a note from the landlady on the bench. He picked it up.

Faith stared at him from the kitchen door. 'Dougall?' she said.

Dougall went on reading the note. He grunted, screwed it up and threw it in the bin.

'What did it say?' Faith bent down and retrieved the note – which was a reminder about the number of times

159

their front step was to be scrubbed per week – and put it in her pocket to dispose of elsewhere, for if their landlady found notes she had written thrown in their bin she became angry, taking it as a mark of disrespect.

'Dougall?' called Faith, following him into their bedroom. 'Dougall, I . . .'

He was sitting on the edge of the bed staring towards the window.

'Dougall?' As there was no response she came and stood in front of him. 'Dougall!'

He continued to stare beyond her.

'I can't bear it when you will not talk to me in the house!' she pleaded, getting on her knees in order to be within immediate range of his face. 'I came in here to apologize for . . . Please, please look at me!' Dougall stared ahead. 'Why will you never talk to me in the house?' Desperately she got up and sat next to him on the bed. 'Please! I need warmth!' If he would only turn or put his arm around her! 'I can't stand this any more!' she cried. 'I need human warmth!' Seeing that she was getting nowhere she got to her feet. 'I'm a child of God!' she shouted. 'You can't treat me like this!'

She knew he would not speak. He only spoke to her in public or in front of guests, becoming then such a different person she was not sure how to treat him. At times she wondered if they were transparent: if people noticed they were different from other couples. Turning to look at him again she found him lying on his back, staring at the ceiling and a rage rose in her, ballooning up and bashing against her skull as if she might, almost without willing it, rush at him with a brick and batter his head till he was finally still; this man who knew his silences drove her to a dangerous pitch of frustration yet knowingly persisted. Occasionally he would speak to her in the kitchen: perhaps because there were always knives around . . .

160

Running from his presence Faith squeezed herself into the large uncomfortable wing chair in the front room, in an agony of self-doubt. Should she write to Ceci? Of course, given that they were married nothing could be done, but to have someone to talk to . . . Could she even invite her? She crossed quickly to the sideboard and drew out a writing tablet. If Ceci agreed to come she certainly dare not tell Dougall for he would make a point of being there, of touching her on the shoulder as he never did in private, confusing her and strongly reinforcing the image he had been at pains to create: that of a caring husband. Touching her, Faith thought angrily, raising the lid of the inkwell? Even when he had been obliged to waken her for the doctor he had been careful to do it with the cold back of his hand rather than the warm inner palm. Lifting her pen she began.

'Look! How nice!' Ceci called. 'Dougall has invited us down!'

Myra tweaked the letter from her hand: 'It's not Dougall – it's Faith.'

'Same thing,' murmured Ginger. 'When people are married you treat them as one person.'

Myra paused, struck by the romanticism of the idea.

'Oh, I think people are still capable of individual acts,' Ceci inserted for Myra's benefit, not having forgotten how neither her work nor her ownership of Old Bowen's land had stood her in good stead when, after Calvin's death, it came time to throw her off Hexham . . . Even her own property had miraculously 'reverted' to Calvin! 'If a woman worked at something and earned it, I think it should be hers.'

Ginger packed his mouth. The eggs tasted good and the argument was of no interest. He liked his eggs fluffy.

Slightly irritated Ceci rose and slipped Faith's letter behind the clock.

'There are two more letters,' Myra reminded her with an enthusiasm which meant one had to be from Olwen.

'Why didn't you bring them in?' Ceci asked, looking at Ginger to determine whether she should open Olwen's in front of Myra. The girl was likely to say the most unthinkable things and Myra was too old to be told to go outside and play.

'Bring the other one first,' Ginger instructed. 'Who's it from?'

'I can't bring it to table because it's covered in mud,' Myra explained. 'The writing is very bad and the name "Hexham" is on the same line as Moke.'

'It must be *Annie*!' Ceci gasped, running from the room.

Ginger wiped his mouth. If that was the female who'd worked in Ceci's pub on the West Coast her letter wouldn't be any less 'educational' than Olwen's. Probably written it sitting in some grog shanty with her back to the light . . . 'Read Olwen's letter first,' he called out.

In the kitchen Ceci hastily scanned the contents of Annie's letter and learned the amazing news that she and Reg were in the backblocks, making a go of it and that as soon as things were 'sorted', they'd like them up.

Giving Ginger a meaningful look as she re-entered the room, Ceci settled down to gladden Myra's ears with news of Wellington. Carefully she sifted the contents of Olwen's letter but it unfolded in a different way from usual. Gone were the flippant comments, the personal views, replaced by a seeming welter of information. The girl told of two theatrical productions, going to lengths to describe the costumes, lighting and general effects; a boat race in which she seemed to be one of a crowd and even a remote picnic spot set in hills.

162

'Oriental Bay,' Myra sighed wonderingly. 'Do you think she goes to all these places alone?'

Ceci glanced through the letter. There was no mention of a man. 'She has Hetty and Muriel, I suppose. Gwen wasn't it? Then there are the girls from her workshop. I expect they make up a party and one or two of the husbands escort them.'

The idea of Olwen and her cohorts being driven like geese into some racing enclosure amused Myra no end.

'Again there is bound to be a Women's Institute in a place like Wellington,' Ceci went on.

'Nice she's getting about,' Ginger observed. 'You see, Myra, if a girl sets her sights on it and works hard, even in this age she can go some way towards educating herself.'

Ceci leaned back in her chair. It *was* good that Olwen should be acquainted with opera and theatre. It was a sensible adjustment to make to life as a single woman.

Myra closed her eyes. How she wished that she too had been at the regatta, pressed shoulder to shoulder with handsome men who cheered as the boats went out of sight and gorgeous women with little dogs they fed dainties! How she would love to have been in the enclosure even if, as Olwen had said, the men kept darting away to queue up in lines where they stood so close their hat brims touched! She would have worn a great long frilled dress with five, perhaps six, layers of frill to the skirt – and a hat with feathers and flowers held down by a scarf! It was well for Olwen to complain that the horses thundered by and were gone in a flash and that the sport was a masculine pleasure shared only by the ladies for the sake of display. Maybe the floor of the enclosure *was* littered with cigar butts and pieces of paper but didn't that go to show how unimportant ordinary tidiness was in an exciting place like Wellington?

'Look at Myra,' Ginger whispered.

Ceci glanced over. 'Hello? Hello?' she called.

Olwen went on to talk about Happi, giving Ginger the irksome sense that he was being 'educated'.

'Her people originally came from a place called Taranaki,' Ceci read aloud.

'Where?'

Ceci shook her head, thinking it was high time they got hold of a map. 'If the North Island is something like a diamond on its side,' she began, 'I think it's about half way along the top left-hand edge.'

'How would you know?' Ginger asked.

'In the days when all thought *I* owned Hexham,' Ceci replied pointedly, 'when I was actually trying to *sell* Hexham, I used to sit in the bank manager's office in Christchurch staring at the map on the wall behind his head. Taranaki was on it. All right?'

Quietened, Ginger listened to how Olwen, going against the trend, had become friends with the Maori girl Happi and occasionally accompanied her to her *pa*.

'Her what?'

'I gather it's some kind of – fortified hamlet inside a fence,' Ceci said, turning the letter over.

'Is she getting into that girl's family?' Ginger asked.

'It seems they receive her quite well,' Ceci nodded.

Ginger shook his head: 'It'll do her no good mixing there . . .'

Although it was not like him to be snobbish Ceci knew what he meant. 'Listen to this,' she grinned, then read aloud: 'Although Happi was born at the top end of the South Island in Waikawa, her people, the Te Atiawa, were North Taranaki people who moved down to Wellington following the *Heke* or Great Migration, led by Te Raupar-aha and his Ngati Toa tribe from Kawhia – which is in the north by Auckland.'

'My God,' murmured Ginger.

'. . . and Te Whatanui and his Raukawa from Maunda-Tautari.'

'Didn't send that girl up there for a university degree,' Ginger grumbled.

'I don't see why those Maoris wanted to go to a sophisticated place like Wellington,' Myra put in.

'Can't have been like that then,' Ginger pointed out.

'The attraction,' Ceci read on, 'seems to have been the swampy lands around Wellington. The Maoris traded the flax for guns.'

'What did they want with guns if they were Christian? You said earlier – '

'Really, Myra! Who gave them the guns?'

'The sealers and whalers,' Myra insisted. 'It wouldn't have been the Christians!'

'Well, maybe the Maoris were fighting each other,' Ceci continued. 'Be that as it may the three migrating Maori groups made an agreement about dividing up the land and Happi's lot got the harbour and swamp land and the Ngati Raukawa got – '

'She used to write about herself!' Ginger said, getting up. 'How many pages of that is there?'

'From the Waikanae to the Rangitikei Rivers,' Ceci read under her breath. 'Waikanae River means the water where you see the million eyes of the *kanae* fish. Can't you just see the stones blinking up at you as the water rushes by?'

Ginger grunted and left.

'And Rangitikei River means river wide enough you need a pole to vault over it.' Myra stared fascinated. 'And they stayed from one *kumara* planting season to the next – '

'Did Olwen write that?' Myra asked.

'She's repeating it as she heard it from Happi I suppose – look,' said Ceci holding the page out to Myra. Myra did not want to look. She much preferred a good story. 'So

Happi's lot moved down to the Head of the Fish,' Ceci went on. 'Apparently that was the Wellington area. And after that when this Te Rauparaha was really powerful, with all the guns he'd purchased off the trading boats by selling them flax fibre, he became a war lord and spent his time going to and fro across Cook Strait in canoes with his warriors until he had taken over all the top of *our* island around Nelson and Blenheim and Picton ... Which explains how Happi was born on our island.'

'Did the north part of our island belong to the Maoris?' Myra asked, scandalized. 'I've never even *seen* a Maori.'

'If you visit Olwen I expect you will,' Ceci replied, folding the letter. 'They seem to be well and truly plentiful around that area.'

Myra's eyes lit up. 'I should like to visit Olwen,' she said, right on cue.

'Well, don't you forget there's been a fair bit of fighting between them and us and we don't want you getting involved.'

'I'm not interested in the Maoris!' Myra retorted. 'I'd just like to go to Wellington.'

As winter lifted and Olwen left her debts with the Notables behind, she found herself going out more and more often with Marshall, affording the Wellington community the opportunity to observe this erstwhile stand-offish young lady walking in public with a man, with the appearance of paying each other serious court. Heads turned, people nudged each other as, impeccably smart yet one step beyond fashion, Marshall and Olwen caught the public eye and held it. When they were alone, however, words and tempers flew for each was strong-headed, powerful in their own right and well-connected by different threads to the mainspring of the Wellington economy. Because it was clear to Olwen that Marshall was serious, she was determined to get herself the best possible deal before 'giving in'. She would be no man's slave yet what precise relationship they were working towards she did not ask herself.

She watched him cross to her mantelpiece. Though he had not been in her house ten minutes his temper was rising as if he wished to control her somehow, yet was unsure whether to set about it with manacles or carnations.

'That's settled then,' he observed, straightening his tie. 'Tonight we will go to Venables' soirée.'

'I'm not going,' Olwen informed him.

'My dear girl!' Marshall burst out. 'Venables and Gwen particularly requested our company! Without wishing to sound vain you must be aware that they will be severely let down – '

'It's up to them to make their own parties a success,' Olwen yawned, annoyed that Marshall had seen fit to accept the invitation without consulting her first.

'After all they've done for you!' Marshall growled.

Olwen crossed to the window and stood with her back to it so that the evening sun could pick out the highlights in her hair. 'In any case I cannot bear those kind of occasions,' she said winningly. 'Let us go somewhere else.'

'If we don't go to Venables', we're not going anywhere.'

'I am,' Olwen said, letting her glance trail down the gully after the creepers and fallen tree trunks. 'There are lots of places I could go to.'

Marshall drew a deep breath. 'Olwen,' he said firmly, 'if the public – '

'If you're so bothered about the public then go out with them!' Olwen shrugged. 'And your tie is crooked!'

'When I marry you – '

'Hah!'

' – your bizarre behaviour – '

'That is positively the worst proposal I have ever had!' Olwen laughed.

167

'You want me to go down on my knees?' Marshall returned.

'Only if you'll do it at Venables'. In which case I'll go.'

Marshall snatched up his cane and left.

Happi came in, her face wreathed with smiles.

'You got rid of him quick this time!' she grinned.

'Maybe I didn't want to,' Olwen said, examining her wrists carefully. 'I actually got him to propose to me . . .'

'Very good, seein' as you already married!' Happi returned.

Olwen flung herself on the couch. 'I can't believe he wants to marry me!' she said joyously to Happi.

'Oh he wants!'

'He *must* be married already,' Olwen insisted.

'You want me to follow him and see?'

Though this gave Olwen an idea she burst out laughing. 'I'm sure he'd never notice you!'

Alone in the room Olwen reminded herself that she had probably done wrong in permitting him to pursue her in the first place. Nonetheless she had felt no twinges of conscience, particularly as they built up to the proposal. Was it that sense of rejection she had experienced when Edmund had washed his hands of her which made it so difficult to believe that anyone would want to take up with her seriously again? Clearly he was in love with her yet . . . Was her conviction that he was already married, hence abusing her, simply a reflection of her own guilt at double dealing? She did not like to view herself as the object of another person's convenience whether or not it served her right. Yet how could a man like Marshall have remained unmarried? It was a well-known fact that everyone in Wellington had come from somewhere else. Indeed some guilty secret, some 'mistake' in his past, coupled with her availability, would go a long way to explaining things!

Sitting at her desk Olwen realized there were two ways

of tackling the problem. First, she would put a detective on Marshall and discover what she could and second, she would clarify her own position by getting a divorce. Nervously she began to write the letter she would send to Edmund's parents to forward to India or wherever he was now stationed. Carefully she figured out the departing boats. Within four months, six at the outside, she would hear from England. She had not seen Edmund for a good three years and their time together had been of the briefest duration. Was it not even possible that Edmund's family had been trying to contact her for that exact same purpose but had not known to where to look? When she had left him, being uncertain of her mother's location she had given no address. Indeed she had consistently lied about her situation and address while she was with him! Oh, to be divorced and to be able to write truthfully to her mother again; to talk of the people she met, the places she went to – not as places but as places visited purely to provide a backdrop for the company of Marshall. How good it would be to tell her mother about him!

The letter posted, Olwen set off for Cuba Street with a distinct lightness of tread. Divorce, divorce, she kept repeating to herself, feeling the freedom of the word ring in her mind. Already the admissions and requests carefully arranged on that piece of paper, written and rewritten, would be moving towards their goal to secure it for her. She felt almost married to Marshall already. How he would love Hexham, would truly appreciate the finer furnishings remaining! If, of course, he were not already married himself, she reminded herself, biting a finger as she crossed the road. The most attractive man in Wellington still single? Well, she would find out. By the time he went to bed that night, though he might not know it, Marshall would be the subject of Wellington's most conscientious detective's scrutiny. In point of fact, she was now looking forward to meeting this man and hoped she would not be late.

At the corner she paused. It would not do to be seen turning up this particular street. Already a group of pick and shovel men and a small boy selling oysters were staring. Olwen hurried on past a hotel which had recently burned to the ground, its wooden front charred, salvage planks and sheets of curling tin piled on the pavement by a mass of broken glass. Carefully she picked her way past, noticing the scruffy urchins in the now damp rubble searching through the ash. She tripped on an oyster shell which cracked underfoot. Farther up, the street looked distinctly mean, a place of tattoo parlours, questionable boarding houses with vaudeville artistes' names pinned in lists by the door; broken-down premises where billiard balls clicked all day and idlers and speculators hung in the doorway. She could not walk much farther without being obliged to turn, Olwen realized, making a sharp left at the next corner. Why a detective would choose to bury himself in a location like this she could not imagine but if she found him she would most certainly arrange to meet in a more savoury venue next time, she told herself, stumbling into a deep hole in the road in which part of a pig's intestines bobbed. Beyond it, children were inflating the animal's bladder preparatory to a game of football and in a small wooden crate an enthusiastic toddler thumped his arms and screamed at a tethered goat while a chicken pecked at his feet. Peck, peck, peck! The child shrieked. Just one block off the main road and already they were keeping animals!

Cutting through an empty section Olwen came upon the street she sought and picked out the house. People no longer looked at her. It was as if being poor they were used to a stream of the better-off tripping up the stairs at number eight. Olwen hesitated. A rat shot across in front of her. There was still time to turn back. From the corner of Cuba Street came the cries of the vendors: 'Rabbit hoh!' 'Milk hoh!' She could see the gigs and cabs grinding by, the Chinamen with vegetables slung from wooden yokes darting between them and an organ grinder, a small monkey on his shoulder, shouting at the traffic to stop. Already a crowd of children were gathering, running past Olwen, heading for the monkey. Olwen made a sharp turn up the stairs to number eight. For a moment the sickly smell of rotting fruit, mixed with the fennel which grew in abundance amongst the trampled tins and old fish heads scattered on the vacant sections of these back buildings, clung in her nostrils. It was a smell she would come to associate with all that was evil in Wellington. As she let the knocker fall on the door a hobo lying amongst the fennel raised himself on an elbow to look at her.

In her heart she wished for a situation – not as the French were rumoured to have – but where she and Marshall could live in complete openness together: an unimaginable idea in virtue-conscious Wellington. Part of her sensed that were it possible Marshall would agree to this, yet she dared not mention it. Nor had she needed to. Yet now the smell of the fennel was making her uncertain . . . Marshall had got her measure, had found what interested her and against her will she had responded. As she waited for the detective to come to the door she was aware that the feelings that had emerged in her were so strong she was afraid to believe such happiness could exist for her. She would have to be very sure of the depth of his commitment before permitting herself to lower her guard even slightly before her divorce came through for, attractive though he was, she must not make a fool of herself. In fact because he was so attractive she must make her instructions to this detective so explicit that not a stone should remain unturned.

Chapter 13

Even as the autumn fennel bloomed on the city wastes, telling Olwen that ten months had passed since that winter's day she had knocked on Marshall's door, the fields in the backblocks were yielding their summer harvest. The ripened cocksfoot had been gathered in and the scythed sheaves thrashed against a frame till the seeds fell off. Coughing and choking in the dust Annie had swept them together with her hands and shaken them through a great sieve Reg had purchased on a trip down. How folk below dealt with their cocksfoot they did not know but for them the sieve was more than good enough. Their seeds were sacked and stacked, their fodder carefully stored for winter and their few cows now returned from the bush were trampling their clearing with relish and twitching nostrils. For a first crop the cocksfoot had provided excellent pasture of a quality and brightness far exceeding their expectations.

'Things keep up like this . . .' Reg murmured, leaving his sentence as usual for Annie to finish. He looked across at her. The woman was better looking from one side and it had always puzzled him. He brushed some chaff from his sweating forehead.

'Come here.'

Annie hesitated. The last few months when work allowed and they were alone together there had been a certain tension between them.

'Get over here,' Reg repeated, still crouched. As she crossed to him he rose.

'I marry you, Annie,' he said solemnly, standing in the middle of the clearing.

'I marry you too, Reg,' Annie answered.

'Annie – Never-Mind-Me-Other-Name,' Reg repeated, teasing. In his heart he knew she would love to be a mother – that to her it was the highest and most noble calling for a woman, one she had always assumed would pass her by on account of her background. 'When we go down we'll get reg'larised.'

Annie looked abashed. She glared at the sky. The weather was coming up dirty and Reg in his unrefined but genuine way she understood so well had saved them both embarrassment by not only proposing but marrying her. Quite recently he had started saying 'Please' and 'Thank you' so maybe it wasn't so remarkable . . . Still she felt shy.

Reg scratched his head. There were things about a woman he would never understand! There'd been that one instance earlier where he'd put his foot in it with her and she'd gone off for a long time like she wasn't coming back but he'd known she was hiding just within sight, had him in view all the time and was afraid to go off and get lost. He hadn't gone after her. No! He'd just let her pick her own time to come back and just pretend she'd been meddling by the woodpile . . .

'I reckon you'll do,' Annie said looking up, clearly moved by his proposal.

Reg shifted a bit. Now they could get together properly and point was, he'd felt like it and he was darn sure she had. Fact was he'd only ever done it that once on the spur of the moment with Ceci and for all the times she'd done it he'd bet Annie could never have shown her private soul to a man. Might be a bit difficult to start with but worth working at.

'Better get on, Reg,' Annie nodded at the sky.

It was wonderful this sense of togetherness – the way they could just say things to each other. With sweat they had cleared their land, chopping and burning until they had looked out on a sea of blackened stumps with the first green shoots springing between them and the cry of the wild birds clear beyond their picket fence. Settled for the first time, each trip to the local grain and hardware had been a serious much-discussed event. And they had been careful with their money for though they had made a small beginning, it was the biggest adventure of their lives . . .

'We can feed the cows those stalks,' Reg murmured looking away.

'I know,' Annie said, again the thrill of being in total agreement with another human surging through her. She felt like a picture of two fish she'd once seen in a pub. The landlord had told her they were swimming alongside each other because they agreed about things, they were in harmony and the one was obedient to the other. Whatever he had been trying to tell her she was not sure but she did remember those two fish.

Reg suddenly turned his eyes on her, unable to make the first move, yet knowing she was ready for him. Annie dipped her head. She could not cross those few yards between them and embrace him! She looked down. Reg cleared his throat. They were married now and that was that! He'd see about Annie tonight.

Because they had not known where their land ended, day after day throughout the summer months Reg had continued clearing and chopping at the cover until by now they were well on the way to the hills. He'd learned the lesson from the other settlers of getting your cover down and firing it during winter, and next spring, thanks to the seed he and Annie had saved, he would plant the entire area out. Each day he had gone farther for there was no way of measuring a boundary or telling where it stopped.

174

That their plot had been much larger than the small plots around the darkened 'boxes' on the survey map he knew: that was probably why it had been left. It was an expensive piece Annie's finger had landed on and being on the outskirts where the flattened pocket gave way to the hills they could, if they wanted, run right up to them. Folks around would have nothing to say for they had only cleared the small bit to help them get started. It was a well-known fact that some people who had bought land in the backblocks had never found it, Reg reminded himself. Others had purchased land in swamps they had been unable to drain or beyond swamps they could not cross! He had pressed onwards. Now all that remained was a simple band of trees between him and the horizon, a wavy ribbon separating the wilderness of chopped and dying greenery from hills beyond, which supported nothing but faint yellow grass and a rocky outcrop. Reg scratched his head. He did not want to cut those last trees down. Although he could not explain why and Annie's reasoning was let's get every inch, a disturbing scene from the West Coast had stayed in his mind. There had been quite some logging in one region to build a settlement yet hardly had the trees come down than it rained and shrubs rushed after them, then the earth – in a great mud slide – and tore down the hill crushing first the huts of the settlement then its church. He remembered the welter of mud, broken branches and rocks. And the baby trapped, the old man buried alive and the child who had been left minding the baby caught in a tree in the fork of a river. He was not going to remove those trees . . .

Faith sat turning the pages of her missal. No one was coming. They were not going to come. She crumpled the wet handkerchief in her hand, remembering how carefully she had worded her letter: 'Don't reply, just come if you are able . . .' Surely a sensitive reading between the lines would have told somebody that she feared a written response? That she was in fact sending out a plea for help? Why, she had most particularly suggested that Ceci visit during the day so that they could go for a walk by the sea, or have a picnic somewhere. She had even imagined Ceci discussing with Ginger who should pay for their lunch should they stop somewhere. She laid her missal aside and crossed to the window. On the far side of the street she could see Dougall and the other upright citizens of Dunedin returning from Dougall's church. She did not bother stepping away to conceal herself in the shadows of the room. They all knew she had stopped going to his church so she might as well stare at them. Who knew if they were even thinking she was better off at home than sticking out like a sore thumb in their church?

The words 'For I poor worm have no manhood left,' spun in her head. 'A byword to all, the laughing-stock of the nation.' Why did this psalm taunt her? 'All who catch sight of me fall to mocking; to mouthing insults and tossing their heads in scorn.' How long was it since she had written that letter to Hexham? How soon were married daughters forgotten? 'Do not leave now when trouble is close at hand and I have none to help me,' the psalm continued. 'I am laid in the dust to die . . .'

She had stopped going to church with Dougall soon after he had stopped speaking to her in the house. There no longer seemed reason to strive to please him. As the situation worsened she did not even seek to avoid his anger and, strangely, found he seemed happier going to church on his own. She had always felt out of place, homesick at his services and now Sunday after Sunday she passed alone in the front room while the citizenry of Dunedin trooped by. Never had she imagined she could miss the Mass so badly! Never had she realized what a central part it had played in her life! That her service and Dougall's, both designed to give honour and glory to God, could begin and end with such different sentiments while traversing similar paths had shocked her. The familiar atmosphere she had grown up with, that comfortable feel of sinking into the Mass as one's feet slid into slippers at the end of a long day, then arising refreshed, was not there and she missed it badly. Even at the most sacred time of Dougall's service – the preparation for Communion – when she had looked around, though she had found heads bowed and hands in unnatural positions, there was no sense of a Presence. How she longed for the Catholic barn in Moke where bodies slipped into comfortable positions and eyes slid closed as inner souls awakened.

If her situation could be described as one of suffering, she told herself, suffering was supposed to chasten and repair, to draw people closer to God – yet though she had submitted on every possible count to Dougall, had exercised depths of humility her family and friends would have had difficulty believing she possessed, there was not the tiniest indication that her efforts were leading her any closer to either Dougall or God. Indeed, when it occurred to her that perhaps she was trying to lead, she had tried the reverse tack. But Dougall remained like a mule halfway between the poles of forces she did not understand. If she had received a penny for each time she had asked what she could do to please him, she would already have been a rich woman.

Coming to at the sight of him at their gate she hurried to open the door and greet him. 'Dougall,' she smiled warmly, the habit of hope triumphing over experience persisting.

Dougall kept his eyes down and walked past her.

'What is the matter?' she cried, running after him. 'What have I done?'

But the back door had closed and he had already crossed the yard to speak to their landlady.

Faith fell to her knees and prayed: 'Mother Mary,' she urged, 'you saw that! How am I to live with him?'

Instantly the words flashed into her mind: 'Love him.' But even as the gentle voice faded, Faith knew she had heard the truth.

'*How* do I love him?' she demanded.

'Live with him.'

'I am trying to live with him!' she said angrily. There was a silence. Faith got to her feet. 'I don't think anybody likes me,' she said with genuine conviction.

'I do,' came a soft voice Faith recognized as the Heart of God.

'Why?' Faith asked, taken aback by the remark, surprised at it. 'If I was any good Dougall would love me.'

'I only make what is good,' answered the voice.

Faith felt a gentleness come over her. She would try again. Day by day by day she would try turning to God for solace, for one could not go on without love and clearly it would not be coming from Dougall. Life without love! She had never imagined such a condition to exist! In fact she had had such a surfeit of love at Hexham that in trying to break away she had pretended an indifference to it; had cultivated in herself a rejection of this warmer side of life. Well, she had dug a pit and fallen into it and life, with an eye to irony, had turned the tables on her till now she longed for love!

Briefly strengthened by prayer, Faith decided to take up her cross in true Christian tradition and walk. She would not be beaten down by Dougall's unkindness and though perhaps it would be wiser to be to him as he was to her, she would continue to give. If there were only some chink in his armour, some tiny crack where the light could shine through and give her cause to hope that when all was said and done, he wanted her. One year, two years ... how many years would it take if he did not turn for her to become so inflamed by her experiences that she would be incapable of a generous word or kindly thought? How twisted would she become if her every normal instinct were thwarted, treated with disdain? They had said the words of the marriage ceremony not once but twice thanks to Dougall's thoroughness in making sure they underwent the ceremony in both churches. She had meant the words and they were well and truly married so why was it like this? Did other people start out tearing at their marriages like dogs at bones? If there was only someone to talk to!

Her letter lay behind the mantelpiece clock at Hexham along with other letters which had been enjoyed or 'dealt with'; letters like Annie's and Olwen's – all of which would remain undisturbed until some special circumstance arose or the clock was pushed dangerously close to the fireplace that it occurred to someone to give it a good tidy-out ...

Gathered at James' and Hetty's mansion for their annual get-together the Notables and their wives were reviewing the events of the year.

'Absent friends,' said Hetty acidly, angry that Olwen had not come. She raised her glass and looked knowingly around till her eyes settled on Gwen whom she had particularly instructed to invite Olwen.

'Do you know she has a *Maori* living with her?' Gwen said, anxious to shift the focus of illwill to Olwen.

Hetty gasped. This was incredible. 'A *man*?'

'A young girl!' Gwen revealed in a voice rich with nuance.

Hetty's tongue touched the tip of her lip: 'As a maid?'

Gwen savoured the moment. 'I don't – think – I would quite say *that*,' she said, lowering her eyes suggestively.

'More as a friend, you mean,' volunteered a voice from behind. 'Isn't that what you were about to say?'

Gwen spun to find Marshall Cavanaugh frowning down at her.

'You forget,' Hetty said directly to Marshall, annoyed with him for spoiling their moment. 'We've all been — *measured* by her . . .'

'She may have got your measure,' Marshall returned, 'but you don't seem to have got hers!'

'How very rude!' Gwen piped as Marshall retreated towards the group of men standing by the window. 'You shouldn't let him get away with a remark like that!'

Hetty considered. James had heard. James would take care of him.

'Talking about Miss Laird, were they?' James grunted as Marshall approached. 'Bothers the women she won't come to their "do's". . .' Marshall shrugged. It was an acknowledged fact that the 'do's' were for the women. 'Thing is, old chap,' James went on, 'she's either with us or against us, don't you know?' He glanced around the room with its preponderance of pink, choosing his moment to draw the women into the talk.

Alerted, Hetty hurried over: 'If she doesn't want to be part of us — if she *wants* to behave as a seamstress . . .' she left it open.

'She's been seen on that Maori *marae*,' James said, taking a cigar from the box and feeling in his pocket for a knife.

'*Marae*?' Gwen asked nervously.

'*Marae*, woman, *marae*!' Venables corrected her pronunciation. 'That open space in their village! Meeting house thing!'

Gwen drew back as if bitten and Hetty, pleased that the evening was finally heating up, leant over. 'One can't be expected to know words like that, dear,' she breathed compassionately. 'Yet Venables was a little over-harsh with you I thought.'

Gwen was annoyed. It was a known fact that to mention Maoris to Venables was like waving a red flag at a bull. Now, no doubt, his acute anxiety which took various forms when he was in the presence of James would rear up and embarrass her. How wretched it was that James' control over the imports Venables needed for his business should leave them exposed.

'What I say,' shrilled the voice of Venables, 'is that we can as easily unmake her as make her!'

The room became quiet.

'Ever the realist, Venables!' James encouraged, cutting his cigar and deciding to play him a little. 'But the girl's established now, mind. Clean bill. No debts to anyone. Don't see you can do anything about that!'

'Aha!' Venables took the bait. 'She's still dependent on us for her cloth! For the import of it!'

The women on the sofa spun to face him.

'Steady on!' cautioned Hetty.

'On the contrary,' said Gwen, spotting the chance to recover face. 'Don't we all have our gowns for the season?'

A titter of 'yesses' ran through the group.

'I believe she's up to Muriel.'

'What a place to leave off!'

'I don't think this is in anyone's best interests,' Marshall began cautiously, conscious that his earlier rudeness had compromised him.

'On the *contrary*,' Venables took up Gwen's phrase. 'We've done it before. You remember that young whippersnapper whatsisname thought he knew it all?'

Gwen smiled.

'That was despicable,' Marshall growled.

'On the *contrary*,' James joined in. 'That sort of chap tends towards suicide.' He poured a drink. 'If it'll please you, Venables, we can certainly "lose" a few of her orders . . .' He refilled the men's glasses. 'Looking a bit green behind the gills. Not actually going out with her are you, Marshall?'

'I – may have seen her couple of times . . .' Marshall faltered.

'More than that, my dear!' Hetty said. 'Been seen. Hasn't he, Venables?'

'We are not saying there is anything *serious* there,' James warned, coming to stand by Hetty and toy with her hand. 'Realize you value your position amongst us – amongst the community.'

Marshall put his drink down, aware he was being threatened. 'This is despicable,' he repeated. 'Because this girl is different from us – because she does not pass her time in the way that we do – is she to be penalized? Has it not occurred to any of you that were she not different she could not design such extraordinary creations? Which of you would sacrifice your gowns, all of them, for the sake of having her sitting here now? I, for one, would change nothing about her!'

Almost before the last phrase was out of his mouth Marshall realized it had not been wise.

'I will have no part of any trickery; any diverting of her orders.'

'Fact is, young man,' James said after a short pause, 'the girl relies on taffeta and it is *I* who controls that!'

'James' meaning is,' Venables elaborated, 'that you had better decide which side your bread is buttered.'

'I'm sure I could find someone else to do my paperwork should it become necessary,' James added.

Marshall swung from the room.

'You needn't have been *quite* so explicit!' Hetty bleated.

'He'll lend Miss Laird money if she's driven out of business!' Gwen promised. 'He's in love with the girl.'

'I won't be denied my sport,' James warned, offering the cigars and restoring the atmosphere of bonhomie in the room.

'That's the spirit!'

'A few months should starve her out,' he continued. 'Bring her round.'

The women nodded and Hetty allowed herself to relax. Even now in his early sixties, with his paunch, the stale smell of smoke which accompanied him everywhere and his scattering of dandruff, there was no doubt about it. James still cut a respected figure and the man loved her. She watched him reach for an ashtray to knock the end off his cigar.

'I'll Paikakariki her . . .' he murmured.

Olwen sat waiting for the detective, Archie, to show. The man was positively the most extraordinary human being she had ever had dealings with, except, perhaps, for her own father! He insisted on wearing eccentric disguises and meeting in unlikely places on the basis that his clientele were all so well known he wouldn't want to compromise them by being recognized in their presence. By her own reckoning she had now been waiting in The Swan for seventeen minutes under the steely eye of an unpretentious barmaid whose trade seemed to consist mainly of filling jugs and bottles for people to take out and consume elsewhere. By the pictures of Galway on the walls she took it the management was Irish. They had a few rooms available for accommodation, their prices chalked on a slate.

Finally Olwen rose. To date Archie had told her where Marshall worked, where he lived, what he earned, who he was mostly known to associate with and other such details which, if no surprise to Olwen, at least proved he was thorough. For some weeks now he had been monitoring

Marshall Cavanaugh's mail, incoming and outgoing, presumably through an 'arrangement' with one of the team of porters who supervised the apartment building where Marshall lodged or perhaps even with a postman or the post office itself. It seemed likely that a man like Archie would have such an expedience. He was not to open any mail: merely to see from whence it came, with what regularity and the date sent. This was because Olwen wished to know whether someone somewhere, wife or lover perhaps, was in regular contact with him. A communication from overseas in particular would alert her to an area which should be enquired into further.

As the hands of the clock moved up to twenty minutes, regretfully Olwen turned to the door and stepped out into the muddy street. Instantly she was accosted by a snake charmer hissing: 'This way!' at her. As Olwen followed Archie around the corner she could not help smiling. 'I'm *so* sorry,' he babbled. 'She wouldn't let me in!' And little wonder thought Olwen, eyeing the suspicious-looking laundry basket in which he allegedly kept his cobra.

'I'm late now so we'll have to talk as we walk,' she told him. 'I can't help what it looks like. You can pretend I'm interested in buying your snake!'

Hurrying back towards Courtenay Place Archie detailed to Olwen Marshall's mailing arrangements. It seemed, as in all other respects, he was clean. His mother wrote occasionally from Wiltshire and there had been a recent letter from his sister in Bournemouth.

'How do you know it's his sister?'

'Aha! Because she married a Michael Parrish and he moved to Bournemouth.'

'How could you possibly know that? It could very well be the man's wife!' Olwen retorted as they stumbled over the tramlines.

'There is most certainly no wife,' Archie said solemnly. 'I know that for a fact.'

'How?'

'Because one of the first things I did was to take the trouble to write to Somerset House in London and enquire!' he said, pleased with himself.

'Can you do that?' Olwen asked.

'I already *have*!' Archie replied, as if his professional standing had been bruised by the question. 'I was merely awaiting the reply.'

Olwen paused. It would have been very unfortunate if he had made the same enquiries about *her* situation. But she hadn't been born in England so perhaps Somerset House wouldn't know. Edmund had, however, and they'd married there ... 'I still want you to stay alert,' Olwen cautioned him. 'There may be a mistress. People are not always what they seem.'

'Olwen,' Marshall began carefully, 'have you ever given thought to diversifying your means of importing cloth?'

'Whatever for?' Olwen replied. 'It has to come by sea!'

'You could use an Auckland agent and have it brought down by – '

'That is *impossibly* roundabout!'

'Or the South Island. You could ship into Lyttelton then up by – '

'Whatever is wrong with Wellington?'

Marshall hesitated. He had no right repeating idle, possibly fatuous, gossip. 'There have been – instances – of agitation on the waterfront,' he said lamely.

Not a good liar, Olwen thought. 'I would like you to repeat to me anything you may have heard which may affect my future,' she began.

'I'm not at liberty . . .'

Olwen walked to the window and stared over the rooves

185

of Wellington. During the past few days she *had* noticed a change in people who dealt with her, the lifting of a brow, a mouth curling. 'What do you suggest?' she asked, turning.

Marshall hurried over and took her hands: 'I would like us to become engaged.'

So that was it! Olwen thought bitterly. His personal servant had advised him that the house porter was receiving tips for inspecting his mail! He was afraid she would find something out and abandon him! His next remark only confirmed this.

'Things could get very difficult around here for both of us . . .'

Olwen's face took on a wry expression.

'I suggest we name a date,' Marshall urged. 'I suggest we announce our engagement forthwith and choose — spring? A spring wedding!' The Notables would have to be more careful with Olwen, he told himself, having him to consider as her husband. Why was she staring so distrustfully? 'I am trying to protect you,' he explained.

To pin me down before I find out something derogatory about you, you mean, Olwen concluded.

'At considerable cost to myself,' Marshall continued.

'Why are you in such an uncommon hurry?' Olwen asked. Marshall touched her shoulder but her face remained hard. Perhaps she could have it both ways, she was thinking. If he was too pressed to enquire about her . . . Staring past him, she counted the months since she had written the letter requesting a divorce. Within two months at the outside she would know and by spring the divorce should be on its way. But suppose it were late? 'I'll agree to announcing our engagement in spring,' she stated. 'But spring is too soon to marry.'

Marshall held her hands: 'Do you realize, Olwen, this could be a very difficult winter until spring . . .'

'You're a romantic,' Olwen scolded, pulling her hands back yet wondering what he had meant.

Marshall shook his head. Romance was nothing to do with it. If James had his way, by the time spring came the girl would be skin and bone! Indeed there would be nothing left of Olwen worth marrying!

Watching his face, Olwen was sure he had a secret concealed there. How she longed to tell him she did not mind, that whatever his circumstances were – once she was free – she would happily marry him.

'I sense I have lost Gwen's friendship,' she confessed, looking up. 'I should like to have been friends.' Marshall nodded. 'But on my own terms.'

'Let us go for a walk,' he said gently.

'The Maoris call Wellington The Headland That Feeds on The Wind,' Olwen smiled as they stepped out of Marshall's building into a veritable gust.

'Very beautiful,' Marshall agreed.

'They call Mount Victoria "Tangi-te-keo, The Cry of the Wind", ' Olwen continued.

'Mind!' Marshall cried, stepping in front of Olwen as a group of work horses, freed from their stable, galloped wildly down the road towards Oriental Bay for their daily swim.

'What a sight!' Olwen sighed seeing the horses rush into the water, kicking and splashing and sending small boys running for land. Beyond them, up to their necks, other horses swam freely.

'They have the freedom of the city,' Marshall observed.

Though they were aware of people watching them watching the horses, Marshall and Olwen dared to link hands.

'Look at that one!' Marshall exclaimed as a young filly tore from the water and rushed for a hillside. 'Find herself a nice bit of green up there!'

'It won't be long before the horses lose all this, you mark my words,' Olwen said sadly. 'Some Know-it-all will take it away from them or say they may only bathe on such a day before such a time, poor things. When you consider how hard they work I'd say they're entitled to a bath every day, wouldn't you?'

Marshall agreed. He would have loved to put his arm around Olwen and draw her to him but it would have compromised her beyond repair.

Sensing it, Olwen smiled. 'That is not the sort of thing we do, is it?' she asked. 'Only the Maoris express affection in public.'

'Let us be content to hold hands,' Marshall said with a great softness in his voice. 'Never forget, Olwen, the future is ours.'

As evening went on they found themselves wandering in Haining Street, the most forbidden, the most dangerous of all locales and one which held out a macabre lure to those in love. From tumbledown ramshackle houses crammed together came the smell of opium, preserved ginger and cries in a strange foreign tongue.

'Packapoo dens,' Marshall observed knowingly. Still scenting, flirting with danger they found themselves in Tory Street named for a ship but now one of the meanest streets in town. Olwen paused. Had she not been here before?

'Is that Cuba Street down there?' she asked. Vague surprise crossed Marshall's face. On they went past the pawn shops of Taranaki Street, those give-away signs of the destitution beyond view.

'This lane,' said Marshall pulling at Olwen's sleeve and leading her up Alma Lane, up Tui Street. Olwen gasped. If ever she had seen despair expressed in poverty, this was it. The sewers washing into the broken houses, leaning one against the other for support, their floorboards mildewed;

the distinct stench of septic puddles that stung the back of her nose, the occasional walled-up house, the bark of a trapped dog behind it, the hopeless attempts of the poor at repairing their rotten structures with pieces of rusting iron salvaged from elsewhere . . . Marshall let out a deep sigh: 'I'd like to do something about this one day,' he said.

Fired by the poverty and their feelings of compassion for fellow man; congratulating themselves on their bravery for having seen it, they pressed against each other in the shadows. Around the lintel under which they stood the rain began, whispering at the open sewer, hammering the strips of tin and litter, washing it into rat holes, under sacking and into the interior of houses. Olwen coughed. The smell was nauseating. As the water dripped from the lintel and ran inside her blouse and over Marshall's chest she felt him become excited in a dangerous way. 'Marshall!' she cried. 'Let us get out of here!'

Roused yet reluctant, Marshall led Olwen to the safe broad streets of Wellington, the streets of Hetty and Gwen and the Notables who had no direct cause to concern themselves with the goings-on in the places like Holland Street or Jacobs Place. Never had Olwen looked so beautiful as she did now, Marshall told himself, wet through, her eyes moved with compassion. It was all he could do to stop himself possessing her then and there on the sidewalk. Never was he to see her looking so beautiful again.

Chapter 14

The sight of Brigham, always on the look-out for a favour, was far from welcome, yet courtesy obliged Marshall to let him into his apartment. 'How was the pleasure trip north?' he asked, feigning enthusiasm and biting back the observation that Brigham could put his time to better use by seriously pursuing the limited employment opportunities that existed in Wellington, even at the risk of getting his hands dirty.

'Capital!' Brigham replied

'Get in any hunting?'

Brigham nodded.

'What?'

'Possum. Amusing actually. Bounder invited me to a local meeting. Bit of a disagreement going on,' Brigham said, wondering why Marshall had not yet offered him coffee. 'I ask you – why should a chap miss out on the fur trade because of some chappy's orchard?'

Marshall caught him staring towards the coffee percolator. 'I don't follow.'

'Got themselves quite excited about the possums at the meeting. Breed like rabbits, you know. The fur trade. But also like to eat fruit – '

'The neighbour's fruit orchard!' Marshall nodded, beginning to grasp the situation.

'Mine host voted with the neighbour against the introduction of possums then dropped off a breeding pair on the way home.'

'Of possums?'

Brigham nodded. 'Direct hit. Straight in the orchard,' he grinned suavely. 'After dark of course.'

About to say: 'I don't mind telling you, Brigham, I consider that rough – ' an idea struck Marshall. In the event James made too much trouble for Olwen perhaps she could profitably turn to fur. 'What's it like, possum pelt?' he asked.

'Fair enough, fair enough,' Brigham replied. 'Put it like this, the Australians have been doing well out of it!'

'How is it to sew?' Marshall asked seriously.

'*Sew*!'

'I'm not a hunting man, I've never seen a possum – '

'Trap them, don't hunt them – except for sport,' Brigham corrected. 'Cute little things. Bright-eyed, feet like cat's. Big ears.'

'The pelt?'

'Thick!'

Marshall became thoughtful. It sounded as if it might be as easy to work with as Persian lamb which – given its tight curly hair – even a child could patch coats with without seams showing. Mink type of furs on the other hand were known to be notoriously difficult and took years of training to avoid waste. Such furs would be too expensive for Olwen to embark on should the Notables decide to squeeze her out of the cloth market that winter but possum ... The experience with Persian lamb-type pelts had proved apprentice girls could be put to work on it immediately ...

'I'll tell you one thing,' Brigham assured Marshall, helping himself to a cigar, 'local brats will get them for you by the handful if you're interested.' He lit the cigar. 'But mind they don't damage the pelts.' He observed Marshall's thoughtful expression. 'Put it like this, if I had the money, I'd consider buying into forest land now, for an acre of forest, at present yielding no income, would – stocked with possum – certainly match your return on pasture land with no permanent damage to the trees. Fine fur too. *If* I had the capital, as I say, I'd establish a fur farm and bring in silver fox *and* musquash!'

'Next time you go up there,' Marshall said thoughtfully, 'find out how much the locals would have to be paid per possum. The skins undamaged of course. Breakfast?'

As the men set off for Marshall's breakfast club Brigham let it be known that he approved the way the pioneers had set about stocking the island paradise with beasts of the 'huntin', shootin' 'n' fishin' ' variety. It had given him pleasure on his trip north, he said, to see the familiar domestic animals from home, the imported grasses and treescapes of his native land. 'A man's got to have something to kill,' he observed, ducking around a tram. 'Next time I'm going for deer. Joined a gun club already. They bag foxes too and when they can't find 'em take the hare instead.'

Marshall held open the door to the club: 'When we came out here you realize there were no mammals at all. Just a few fish and a lot of unusual birds – '

'You've done well, done well,' Brigham condescended, stepping in front of Marshall, hungry for breakfast.

Marshall did not entirely agree. 'So you like the rats we brought here?'

'All ships bring in rats,' Brigham said, conscious he had not pursued the introduction Marshall had arranged for him with the Inspector of Nuisances.

'But have you seen the children playing with them?' Marshall went on. 'Piling up rubbish in the poorer quarters, leaving it for a few days then surrounding it and waiting for rats to run out? They dare each other to go into the middle and remove the rubbish a piece at a time and fling it over their heads and when the circle is seething with animals – '

'If children want to get bitten . . .'

Marshall signed to the waiter, aware that for some reason he was tying up his walk through the slums with Olwen, and his desire for her, with anger at the remarks Brigham was making.

'Can see the bounders dashing up the hawser ropes straight off the boat and on to land!' Brigham was saying. 'Natural'.

Marshall glared.

'Let the government come up with a Bubonic Plague Prevention Act,' Brigham continued, eyes on the approaching waiter. 'From what I hear you've got leprosy here already.'

Marshall felt like hitting him. 'I take it you didn't avail yourself of my letter of introduction to the Inspector of Nuisances?' he said, snapping the menu open.

'Appreciated it at the time, old man,' Brigham replied, indicating to the waiter the full set breakfast with two fluffy eggs. 'But hardly my cup of tea.'

'You do have something in mind then? In the way of work?'

'Actually yes,' Brigham nodded vigorously, tapping the word 'coffee' with his finger. 'And it doesn't include abusing immigrants who can't speak English for relieving themselves against walls!' His finger moved along the row suggesting fresh rolls as opposed to muffins. 'Or getting dogs and a certificate as a professional rat-catcher. No! I've a much better idea this time,' he said pushing back on his chair and reaching to unfurl his napkin. 'I am going to involve myself in the insurance of cargo. I feel a man like James could make use of me. He has given me a little job to do already.'

Marshall frowned: 'I hope you considered carefully before accepting. What was it?'

'Bit of this, bit of that,' Brigham replied evasively. 'I mean to get into shipping.'

'If you are helping James in a matter of the *cloth* trade,' Marshall warned, 'Then tread most carefully.'

Brigham leaned forward and flicked a pat of butter on to his plate.

'What James requires you to do,' Marshall continued as the butter sank into Brigham's toast, 'may determine whether or not we will be in a position to continue as friends.'

'And I would advise *you*,' Brigham replied in an equally soft voice, 'that you might have to tread a bit carefully with your possum skins. I'm not entirely sure that it's legal to get them.'

Marshall laid his knife down and watched Brigham put food in his mouth. While he hoped he was wrong there was very little use a man like James could possibly find for Brigham unless it involved skulduggery of some sort such as entering a warehouse and removing – 'losing' they would say – materials ordered by Olwen . . .

As winter led on it was clear to Marshall that Olwen was in difficulties but as she was too proud to mention them to him, he could not find grounds for involving himself. Further, bound as he was by the consideration to not repeat matters heard as idle gossip, with his hands tied, Marshall could only long for Olwen to confide him, to explain at what level she was encountering difficulties in order that he might advise her. Clearly, this was not her way. Hence he was obliged to watch from the sidelines as she became paler and more fraught. Yet they were not far into the winter when some change occurred which led Marshall to believe he had misjudged both Brigham and James. Unknown to him, aware that something was wrong and that it was no coincidence, Olwen had made an appointment with James and confronted him directly.

'There seems to have been a great deal of trouble with my orders during the past several weeks,' Olwen told him. 'Which I would rather imagine would come as no surprise to you.'

'Well, well,' replied James, leaning back in his chair.

'If you think that my business, my expertise, is founded solely on your goodwill, James,' she said, seeing him flinch at the use of his name, 'you are sorely mistaken.'

'Making alternative arrangements, are we?' James enquired. 'Auckland is a long way as is the South Island and taffeta mildews.'

'My dear sir,' Olwen replied vehemently, 'there's enough muslin in this town to clothe the entire country! Do you wish to see your wife running around in a muslin shift?'

'None of the women on whom your trade depends, my dear, wear muslin,' James pointed out.

'Is that what you think? Suppose I were to tell you that this time next year your wife will be clamouring for one of my new muslin chemises; that I have come up with a completely new fashion line which will make taffeta so redundant that neither Hetty nor Muriel nor Gwen would be seen dead in it in public! In fact, I doubt, once my first models are revealed, they will have the face to wear this season's gowns!'

'If you choose to design for the masses – '

'Then the Notables must wear their cast-offs!' Olwen completed the sentence for him. She crossed to the door. 'I merely came to thank you, *dear* James for stimulating me to think in a new direction.'

As the door closed behind her James struggled to grasp what she had said. Was she going to create some new style his wife and her friends could not wear? Her prices would have to drop to meet the masses . . . but then again, if less work went into the product and it was turned out faster and actually took the working girls' minds he could be in for a run for his money. Quickly he twanged his desk bell.

The door opened. 'Get me Brigham at once,' he demanded. 'Send a boy to his apartment and fetch him!'

'Am I right in thinking you have the ear of our good friend Marshall?' James asked affably. Brigham nodded. 'Wouldn't by any chance have any idea of the man's current thinking towards his – lady friend's enterprise? Any new – change of direction?'

Pleased with himself, Brigham stepped forward smiling. It was exactly the opportunity he had been waiting for, in fact he could hardly believe his own good fortune. He bent his face toward James and whispered: 'Opossum fur . . . Fur!'

To his amazement James smacked his desk and roared with laughter.

'I assure you I am not joking, sir.'

James nodded, tears of relief filling his eyes. No wonder the mindless girl had said muslin! Simply trying to lead him in the wrong direction!

Although she had been serious when she spoke about muslin, in a very short time the rumour that Olwen was going into fur brought a rash of invitations she had the greatest difficulty in understanding.

Ceci woke up and went straight to the clock, pulled out Faith's letter and re-read it and, although there was nothing untoward in it, found she could not shake the feeling that Faith had a need of her.

'I think I'll go down and see Faith,' she told Ginger.

'Why?'

'Why not?' Ceci shrugged. 'It's ages since we've seen her and we got on so well last time. I think I'll just – turn up and take it from there.'

'Write and say you're coming.'

Ceci hesitated. She felt that was not the thing to do. 'I think I'll just *go*,' she said softly.

Hardly had she been walking any time on the beach with Faith than she began to suspect that something was very wrong. The girl to'd and fro'd like water in a ditch – towards her and away again – coming out, hiding, stating then denying.

'Let us stop playing games, Faith,' Ceci said, grasping her wrist. 'Tell me the truth.'

At the physical contact, Faith broke and although she felt a hideous sense of betrayal, out came the storm. 'It's Dougall. I can't stand him.'

Listening to Faith's voice crash around her it occurred to Ceci that the girl might be disturbed until she remembered that that was always Ginger's response to her own deepest needs.

'He has a terrible temper,' Faith was saying.

'You mean he shouts at you?' Faith shook her head. 'He hits you?' The shake again. 'How does he show his temper?'

'He – he –'

'Does he do *anything*?'

'No.'

'Oh I see,' Ceci murmured.

'It's just, he keeps other people at arm's length by being nice to them, but me whom he lives with – '

'He keeps at bay by anger,' Ceci finished for her.

197

Faith looked relieved. Relieved and incredulous.

'Why did you marry him?' Ceci asked. The girl hung her head. 'I'm asking as much for my own reasons as yours,' Ceci confided. 'I still can't explain to myself why I married Calvin . . .'

Encouraged by a shared circumstance Faith went on, the picture emerging of a party who had misunderstood sign after sign. Gone were the dour looks, the critical disdain, the clever turns of phrase which had so wilfully stung Ginger. Gone that sense of absolute timing.

'I didn't feel good about my father and you,' Faith said honestly. She had been the babe on Maureen's hip, Ceci remembered, who had caught her eye when she had entered Ginger's home for the first time and found him amongst his brood. Was it possible for a tiny baby to sense the destruction of its family the instant a stranger stepped into the room? 'A lot of things about my father I didn't approve of,' Faith was saying. 'I may have been too young to understand about our mother but I felt he wasn't right with her,' she hesitated. Obviously there were no jibes lined up for her, Ceci realized. 'Then Lizabeth married that laggard – that was hard to take . . .' Her voice trailed off. By the distant look in her eyes Ceci guessed she was thinking Lizabeth might have been the happier of the two. 'I just don't know if I'm *normal*,' Faith mumbled.

'What do you mean?'

'He never touches me.'

Ceci shifted slightly. This she found difficult to believe. Dougall had been the heart of friendship with them and there had been no shortage of little gestures – the drawing back of a chair, the squeezing of an elbow, the hand placed in the small of a back . . .

'You don't believe me, do you?' Faith said dismally. 'I

thought you wouldn't.' A sense of bitterness swept over her. 'I've made a fool of myself for nothing!'

'You were telling me what attracted you towards Dougall,' Ceci pressed her. 'Apart from irritation at your father and a dislike of your religion – '

'I don't dislike my religion!'

'I could understand it if you resented *me* – '

'Dougall never *touches* me,' Faith repeated in an urgent voice.

'What do you mean?'

'That.'

Ceci frowned.

'It's all right at your age,' Faith said naïvely. 'But for us the whole day builds towards it . . .'

'I don't want to insult your intelligence, Faith, but have you tried everything?'

Faith looked as if she could have struck her.

'I can understand someone as outspoken as yourself finding marriage difficult to adjust to, yet – '

'As soon as I get into bed he puts the lamp out.'

'And then?'

'*Nothing*! When I first objected he said that that was what people did. They went to bed, they put the light out, they went to sleep! I tried getting to bed first and I found he didn't come in. He would sit in the front room until I fell asleep. If I rolled towards him during the night he would roll farther and farther away until he reached the edge.'

'Then what did he do?'

'Got out and went into the front room!'

'Maybe you touch him too much – '

'I *knew* you'd say that!' Faith said bitterly. 'For six weeks I would be careful not to let even the tip of my little finger near him! Sometimes I would long to fling my arms around him and say how wonderful life was ...' She paused.

'Maybe you should have.'

'As soon as I did he'd quickly turn his head away and I'd find myself kissing his hair, then he'd turn back again and ignore the incident.'

Ceci frowned, her immediate response being not to believe any of this yet something nagged at her mind, some small detail she had subconsciously noted that suggested the girl might not be lying.

'After a while I got worried about him so I reached over and held him fast in my arms one night. He went absolutely rigid.'

Now Ceci had it! It had been when she was dozing in the wing chair in their front room and had come to on Dougall staring from the window while Faith was calling him from the doorway. At the time she had had the impression that Dougall had distinctly heard yet was pretending not to ...

'Have you talked to him about this?'

'In the mornings,' Faith's voice went on, 'I jump out of bed and run into the kitchen after him begging him to say good morning to me but he won't speak! He won't say good morning and he won't say good night! I just stand there in front of him saying please Dougall say good morning to me. I can't go through the day if you leave the house without speaking to me again. Just say good morning, *please*.'

Ceci frowned. This was a bad situation and something would have to be done.

'Would you like me to speak to Dougall?'

Faith shook her head. 'You'd end up believing him and not me! He's far too convincing!'

They walked on for a while in silence.

'I don't know what I can do to help you,' Ceci admitted.

'Nor do I.'

'I'd say I'd pray for you if I knew how,' Ceci began, deciding not to add that there had probably been too much of that going on already ... It was ridiculous that in a situation like this two young people should be bound together for the rest of their lives. She would speak to a priest. 'Have you been attending your Church down here Faith?' she asked.

The girl shook her head. 'We went to get it regularized – the marriage you know – just a repeat of vows; but you mustn't go near the priest,' she begged. 'Promise me you won't do that. And promise you won't tell Father!'

'I might get an opinion from a priest without mentioning names but I won't tell your father.'

'Please don't tell them how unhappy I am,' Faith pleaded. 'I couldn't bear to have Myra and Lizabeth and the boys know what a terrible life I have.'

After all the trouble you took to impress them, Ceci told herself. 'Do you feel a little better for having talked?' she asked kindly.

Faith nodded, her eyes filled with tears.

'Come here,' Ceci said, putting her arms around the girl and hugging her warmly. 'There now. Cry if you like.'

Faith sobbed and shook against Ceci, the anger and hurt flooding out of her, the warmth of another human being feeling more precious than she had ever remembered it.

'Next time shall I bring Ginger?'

Faith shook her head violently.

'If things get too bad, you come up to Hexham,' Ceci suggested. 'Just tell Dougall where you are. You don't have to tell us you're coming. Nor do you need an excuse.'

'What will I tell Father?'

'That Dougall's working. That he can manage without you.'

'*That's* certainly true,' Faith observed.

On her way to the priest's house – or presbytery Ceci reminded herself – she ran the phrases through her mind: priest/presbytery for the Catholics; minister/manse for the Presbyterians; vicar/vestry for the Church of England – and in case of difficulty, the word 'reverend' was generally useful except for a priest who should be addressed as 'Father'. In an era when people were touchy about such things, she was determined not to create offence at the outset.

'Did they marry in the Catholic Church?' was the first question the priest put to her.

'The person on whose behalf I am speaking is a Catholic,' Ceci began. 'But the other person is of a – a – different persuasion ...' How she hated that ridiculous phrase which suggested they persuaded each other rather than fought about it!

'But they married in the Catholic Church?' the priest went on.

'The vows – but no nuptial mass.'

'That wouldn't have been allowed.'

'The main ceremony took place in the *other* Church.'

'If the vows were taken in both Churches then your "certain person" is well and truly married,' the priest advised.

'But it hasn't been consummated.'

'In that case,' said the priest brightening, 'and we would have to be under oath – there is a chance of an annulment. After the divorce.'

'Divorce?' Ceci gasped.

'We don't like to get out of step with the state.'

'I thought your Church didn't believe in divorce?'

'We don't. In fact you can simply disregard it. Afterwards.'

'But she – this certain person – has to get a divorce before you can grant her an annulment?'

'That's correct.'

Unwilling to state that it struck her as the ultimate hypocrisy for an institution that did not recognize divorce to make it a precondition of the annulment to which a person was entitled, Ceci fell silent.

'In point of fact they would be awarded concomitantly,' the priest was saying. 'It's the best we can do. We have always advised against "mixed" marriages.'

'My husband and I are "mixed",' Ceci replied with indignation.

'Ah,' the priest paused. 'That's *quite* different.'

'I can't put the girl through this,' she said, rising. 'Annulment she might accept, divorce never. Her father would never accept a divorce! It would demoralize him! And ruin his position in the community . . .'

The priest looked at her sadly. 'My dear, when you say you are "mixed" you mean no more than that your husband is a Catholic and you are not. There are others whose attitudes, particularly to do with forgiveness versus despair or trusting in God rather than trying to outwit him with merit, have ways of life very different from yours and ours. If ever – God forbid – the Reformist community and ours should come to blows, it will not be about whether Mary was a virgin or any other doctrine. It will be our different ways of life. Our Church may modernize. We do not re-form.'

'It's a terrible thing to see a young couple who can't get on because of religion,' Ceci complained.

'It is for this precise reason, for the happiness of the couples and the homes they will establish that the recommendation is to – if you like defer the battle – to let it be fought out by clerics and not on the parental hearth. When two children have been reared in very different conditions regarding such attitudes as the place of friendship in love or spontaneity versus control – even a laugh in a marriage can be a dangerous weapon . . .'

Ceci found herself beginning to like the priest.

'My brother, who is a planter in Malaya,' he went on, 'tells me that the natives there are so deeply appreciative of Allah's goodness they do not wish to appear so untrusting as to dig around the bases of trees already plentiful with fruit . . . Had we been born there doubtless we too would lie happily in the sun. But our history has been different. The North Europeans responded to their harsh climate by deciding time must not be lost. It was *they* who brought about the perpetual anxiety underlying the Reformist fear of being caught idling, that fear of enjoyment or relief of any kind. That such beliefs took root with the materially impoverished Scots is not surprising. You are particularly fortunate that there is a way out for this child.'

Ceci got to her feet. The morality of it was beyond her but if there were a way forward permitting both Faith and Dougall to get on with their separate lives surely it would be wrong to not hold it out to them.

'If you decide to go through with the annulment,' the priest said, coming to the door with her, 'it is a long, extremely painful and public business almost as bad as the divorce. It needs fortitude and courage. I do not doubt that you, my dear, possess it but think twice before subjecting a young girl to this. Ask yourself is there not some way their situation may be mended? Often the young when they are married find the going hard. Sometimes it is kinder to turn a deaf ear . . .'

Ceci closed the presbytery gate.

He was right of course. She had no particular affiliation: merely an idea of God she'd picked up from seeing her mother on her knees or hearing a spontaneous: 'God give me patience!' when she'd wanted to slap them. She could not even describe herself as a Protestant as there was nothing she protested about and the name only suggested Henry VIII to her. But given a choice she did not like the idea of using hard work to restore a 'broken' link with God: she preferred to live with a God who liked her and understood her weaknesses.

Poor Faith, she told herself as the tin rooves of Moke bumped into sight. She had tried to wear Dougall like a brooch and blind them with his brilliance. Lizabeth had simply taken her independence; the boys didn't acknowledge Ginger's authority; Myra cheated . . . Everyone had escaped but Faith who had decided to do it by finding harder rules to follow! Looking back at her own situation Ceci realized that unlike Faith she had never had the courage to speak out against her unhappiness with Calvin but had kept quiet for the shame of it; the feeling of personal disgrace. Like Faith she had not expected to be believed by others. But unlike Faith – in staying too long – she had developed the conviction that she was at fault. Therefore it was essential that Faith be rescued forthwith.

Reaching Hexham she put on a bright face lest Ginger suspect anything. Even honesty, however, became hard for the double standards Dougall had succeeded in establishing kept tripping her, leaving the uncomfortable feeling that they were arguing.

'How are they getting on?'

Ceci hesitated. 'I thought the landlady was a bit of a tartar,' she offered carefully.

'From what Dougall said she sounded marvellous! Their place fallen down yet?'

'Actually,' Ceci said, hating to contradict him, it's in excellent order.'

Ginger looked at her quizzically.

'I asked Faith to come up and see us sometime. Be nice, wouldn't it?' Glancing at Ginger she saw the remark hadn't registered. 'Did you hear what I said? I invited Faith up.'

'I've been thinking of going to Christchurch,' Ginger began.

'Oh?'

He glanced down. He wanted to keep this one a secret.

'Well,' Ceci said carefully, 'I might go back down to Dunedin myself.'

'What for?'

'I can have a little secret too, can't I?'

'So you don't mind my going to Christchurch?'

'Why should I?'

'Well I'm glad Faith's all right,' Ginger said, relieved at not being questioned about Christchurch, yet annoyed by Ceci's lack of curiosity.

'Will you be looking for Lizabeth or checking on the boys down there?' she asked directly.

'You tell me why you're going to Dunedin first,' Ginger retorted.

Ceci folded her arms and considered. 'Young girls,' she said slowly, 'need a certain amount of advice in marriage. Need I say more?'

Ginger shook his head. Coming from a sheep station it was hardly as if Faith didn't know the facts of life! Still, if Ceci was so taken up with the girl's situation that she was not going to press him about his affairs, so much the better. She'd even seemed relieved he was going. Aware that an atmosphere had arisen between them Ginger shrugged.

'All right. You go and I'll go,' he said, managing a smile.

'Agreed.'

* * *

Sitting in Christchurch in the bar of The Commercial Ginger let his eyes rest on the back of the barmaid's neck. *She* wouldn't need telling the facts of life either! Her dark hair was pulled upwards and her skin below had the paleness of the underbelly of a fish. He wiped his mouth. He'd already done the rounds of The Lion, The National, The Railway, The Cecil and The Central and was beginning to feel a little sleepy. It occurred to him for a moment that the barmaid might have been a 'lady of pleasure': if so her customers were lucky! He had never had a really black-haired woman. Maureen had tended towards red, Ceci was brown . . . In fact he'd never *had* another woman. So why the black hair? Ah! That poor woman in the shack beyond the railyards in Dunedin, he remembered! Frank's wife. Twice that day at the racecourse he thought he'd glimpsed Frank but each time he turned out to be mistaken . . . Of course he'd been there on the pretext of looking for his sons but it was Frank he'd come for. He wanted to put it to him man to man about the photographs and the wife and simply give him the chance to return Lizabeth. Wasted journey! And now it was time to go to bed and he had no one to go to bed with. Poor old boy, he said, beginning to feel sorry for himself. No one to go to bed with. Gradually he managed to build up the sensation of deserving a companion, of needing one . . . Ceci and Hexham were far from his mind as he stared at the back of the barmaid's neck wondering, just wondering. It was a shocking thing that a man should go through life knowing only two women, he told himself, the one of them currently all taken up with the glamour of his daughter's new home in Dunedin. Getting unsteadily to his feet he beckoned the barmaid over.

* * *

As she stood by the wash-stand in his room removing her blouse again he marvelled at the hairs on the back of her neck, so soft and shiny, so downy smooth. His own hair was old, that was the trouble. Coming up towards forty it had got dry and brittle and although others might not notice, it took only the sight or touch of young hair, the feel of young skin, to make a man aware. Lying on the bed he opened his arms. The girl turned from the wash-basin and stepped towards him . . .

Chapter 15

As the mist lifted over a patch of shaved land in the backblocks Reg delivered Annie of a baby, a little girl.

'Is it all right?' she asked.

'Little girl,' Reg murmured.

Annie sat up. She had been terrified of this delivery, certain the child would strangle on its cord, and had in fact begged with Reg to let her have some woman up from the hamlet, but his response had been: 'I pulled out plenty sheep in my time,' and 'We don't want none o' them peculiar people with headscarves meddlin' up here.'

Reg stood holding the baby then walked to the door with her.

'Bring her here! Bring her here!' Annie cried.

'Just gettin' some light on her,' Reg drawled, his own frame blocking any light that had been in the room. 'Looks like me.'

'Oh, you mean she looks intelligent,' Annie teased, struggling to her feet and coming over. 'Give her here.'

Reg handed the baby to Annie and watched her study its wrinkled face as if she were reading there a message of great importance.

'We are lucky, Reg,' she said softly. Reg put his hand on her shoulder and dipped her head.

'Call her Annie,' he said gruffly. 'After you. Little Annie for now.'

Annie nodded. Why not? Since she had been five months gone Reg had been extremely solicitous of her, allowing her to lift nothing, never strain and even give up woodpile duties.

'We better christen her, Reg.'

Reg nodded and they stepped outside. This was a very important, a sacramental, act, so they used the original billy they'd cooked the chicken in on the way up just to be sure.

In the weeks to come in their small home, still little more than a shed, Annie found herself sewing – a skill she'd always considered 'uppity', having herself led a life of hand-downs where the manner in which you wore the clothes that didn't fit, the way you 'carried them off' was more important than the cloth. Reg carried baby Annie about all the time and would not put her down. He had to be chased out of the house with a stick or see Annie, her nightdress billowing about her and the spade in one hand, heading for the field, her large bare feet planted in the mud. Then he'd shout that she had to come back and keep warm 'because she was the child's precious mother'. Excused of harder work Annie took to wandering, Little Annie strapped to her back, collecting Jew's-Ear fungus, at least that was what she had heard it called. It grew on logs and the stumps of fallen trees as they rotted. Reg had no objection to these excursions. 'Please yerself,' he'd say, or, 'You're the boss.' He watched with amusement as she strung the fungus up in the eaves to dry.

'What you going to use that for?' he asked.

'Pad out soups and stews come winter. You're not the only one knows a thing or two!'

'Have it yer own way,' Reg nodded.

Annie's wanderings also took in the collecting of various leaves and berries she believed had values.

'Manuka berries!' Reg scoffed

'You'd be grateful if you had diarrhoea – '

210

'And the flaxroot?'

'You'll know when you get constipation!'

'If you say so,' Reg said, giving in to her superior knowledge. Well, he did know a thing or two himself. Hadn't he known to wash her with woodash water where she was bleeding after the baby? Nothing like woodash water for cleaning wounds, not to mention taking the pain away.

'I suppose you got all kinds of plans figured for getting that child educated already,' Reg teased. 'Taking her out and picking up bits of fungus!'

'I'm getting stocked up on things that'll save me time later,' Annie informed him. 'Now don't you touch that can!'

'Only a bit of fat – '

'I'm making soap out of that. So you can pass down the soda and go outside and get some woodash.'

'If you say so.' Reg got to his feet.

'And if you see a woodhen while you're out,' Annie called after him, 'I wouldn't mind a bit more fat for rubbing on bruises.'

'Nobody bruised around here!' Reg said from the doorway.

Annie nodded. The man was certainly overdoing it and it would only be a matter of time before he brought a great branch crashing down on his head. 'You just get that woodhen,' she called after him.

Reg decided to keep an eye out for a woodhen while chopping the *rata*. Could have been a woman's thing she was talking about. It was only early summer and he'd never got in such a great woodpile before. Wait till Annie got back to woodpile duty: *manuka* ready for baking; birch and beech being good 'steaming wood'; the *rata* for heat and backlog; silver pine for kindling and for a good flare-up when needed; *matai* – good old black pine – to see them generally through winter; and a fair helping of broadleaf to keep the blaze going. What's more, he'd arranged it all properly in sorts and sizes. He stood up and tried with a dirty knuckle to rub some bark dust out of his eyes. That baby was the most beautiful thing he'd ever seen and it was all his and Annie's. If he had been a singing man, a man with a bigger chest, he might have sung out till his voice rang in the hills. Problem with that was folk in the hamlet would hear him. Enough of the woodpile! He must get busy carrying up more water from the creek for Annie to wash baby in. Lately he had seen cleanliness like he'd never believed existed and the more empty kerosine tins of water he struggled up the hill with, the more he felt inclined to make short work of it by boring out a hardwood tree trunk and sinking it as a pump. The effort would be back-breaking and tedious but it would be a nice surprise for Annie and worth it in the long run.

Although he had lived a long time and thought he had seen everything, James had been surprised that Olwen had not gone into fur. Equally he had found his estimate of Brigham's usefulness declining, for the false fur rumour had damaged his standing amongst the women, all of whom had invited Olwen to their parties, only to be snubbed in the first instance, infuriated by the non-appearance of her rumoured fur line in the second, and insulted when, in spring, her new line appeared and was actually based on simple cotton. The look took Wellington by storm, the wearing of it requiring a demure attitude which left no room for pretension. If worn humbly, it was so ravishing that many of the haughty ladies wondered how they could in a short time develop the trait of humility in order to benefit from the fashion which was presently laying Wellington gentlemen at the feet of the more modest ladies. Though in his time James had seen bowlers replace bell-toppers, dinner-jackets do away with the elegant smoker, the appearance of pyjama suits on men who had previously been quite happy with nightshirts and, perhaps worst of all, washable celluloid collars replacing starched linen – amongst these reversals of taste, never had he seen anything quite so extraordinary as Miss Laird's new design. He had puzzled long hours over a motif apparently borrowed from Maori culture which she used frequently and which particularly inflamed Venables. No doubt she would have them tatooing their chins next, Venables' wife Gwen had observed. The only vanity Olwen permitted her women, apart from occasionally padding the cotton, was a forehead ornament fixed on a ribbon which drew the hair from the face and could also be worn mounted on the head or simply tied as a band. All it needed was some feathers poked in the front, Hetty had said callously. James could see Olwen's designs required women to change to wear them and he was not sure that this was a bad idea. Further there *was* a freedom to them, a way of making the women 'at home' or in their 'natural place' in the environment rather than at odds with it. In the inner recesses of his mind, though he would *never* have told Hetty, James felt such thinking, though bad for the taffeta trade, had a lot to recommend it. And this, coming from a man who could remember the invention of the safety pin and had found time to object to it, James told himself, was high praise indeed!

Yet, he puzzled, Olwen did not seem particularly grateful for the success her new work had brought. Nor, now that he had regularized her taffeta supply did she react in any way. If people wanted taffeta she used it. She disregarded the fact that their game of cat and mouse was over and simply got on with her work. Yet she *had* changed, James realized, watching her from a distance. Their spat had increased his appreciation of her dogged professionalism. In fact it was his heightened respect for her which had induced in him a sense of self-disgust at involvement with the hanger-on Brigham and caused him to firmly reject further offers to interfere with the girl's cotton supply. Amazing that Miss Laird should realize that fashions were all very well for other people but one had to be just beyond them oneself in order to hold public respect and retain one's place in Wellington society. She dressed quietly. James admired that. Whether she was going with Marshall Cavanaugh these days was difficult to say, so discreet was she. Why, she maintained such a touchingly low profile even the most difficult of his wife's friends had problems picking a fight with her. In fact these days the girl went about like a positive mouse.

Olwen closed the window and stepped away from it. It had been a hard winter but few, she hoped, had realized this. In all probability the girls in the workshop had put her pallor and gaunt expression down to her 'flash of inspiration' rather than worry over the diversifications market conditions had forced on her. And she was thankful the line had gone over well. In truth she had never felt less inspired than sitting before that first bale of muslin! Naturally she had not told Marshall of her difficulties or of James' role in them for it would be unfair to embarrass him and might well promote conflict between the two men. She had simply said she was switching to cotton. His earlier remarks about the desirability of 'varying her import arrangements' had led her to believe that he had a conflict of interests, so the less he knew about her situation the better. Because of work she was seeing less of him and sensed he had fallen out with Brigham but her real cause for concern remained Edmund. There had been no letter from him. Did divorce perhaps take a lot longer than a year, perhaps three years or even ten? He could at least have written saying he was not averse to the idea of granting her one. That would not have taken a day! Indeed it would not have taken five minutes! Then she would have been free to respond to Marshall with complete openness instead of holding back all the time as if expecting him to produce a great diamond! How painful it was! The chilling thought arose that Edmund had received and destroyed her letter because, previously unable to contact her, he himself had entered into a liaison to which the acknowledgement of her existence now would come as a serious embarrassment. It was difficult to imagine Edmund staying single for long: he was far too lazy to care for himself. Further, there would have been no reason for him, on returning to England, to remain unmarried, for the constant round of social engagements – the means by which wheels were oiled and people rose in this world – were part of a system which worked distinctly less well for the unmarried. Might he even have said he'd divorced her in India? Olwen wondered with a shock. And where would that leave her? Hastily she had written to a firm of London lawyers asking them to make enquiries. She now waited.

Nor had she been able to reduce the expenses of her private detective, Archie, for the difficulties she had encountered in trying to launch her new designs had made her realize objects were being placed in her way which must be met head on. Although these had stopped and it had been a relief to know that Marshall had not been involved in any shenanigans, the climbing over one hurdle after another had taken their toll, and as she had come to rely more heavily on Archie, she had feared someone would see her entering or leaving his premises so had resorted to wearing a black face veil when she visited. Added to this tension was the fear that Marshall would doubt her sincerity in that she had given her word, had consented to the announcement of their engagement in spring and spring was on them – yet she'd held back. For a while the new design and her professional survival had provided an excuse but now when she met Marshall in the evenings she detected a slight cooling. He spent more time with Brigham – having mended fences – and less with her. Though she could not put her finger on it, Olwen instinctively disliked Brigham.

'Why do you tail him around with you?' she protested when Marshall announced that Brigham would be joining them for supper.

'He's harmless enough,' Marshall shrugged. 'A man has to find some way to fill his time.'

Olwen bit her lip.

'I appreciate forthright speaking,' Marshall said pointedly. 'I like people who feel they can deal with me directly.' Olwen felt reproached. 'The man certainly laid his cards on the table when he arrived here without a friend,' he continued. 'It's not as if he had any connections to start him off.'

'He gives me the creeps.'

'If it's any consolation to you, just when things were looking up for the poor chap James got tired of him.'

'One wonders what he was doing for James.'

'Told me he wanted to go into cargo insurance,' Marshall said pityingly. 'Can you imagine? In fact I thought quite ill of him at one time and let him know it – without cause as it turned out.'

'You don't need to be sorry for Brigham.'

'He hasn't seen Khandallah – '

'Don't bring him to my place!'

'Just for tea . . .'

Olwen shook her head. She did not want Brigham in her house, yet, sensing how little of Marshall's goodwill remained, felt obliged to agree.

'An unusual name, "Olwen",' Brigham said, looking directly at her. 'A name, once heard, that would – stay in the mind . . .' He paused.

'Have you heard my name before?' Olwen asked coolly.

Brigham toyed with a teaspoon. 'Only once.' He cocked his head. 'But it couldn't have been you.' He glanced salaciously at Marshall as if the reference were beyond repeat in the presence of a lady.

Olwen began to feel uncomfortable. In her state of turmoil when leaving Edmund and returning to New Zealand had she been in any way 'indiscreet' with the cabin staff on board ship? Had she left anything 'personal' lying about to be read? She dared not press Brigham for details such as had the Olwen he'd heard of been the wife of a gentleman who had gone to India? Had she been packed off in disgrace to New Zealand? Or had Brigham heard the story in London or was it simply a piece of pub gossip he'd picked up?

'What was the name of the ship you came out on,' she asked carefully, hoping against hope that it wasn't the *Pomayne*.

'The *Kumara*,' Brigham replied. 'An old three-master with sails. All of six weeks to get here. Only between eleven or twelve knots a day at times,' he went on. Olwen breathed out.

'Not very good, that,' agreed Marshall.

'But it gave one time to think,' said Brigham, looking

217

pointedly at Olwen. 'Time to meet other travellers.'
Olwen's breath caught.

'Got here in under a month myself,' Marshall confided.
'At least that's what Mother tells me!'

'I believe you were educated in England, Miss Olwen?'
Brigham asked politely.

Olwen nodded.

'As I say, it's not a name – once heard – that would be
forgotten . . .'

'Why did you bring him here?' Olwen demanded, as
soon as Brigham had left.

'He originally asked if he could come!' Marshall replied
hotly. 'And I don't feel you were altogether civil to him.'

'He makes me feel uncomfortable.

'Be that as it may, now that he has been introduced you
can expect him to call.'

Olwen glared. 'By widening our circle – are you trying
to punish me for not having become engaged to you
already?'

Marshall picked up his hat. 'It's getting late,' he said. 'I
must be leaving.'

'Meaning of course that if we were married you
wouldn't have to go? Am I to reckon on further grand
exits?'

Marshall withdrew abruptly.

Once he had gone Olwen sat down with a cup of tea.
She had felt threatened by Brigham's suggestion that hers
was a name 'once heard never forgotten'. Now surely the
man was being charming. The name was unusual and
whatever name she had come up with he would probably
have said either how pretty it was, or it has in it the sound
of tinkling water, or I have an aunt called that, or some
likely phrase? Surely 'once heard never forgotten' was not
so extraordinary.

* * *

218

From the top of a sand dune Faith peered down on St Clair beach noting the large number of children paddling, their mamas occasionally calling out to them to mind that their hats did not blow off. On the rocks beyond she could see a girl her own age walking with her mother and in front of them three small boys, squatting in Sunday suits, picking at pebbles between the rocks. The sea was a long way out, coming in in great grey waves under a dull sky. Behind her lay the town, quiet, deadly – and to one side of it, an even more depressing thought, the house no different from its neighbours to which she must now return. She was going to tell him. She had made up her mind. Gathering her courage she got to her feet and stumbled down the dune.

During Ceci's second visit to her they had struggled with the idea of divorce and annulment. The annulment she wanted, for she could not endure living with Dougall and wanted to be single again. But the divorce she did not want. Nor did she see what it had to do with the state if the Church annulled her marriage. They'd only registered it with the state. The state hadn't married them. God had. But the priest had said she couldn't have the annulment without a divorce. Apart from it being a wicked thing to do, she *could* not divorce Dougall. That would make her a divorced woman! Kicking her way through the sand Faith ran all the worst phrases she could think of through her mind yet none sounded so deformed as the phrase 'divorced woman'. She would not mind being described as an 'abandoned' or 'ugly' or 'wicked' woman: these words did not sum up in her the coldness and terror of the word 'divorced'. Divorced woman. The word 'divorced' cancelled out the word 'woman' and suggested a vanity, a disregard of all that natural folk cherished. It cut like a knife. Yet without it no annulment. She was being asked to do something very wicked – but by the priest himself – so it must have been all right. Yet people would say the most terrible things about her. She would be daring God down out of heaven ... To secure an annulment was a sign that she was an innocent party and not at fault. The Church would unmarry her and then people would understand. She would still be one of them – still be a person ... But a divorced person ... ?

Crossing the road Faith wondered why her father had not insisted on coming with Ceci. Ceci had said he'd gone to Christchurch on business. Indeed she had been lucky no one had seen Ceci in Dunedin and reported it to Dougall. Part of her wanted to ask the priest if it was because they had married in both Churches that a divorce was necessary: because the one Church could not annul the other Church's marriage too. But Ceci had asked him twice and seemed very sure of her facts whereas she, Faith, did not have the courage to open the presbytery gate.

She, who had never even had sex with a man, would be known as a 'divorced woman', as if she had done the rounds of all the pubs in town! She would go out looking for love bearing this great stigma. It was impossible that her father or anyone in the Catholic community would accept that the divorce had been a precondition of annulment: she knew them too well. The word 'divorce' would blind them. In fact she dreaded the word more than the painful process leading to it. Glancing back at the beach she realized that with her decision, she was leaving behind every part of the previous life she had known. Yet she would do it. She would take steps one at a time, however terrible, alone in Dunedin. Hopefully her father would not hear about it till all was over.

Though she had been in an agony of self-doubt, now that she was leaving Dougall she felt almost sorry for him.

How would he cope? What would people think of *him* after the annulment? Even the fact that he would miss her helped build the feeling of love she felt rising as she walked up the slight incline towards their house. By the time she opened the front door she felt almost sufficiently well disposed towards him to stay, but the sight of him standing in their hallway, his back to her, knowing full well it was she who had entered yet ignoring her, refuelled an anger which saved her from self-doubt, carried her beyond intimidation. Though the moment was hers and she should have felt power, a childish urge to run forward and thump him in the back and make him turn around prevented her concentrating. Already he had walked on into the kitchen.

'I'm leaving you, Dougall,' she said excitedly.

Dougall glanced up at her and continued pouring some water into a small pot.

'I've had enough of this and I can't stand any more!' Faith insisted, sitting.

Dougall struck a match under the pot.

'I hate to do this to you,' she said, flinging an arm across the table. 'But you must understand, there's really no point in going on like this.'

Dougall opened the cupboard and reached down the tea.

'If there was the slightest sign of any warming on your part . . .' Her voice trailed off. 'I mean, what do you think it's like for me?'

Dougall lifted out two tea cups and placed them on the saucers, and the fact of watching this gave Faith a warm protective feeling towards him. How tragic it was that she was leaving just when there seemed some possibility of fondness between them.

'Don't you think we could really try?' she asked earnestly.

At that moment Dougall's cat walked into the kitchen.

'Hello, my tiny!' he said, bending, picking it up and smothering its face in kisses.

'Have you been a good girl today?' His hand slid along its spine making the small animal squirm with pleasure and rub against his chin. 'Who's my little favourite, then?' Dougall asked. 'Do you want a treat?'

Watching this familiar display of affection reserved for his cat, Faith felt her anger mounting. 'You say hello to that cat every time it comes into the room!' she accused. 'You look up and follow it with your eyes and take it on your knee . . .'

'Let's get that sweetie,' Dougall said to the cat, carrying it out past Faith and out of the kitchen.

'I'm divorcing you!' she shouted.

Dougall went on into the front room where he kept the small tin of treats the cat enjoyed. He placed the cat on his desk, unlocked the drawer and pulled it out sufficiently to allow the cat to reach inside with her paw and draw the tin towards her.

Faith came running in. 'How can you *do* this to me?' she shouted.

The animal rolled on the desk displaying its stomach which Dougall scratched with the fingers of one hand while undoing the tin with the other.

'There's my beauty,' he murmured, snapping a treat in half with his thumb nail.

Faith sank in the wing chair and began to cry.

'A little drink of milk?' Dougall asked the cat, picking her up and carrying her back towards the kitchen.

Faith blew her nose. So it hadn't been a nice thing to say, that she was divorcing him. He might at least have shown some surprise or been moved to talk to her about it. Where was his anger, his fear of rejection? She heard water being poured, teaspoons chinking, and knew the brew was made. Maybe this cup of tea was the best he could do towards saying he did not want her to leave?

'I'm sorry, Dougall,' she began, hurrying into the kitchen. 'I didn't mean it, I – '

'Women can't put their husbands aside,' Dougall assured her, passing the tea.

For a moment her tendency to believe everything he said confused her. Could this be right? The fact of him speaking to her in the house made her feel dizzy.

'But you can get out any time you like,' he said quietly. 'I shall see you get nothing.'

'How can you speak to me like this?' Faith asked, stunned at the undertone of absolute hatred in his voice. 'I'm only doing what has to be done for both of us. It doesn't mean I don't love you – '

'Love me?' Dougall snorted. 'I doubt you'd know the meaning of the word!'

'Me?' Faith gasped. 'When have I ever been anything but loving? Who has opened her soul up to you and made herself a doormat for you to jump on? Who has brought your slippers only to have them kicked away? Who has come to greet you at the front door and been walked past?'

'If there is any divorcing to be done around here, it will be *me* divorcing you.' Dougall assured her.

'But why?'

'You want everyone to think it's *my* fault? You want them to think there's something wrong with *me*? Or is it just that *you* thought of it first?' he said belittlingly.

Faith stuck to her part of the agreement not to mention Ceci's name. 'I decided what I decided,' she said stubbornly.

Dougall took his tea cup to the sink and tipped some

223

water into it. 'You're quite pathetic,' he said, shaking water from his hands.

'I'm getting a divorce, Dougall, because I am having this marriage annulled,' Faith said calmly from the table.

'Annulled?' Dougall whirled.

'Yes,' said Faith quickly. 'And for the annulment I need a divorce at the same time.'

'So you're bringing your filthy Church into this?'

Hurt at his savage words Faith covered her mouth.

'Nothing they say will make any difference.'

'That's why they're wise enough to insist on a divorce!' Faith retaliated, suddenly finding the idea did not rankle. 'I have always been bred to see divorce as the last resort of an unfeeling and godless person, Dougall,' she went on. 'A wicked thing to do. The annulment recognizes that we were not married in the first place –'

'So how can you cancel out something that has not happened?'

'I married you! You didn't marry me! I don't know what you wanted with me,' she stammered. 'But I have to divorce you, to go through all this – this – ugliness – to be *free*!'

Dougall picked up Faith's cup and put that also in the sink. She looked at his bent back. If he would only turn even now, open his arms and take her into them!

She felt the tenderness rising: 'If I knew some way to help us . . .' she began.

Dougall strode from the room.

When she awoke the next morning he was not there. He had taken his work clothes into the front room the night before and it had come as no surprise to Faith that he had slept there. She had not slept a wink. She had wanted to go to him. She had not heard him going into the kitchen

224

to get his breakfast so maybe she had drifted off in the end. The fact that he was not in the house now filled her with a heady lightness and as she slipped into the clothes which always felt damp from the landlady's bedroom she sensed she had taken control. She had faced up to an impossible situation.

Going into the front room she almost hoped there would be some indication that he had not slept there the previous night but simply gone; that he had taken his work clothes and walked out. But there it was – the blanket kicked from the sofa to the floor – his slippers and book – and that stamp and seal of a comfortable night, his cat sleeping on the sofa.

She swished back the curtains and gazed out at the bright light coming up off the sea beyond the houses then turned to look at the room behind her. She would never want to see this room again. Nor to see him in it or in her life. By now he had known for sixteen hours that she was getting out. It was a Monday. The idea of one more Monday, let alone as many Mondays as it would take to make a divorce was heavy. How could two people exist within four walls with a thing like this between them?

Monday, Ginger murmured to himself, conscious of the fact that Ceci would have returned from Dunedin on Sunday evening at the latest, more likely on Saturday. What could he have been doing in Christchurch on a Sunday she would ask. What possible excuse could he give for delaying his return till Monday? He had no friends he could afford to mention, for sooner or later they would bump into them and his lies would become public.

'To be frank,' he told her, unconscious of the pun, 'I just lay in. I felt like lying in the hotel and sleeping.'

'I don't see anything wrong with that,' Ceci said

225

brightly. 'It does a person good to have a break.' For all that, he looked tired, she thought. And hung over.

'How was Dunedin? How's Faith?' he enquired.

'Oh, getting there,' Ceci said carefully.

Ginger hurried upstairs. He needed a thorough bath and he'd better examine his garments and body minutely to be sure there was not the slightest trace of his misbehaviour. On the ride up he had begun to feel horridly guilty about the episode with the barmaid, full of disgust and self-loathing. Having drunk too much had added to his remorse to the extent that he felt a genuine need to make amends. What's worse he couldn't remember the details.

'Did you achieve what you set out to?' Ceci smiled when he came down to lunch.

'It was a blind lead,' Ginger confessed. 'I was looking for Frank.'

Relieved that she would let it go at that Ginger listened to Ceci enthusing about a second letter that had arrived from Reg and Annie. It was as if *she* was keener to fill the silences than he . . .

'You recall Annie used that quaint phrase about an "intention of becoming sincere"?' Ceci was saying. 'They've actually had a baby!'

Ginger made an instant note to get Ceci pregnant as soon as possible. 'They became cow cockies in the back-blocks, wasn't it?' he asked, trying to keep the conversation going.

Ceci nodded. 'It's a little girl and they've called her Annie . . .'

Ginger's mind trailed off. Little Annie . . . Little Frank . . . Frank . . . Frank's wife . . . The barmaid . . .

'It's difficult to believe Reg finally married! That makes Annie and I as good as sisters,' Ceci observed, 'given we've each mothered one of his children!' Looking up she found

226

Ginger wearing an expression like a spaniel who had messed the favourite rug. 'Cheer up!' she urged.

Was he imagining it or was she a little brighter than usual?

'Tell me about Christchurch,' she was saying.

As the day wore on, a feeling of guilt stabbed at Ginger every time he saw Ceci in some familiar activity, ironing Myra's dress, pegging out the boys' shirts, lifting a cake from the stove ... By tea time it had become unbearable. 'Ceci,' he said in a broken voice, placing his hands on her shoulders.

'Wait,' Ceci murmured. 'Listen.' Both cocked their heads. Yes, there it was – the distinct sound of the Moke trap on their gravel driveway.

Ginger peered from the window. 'You won't believe who this is! It's Dougall!'

Quickly Ceci rose from the stove. If ever she had felt acute discomfort it was now.

'Come in,' she heard Ginger say from the front door. 'What is it?'

'Sir,' said Dougall, hovering in the entranceway, 'I have something very serious to impart. Faith wants a divorce – '

Ginger stepped back as if smacked. 'A *divorce*?'

At that moment Ceci appeared in the hallway.

'I'm sorry to trouble you at this time of day, Ceci,' Dougall said with a warm smile. 'I really wouldn't if it weren't a matter of the utmost concern.'

'Come in, come in,' Ginger was saying, reaching forward and taking Dougall by the elbow. Ceci noted Dougall pause and allow himself to be pulled into the hall. How ridiculous it was!

'Perhaps your wife should sit down,' Dougall was telling Ginger, as if the news Ceci already knew might cause her to pass out. With relief she realized Faith hadn't blabbed, God bless her. As well she had visited mid-morning when the landlady was out shopping! As well they had talked on the beach and amongst the sand dunes! And as well she had departed directly for the coach station!

'Under no circumstances,' she could hear the righteous voice of Ginger, 'would I permit Faith to entertain the idea of divorce!' How clever Dougall was, Ceci thought, watching him. All smiles and politeness, all concern for all concerned! Had she not witnessed his indifference to Faith when she was concealed in their great wing chair in the darkness of a winter's afternoon, she would never have believed him capable of those attitudes Faith had described.

'Do you hear this, Ceci?' said Ginger, turning to her in amazement as she entered the drawing room. 'We shall have to get that girl up here and talk some sense into her!'

'When I last saw her,' Ceci quickly put in, 'I think you will agree, Dougall – '

'Everything was fine!' he interrupted.

'You can rest assured, Dougall,' Ginger insisted, 'she will get nowhere with that attitude in this house. I never thought to hear the word divorce in my family. In fact there has never been a divorce that I know of in Moke or amongst the Catholic community anywhere . . .'

Ceci looked down. Had he forgotten Frank was a Catholic?

'I can't apologize enough,' he was saying.

From an upper window Ceci watched Dougall leave and sensed he was pleased with his visit.

Behind her Ginger brooded. In truth he had found the chance to lambast Faith a convenient gambit to distract himself from the acute discomfort caused by his own misadventures in Christchurch. It provided an excellent excuse to stay off sex with Ceci whom, after his behaviour, he felt he could not approach with intimacies. 'Would you believe it of the girl?' he murmured, getting into bed. 'After all the trouble I went to for her.'

Throughout the night when Ceci turned to him, herself troubled, Ginger kept the girl's 'wilfulness' as a barrier between them as if, with such serious matters afoot, affairs of the heart must wait . . .

'Ginger, I'd like to talk about Faith,' Ceci began, but soon realized, having 'connived' with the girl, she was hardly in a good position herself. She lay listening to his forced breathing.

Hardly had the sky lightened than Faith, too, arrived, having learned from her landlady exactly where Dougall had gone and, having begun her journey the previous afternoon. She flew into the house denying, accusing, creating the impression that she was indeed a hysterical person no sane man could be expected to live with.

'He believes Dougall and not me and I'm his daughter!' she shrilled after an exchange with Ginger.

'Try and control your voice . . .'

'You expect me to behave dispassionately when I'm being attacked on all sides? He said Dougall was a martyr to me!'

'But you can see the effect your words had,' Ceci cautioned, putting an arm around her. 'You were not believed! So be careful when the time comes,' she urged, taking the girl's wrists. 'Don't speak to the clerics or officials like that.'

'Why?' Faith begged tearfully.

'Hold back. Speak as calmly as you can manage. I really mean it, Faith – if necessary you must act a lie.'

'It was his fault for shouting at me,' Faith protested, glaring. 'Where is he?' she demanded, pulling away. 'I'm

229

going to tell him that if I'm annulled, then in the eyes of God I'm free!'

'Wait!' Ceci called, but Faith had run from the room. In the next minute her voice was heard shrilling from the study.

'But I have a *right* to an annulment!'

'If I have to take you down to Dunedin myself,' Ceci heard Ginger shout. 'My bag is still packed! I will return you to your husband.'

Faith began to cry loudly. Ceci stood in the doorway biting her knuckles.

'This is a fine mess!' Ginger accused, whirling.

'You don't need to be quite so unfeeling with her,' Ceci pleaded. 'She'll think you don't care.' She mopped at Faith's face.

'What do you expect me to say?' Ginger demanded. 'After all the trouble I've been put to in these parts agreeing the marriage.'

'Leave her – '

'I'm not staying here!' Faith shouted, running for the door. 'At least I've a home to go to even if I'm not wanted there!'

'Won't have it for long though,' Ginger hurled. 'Carry on the way you're carrying on.'

Ceci crossed to Faith and took her wrist.

'Let me go!' she protested.

'Don't change your mind!' Ceci whispered, holding the wrist firm. 'Congratulations. Be brave!'

'What are you two muttering about?'

'She wished me a good journey,' Faith lied.

'From now on,' Ginger said, coming over, 'we'll keep a strict eye on you. If necessary we'll have *both* of you living up here at Hexham until you learn to respect your husband properly.' From behind Ginger Ceci winked and shook her head at Faith. 'I'm not having you bring disgrace on this family,' Ginger went on.

'You're just afraid of what local people will think of you.' Faith stated. 'You're a thoroughly selfish man!'

Ginger stopped short of hitting her.

'Leave her!' Ceci ordered. 'Don't interfere – '

'How dare you raise that phrase after the damage it did with Lizabeth,' Ginger accused. Ceci looked at him steadily. 'That's the phrase that got us into all this trouble in the first place. I should have put a stop to the marriage.'

'Leave Faith to run her life,' Ceci said in a low voice. 'Believe what she says. I do.'

In bed that night Ginger rolled away from Ceci. He had been an utter pig and knew it. First with the barmaid in Christchurch and now Faith. He'd been using her as a scapegoat for his anger.

'Ceci?'

'You were horrible to Faith.'

'I had things on my mind.'

'If you will just give the girl a chance to – unburden – '

'I didn't mean to fly off at her.'

'It's unreasonable to assume that a – sensible girl like Faith would behave like that without cause.'

Ginger blew out loudly. It was unlikely he'd get a chance to explain now. 'Let's leave it, Ceci,' he said. 'Let's get some sleep.'

Facing their different sides of the room, they dreamt separate dreams.

Dougall got into bed with Faith. 'It's because of this, isn't it?' he said.

Faith lay icily. If he thought she was about to start making up after all she'd been through he had another think coming.

'Faith, I'm ready to try . . .'

'You've done me far too much harm,' Faith murmured into the blankets. In her heart she wanted to turn to him but Ceci's warning that the annulment hinged on non-consummation, so she had better not do it now, played in her ears.

'I shall tell your Church Commission you kept touching me and that put me off, shall I?' said Dougall. 'And that you behaved in a hysterical fashion. I can rely on you to give that impression, can't I, Faith? So no one will blame me for – for making you wait till you could "respect" sex?'

Feeling she need not reply Faith listened to his silence and knew he was troubled. He *would* be convincing if he told the Commission that he had been exercising his duty as a husband and waiting for her to behave in a 'womanly' fashion and accept subjugation to their marriage vows. The Commission, all men, would doubtless agree with him. Doubtless he would pull back her chair and smile at her and pat her hand and say reassuring things like he had done at Hexham; create an impression and display all those virtues which would tell the Commission that he was a loving husband and she an unbalanced, aggressive, possibly sex-crazed woman trying to draw others into her situation and that there were no grounds for them to interrupt his conduct of their affairs. She could sense him plotting, could sense that he did not desire her.

Suddenly he made a grab for her, the speed of it taking her so by surprise that the shock of physical contact was embarrassing and painful.

'Dougall!' she gasped, ready to give her body to him though the words: 'Don't let him do it now!' hammered in her brain. He was saying her name over and over again, his voice cracked and breathless as if the proximity of their bodies was frightening to him. *Now* was the time; *now* she should pull away . . . She did not. But as Dougall lay on top of her she discovered the incontrovertible evidence that it was his voice only and not his body that was hungry for her. Limp and exhausted, too tired even to cry, she lay while Dougall sat up angrily. Even looking up at him she realized it had not even been so much his voice as his social position which had wanted her. And it was only the disgrace of his being revealed to the world as impotent which had driven him to even bother to reach for her now.

'If you'd only told me – ' she began pityingly.

'Don't you dare pity me,' Dougall warned. 'I knew I was impotent when I married you.'

'I don't believe that,' Faith said sadly. 'And you've done me so much damage, Dougall. We could have managed without sex if you'd only been friendly.' She began to cry. 'Ugliness has become a habit between us.'

'No doubt everything will go your way now, won't it?' Dougall said coldly.

'I won't mention your condition,' Faith promised. 'Unless I need to.'

'Mention it!' Dougall retorted. 'You won't get an annulment anyway because I'll say I told you about it before we married and you'd agreed!'

'Is there any reason why this should be so?' the priest asked of Faith.

It was her first visit to him and he was putting her through her paces before taking her to the Commission. Hobbled by uncertainty as to whether the contract would be valid had she been aware of Dougall's impotence at the time, Faith shook her head.

'No.'

'He is simply unfriendly towards you and will not touch you?'

233

'Yes.'

'You do not seem very grieved about it.'

'I am trying not to display emotion.'

'Do you display emotion at the right times?'

Faith felt anger rising in her arms, her hands gripped the chair edges and she saw the priest notice. 'I do my best within the confines of the marriage.'

'And are you prepared to continue trying?'

Faith paused. She would have to say yes but that would terminate the interview.

'Shall I have the young man in and talk to him here?' the priest asked kindly.

Faith shook her head, lips clamped together, eyes filling with tears.

It was a picture the priest had seen before: one he recognized. 'Kneel down with me now and we will pray for guidance,' he said gently. The girl obviously did not want guidance, she wanted out. However, before flinging a marriage away ... 'Are you sure there's nothing you're not telling me?'

Faith shook her head. The way ahead would be dark, long and difficult, but her mind was set.

Chapter 16

Because he had heard nothing, Ginger assumed the trouble between Faith and Dougall had died down. The extent of Ceci's involvement had never occurred to him and though she had longed to confess her part, wisdom had counselled she keep quiet. Neither had Ginger confessed to her about the barmaid. Instead, part motivated by guilt, his displays of affection had become increasingly warm and more genuine so that, had he been able to take a balanced view of the situation, he might have concluded the incident in Christchurch had done him good. He could not shake the feeling he had a debt to pay Ceci which he took to be a child.

Things were going well between them until the morning of their planned visit to Reg and Annie's when he read in the paper that a young Catholic woman, *his* daughter, had achieved a divorce in an Otago courthouse. Feeling different about the entire world, he went back to the beginning of the article. No mention of an annulment.

'Well they wouldn't put that in the paper, would'they?' Ceci reasoned with him. 'That's not what papers are interested in.'

'What do I care if she got an annulment?' Ginger fumed. 'I would have thought that was the whole point.'

'I hope this is nothing to do with you,' he warned, pushing his chair back and standing.

Ceci kept quiet.

On the way into the hills Ginger continued to sulk about Faith.

Ceci tried to cheer him: 'Leave Faith for now. About the child – '

'You're too old,' Ginger barked. 'No woman over twenty-eight should have a child. Looks ridiculous!'

She had been about to ask should they get something for Annie's child and felt distinctly hurt, for his words were unkind and quite at variance with the sentiments he had expressed since returning from Christchurch. 'So you never meant it, anything about our child?' she asked carefully.

'Do you think I really want another family after I've just done raising one?' Ginger said in a rough voice.

Ceci swallowed. 'I think you might have been a little more honest – '

'Well I *don't* want one. I said what I said to please you. Men do.'

'That's nice,' Ceci said, turning her head away.

'I don't know where she thinks she's going to live,' Ginger continued on the topic of Faith.

'We'll have her back. You know perfectly well.'

They rode on a little.

'She'll certainly be in great demand in Moke.'

'Possibly.'

After a while they came to a fork in the tracks and took it to the right.

'I can't see them sticking at anything either' Ginger said, now switching the subject of his grumbles to Reg and Annie. 'Complete wasted journey.'

'There's a store over there. Can't be far now.'

'Don't you believe it. That store's only there because of the fork.'

'Well I'm going in and see if they've anything to eat. It doesn't do to turn up empty-handed.'

'Whatever you buy, get it *live*,' Ginger shouted after her.

No point buying something dead that had already started going off. Besides, if they had left the area, they could use it themselves. Pigeon was nice. 'Get two!' he shouted.

Ceci looked around the building's darkened interior, which did not promise much of any provender, especially fresh stock. Was it even a store or had she blundered into some poor settler's private shack? Finally she noticed a thin man sitting in the dark watching her.

'Out back,' he nodded when she asked for food. 'Got just the ticket.'

Following him, Ceci saw amongst the man's jumble a large box with holes punched in the sides.

'Thatter do you right, Missy,' he said, flipping the lid open and pulling out two rabbits by the ears.

'I hope they're not your last ones?' Ceci enquired, afraid they might even be pets.

The man shrugged as if that didn't matter and, looking at his few belongings, the straw oven in which presumably he made his bread, she sensed he rarely had visitors. Rabbit was bound to cheer Ginger, Ceci thought: he was most partial to it – especially if Annie would make pastry or allow her to make some . . . The man was now staring at the toes of his boots, a rabbit in each hand, waiting. When she nodded he plopped them in a small wicker crib and secured it with twine. She could imagine him sitting all day, waiting by his oven for things to cook by the heat of the straw.

'Do you want this crib back on the way down?' she asked.

'You choose,' he said shyly.

'How much?'

'I'm easy.'

'Is this enough do you think?'

'Suit yerself.'

'I don't want to underpay you. Now tell me how much they are.'

'Whatever,' the man said expansively, leaving Ceci the impression that, possibly because of his isolation, he had no idea of the current market price for rabbits and did not think it right for a man to charge money to a female who asked for food in a pioneer society.

'This is fair,' she explained, giving a little more than the general price the at-doors man asked when he brought rabbits around to the kitchen at Hexham – which itself was twice the going price in Moke, though well below Christchurch.

'You better keep that crib,' the man said flushing and genuinely delighted.

'We'll be coming down tomorrow if you've letters to go – never mind the stamps.'

'Where are you?' Ginger shouted from the doorway, the thought of food making his stomach rumble but his humour improve. 'How far is it?' he asked the man, explaining where they were bound for.

'Good way,' the man said.

'Get there today?'

'Could do.'

They resumed travelling. Although the land so far had been dry and gnarled, the breeze which now sprang towards them was moist, soft on the skin. In the far distance trees could be seen scrambling towards a low ridge of hills and even as they neared them the sounds of human activity borne on the wind reached their ears. Soon the land had opened up into small holdings, now well developed, the year's crop sown, the remains of the winter woodpiles stacked under bark-cover awnings, the vegetable plots planted out and the cows standing together in muddy paddocks for warmth.

'Cow cockies,' Ginger grunted.

Gradually they began to see people, some of the women with headscarves, the odd pig, dogs.

'It must be backwards up here,' Ginger observed.

Ceci put her head on one side listening to the birds. Obviously these people would be short of quite a few things but they seemed happier than in Moke. She could hear someone laughing loudly and from a shed came the sound of water being slapped about and a young girl singing. Further up the track children were playing with stones.

'Hey!' Ginger called to them. 'Where's 442?'

The children got to their feet and observed him solemnly as if he'd spoken in a strange tongue.

'We're looking for a scrawny-looking man and a dumpy woman,' was what Ginger would like to have sung out but he knew Ceci would give him one for it.

'It's Mr and Mrs Reginald Bowen we're after,' he said.

The children pointed up the hill.

After they had ridden a while they ran out of road.

'You can't expect Reg to come out and put up a signpost just for us,' Ceci defended him.

'The road has finished!' Ginger complained.

Tethering their horse and taking their belongings, they left their cart and began to slash inwards through the undergrowth, gradually climbing until, cresting a small hill, they paused for breath and Ceci put her hand to her mouth and called: 'Re-eg! An-nie!' Turning on the spot they saw below them cleared land which, except for a belt of trees, ran all the way to the hill line. Smoke could be seen rising. 'Ann-ie!' Ceci called, running forward.

Annie was balancing a kerosine tin on the open fire to heat washing water when she heard Ceci's voice on the wind. She gave such a shout she almost knocked the can into the fire.

'Ceci!' she screamed. 'Reg! Reg! Get in there and watch Little Annie.'

Reg, who had been salvaging ash from Annie's fire and emptying it on to a fresh skin he was curing, calmly spread the ashes, folded the skin in half, dusted his hands off on his britches, dipped them into the clean water and smoothed back the remains of his hair. He looked around. The day of reckoning had come: the day when she would see how good he had made. Quickly he hurried into their home to take the child in his arms. Already he could hear voices coming towards him.

Ceci looked up. There across the clearing was Reg standing in the doorway, holding a baby. She could not recall having seen him without his hat before: to see him with a baby was a further shock. 'Oh Annie,' she cried, hugging her.

Annie burst into tears. 'It's so good to see you, Ceci! When I ran out of Grevillton I never thought we would meet again, do you know that?'

Ginger watched the two women and beyond them – Reg. It had been a very, very long time – all of twenty – perhaps twenty-two years? The last time he had seen Reg, the man had been tearing down wedding banns, crumpling and flinging them in the ditch before riding away from the pregnant Ceci and leaving Moke with its biggest mystery in years.

'Do you remember Reg?' Ceci was asking, amazed at her urge to fling her arms around Reg and embrace him as if he, not Ginger, were her husband. Reg's eyes were moist and in his arms the child he would not put down twisted and turned.

Ginger watched Ceci take the little girl and hold her,

utter delight, joy for Annie and Reg on her face; not the slightest trace of jealousy. Annie looked all of thirty-five. How bitterly ashamed he felt for his unkind words to Ceci!

'I'm so happy for you,' Ceci insisted with glistening eyes. 'I just can't get over it!'

'Come in,' said Reg in a broken voice.

Ginger stepped into the shack after them.

'Bit different from Hexham,' Reg observed, glancing back at him.

'You could do with a road,' Ginger pointed out.

'Don't need one. What for?' Reg replied, making Ceci realize the two men would get along like a house on fire. 'Had your wits about you, you could have come by the path.'

Ceci looked around the cottage, its very simplicity a mighty strength. How it reminded her of Old Bowen's! The strange-shaped bits of meat smoking in the rafters, the slab table, now permanently in place in that its legs were hammered into the earth, picture sheets from the *Weekly News* pasted along the best wall, the wall seen as you entered the door, a few pans on the floor, no chairs but some sawn-off tree lengths.

'Ain't quite finished in here,' Reg said, scratching the back of his neck.

'We live outside most of the time,' Annie explained, returning to linger in the doorway beyond which a line of unwashed pots, old porridge ringing them, nested in the earth and cradled rain water at crazy angles.

'We have something for you,' Ceci said turning. 'Ginger?'

Ginger held out the wicker crib.

'Oh look at their sweet little round little heads!' Annie cried, clasping her hands.

'Give 'em here and I'll brain 'em,' Reg murmured.

241

'You shan't, Reg!' Annie told him, surprising Ceci by the confidence in her voice that he would obey her. 'You will build me a nice hutch instead.'

Ginger frowned. What was for lunch? But Little Annie gurgled and pointed delightedly at the creatures, poking her fingers at them.

'Make the kid a nice hat,' Reg retorted, feeling that in front of Ceci he should still act tough.

Ceci smiled. Motherhood had filled Annie with such tender and compassionate thoughts she could not face killing a rabbit!

'We've plenty of food,' Annie said proudly. 'Potatoes of course.'

Oh potatoes! How Ceci remembered those potatoes! When she had been almost starving herself and Annie had arrived at Grevillton and that was all she could offer her, Annie had said: 'My Lord! Is that all you got, potatoes?' Ceci started to laugh.

'That all you got, potatoes?' she teased.

Annie burst out laughing and came to put her hands on Ceci's shoulders.

'We got meat in brine,' Reg said seriously. His knees creaked as he bent and lifted a wooden cover from a pail. 'Goat.'

Ceci's eyebrows raised. To Reg 'goat' had always meant stolen sheep.

Annie saw the gesture. She shook her head: 'No, Ceci,' she said. 'We bought that in the hamlet. Reg don't do that no more.' Once, when times had been hard, she had caught him smearing borrowed goat dung on trees in a line leading up towards their place in an effort to 'encourage' a couple their way. But she'd put her foot down and the lesson had been learned. She would love to have told Ceci but loyalty to Reg came first.

'So how's gardening up here?' Ginger asked, filling the gap.

'Birds do a lot of damage,' Reg replied.

'What sort?'

'Blackies, chaffs, *keas*.'

'You know,' Annie joined in, 'I had a *kea* rip right through a pillow case I was draining fruit on the clothes line in. All the fruit went splat on the earth!'

'I'll shoot that *kea* one day, if I can get it,' Reg said grimly. He went to stand by Annie and put his dirty mud-caked hand on her shoulder, his eyes shining with pride as she smiled up at him.

'So how do you like our bairn?' he finally got around to asking Ginger.

'You stay,' Annie urged Ceci. 'You stay some days with us.'

'I think we can,' Ceci said turning to look at Ginger. The change would do him good and the four of them together, why, it was too wonderful to believe.

'I'll get down and bring your cart in,' Reg said. 'Not that anyone'd pinch it up here. Folks here know how to be decent.'

'If there'd been a track,' Ginger began.

'Clear as daylight, that track.' He strode out of the hut, soon to be followed by Ginger.

Ceci crossed to the slab chimney. 'Funny how one puts you in mind of another – these slab chimneys. They're all much the same . . .' She was not about to describe her own life with Reg or how the distinctive features of Bowen architecture evoked such memories.

'Give me a hand to get this camp-oven on the fire I got going outside. Winter may be passed but I'm not wasting wood lighting it here! I'm glad your Ginger's come,' she confided. 'There's things need doing and you know how Reg is – won't go down to the hamlet and ask.'

'Ginger could do with some honest work to occupy his mind.'

'I'm not sure which of us will have the most to tell.'

'I'll match you blow for blow!'

As the women carried the oven out and stood it on the live embers they saw Ginger starting off into the bush. Annie shovelled a few embers on to the oven lid.

'I'm going to put this in here,' she said, putting a large pudding in. 'That's Reg's jam roly poly. Very fond of that is Reg. I had it standing there doing. Give it a nice slow cook and plenty for everyone.'

Ceci glanced at the split palings their house seemed made of and saw a battered billy under the eaves. 'Is that your billy?' she asked, hearing the ghost of condescension in her own voice.

'That was about all we had when we come up here,' Annie said truthfully. 'Fact is, that's sacred.' She paused. 'Ceci,' she said shyly, 'wait a minute.' Going inside she picked up Little Annie and came out holding her. 'Can I ask you something?' What she said was not what Ceci expected to hear. 'Will you teach me some nursery rhymes? I only know bar songs and we don't want Little Annie learning them.'

'Don't you know "Ring-a-Roses" or "Cry Baby Bunting" or "Golden Slumbers"?' Ceci asked, amazed.

Annie shook her head. 'All I learnt as a child was "She'll be Coming Round The Mountains". And "Clementine".'

'Right,' said Ceci taking Little Annie and nestling her in the crook of her arm. 'We'll start with "Jack and Jill" and then "Little Jack Horner".'

Annie squatted opposite.

'You rock them while you sing, look,' Ceci smiled,

244

bravely launching her voice up the scale with 'Jack and Jill' till Little Annie opened her eyes and blinked.

Coming back with the horse, Ginger and Reg made their way to the clearing.

'I tried to fill 'er in on who you were,' Reg explained. 'Being as they were together runnin' that pub about the time you and Ceci was soft on each other.'

'I expect you'll be wanting to hear about your own daughter,' Ginger said pointedly.

'Oh, ah,' Reg smiled. 'Got to write to that girl. Keep 'er on the straight an' narrow. Heer'd you gave her an allowance. Thank you.'

Thank you. Did Reg Bowen say *thank you*?

The horse began to pull appreciatively towards the sweet scent of the new cocksfoot.

'You leave that alone, boy,' Reg warned. 'Got some ready picked for you.'

At that moment the voices of the two women singing reached them.

'What's that?' Reg asked.

' "Humpty Dumpty".'

' "Humpy Dumpy"?' Reg repeated. 'You know it?'

Ginger nodded.

'I don't think I never heard that one . . .' His voice trailed off. 'Got a nice lilt to it though . . .'

Chapter 17

It was damnable the way Edmund had not replied. It was the most spiteful act of a selfish young man – just because she had been foolish enough to tell him she had finally found happiness; had been so stupid as to think he would be glad on her behalf. Inevitably as she became more worried about maintaining Marshall's commitment, she felt herself becoming more dependent, less attractive to him. It was the way of love. One loved; the other was loved. Her hope had been to be the indifferent one inspiring love in the other; convincing him he would not be happy until he'd possessed her.

Naturally, Marshall spent less time with her, and more with Brigham. His cargo insurance idea had not come through, people placing little credence in either his home 'contacts' or what was basically a form of poaching on established companies. As James had said: 'If the chap's *that* well connected he wouldn't have been sniffing round the Inspector of Nuisances . . .' How dare Marshall imply that she and Brigham had things in common! Perhaps there were certain similarities: each had silences, each slipped off into their own thoughts, each asked personal questions, yet while Olwen was direct with hers, Brigham was circumambulatory – crafty one could say. She felt extremely uncomfortable when he was around yet politeness would not allow her to make an issue of it, for she frequently left Marshall to his own ends and who was to console him if not Brigham? At times, however, his very presence chilled her.

She strode angrily to her bureau, pulled out a writing tablet and sat down. Just let her get a divorce, marry Marshall and be rid of Brigham! She would chase up the matter with her London lawyers.

'Dear Sirs,' she wrote hastily, 'I am dismayed to have received no response to my enquiry in the matter of – ' She could not say 'my husband'; better to spell Edmund's name out. 'The waiting is intolerable,' she continued.

At the sound of steps mounting to her porch, she tore out the page and flung it into the waste basket. Damn!

Marshall stepped in. 'No Happi?'

'She's in the South Island with her mother. Or rather, her mother sent for her and she's gone.'

'You've got a vacant property across the road,' Marshall observed. 'Brigham's taking a look at it. Advertised as a gentleman's residence of seven rooms, one floor and every convenience – which I doubt he can afford!'

That it should be vacant hardly surprised Olwen after what had been going on at her house and while she did not want Brigham as a neighbour she could well imagine the place opposite being offered at a substantial discount, despite its 'nicely laid out shrubbery', its 'few minutes' walk from the station' and its 'sunny location'.

'What's been going on here?' Marshall demanded.

'Before she went – well, I'd better begin at the beginning. Happi's brothers and sisters did well in school: at least they're all literate. Her mother asked her to go back to take over her own job as *hawini* on a plantation in Picton while she went to visit a sister somewhere. She's a house servant you know – the husband fishes. He does better selling the fish to the *pakeha* farmers than working the land so his brothers grow for him. In any case the *pakehas* are too busy to fish themselves. Happi's father trawls – '

'From what I've seen of your girl,' Marshall interrupted,

247

'I can't say she'd be much use in anyone's house. Did the people her mother works for know she was coming?'

'I asked the same question myself,' Olwen smiled. 'I said, "Will your mother have told that woman to expect you instead?" Happi said "Of course not!" and asked what difference it made. For her it came down to the fact that her aunt needed her mother so she would go. In fact when I said, "Are you going to go?" she seemed more surprised I'd asked and said: "She's my mother, isn't she?"'

Marshall laughed. He opened the door on to the verandah. 'Come out here, Olwen.'

'But you should have been here when the invitation came,' Olwen smiled. 'There must have been about fifteen of them! I have no idea how long it took the message to reach us from Picton – perhaps her mother no longer even needed her by the time it got here.'

'Bit of a shock for you, fifteen Maoris turning up,'

'Well they moved in of course – Happi made them very comfortable. She pulled all the covers off the chairs and took down the curtains for them to sleep on, rushed about picking up every last piece of edible matter in the place plus half the fern roots and the roots of various other plants and trees in the gully, *flowers* even and birds' eggs. I had no idea so much of the gully could be eaten!'

'I expect she missed a couple of rats.' Marshall grinned kindly. 'I understand the native rat is quite delicious.'

'Well naturally they got to chanting and singing. They say things three times, you know; you count words being repeated and begin to recognize them. There's a definite sense of ceremony –'

'All this with no curtains up?'

Olwen nodded. 'But it was beautiful. A man would suddenly get to his feet and speak in a most impassioned tone while everybody listened, then a woman would burst into song at perfect pitch with that fine rich voice they all seem to have. The next minute they would all be on their feet, swaying and singing as if the South Seas had come to Khandallah! Happi was bent on making it clear "her" home was their home. In any case I knew it would not last forever and have received exactly the same degree of spontaneous love – *aroha* they call it – when I visit their *kainga*. Even here, between crying and laughing, someone would always take the trouble to explain to me. They cry for joy, happiness, for any emotion. I wish you had seen them swaying – the women in front and the men behind – their movements saying "Come to me" or "My poor heart is beating faster." You could just see those men crammed in canoes, their huge trunks swinging from side to side as they paddled down the seas from their Polynesian homeland. I could actually imagine them coming from Hawaiiki with their sweet potatoes, *taro* and yams, leaving overcrowded islands behind to – '

'Find the Moriori already here,' Marshall interrupted.

'You can try to spoil it, but it was beautiful,' Olwen said quietly. 'I felt enriched by their presence in the house. Tears publicly rolling down cheeks, publicly wiped away . . . Turning to each other offering comfort.'

'When you talk like this,' Marshall said solemnly, 'I want to marry you more than ever, Olwen.'

Olwen decided to keep on talking. 'I think they delivered more than the news that Happi's mother wanted her. They could have been travelling to a wake – just picking up news as they passed through places where they had relatives, you know? When they left, Happi and I stood on the porch farewelling them. Each of them pressed noses with her, first on the one side then the other. Then me. I can't tell you how intimate it feels: more deeply personal than kissing.'

Marshall took a step nearer and looked down into Olwen's shining eyes.

'The next day the people opposite complained.'

Brigham stepped into the room and saw Marshall and Olwen beyond the glass door on the verandah. His eyes moved to Olwen's chair, slightly back from her desk, the pen as it lay by the opened inkwell, the recently scrunched letter in the basket. Instinctively his hand reached for it, drew it out, uncurled the paper, read what was written there, scrunched, then threw the letter back . . .

'You cannot imagine what this waiting does to a man,' Marshall said softly. 'I had made arrangements to increase my fees – since you improved your relationships with the – the people my work forces me to associate with,' he fumbled. 'And I put in for provisional leave with the companies I am contracted to. The leave still stands. In some cases it had to be cleared with the home companies – '

'Give me time to make the dress,' Olwen said quietly.

'What?'

'The cloth is ordered,' she lied. 'As long as there is no interference with its delivery . . .'

'And will you invite your parents up?'

Olwen nodded. Her mother certainly need know nothing about it but should Marshall force her hand, well, Ginger could surely develop a 'sore' throat . . .

'My life,' Marshall said, holding her to him. 'You are my life!'

Beyond the dividing doors Brigham watched them. Who *was* this Edmund? he asked himself.

The weight of responsibility for Marshall's happiness sat heavily on Olwen but still she could share his joy.

'Nothing need be changed,' he exulted. 'Nothing altered.'

'How long do I have?'

'Have?' Marshall repeated.

'To make the dress.'

'Two and a half months.'

'Better get my riding boots on then.' Olwen smiled.

At that moment Brigham joined them on the verandah.

Without the slightest qualms Olwen set about ordering the material for her wedding dress. Although previously these dresses had been in a variety of colours owing to the fact that no girl could expect to have an expensive dress for just one occasion, for the past five years the emphasis had definitely shifted to white to the extent that white wedding dresses were coming to be regarded as the *sine qua non* of a respectable society wedding. Olwen chose black. If she were to be married, let her take Wellington by storm. Let her confound their conventions both old and new with delustred black silk and glistening jet trimmings. Nor were the girls who worked in her cutting room in any doubt as to whom the fine tulle was intended for, the dusky shoulder ornament, the zig-zag line reflecting a macabre cynicism which on anyone else would look ludicrous, but on Olwen – the height of glamour. There was just the tiniest hint of eroticism where the hem curled to one side, yet with the attention drawn to Olwen's haughty profile, all agreed the effect would be stunning.

As each stitch fell into place, Olwen's decision to proceed without her divorce papers became more irrevocable. Nor in the quiet of her heart did she regret taking the bull by the horns. She was about to sin on a big scale. And do it in black for insolence.

Moving silently across the Cook Strait Brigham travelled away from Wellington. Since Olwen had 'agreed', Marshall had been spending less time with him and would think nothing of the fact that he had vanished. Indeed he was so deeply involved in plans for his future, he would probably not think twice to find him 'out' should he call.

Brigham crossed to lean on the rail of the *Penguin*. Built in 1864 on Clydebank in Britain she had originally served the Glasgow-Liverpool run for which, Brigham feared, she was greatly more suited than the unpredictable and dangerous Cook Strait whose floor was known to be peppered with wrecks. He was not a good traveller. In fact, had he not felt this trip to the South Island might pay off handsomely, he would have remained in Wellington. The steamer rolled, sending her smoke at a giddy angle into the clouds. According to a plaque in the saloon, after fifteen years' service in Britain she had been bought by the Union Company since which time she had been used for excursions from Dunedin to places as far afield as Milford, Dusky and Doubtful Sounds – none of which Brigham had ever heard of though he understood the word 'sound' to mean a sort of fjord. That it had survived these journeys was some comfort though the naming of a sound 'Doubtful' suggested very poor attention to the topography. It was only to be hoped that the pilot had a better idea of the coastline than the person who had named that sound. He walked to the other rail. Already the North Island had sunk from view in a roll of waves which rose to meet sheets of sleet lashing downwards. The storm was some way behind them now and seemed to be battering Wellington's headlands. Whether the front or the back of the steamer were the best place to be he could not decide: going below made him feel positively bilious. BOOM! BOOM! went the hooter. What did that mean? The *Penguin* made the journey between Wellington and Lyttelton once a week: by now surely she would know the way? If an accident were to befall them they were horridly overcrowded . . .

Gradually from the mist ahead the shape of the South Island appeared, a brightness behind its clouds unlike the heavy darkness in which they had last seen the North Island sinking. Bit by bit the rugged outline of the Kaikouras emerged, cutting viciously into the water, allowing neither rock nor beach for man to make a landfall. The closer in the little steamer got the faster they seemed to be going, until their very smokestack gave the effect of carving out the crest of Banks Peninsula as they rounded before it and headed inland, rather than make their way out to open sea and continue south. In more sheltered waters they proceeded until the headlands and Port Hills of Lyttelton harbour could be made out, heralding their imminent arrival. Already Brigham felt better. The words 'Christchurch Club' came to mind along with a string of other names he had heard loosely mentioned in the company of James. He would follow the passengers from the boat and casually board the Lyttelton–Christchurch passenger train which conveniently cut through the Port Hills. He would do it as if in the habit of travelling to Christchurch. Once in the club introductions would be easy to obtain, possibly also a saddle horse . . .

Myra had the fidgets. It was hardly fair to leave a girl coming up eighteen years alone in the house with two boys who talked of nothing but horses. Certainly she did not mind cooking for them but there must have been a great deal more to their lives in Christchurch than they were telling. There was a knock at the front door. If that was the rabbit man she would give him a piece of her mind. Just because her father was away people felt they could come to the front door. Opening it with a glare she was quite taken aback.

'Good afternoon, Mam'selle,' said Brigham in his most

charming fashion, clasping his hat to his chest as if the very sight of it might offend one as delicately beautiful as the lady he was addressing. Myra drew in her breath and in the space of a few minutes learned that this living marvel was a close friend of Olwen's who was visiting the South Island from Wellington and had determined to pay a courtesy call on the household as he travelled south.

'Please come in,' Myra gasped. The boys were not home and it would fall to her to entertain him. 'Please come into the drawing room,' she begged. 'I'll make some refreshment at once.' Leaving Brigham in the drawing room Myra hurried to the kitchen to boil water then went straightaway to her bedroom to make the best of her appearance.

In the drawing room Brigham browsed. Here was a photograph, here another photograph, here another ... Were the object of his visit other than the pursuit of information he might even have considered pocketing several of the trifles which lay undusted on the shelves.

Myra entered with the tea.

'I first knew Olwen when she was in England,' Brigham said confidently. 'You can imagine how delighted I was to bump into her again in Wellington.'

Myra smiled dreamily at him.

'You wouldn't have known Edmund yourself, I suppose,' he went on, accepting a tea and allowing his eyes to linger almost with passion on Myra as the effect of the strength in his voice made her wilt and co-operate before him.

'I've never been to England,' she said weakly. 'I've just barely been to Christchurch.'

'Too bad, too bad,' said Brigham, stirring his tea. 'I'll speak to Olwen. You should come to Wellington.'

'I would like that very much.'

'Olwen is very happy there. She never mentions her previous marriage.'

Myra lifted up the plate of biscuits and offered them to Brigham. 'My brothers are quite sophisticated,' she said. 'They are often at the race track in Christchurch. I have an elder sister who's married in Dunedin. Her husband is extremely handsome and they have a modern town house,' Myra prattled on.

With little difficulty Brigham drew from her that Olwen was not her sister, that Ceci was Olwen's mother but that her own mother had been someone else.

'They moved into our house. We didn't move into theirs,' she explained, then suddenly felt uncomfortable. Was she being disloyal to Olwen? After all, it was hardly Olwen's fault if her mother had accidentally 'lost' Hexham and, after all, Ginger was her stepfather. 'Perhaps I shouldn't have said that,' she said. 'It was hardly kind.'

'One cannot imagine you being anything but kind,' Brigham reassured her. He was not listening now but thinking. The girl had not actually stated that Olwen had been married – but she had not contradicted him when he'd said she had. He had what he'd come for. Perhaps he'd better be going before anyone else should arrive. Or should he question her more closely?

At that moment the door opened.

'Michael!' Myra cried, jumping up. 'This gentleman is an acquaintance of – '

'Of Miss Laird's,' Brigham interrupted, extending his hand. 'Met her in England, don't you know. When was it?'

The boys looked at each other. It was plain that Myra had been talking to this person for quite some time and although at first they fell for his man-to-man charm they soon began to feel distinctly uncomfortable with Brigham.

255

'Don't know.'

'You'll have to wait till Ceci gets back,' they fell to replying. But it seemed Brigham couldn't or wouldn't wait. When he pointed at a picture of Olwen on the mantelpiece, nodded at it and smiled, an uncomfortable feeling filled the room as the boys became aware he was after information.

'Why did you let him in?' they demanded, rounding on Myra as soon as Brigham had gone.

Covered in shame she tried to convey how different was the diffident man who had come from the self-assured man who had left.

Pleased with himself Brigham made his way back across the plain towards Christchurch. He had what he had come for. At least, if Olwen reacted properly, he would be home and dry. With a smile on his face Brigham set sail for Wellington.

Chapter 18

With the sight of Annie cradling her baby fresh in his mind, on the journey home Ginger repented his cruel words to Ceci, the poignancy of what he had seen having made a deep mark. In addition, Ceci's generosity in sharing Annie's joy had stung him to the extent that in his heart he resolved he would try and that the idea of a child was not so ridiculous as he had first imagined. His own children were hanging by the merest threads to Hexham, Olwen was established . . .

Glancing across as their cart bumped out of the foothills, Ceci sensed the change and was pleased. Before visiting Reg and Annie's she had found herself comparing Ginger with Billy, the dear man who, but for a mining disaster, she would have ended her days with on the West Coast. Still married to Maureen, Ginger had come twice to visit her – and been turned away. Though she had long since recovered from Billy, when at times she found herself comparing the two men – Ginger had often come second, perhaps because they were too comfortably off at Hexham . . . She had even been remembering with nostalgia awful days in Grevillton when they'd had nothing to eat. Smiling, she turned to Ginger as their cart swung on to the main track. He grinned back. It was so good to see him looking manly again, to see splinters in his hands, to have heard his deep laugh rock the hills along with Reg's high, peculiar whine. What a time they had had, the four of them.

'That was really spectacular, wasn't it?' she asked.

For answer, Ginger stopped the cart and kissed her and

257

though he could not have chosen a worse moment, decided now was the time to clear his chest. 'Ceci,' be began, his hand on the back of her neck, 'when I was in Christchurch . . . Remember that weekend you went straight back down to see Faith again?' Ceci turned her head towards him. 'I didn't have a lot to do. Fact is, I spent most of the time in pubs . . .'

Alerted by a quickening in the atmosphere Ceci found herself concentrating hard.

'On Saturday night I got to staring at this barmaid –'

'And you slept with her.'

Ginger nodded.

There was a pause.

'What was she like?'

' 'Bout Lizabeth's age, possibly older. Dark hair – '

'Are you sure you didn't imagine it?'

'It's all very clear.'

Ceci began to cry.

'I'm sorry, Ceci.'

'I keep seeing you on top of her . . .'

'I wouldn't have done it if I'd known it would hurt you so much,' Ginger urged, himself close to tears.

'I still keep *seeing* you . . .'

Amazed at the way it hurt they clung to each other in the stationary cart, scarce able to believe it had happened. Looking back, Ceci recalled that Ginger's behaviour *had* been peculiar for the three weeks after he'd returned – but as she'd been worried herself about Faith she had not found time to pay him attention.

'Did you know?' Ginger asked.

'Not until just then. When you said there was this barmaid, I just knew you'd done it. Perhaps I guessed what you were going to say . . .'

'I'm sorry,' Ginger repeated.

258

'I don't mind,' Ceci insisted. 'She looks up, you're looking at her. In an instant it's decided.'

Ginger nodded. That was exactly how it had been.

'You're a good-looking man,' Ceci went on. 'You probably had that look in your eye. It would be part of life's experience for the girl. Did you pay her?'

'Didn't think to,' Ginger mumbled.

'Very nice for you!'

Ginger bit at his nail: 'Say you forgive me.'

'I can't because you haven't wronged me. But I don't suppose I shall forget it. I can say I don't mind – but I feel awful!' With that she burst into tears.

Quietly they followed the main track, their horse knowing it could slope off and drag them over ruts and ditches to satisfy its thirst or pull at a newly green plant. The silence now was not rich and did not pulsate with expectancy. It was the tired silence of a day's work, of burdens taken up again.

'I wonder how Faith is getting on,' Ceci offered, remembering how angrily Ginger had spoken of her on the way out. 'She'll be divorced and annulled now.'

Ginger snorted. Given his own failings he found it a little easier to come to terms with Faith's.

Ceci reached across for his hands. 'Better get this horse organized, hadn't we?' she said, slipping the reins into them.

Ginger laid the reins down. 'Ceci,' he said with deep feeling.

'Look out!' she cried.

Ignoring her, under the open sky, he proceeded to prove with vehemence where his loyalties lay.

'There is no need for this!' Ceci protested as the horse, conscious matters were in train, took off at a gallop down the road. 'Someone will see us!'

259

'Let's hope,' Ginger gasped, 'they'll stop the horse if they do!'

'Faith's here,' said Myra, coming to greet them as their cart turned into the stable yard at Hexham.

'Good!' Ceci replied, jumping down.

'And Papa,' Myra rushed on, 'there was the most wonderful man here. Only I may have been a little forward with him.' Ginger glanced at her stomach. 'The boys said I talked too much about our family.'

'Who was this man?' he asked.

Myra felt uncomfortable. 'Someone who knows Olwen in Wellington,' she said, wanting them to change the subject.

'Did you hear that, Ceci? Is he staying around here?'

Myra shook her head. 'He popped in to pay his respects. He was going south.'

'Well no doubt we'll hear about it,' Ceci said, lifting their bags down from the cart.

'Where's Faith hiding?'

'She stays in her room all the time.'

'Is she all right?'

'She's all right.'

Ginger strode briskly towards the house.

'Ceci,' whispered Myra, running forward, 'was it all right for me to talk to that man from Wellington?' Ceci smiled at her anxious face. 'Only the boys said I shouldn't have.'

'There's a lot of things they shouldn't have done either,' Ceci said, squeezing Myra's hand. 'You take no notice.'

Sitting alone in her room Faith nursed her secret. She had told no one, not even the priest, that Dougall was impotent and now that the Church had annulled her marriage on the grounds that no relationship existed and the state had given her a divorce, she found she could not enjoy her freedom. She had concealed the truth and profited from it. By her silence she had acted a lie. Skulking around the house she knew her behaviour was a mystery to the family but the courage she had summoned in Dunedin had vanished. She took no notice of Myra. No longer was there any advice based on sobriety: she was even seen sipping a Scotch. Strangest of all to Ceci, after the trouble Faith had taken to clear things with her conscience, she would not go to church. White and anxious, she looked as bad as had Maureen on her worst, her 'mental', days but Ginger was determined she would come through better than her mother ... Faith would have nothing to do with any social activity. Like a mute rock she stood while the ripples of the scandal washed about Moke and the local community; Catholic and Protestant alike disapproved.

'Why is she moping?' Ginger asked Ceci. 'She ought to be out enjoying herself.'

It was amazing, Ceci thought, that Ginger could now see Faith's position so clearly that he had to be restrained from going down to Dunedin and personally thumping Dougall.

'There is something strange about her behaviour,' Ceci assented. 'But so was there about yours for a good three weeks after your Christchurch weekend!'

Ginger shrugged.

'Leave me a while and I'll put my finger on it.'

Gradually it came to Ceci. Out of the blue Ginger had not been to Communion for the three weeks it had taken him to see a priest and get confession. She recalled Theresa mentioning it to her in dribs and drabs as if hinting or trying to communicate something she could not grasp. It was not worth going to Mass if you could not go to

Communion, Theresa had said, adding that if someone did not go up when the time came, this was either because they had broken their fast from the previous midnight or had committed a mortal sin, which would put their souls in danger ... The first Sunday after his Christchurch weekend Ginger had coughed loudly outside the barn, Theresa had said, just as the congregation were gathering for Mass, had produced a peppermint from his pocket and popped it very publicly into his mouth. Apparently this had caused a stir and, according to Theresa, when Ginger had failed to go up to Communion people had looked knowingly at each other but with good-natured shrugs. The next Sunday Ceci recalled Ginger had awakened early complaining of stomach cramps so that she had made him a cup of tea and finally been allowed to cajole him into drinking it – although that meant breaking his fast and missing Communion. It was she who had mentioned that to Theresa. The third weekend he had managed to drink far too much for no particular reason on the Saturday night and develop a disabling hangover to the extent he had actually missed Mass. When Myra had then commented that he had not been to Communion for three weeks his temper had become badly frayed, and shortly after he had closeted himself with the visiting priest only to come out radiant, relieved presumably of two mortal sins – one of them being the barmaid, the other the missed Mass – and a string of venial ones.

'She's not going to Mass because she doesn't want people staring at her, that's all,' Ginger stated.

'It would take more than that,' Ceci contradicted. 'I believe Faith thinks she's committed a grievous sin.'

'What do you keep to yourself, Faith?' Ceci asked. 'What did you not tell the priest?'

'That Dougall was impotent,' Faith said immediately. 'He said he'd say I knew and then I wouldn't get the annulment.'

'You *would* have!'

Faith burst into tears. 'I feel terrible! I married a Protestant, then I lapsed – '

'Lapsed?'

'Then committed perjury.'

The mortal sins were piling up.

'By the time I knew he couldn't – things were advanced. I wanted the annulment – and now I feel I haven't got it – '

'Because you obtained it by deception do you mean?' Ceci completed the thought for her.

Faith nodded. 'Now I feel I'm still supposed to be with Doug.'

The two women began to walk.

'Go back and tell the Commission that he was impotent.'

'Then they'd say I'm not annulled.'

'So what? You're divorced!'

'I don't care about being divorced!' Faith burst out desperately. 'Can't you see if I'm annulled it means in God's eyes it wasn't my fault. I'm a decent person. I – '

'And if you're divorced?'

'Just a couple that can't get on.'

Turning out of the garden they proceeded down the track towards Bowens Gully.

'Annulment isn't just a Catholic word for divorce, you know,' Faith said bitterly. 'Anyone can live together, like Lizabeth and Frank, but when you marry, God puts a seal on it that only God can take away – '

'Are you telling me, Faith, that you think the state doesn't have the power to end a marriage?' Ceci interrupted. 'That only the Church does?'

'What state?' Faith shouted, tripping on a stone. 'The French state? The Dutch? Some human who's been elected?'

So that was it! They were back to the authority of the Catholic Church again, the Church's 'leadership', descended from St Peter who had been appointed by the Son of God. It was something Ceci would never understand but which penetrated the lives of the Catholics she knew to the core of their being. It was in bed with them, between them and their actions, and following them afterwards. Their belief was like a stone they either swallowed and made part of them – or it crushed them.

'What about Dougall, is he annulled?'

'Of course not!' Faith snapped. 'The poor thing's just divorced.'

Because his Church won't accept your Church's ruling, no doubt, Ceci thought.

'That should suit him very well though. He won't have to marry anyone now – but he'll certainly be accepted back.'

Faith slowed down. 'I had to say some horrible things about him. I would never have even *thought* them if the lawyers hadn't made me.'

'But were they true?'

Faith nodded. 'It was the Church Commission I acted the lie to.'

'Do you think Dougall would have wanted the whole town to know he was impotent?' Ceci asked. 'It seems to me you were protecting him –'

'I acted a lie.'

'Stop being so precious, Faith, and grow up. You can't climb on a dry pyre, fling the flame of truth into it and expect to survive. This is the real world!'

'We Catholics don't live in your "real world", Ceci,'

264

Faith said quietly. 'By doing exactly what you said we couldn't, by flinging truth in, we believe God opens ways for us – '

'To court self-destruction?'

'We lose ourselves to find ourselves. We are supposed to die to our own selfishness. I saved myself,' Faith railed. 'And I involved others.'

Pausing on the ridge overlooking the gully Ceci realized it was not going to be easy to cut Faith free from her guilt. 'Go to confession,' she said boldly.

Faith looked at her with exhaustion. 'It doesn't work like that. It's no good saying you're sorry.'

'But you *are*!'

'You have to make restitution.'

'So everyone has to know the truth about that poor boy?'

'If you've damaged someone's character – you have to un-damage it, you see?'

'So you have to go back to Dougall because you kept quiet about his condition?'

'Do you mind leaving me now? I want to walk.'

Ceci sat down and watched the girl wander away from her to the dip in the centre of the gully where the old dwelling had stood. She watched her as she became smaller and smaller, almost sinking into the grass, then turned and hurried back towards Hexham.

'I'm not clear why it bothers her so much,' she confessed to Ginger.

'No priest would like the way she manipulated the situation.'

'You couldn't humanly expect her to take a chance on Dougall's not lying.'

'Talking to a priest as a representative of God – you're

not talking about humans. The priest would have had guidance. Faith tried to give it to him by setting him up.'

'Couldn't you discuss it with a friendly priest and see if he didn't take a more kindly view than you?'

Ginger scratched his head. He was thinking that if Dougall had been so 'right living' he couldn't have known he was impotent before the marriage. 'If we can get her absolution, God's word that she is forgiven,' he said, 'she'll come right. I just hope the priest doesn't forgive Faith but re-instate her marriage.'

Not happy with the situation, Ceci waited for Faith to return.

'You can stop punishing yourself now, Faith, because I've figured it out,' she informed her. 'When Dougall reached for you in bed, even knowing that consummation would exile forever the faintest ghost of an annulment for you, did you hold back on Dougall or offer yourself to him?'

'I gave,' said Faith.

'Then what have you to accuse yourself of? That was the moment when you chose between honesty and a technicality: not in the Commission . . .'

Slowly the light came back into Faith's eyes. Running forward she grasped Ceci's hand. 'But I think I'll still go to confession,' she said warmly.

Brigham walked slowly up the hill towards Khandallah. He had decided not to take the train. It was a day he wanted to remember. Already he had risen high enough to see beneath him the harbour and the city he intended to make his own. Some children ran past. They thought nothing of the man walking up the hill instead of coming by train; smartly dressed but neither in the city nor bound for it.

'I thought I might find you here,' he said when Olwen opened the door. 'I called at your workshop – '

'Has something happened to Marshall?'

'Not yet.' Perhaps, he thought, he could even manage to marry her himself. She could afford to keep him.

'Is it something particular?' she asked.

Brigham stepped in. 'You must be very happy.'

'I am.'

'With your wedding about to happen.' He looked piercingly at her. Olwen gave a slight smile. 'Many girls would envy you I am sure.'

'Marshall could choose who he wanted.'

'But it was *you* he wanted.'

Suddenly Olwen became ill at ease. This man had no right discussing her intimate affairs, yet she felt were she to say so or to anger him in any way, she would be the worse for it.

'He has often told me how fond he is of you. It seems no one else would do at all.'

Olwen shrugged. It was essential to get into the company of others without delay. 'I am going into town,' she lied, reaching for her workcase.

'You find my company onerous?'

Olwen managed a smile. 'You will create a scandal by lingering when my girl is out.'

Brigham closed the door behind Olwen. 'That is something we must avoid. Would you agree?'

Olwen had in fact intended remaining at home that day and piecing together drawings.

Brigham reached for her case. 'Allow me.'

'I'd rather carry it myself.'

Instinctively she headed for the station. The 11.42 would be along soon.

267

'I would prefer you do not visit me without Marshall,' she said abruptly.

Brigham paused. 'Where then do you suggest we meet?'

Gaining courage from the familiar sight of the Station Master Olwen decided to give Brigham his cards and see to it that Marshall felt the same. 'There is nothing about you that is necessary in my life,' she said vehemently.

'Edmund.'

Olwen stood staring up the line. He had waited all this time! Possibly he'd even known before leaving England! Possibly he'd come out looking for her in case she'd made good!

'Edmund,' repeated Brigham. 'Suppose I were to tell you that Edmund is on his way out now?'

'He isn't!'

Brigham swallowed. Play her carefully.

By the time the train reached Wellington, even though she had chosen an occupied carriage, it was clear to Olwen that Brigham knew. It occurred to her he may have written to Somerset House. The insolent way he had 'toyed with' her on the crowded train had made it clear how close to the wind he was prepared to sail, had left her only one question to ask and she could ask it in two words. As they passed out through the ticket gate she put it to him: 'How much?'

'As much – and as often – as you can afford.'

In the next minute he was gone. Olwen did not dare to think. She walked as fast as she could out of the station, across the road, through the lane, down Lambton Quay, across Post Office Square, past the junction of Cuba and Manners Steets and towards Courtenay Place. Although the girls lifted their heads when she entered she did not see them, nor did she hear the clock chiming over by the waterway. Just nine words in a voice she now hated with a passion rang in her ears: 'As much – and as often – as you can afford.'

Badly frightened, she hurried towards Marshall's that night. It was damnable that he should be friends with Brigham. She could not tell him what had happened but could at least receive some reassurance, some human warmth from his presence. About to cross the road she saw Marshall and Brigham step forth together from the entrance of Marshall's apartment building, deep in conversation and no doubt headed for his club. The atmosphere between them was convivial. That Marshall could not *see* the snake he was entertaining; that he should be so nice to someone who was causing such disharmony and running amok in her life filled Olwen with distress. Though she could not escape Brigham, was there not some way she could drive a wedge between the two men to make sure that the little she possessed remained her own? As they passed by her Brigham glanced into the shadows and Olwen sensed he saw her and at that moment found she hated him more than she'd thought possible.

In the days to come she could scarce get near Marshall for he seemed always in Brigham's company and as their wedding drew closer, from a distance she saw Marshall's eyes become brighter and more concentrated.

By now she was putting out tenders for more work to defray Brigham's expenses. His wardrobe was increasing steadily; he had moved out of the hotel and taken an apartment where even Marshall was entertained. No longer did she employ the detective: she could not afford him. Driven by fear she made her own observations.

Like a gambler, the relief of having paid Brigham off and bought a few days of respite made her heady with joy. When he came at her again she would speak harshly to him: 'Take it and get out.' There was no longer the need to speak courteously and, freed from this restraint, she spoke in a way he had never been spoken to by a woman before. This excited him. He found himself unwilling to leave. Gradually it came to him that, though she was paying him to keep quiet so that she might get married, he could take payment in services as well as cash. He put it to her: 'I could make things easier for you, Olwen.'

'Don't call me by name!'

He touched her.

'It would be difficult for me after you're married,' he said pointedly. 'Marshall might find your housekeeping a little – ah – expensive.'

'You said – *until* I married.'

'I thought we might try a little something else. It would require my sampling the goods before making a forward commitment for I would be out of pocket and if the goods weren't worthwhile . . .'

'Out!'

'Think of it.'

How could she have been so stupid, Olwen moaned, hurrying up Manners Street towards the Turkish baths, the sole place she knew Brigham could never trouble her these days. Of course he would not say goodbye to his living so easily. The charge of bigamy would be worth even more to him, being more necessary for her to conceal than the intention to marry before obtaining a divorce. Why the banns were not even up yet and she was paying what must surely have been a top rate for his silence.

She turned into the bathhouse. On two days a week its use was given over to ladies only. Paying her money she retired to a cubicle, removed her clothes and laid them on a bench. Although the bath itself was little more than a steam cabinet or metal box she sat in with her head protruding while the hot vapours poured all over her, the sense of relief as the sweat and anxiety of the day ran off her was magnificent. Further, in the steam it was easy to cry for none could see. Should the lady enter to increase the steam what was a little more water running down a woman's face with the beads of sweat already dropping from her hair? Yet she would not let her face crack; would not give way to grief. How lucky were the Maoris with their lack of secrets, their easy crying in public. If only there were someone to turn to!

Chapter 19

'Miss Laird is taking on a lot of work for someone about to be married,' Hetty observed, sitting up in bed.

James grunted that weddings did not come cheap.

'Do you think she means suddenly to quit?'

'Quit?'

'How many dresses do you think I should order? In case. Given one does not know fashions to come.'

'Once she's settled down she'll go back to it.'

'Gwen was wondering if we shouldn't perhaps show a little more friendship towards her. When is the wedding to be? How can we help when it's all so hush hush?'

'Maybe she doesn't want help.'

'Would you have a word with Marshall?'

'If the poor girl is making dresses for all the guests as well as herself . . .'

'For every reason we must mend fences, James. It will be hardly possible to avoid her once they are married.'

May as well get up, thought James. There was no rest to be had when Hetty awakened with her mind blowing like a rag in the wind.

'Oddly enough, I am quite prepared to like the girl, she has changed so much of late,' Hetty said plaintively. 'But now that Miss Laird is to become Mrs Cavanaugh, she must surely respond to us.'

'Life could go on y'know, Hetty, if they kept themselves to themselves.'

'Married women cannot be solitary.'

She wouldn't be if she'd married him, James told himself. And where would the couturière business be then?

'It would be inconsiderate,' Hetty continued, 'for the Cavanaughs to remain apart. Entertainment would be difficult.'

'Marshall could come on his own,' James offered, envying him both the chance to go out alone and the opportunity to bed Olwen.

'That,' said Hetty, 'is a positively dangerous idea. Marshall will not advance his position with you, James, if he gives in to Miss Laird's selfishness. In Wellington, married women accompany their husbands.' James yawned. 'In my heart I should like to be friends with Miss Laird. I really should.'

And so should I, thought James.

'She could farm her work out entirely and spend much more time with us . . .'

If her father were there he would give Brigham a good crack, Olwen told herself, half wondering if she should invite Reg up. Was Brigham bluffing? By prying she had discovered he received no mail from England. Was he just a ne'er-do-well come out on the off-chance with a piece of purloined information, possibly overheard in a public house, that Edmund had sent an attractive wife packing to New Zealand? Had he perhaps intended to play some other confidence trick on her but finding her so well situated and about to entertain matrimony . . .? Dates and times whirled in her mind: he had not known she was in Wellington: he had bumped into her. Whether it was a clever guess or not she had played right into his hands. Happi had not told him Edmund's name: Happi did not know it.

She moved to open the front door. 'Marshall!'

273

'You look tired,' he said, stepping in. 'I thought we might take a picnic somewhere.'

'To tell the truth – '

'Yes, Olwen. Always do that.'

'I don't feel like it.'

'Come,' he said gently. 'The fresh air will do you good.'

As they walked to the station Marshall counselled her: 'This is supposed to be the happiest time of your life. Why are you working so hard? Is it the expense of the wedding? I don't like to see you look so pale.'

Olwen hung her head.

As the day wore on she saw how carefully Marshall had planned it. Having left the train and travelled some way by carriage he led her across farmland and began to climb with her up into the hills. In the distance the *rata* could be seen blooming, and from here and there came the sound of sawmills. As they climbed higher the trees gave way to fern, then scrub with boulders in it.

'I'm quite breathless,' said Olwen, gasping and sitting down. As she looked up at Marshall standing above her the clouds seemed to brush his very head as they rolled on past neighbouring hills to stretch out over the bay and the Cook Strait beyond.

'It's very clear up here,' said Marshall in a firm voice.

Olwen breathed deeply. It was a long time since she had been out. Here she felt free from her troubles, from the noxious influence of Brigham and the daily cares of the city itself.

'You would tell me if something were wrong, wouldn't you?' he asked gently after they had picnicked.

Olwen stared out at the clouds below covering, she knew, the water.

'Is anything troubling you?' Marshall asked.

'Nothing.'

274

'But you would tell me.'

'Of course.'

Marshall looked uneasy.

'Come and sit by me,' Olwen said, smiling up and patting the bracken beside her.

As if his mind were elsewhere, Marshall pulled his hands from his pockets, came over and sat down. 'I was thinking of posting the banns next Tuesday,' he said. 'Do you object?'

Olwen shook her head. 'Post them.'

Without looking at her Marshall began replacing the items in the picnic hamper.

As they climbed back down he moved ahead of her, having lost the original track and making use of a stream bed to descend. Olwen watched him swing from one side to the other as if she were losing him, his boots scratched by thorns, a tear by his knee and a bleeding finger he seemed not to notice. He walked straight on through the mud when he came to it, scarce bothering to glance back for her welfare. On the way home on the train he said practically nothing.

'Leave me here,' she said at Khandallah Station. 'I can manage.'

'Will there be anybody at your house?'

'Happi may be back.'

'It's not good for you to be alone,' Marshall said solicitously. 'What about Brigham? Does he visit?'

'Why should he?'

Marshall shrugged. 'Your girl seems to be away a lot of the time.'

'She's hardly my girl.' Olwen said wryly.

Wearily she stepped on to the porch and slipped her key into the lock.

'Were you out with Marshall today?' Brigham demanded, appearing from the bushes.

Olwen nodded tiredly.

'Did you tell him about us?'

'Get out,' she murmured.

The following Tuesday when Marshall posted the banns Brigham arrived like the proverbial bad apple to demand instant gratification.

'Leave me alone!' Olwen screamed from the privacy of her back room overlooking the gully.

'I'm not asking for money,' Brigham informed her. 'Just a taste –'

'You disgusting creature!' Olwen cried, striking at him with her fists.

'It will do you no good to scream. You will only attract attention.'

'If I ever give myself to you, it will be in a form you don't enjoy!' Olwen assured him. At that, there was a sound at the front door.

'I'll have my taste before he does,' Brigham promised.

'You're wrong! That's my girl back!' Olwen shouted, pulling away and running into the hall.

'Excuse me, Happi,' she said as the girl entered. 'I have to go somewhere.'

Happi cocked her head. 'Who went out the back?' she called.

Running with all her might Olwen caught the last train into Wellington. It would mean walking back but never mind. In a short time she was knocking on the door of Marshall's apartment.

'It's my mother,' she pleaded, accepting a glass of water. 'I have heard that she is unwell.'

'Will you go to her?'

'No,' Olwen blew her nose. 'But she will not be able to come.' She wiped her eyes. 'Could we delay a little?'

'What difference will delay make?'

'To our love you mean?'

'If she's too unwell to attend the wedding, how will the delay help her?' Marshall laboured the point.

'Oh. It – it's out of respect.'

Marshall stared past Olwen at the rain which had begun hammering on the window.

'I wouldn't be happy under the circumstances,' Olwen pleaded.

'Respect for me?' he said softly. 'Do you trust me at all, Olwen? Do you care about me?'

Olwen looked down.

'I'll get you a carriage,' Marshall said almost gruffly. 'Get some sleep. You are going to need it.'

Her heart in a turmoil, Olwen climbed into the carriage. She must rid herself of the limpet Brigham.

'I can't stand this for one moment more!' Olwen screamed, bursting into the house. 'I cannot go on!'

'My word! You pretty excited tonight.'

Olwen covered her face and started sobbing. Happi at once burst into tears of sympathy.

'Oh, Happi! It's such a mess. I wouldn't know where to begin telling you.'

'Olwen, you better get to the *marae*. Only one place for you, girl. Back to the family.'

Olwen blew her nose. Typical that whenever anything went wrong Happi would run straight back to the bosom of her clan.

'You come on,' she said. 'You don't need nothing. You better hurry.'

'Me?'

Suddenly it dawned on her what Happi meant. In the

same way as she had made *her* home Happi's home – in the same way that Happi's relatives had always accepted and welcomed her amongst them – they would now take her in and look after her.

'Hurry up,' said Happi, as if as an individual she had nothing to offer; as if no Maori needed ideas beyond belonging, beyond getting back to the *marae*. 'You better come home now, Olwen,' Happi was saying from the doorway. 'Everything will be all right. You will see.'

It was a bedraggled Olwen who arrived on foot at Pipitea early the next morning. Already the cocks were crowing, there were the first faint stirrings in the mud as figures emerged from huts, dogs had their first scratch of the day and fires lazily crackled to life. Nothing had changed since the last time she was there: the few little houses arranged in a vague semicircle, the Meeting House across the space with its decorated columns and carved headpiece; the huts, about the size of settlers' cottages, built of a mix of local and *pakeha* materials, the walls and roofs of *raupo* and the crest of the roofs covered with bent corrugated iron secured by wires tied to logs which rested on the actual roof to prevent the structure blowing away in a strong wind. Most doors and windows were made of wooden planking and hinged, the glassless windows closing against both rain and light. They were not high houses. One or two, quite modern, were built entirely of corrugated iron – hardly surprising given their proximity to the storage yards by the harbour ... One, in fact, Olwen was told, had been built by a previous generation *pakeha* husband of a Maori woman, a big trader who had been given the plot and permission to build by the Maoris because he had helped them repel the attack of enemy Maoris it seemed. In the days when traders and seal hunters had taken Maori

278

women, they had willingly joined up with their tribes and been held in high esteem for they could defend the tribe, provide them with guns. Indeed this spot, Pipitea, had been reserved for the Maoris because, thanks to the guns of the white man who had married into their tribe, they had been able to hold it at all times. Men or women, it seemed, the *pakehas* had always chosen to go with the Maori side in cross-marriages and these houses stood as a reminder. And by all accounts they had fought bravely alongside their new brothers in internecine wars.

Olwen waited patiently while Happi went in to speak to her aunty. She could hear pots being crashed about and the yelp of dogs as the occupants of the *pa* prepared to cook breakfast.

'Olwen! *Haere mai*! Come!' the aunty cried, rushing forward to embrace her. Olwen burst into tears. At once the aunty started crying too and soon a crowd of women had gathered around, all hanging on to each other and crying supportively, as slowly their men — at first grumbling for their breakfasts then driven by curiosity — drew closer and Happi's voice rose in a great chant telling what Olwen had suffered at the evil hands of this *pakeha* stranger.

'He should be stung by a *katipo* spider!' screamed Purotu.

Olwen had heard of *katipos*. They had red rings on their backs and were plentiful on the coast around there, especially on old logs on the beach.

'Get him here,' shouted Mutu, 'that I may stand thigh to thigh with him and struggle!'

The crowd swelled, cooking fires were abandoned as the listeners wrestled with the peculiarly *pakeha* concept of blackmail, so difficult for their direct natures to comprehend. Olwen sensed it was a thing which never occurred.

They ambushed, they killed, they put curses on each other, they made up, they cried, they took each other's things – but they did not blackmail. Was this because they had no secrets; because as children they grew up seeing and hearing everything; because without privacy the idea was ridiculous? Yet they had a capacity for subterfuge; this was known by their uncanny skill on the battlefield, their use of decoys and their ability to outmanoeuvre an enemy. Already people were shouting for the *tohunga*. 'He can stand outside this man's building and shout: "Die! Ingrate!"' Happi's aunt shouted.

Olwen did not want to appear an ingrate herself but she doubted the efficacy of that. It was all very well for Maoris to fear the *mana* of the *tohunga*, his skill at *makutu*. True there had been the case of the young drunken Maori returning past the *tohunga*'s hut who had dared to make fun of his baldness. 'May a cancer squeeze your heart!' the angry *tohunga* had shouted. Becoming ashen the young man had run to his hut only to die within hours. As the old *tohunga* walked slowly towards Olwen she imagined his effect on Brigham would be slightly less monumental. 'It hurts, it hurts,' he sighed. 'Our own very dear child has come back to us suffering.'

Olwen smiled at the good old man, each wrinkle telling of his great learning and history. 'Grandfather,' she said, 'I salute you.'

'We will call a *hui* – a public meeting,' he announced. 'Our child, the friend of our hearts, will not go unavenged.'

At that Olwen wished to rush into his arms, the strength of his feeling – the passion shaking him on her behalf – truly moving her. Although their own breakfasts were not cooked the women set about preparing a *haangi* – an oven dug into the ground, the pit of which was lined with sticks, round rocks placed on top of the wood, that the stones might sink slowly into the pit as the wood burned. By experience Olwen knew the stones would become hot, the burning wood removed as water was sprinkled on to the stones to create the steam in which the *kumara*, the *puha* and pork or whatever else was to hand would be cooked under a cover of leaves with dirt to seal in the steam. Meanwhile the young men would be sent to the surrounding *pas* – to the beautifully named Moe-ra which meant 'Sleeping in the Sun' – for it was the first to receive the morning rays which touched it before its inhabitants awoke; to Karaka Bay; to anywhere else her Ngati Awa peoples had relatives, and summon them.

As the day wore on Olwen began to appreciate what the Maoris' friendship meant to her. Not only had a pig been slaughtered but chickens killed, fish caught and a fine selection of the *pipi* – the shellfish for which Pipitea was named – had been collected by the children. *Tea*, Olwen understood, meant 'white'. Nobody stared at her. Nobody asked questions. All around was activity. The children ran and laughed, picked up puppies and kissed them, were chased away from the food preparation area – itself some distance from the fire for there was always the danger stones would split, shoot off and strike people. She began to feel very relaxed. Brigham was far from her – he came from another land. She was surrounded with love and affection, that great Maori warmth which defied the insidious meanness of Western individuality. She strolled over to the working women. All had forgotten the problem. All were busy in preparing for the *haangi*, the clan meal which would be eaten after the visitors had arrived, greetings had been exchanged, the meeting had taken place, decisions had been reached and it was time to feast before embracing and departing.

'May I help?' she asked.

Happi's aunty patted the ground.

'Shall I look at the *umu*?' Olwen asked.

'You stay well away,' Happi's aunty teased. 'That oven very dangerous. You sit here.'

Olwen sat and scraped some potatoes, glancing across at the pigeon, eels, pumpkin, thistle and native cabbage ready for the fire. Behind her children were running with fern and flax leaves, giving them to the older women. Happi's aunty got up and went to take a look at the fire. Olwen hated the way eels were thrown in live, so that as they squirmed in the embers their slimy skin would come off.

'Give me *pare pare*,' the aunty called. A child brought over a thick rope made of twisted grass which the aunty used to encircle the oven. Quickly she splashed water over the stones, and in the ensuing steam poured in half the potatoes, the pigeon, pork, fish, eels and other meat, carefully smoothed all with a stick, packed the gaps with pumpkin and thistle, then tossed in more water, backing away in a great gale of laughter and steam.

Her sister came running forward. 'My word,' she said good naturedly. 'We almost had you in that *haangi*!'

Together the women spread various bits of old basket and matting in the pit, just enough to stop the earth falling on top of the food. On to that they piled the dirt so that the oven was completely closed to the sky and not a hiss of steam escaped. Laughing, they fell away, sweat streaming from their foreheads. Suddenly Olwen realized she had completely forgotten her troubles. She had seen a perfectly built *haangi*. The food, when ready, would be dry and clean, with a hint of a European roast but the flavour of everything, indescribable and unique.

When the *haangi* was opened her expectations did not prove false. No grease, no juices, no great lumps of fat.

Her teeth slid easily through the delicious pumpkin and pigeon. Women smiled at her, at that moment intent on their food. Nothing beyond the joy of eating was in their minds – the joy of being together. People came up and congratulated her.

There had been a meeting. Everyone had spoken together. Her problems were solved. Olwen took a piece of chicken and smiled. If she could remain on the *marae* forever indeed her problems would be over, for here you were loved simply because you existed. There was no strength like that of the *marae*: there was nothing in *pakeha* culture to even come near this sense of total oneness, this willingness to pull together to help when times were hard. No wonder Happi had torn down all her chair covers and curtains to accommodate her relatives! Did they even have any sense of individual existence, she wondered? The individual pain known to the European seemed only to touch them in matters of thwarted love, situations of unjust result. But soon it would be time to be pressing noses. Soon they would be gone.

Walking some distance from the gathering she sat quietly with her food which the aunty had served on an enamel plate and picked at it with a penknife the uncle had provided. In the distance the food line tailed off into the dark, at the far end of it – she knew – the elders. How touching it was that the most important people always ate last; always made sure that the guests and the workers and the humblest of all should have their fill. Towards the back of the line she saw the *tohunga*. What a dear man he was! Indeed his idea had been most touching and though she would try it out of politeness, clearly it would not work. But paradise could not go on forever: she must return to Khandallah and, despite the love she had experienced with these people, pursue her battles alone. How amazing they were! How paltry and insignificant the trait of individuality her own forbears had brought to this land. Christianity? Did they not have it down to a fine art? Did they not instinctively share everything without even the concept of personal ownership. A woman did not even own her children: her mother, her aunt, her own sister could come and take them should she feel the need. How was it possible that a people could receive her, with her different skin colour, her different language and ideas – and all those things she could think that they did not know. One thing was very sure: her own race would never receive an individual Maori like this.

Olwen felt the hollowed twig in her pocket. What had the *tohunga* said it was? A paralytic juice? Made from – what roots? No doubt their woods were full of strange fungi and berries which created convulsions, excitement, exhaustion and vomiting. Why, Karaka Bay, she had learned that very day, had been named after the deadly berries which grew there. *Tutu* was well known for hallucinations; *poro poro* for abdominal pain, vomiting, diarrhoea and depression – not to mention the native stinging nettle. Yet if what she had heard from Venables was right, this hollowed-out twig probably contained nothing more than the venerable old man's urine. But it would give her great pleasure to slip it into a cocktail for Brigham. Great pleasure to think of him drinking this venerable man's piddle. So far as she had understood it *tohungas* turned up at houses where children were dying of whooping cough and rubbed their bodies with little else. Of course the children did not recover. Her own headache remedies, carefully taken by Happi, had done far more good.

Olwen bade Happi's aunty and the *pa* goodbye. The farewells had taken almost as long as the welcoming – the nose pressing, the crying, the loving attention to detail whereby each person must be greeted, served, looked after. That all should receive the same care struck Olwen by the force of its rarity where she came from. Finally she and Happi were on the road home together.

'You got it? That thing?' Happi asked.

'Of course I have,' Olwen chided. 'Do you think I'm stupid?'

'Good. You just be careful, do like he says.'

Olwen glanced across at Happi. She seemed frightened. Why? 'Everything will be all right,' she began.

Happi frowned.

Suddenly it occurred to Olwen that, away from the *marae*, any individual act was a great threat to her. She, Olwen, had embarked on an individual course. Happi was very badly frightened.

Chapter 20

'Funny how your Olwen didn't take after you,' Annie began. 'She seems all for the city.'

Reg shrugged and looked at Little Annie up ahead of them, wobbling between their marrows, about to flop down on her behind and start beating one like a drum. It seemed everything she did enchanted him. Annie too. The child had brought a joy beyond imagining to both of them, to the extent that they were thinking of flying in the face of God and having another.

'We could get headscarves,' Annie said. 'We could turn religious.'

Reg shrugged. He didn't see that had anything to do with anything. He'd been in and out of the hamlet a few times and been kindly received but enough of a good thing was enough.

He looked over their garden. It was a testimony to the amount of water he'd carried up the hill. This year they would have dried peas, their very own, which Annie had spread on flat ground in the summer sun and lovingly turned daily. A few peas in a winter stewpot made a hefty difference. With Little Annie weaned, coming on for two years and doing mighty well on homegrown food, things were getting on famously, he told himself. Give the kid a little sister or brother to waggle her toes at and they'd be away.

Watching him, Annie too felt proud. On the doorpost she had notched up the different dates they had planted their sets of peas, early potatoes, carrots, turnips, more potatoes and then more peas. The big mark was where the young gooseberry bushes had gone in before the last lot of broad beans, then came the winter carrots which would be slow, the cabbage, the Brussels sprouts, more parsley and silverbeet. The lettuce they'd just kept sewing all along. Somehow she hadn't notched up the rhubarb but there it was, large as life, waving its fronds at them as summer closed in. Next year maybe they'd have raspberries, black-currants and flowers. Any number of flowers would have done well up there despite it being so high, for the sun, when it rose, was burning hot and the rain, when it fell, plentiful. It was just a pity it all ran away into the earth.

There were two areas where he had blotted his copy-book, Reg told himself, the first being the badly con-structed rabbit hutch and the second the waterpump — which had not come off. This was a shame for he would love to have shown it to Ceci and Ginger when they'd come up in spring. He'd really wanted to please Annie when he'd set about boring that tree trunk with an auger to make it hollow so they could sink it in the ground like a pipe, but night after night of the monotonous work and he'd decided to have a go from the other end and had succeeded in cracking the bloomin' thing clean open.

It would be almost worth walking back to Bowens Gully and digging out his old one, Reg thought, rather than start this ding-dang scraping and hollowing again, but there it was — they couldn't afford a metal pipe. Hardware was a major investment and the government man had said the first seven years were a testing ground and they had to 'make improvements' so they'd better get the best use out of their capital. It was the same story with a nice sheet of wire for the rabbit hutch — his second piece of bad carpentry.

He watched Annie take Little Annie around back to get

cleaned up for her tucker. Since she had come along he'd learned to be careful with his axe and slash-hook, never to leave anything dangerous within reach of the child. Even his gun, which he had always felt right about resting on its head against the house wall had now come to be stored inside, across the rafters. Inconvenient when there was an escaped rabbit poking its head out, looking at you and just asking to be shot. Of course Annie objected but she didn't know the half of it. Supposed to be about six rabbits in that hutch – at most eight. But he'd made himself another hutch in the wood where he kept the overflow which, because Ceci's original pair hadn't both been male, went down very well in the hamlet. In fact he was beginning to be known as a bit of a 'rabbit-hoh' man himself, a nice rabbit pie being just what the doctor ordered of a Saturday. The money from the rabbits he was saving for Little Annie's education, though a meaner man might have put it towards a metal pump. It was all very well teaching a child nursery rhymes but there was more to life than that and one day Annie would thank him for it. He did not feel guilty about hoarding the money, for Annie could not regard this income as part of her original nugget because the 'extra' rabbits hardly belonged to her. And they had won him gratitiude in the hamlet for though the delicacy was more than common around Moke, it seemed up here they'd never had any till he'd helped out.

'Where are you going?' Annie called as Reg trumped across the clearing.

'To fix the 'utch,' he grunted.

Holding Little Annie to her, Annie twisted to watch him retreating through the bushes. He was a good man and very patient with that hutch – which always broke. Re-weaving the saplings was all very well till the moon rose –

but what they really needed was a sheet of that good modern wire. But that would be too expensive.

With the wild plums weighing down the trees she had the last of the jam making lined up for that day. Stretching, she glanced through the hinged wood-flap window up into their rafters and saw Reg had taken his gun.

'You catch 'em and put 'em back in, Reg!' she shouted after him.

Reg stood beyond the clearing scratching his head. A good thirty-four rabbits if you counted those Annie knew about, the ones he had and those running loose. Blasted burrowers! Despite Annie's murmurings there were a few here that would end up in the hamlet unless they got that cheeky look off their faces! His little 'un 'ud get a schooling one way or another and for a jack rabbit to sit there scratching its ear in that insolent fashion was as good a way to start as any. BANG! One for the impertinence. BANG! One for the hamlet. BANG! One for their stewpot. He could always get away with saying it had taken three bullets to get the one rabbit. Truth was, if he weren't afraid Annie would come on them, he'd've hanged a few. It made their hair stand out as they died and that was good for the pelts. But women being the sentimental creatures they were he didn't want to upset her. BANG! There went another. He'd tell her he was teaching them a lesson and driving them back towards the hutch. Come to think of it the folk in the hamlet had a metal pump but they'd saved up for it together.

Faintly Annie heard the sharp sounds and assumed that would be Reg making jars for her to preserve the home-made jam she so craved in his roly poly. The way he did it was novel to her. He would take an old bottle, loop a piece of string around it, set fire to the string then – as the flame ate its way along the string – plunge the bottle into

cold water where it snapped neatly in half, the part Annie
wanted sinking to the bottom. It made a good preserving
jar and any kind of jam pleased Reg. Further, it was clear
to Annie that there was no kind of fruit or vegetable that
grew or could be collected which could not be made into
either jam, chutney, sauce or – if Reg got his hands on it –
liquor. Not that she was averse to a spot of parsnip
brandy, but his brewing had a long way to go before she
would be sampling it. His first sip had sent him choking
and clasping at his throat as if a bug had been dancing
there.

On the table's crude edge Little Annie was smearing the
flour paste which Annie would use to seal the lids, cut
from the precious newspapers, over the jars. The season's
jam making had left its scars: jam scalds, blisters from hot
pot handles, a history of red eyes from peering into the
smoke to see how things were going. There had been the
whole business of lugging sugar up from the hamlet's store
and infuriating days when Reg had rested his cans of water
on the woodpile and they had toppled in and drenched all
the wood. Though she was long used to the wild things
that ran from the logs and sheltered there in the rain, her
personal battle with unwilling fires in the early morning,
the soot in her eyes, her hair, down her nails and covering
every inch of their shanty, at times made her long for a
proper stove with a chimney.

Little Annie wandered towards the fire.

'Don't you touch that pot! You come away from there!'
The toddler turned and smiled.

'You get outside and look for your pa,' Annie urged.
'Here,' she flipped a biscuit through the door into the
sunlight. Little Annie ran after it. If she had any sense she
wouldn't be jam making indoors but with the weather so
changeable; besides, she needed the smoke to cure the

meat. Reg had the right idea all right, wandering about in the greenery with a clear sky above. Sometimes the struggle of it all made her bad tempered and angry with him though it was not his fault for liking jam. It was nothing other than the smoky fire which made her so cross and this she realized.

'You finished fussing in there?' came the voice of Reg from the door.

'Fussing?'

'Tea time!' Reg announced, swinging a rabbit at her.

Ignoring him, Annie scooped a little of the jam on to a plate she had been chilling in water. 'Now you just go outside and leave me alone.'

'Got something for you.' He waved the rabbit at her.

'How *could* you?'

Reg shrugged. 'You got your dried meat for winter, girl. Can't afford to be fussy. Try packin' this in salt. Corned.'

'Don't be silly, Reg. You don't corn rabbit!'

'You corn beef,' he replied, then stepped away. She was always irritable when she made jam.

'Happen I'll get you a couple more jam jars,' he said wisely, stepping out. 'Here, Titch!' Annie heard him call.

She went to the door to see him striding off into the undergrowth, Little Annie perched on his shoulders. Where precisely his bottles came from, she did not know. A woman couldn't be expected to know everything. Most things they did discuss and agree on though, for example that they should reduce their number of cows to suit only themselves and complement the local situation by growing more crops. They had been lucky with their land, more so than their neighbours. With the passing season it grew crops as if it could not be stopped. So fertile was it that Annie had even thought of getting in bees for honey to sell locally, but as she and Reg had no experience of such

291

things it was an idea which for the time being had been shelved. Taking a last deep breath of clear air into her lungs Annie stepped back into their 'shed' to resume her jam making.

In the opulence of Hexham Ceci looked up at the space where the porcelain collection had been. It had taken up almost an entire room. She could remember it sitting there in need of a dust when they had returned from Reg and Annie's, could remember how, after they had settled Faith, they had disagreed about whether or not to sell it so that the boys might buy a decent racehorse and how Ginger, almost in response to his changed feelings about Faith and the local community, had suddenly done a right about turn and agreed that it should be sold. 'What the hell!' she could remember him saying, and 'Just a few plates and cups! Let's take the whole thing to Christchurch to the auction.' The 'few plates and cups' had fetched an extremely good price and the week in Christchurch – so refreshingly free of sectarian rumblings – had done Faith a world of good, and Myra, too, desperate for a chance to display herself, had thoroughly enjoyed the event while she and Ginger, each for their different reasons, appreciated the auction.

''Tis a joy to see people with no sense spending money,' sighed Ginger.

'That porcelain collection was worth every penny of it,' Ceci said knowingly.

Their week was spent in a rather fine house the boys used whenever they stayed in Christchurch. It belonged to a member of a brewing family who had returned to England for six months and had left it to them without charge as a token of his appreciation of their expertise when it came to putting his money on horses of their recommendation.

'What a fine house!' Myra cried, dancing from room to room. Faith trailed after her, carefully feeling the edge of a curtain, tapping a chair.

'What about this, Faith? What do you think, eh?' Ginger asked. Faith smiled.

Watching, Ceci thought it was beautiful the way he had taken a special interest in her since she had returned to live with them. Apparently she still occasionally felt she should have stayed with Doug; that his impotence might have passed; that he might not have been impotent except for that particular night; that it was all still somehow her fault and that she had deliberately side-stepped whatever God had been trying to teach her. But gradually Ginger had lured her from the house on the grounds that now she had received absolution she had better start attending Mass at once. Indeed it had been her fear of creating additional mortal sins which had driven her forth, for Mass was the place where the community saw each other, and where their consciences were inevitably paraded in public. Taking her arm, Ginger had shepherded her through the ordeal, careful to keep her by him, going up the aisle as if she were a bride about to be given away, reassuring her, patting her hand. He kept her hand as they went up to Holy Communion, knelt by her, helped her to her feet afterwards and, as Theresa had said, it was a moving, a touching sight. Yet though Faith was being peeped at with curiosity as she passed, still none would go near her.

'Had she been a man,' Ginger said angrily, 'she could have left a wife and five children and still be accepted!'

'Yet it took her own father time to accept her, didn't it?' Ceci pointed out.

For her part, after the first visit to the barn for Mass,

Faith found she did not care about the parishioners. They were very small; they were beneath what she had been through — no more than casual bystanders at the great accident of herself. She felt disdain for them. She knew she would not stay in Moke for ever. And now, patting the furniture and looking up at her father smiling at her, she felt she would very soon be gone.

'I should like to "care for" this house in your absence,' Myra informed the boys. 'While you are in Australia buying your racehorse.'

The boys grinned and Ginger shook his head.

'We won't be gone long,' said Michael. 'If our information is right.'

'I don't have to go to Australia with Michael, I could stay and — and . . .' Kevin did not finish the sentence.

'Funny about Kevin,' mused Ginger on the way back. 'What do you make of him wanting to stay back?'

'He's upset about me,' Faith informed them.

'You talked to him?'

'Everything. You're both too embarrassed to ask.'

Myra looked away. She wasn't embarrassed. She just didn't want listening to what a mess Faith had made of *her* life to spoil her own!

'Kevin thinks I had a rough ride from the Church,' Faith went on.

'Well,' said Ginger, 'If he thinks he can change anything there, he's another think coming!'

'Faith could have gone with the boys to get the racehorse,' Myra pointed out, adding, 'So could I.'

Ginger rolled his eyes.

'I am *so tired* of Hexham.'

'I've been thinking,' Ginger said to Ceci as they prepared for bed that night. 'We can't keep Myra here much longer.'

'The place will be like a morgue without her.'

Ginger gave her a surprised look. 'What I've been thinking is — would Olwen agree to our sending Myra to her in Wellington?'

In her heart of hearts Ceci thought it was wrong of him to ask, for what could the girl say but yes? Myra had always admired Olwen but whether Olwen would want Myra trailing around after her, making sheep's eyes at everything in trousers was another matter. 'I have never thought of that,' she said truthfully.

'What do you think?' Ginger asked.

Ceci hesitated: 'I think I'd like to think about it.'

It could not be denied that Myra was wasting in Hexham and that Moke was no place for a young girl. She was all of eighteen years old, Ginger pointed out, and while he was in no hurry to be rid of her, she was the only one out of all his daughters whose life had not yet been 'decided' or 'spoiled' by circumstance. The boys were blowing away, Lizabeth had gone rotten on the branch and Faith had jumped. Myra at least should have the chance to be 'picked'. She was also the only one they could help and under Olwen's guidance — provided there were not too many Maoris involved — she could probably develop useful social skills in Wellington.

'I know you want what's best for her,' Ceci said understandingly. 'In fact I am surprised you can see so clearly it's time she left.'

'She could help Olwen in her work.'

Ceci doubted this but said nothing. Olwen had never been the sort of girl who liked to be helped with anything. However Ginger *had* given Olwen an allowance to get started with so what could she say? 'Very well, Ginger. We'll send her.'

* * *

It was considered that it would be good for Faith to be involved in the exercise so she was to accompany Myra to Christchurch, stay with her while she 'fitted out' and put her on board ship at Lyttelton. For her part, though she dared not mention him, Myra had not forgotten the handsome gentleman who had called in her parents' absence and whom she sincerely hoped to see again.

'Have you posted that letter?' Faith asked as they descended from the hills to cross the great plain together.

'From Christchurch, silly! It will be quicker from there.'

Faith looked at Myra. She could be quite sly at times and their father had particularly told them to alert Olwen in advance that Myra was coming. He had seen Myra's point of view that there was no point in posting the letter in Moke; that old Moribund would steam it open, read it, copy out the details and create further delay hunting around for the necessary postage. Yet they had been trusted and instructed to post the letter en route.

'Mind you, I still think,' Myra said in a grown-up voice, 'I should post the letter in Wellington. I can take it on the ship with me and post it when I arrive.'

'You certainly aren't spending a night alone in Wellington, so don't think you are,' Faith pointed out. 'You're being met off that ship.'

'I simply meant that I could have it delivered by hand.'

'Listen, Myra. That letter has to reach Olwen at least four days in advance, do you understand?'

Myra looked down. She had no intention of posting the letter.

'It's a matter of courtesy. People have a right to know you're coming. Arrangements may need to be made. Olwen might have planned to go away.'

'Where would she go?'

'Just see you post it.'

'I wanted to call in at her shop as soon as I arrived in Wellington,' Myra protested. Why would nobody let her have a surprise?

'Just see you post that letter,' Faith repeated.

In Christchurch the girls put up at a respectable hotel and set about refurbishing Myra's trunk and making arrangements for the steamer. Tolerant of Myra's impatience at her every suggestion, Faith was aware of seeing the girl off on a 'new life' and conscious of her wanting to be gone. The experience of having lain in bed with a man had changed forever the way she felt about everything. It had even driven a wedge between the sisterhood she had known with Myra, making her feel years older. What did life hold for her now? And with whom? With the boys — as their housekeeper — till a wife came on the scene? Ceci and Ginger had made her welcome but she could not continue with them. 'I wouldn't mind coming with you,' she had started to say to Myra but the look on the girl's face had made it clear that would not do. Could she fashion a new identity for herself? Her idea that God had something in store for her had taken a severe knock. Surely she must still be of some use somewhere? When Myra had departed, what answer would she find in the dry hills of Hexham?

On the last morning they hurried to the quay and gazed at the choppy water, the wavelets with their dark undersides crashing together and stretching to a solid wall of cloud which had closed down as if a fire curtain had been lowered between the North and South Islands. The Christchurch weather, which always came up from the south, was bright, yet ahead on the ocean lay large sombre patches, almost like carpets waiting to be trodden on. Though Myra could not wait to be gone: could not wait to step on to the steamer and free herself of everyone — of her family, of Faith, of Christchurch and Hexham – of the whole countrified, not remotely glamorous, South Island – she shuddered.

'Be careful and don't speak to strangers,' Faith warned, realizing even as she said it how ridiculous it sounded for, from now on, apart from Olwen, everyone would be a stranger to Myra. 'You will write, won't you?'

Myra nodded, wishing Faith would be gone. Already people were looking at them. If only Faith would not hug her and hold on to her as if it were the end of the world. Khandallah! She rolled the word on the tongue of her mind.

'Can I get you anything? Do you have everything you want?' Faith asked anxiously.

The hooter sounded.

'I'm going to miss you, Myra.'

Myra pulled away and began to hurry up the gangplank. Ahead of her a woman with two children was complaining that they were not holding each other's hands properly and Myra felt their impatience at their mother, sensed their excitement, so like her own, as they hurried on to the steamer.

Suddenly it hit her she was alone. She had not thought to turn around and look back at Faith and now she was in the bowels of the ship being jostled and pushed by all manner of people. Frightened, she struggled towards the light of the open deck and scoured the quay for Faith.

'Faith! Faith!' she called, but could not see her.

Suddenly she felt the boat roll. The shouts from below became louder as last-minute trunks were rushed up the gangplank -- itself now being unfastened; money was thrown to someone below without their fare home. The hooter boomed again, sending clouds of black smoke to be blown down amongst the onlookers. Myra's cheeks felt wet. Already her old life was floating away from her and a new one about to begin. She would be in Wellington. She had not posted the letter but lied about it to Faith. Nor did she intend to send word to Olwen or go first to her workplace. She intended to change into her best dress so none could say she was a hick from the South Island and make her way all on her own to the dwelling in Khandallah and knock on the door. What a marvellous surprise for Olwen who would no doubt be giving a party with young men. She might even be wearing a daring evening gown or perhaps smoking a cigarette in a holder.

'This is my – "sister",' Olwen would say proudly as Myra stepped in.

Chapter 21

Already fraught by a situation wherein Marshall was 'doubting her sincerity' and showing a distinct cooling towards her, as the days closed in, though she tried to hide it, Olwen's inner panic increased.

'I tell you,' said Happi, pointing at the hollowed stick containing the *tohunga*'s gift. 'This thing make me feel much better.'

Olwen smiled tiredly. In a strange way she too felt reassured by its presence in the house but Happi truly treated it as if it were some kind of sacrament because it had the old man's *mana* in it. Every time she passed it she nodded to it: she never turned her back on it – in fact was always careful to face it when she spoke, and backed from the room as if it were Queen Victoria.

'You better hurry up and use that stuff,' she warned Olwen.

'Why? Will it go off? Will it start to smell?'

Happi explained that there could be anything in it and provided a nauseating litany of private and public matter which she seemed highly to recommend. The main ingredient, of course, was the old man's *power*, his ability to instil life force and effect change. Olwen shrugged. When all was said and done it could not do Brigham any harm to drink some poultice scrapings liberally peppered with pus from infected sores.

'You got to encourage him first,' Happi told her.

'I despise and fear him.'

'You get friendly with him, bring him out a bit. You

300

make like . . .' Happi waggled her shoulders and bottom seductively so that Olwen fell about laughing at her imitation of a high *pakeha* lady seducing an indifferent man. At that, the door went. Because Happi had collapsed with laughter Olwen crossed to open it but was unable to wipe the smile from her face even at the sight of Brigham, who had arrived, excited by the idea that he could possibly compromise her to the extent of marrying *him*. He had noticed that she had been so much quieter lately: obviously she had been about a bit in the past so could not be too shocked by the idea. All that remained was to put it to her. With force. Yet this laughing apparition in the doorway confused him.

'You may as well come in,' Olwen said, still wiping tears from her eyes.

'Him again!' Happi chortled. Brigham glared. 'You want me to cut your fingernail for you?' she asked, crossing to him. 'How 'bout your toenail then?'

Out of his depth Brigham could only frown. 'Look,' Happi went on. 'He got loose hair on his shoulder.' She carefully picked a hair off and held it between finger and thumb. 'I got it!' She winked at Olwen.

'She's becoming houseproud,' Olwen explained.

Behind Brigham, Happi gesticulated that with a bit of Brigham's personal 'dirt' the *tohunga* could work wonders. She mimed a 'You be sure and scratch him and get some skin shavings under your fingernail' at Olwen.

'I don't know why you keep that girl,' Brigham muttered as Happi left the room.

'She's not so bad.'

'You're different tonight.'

'Yes.'

In the present atmosphere Brigham did not see how he could begin the seduction. He had imagined, in fact depended on, Olwen's exhibiting a certain amount of repugnance, backing towards the wall, clutching at her throat and screaming, 'No!'

'I accept your terms,' Olwen said briskly. 'If we are to do it, we may as well begin.'

Brigham swallowed. 'I had come to tell you that unless you – obliged me – this evening I would feel it my duty to speak out during the wedding service.'

'I see.' Olwen laughed lightly. 'You wanted to seduce me from a position of power. Do you have difficulties getting erections? Usually they say only men who are weak need fear to stimulate them.'

Brigham found himself becoming very excited.

Thinking of him swallowing rat droppings Olwen gave an infectious smile. 'Come along, Brigham, I'm sure you've done it before.'

As anger and a lessening of desire crossed Brigham's face Olwen again experienced an uncontrollable urge to giggle.

'Are you laughing at me?' he demanded angrily.

'This is far too serious for laughter,' Olwen assured him. 'Why, you are about to rape me!'

Brigham sat down. Behind him in the doorway Happi appeared, motioning to Olwen to be sure and give him the *tohunga*'s magic.

'Would you like a drink?' she asked politely. 'I can't stand to see a man lose his nerve.'

'I'll have a drink,' Brigham told her. 'Then I'll flay you alive.'

Olwen folded her arms and looked at him seated on the sofa glaring up at her. 'A quick scuffle between the cushions should do us good, don't you think, Brigham? I shall regard it as my last taste of freedom before years of domestic bliss. It had better be good.'

'Where's my drink?' Brigham fumed.

'We shall drink, then we shall bathe and then you will try your best to please me.' Olwen informed him. 'Excuse me.'

As she mixed the drinks Olwen wondered if she were on a high of hysteria, given that the gravity of what she was doing did not seem to be sinking in. She was going to have sex with Brigham in the hopes that it would shut him up. Of course he would be back. Why, then, was she doing it? Did she intend to keep both him and Marshall happy for the rest of her life?

'Get the medicine,' Happi warned her as she dreamily poured gin into two glasses. Olwen poured the drips from the *tohunga*'s stick into Brigham's glass, strained it, stirred it around. It did not look anywhere near as disgusting as she had imagined, being in fact a colour somewhere between bright carmine and sap.

'You better put something in yours,' Happi warned.

'Pass me the Angostura.'

'Look, I got it here. Some of his hair,' Happi whispered. Olwen nodded. 'Once the *tohunga* get this, he can make a special powder that will enter by the roots of his hair and strangle him!'

'The enthusiasm is appreciated,' Olwen murmured, picking up the tray and stepping from the kitchen. Maybe she had made the wrong decision but this was one battle she was going to win. She would make this experience *so* unpleasant for him; she would scratch his face and bite his neck so badly in the 'passion' he aroused in her that he would be obliged to remain in his own apartment from this day until well after the wedding and then for some time till the scars should heal. At the thought of the physical battle for so long avoided with Brigham all repugnance left her. If she was a cornered rat — let him beware! — she would fight like one.

'Your drink,' she said coolly, turning the tray towards him.

Brigham at once noticed the change in her manner. The girl was becoming afraid. 'Thank you.' Once she had given herself to him she would do it again and again. Women were like that. They complained but . . . He watched her cross and stand by the window.

'I think I shall bathe now,' she said, her back to him.

'May I watch?'

He saw her head sink slightly.

'Drink your gin.'

He took another sip. 'You know how to mix your drinks, my dear.'

'Gin is a woman's drink, Brigham,' Olwen said without turning.

Brigham crossed to her and placed a hand on her shoulder, the shoulder he would soon uncover. He felt it tense.

'Let me bathe.'

'Do you find me repulsive?'

'Would you prefer I did?' Now she was facing him. 'Look!' she said, boldly beginning to unbutton her bodice.

Brigham took another gulp at his drink. He was becoming flushed. Slowly Olwen unbuttoned, eased then stepped from her dress, leaving it a pile of softness on the wood floor. Let him come on!

'I'm ready, Brigham,' she said coldly.

But Brigham's hands had started their journey to his throat only to fall halfway, his glass crashing to the ground in a shimmer of light, his face became redder and redder while his eyes darted about in panic. Olwen frowned intensely. The man's neck was thickening but his arms and legs were not moving – no part of his body but for his eyes moved, not even his chest.

'Happi!'

Happi appeared in the doorway. 'It worked!'

She watched Olwen run towards Brigham yet, as she grabbed him, he keeled over, his face becoming blue, unable to breathe. His panicking eyes seemed ready to burst.

'My God!'

'I seen this before,' Happi explained. The main constituent apparently was not the *tohunga*'s *mana* but a paralytic fern juice used for poisoning fish in times of war. 'Probably because he come from the sea with evil thoughts,' Happi added, insisting that Olwen be grateful for the singular honour shown in making a wartime remedy available to her.

'But what are we to do?' Olwen gasped.

Suddenly the everyday objects in her room took on an awful significance for, whether she meant it or not, she had killed a man.

'Well, he finish now,' Happi observed dispassionately.

'But what shall I do with him?' Olwen persisted.

'You prop him up on a chair in case anybody comes.'

'This is awful.' Olwen murmured, struggling back into her dress.

'He do anything to you?'

'No.' She shook her head. 'But I was ready . . .'

Together the girls lifted Brigham on to the sofa, put a cushion beneath his head and left his feet sticking out as if he were resting after a glass too many.

'Nobody will come at this time of night,' Olwen said with relief. 'At least we've time to think.'

At that there was a knock at the door.

'Marshall!'

305

'You go.'

'No, you.'

The knock sounded again.

As she moved into the hallway Olwen saw the shape of a woman pressing herself against the glass and trying to see in. She opened the door. 'Myra!'

Myra glanced at the anxious face opposite her, so different from everything she had expected. Where were the chandeliers? The cigars? The sound of blackjack and roulette going on? She was wearing her very best clothes and had caught a considerable chill walking up the road to Khandallah, having twice missed her way and been obliged to knock on strange houses in the dark.

'What you are doing here?' Olwen gasped, not asking her in.

'I – I . . .' Myra faltered. She felt like crying. Standing on the verandah there was not a light to be seen. It was as dark and rural as Moke.

'Who is it?' came a voice from behind the door.

'My – my – sister,' Olwen murmured.

In the next minute Myra saw a wheat-coloured face peering anxiously at her. She was seeing her first Maori.

'Your sister?'

Olwen nodded.

'Better come in then,' Happi said in a resigned fashion, ambling back to where they had left Brigham.

'Wait!' Olwen called, but already Myra had stepped into the hallway and was heading after Happi. 'He – he's had too much to drink,' Olwen apologized.

Myra looked at Brigham. 'He hasn't,' she contradicted. 'He's dead.'

At that she burst into tears and flung herself on a chair sobbing, informing all that she had travelled all day and all night and for a week before that and she had come all this way and Khandallah had turned out to be nothing more than an unlit hill top and she had caught her death of cold and here was the man she had been dreaming about for weeks – dead!

'Take off that ridiculous hat and be quiet, Myra.' Olwen said tersely.

For a while Myra defended the hat then fell into a sulk. She had left her trunk in town, she informed them, and was not carrying it another inch.

'What do you mean, you've been dreaming about this man?' Olwen asked.

'I know him. He's a friend of mine. I met him when he came to Hexham. We took tea together!' Myra protested.

Olwen sat down.

'You have been talking to this man?'

'He was very charming to me.'

'How *dare* you come here criticizing my arrangements when you have done so much to destroy them!' Olwen shouted.

Myra was aghast. 'He called to pay his respects. I was only civil.'

Happi looked from one of them to the other then wandered into the kitchen.

Olwen dropped at her desk: 'This is a mess.'

'He's supposed to be a friend of yours and here he is dead in your room!' burst out Myra. 'Why?'

Olwen whirled. 'Perhaps you aren't going to get an explanation! Perhaps, young lady, now that you've come to Wellington you will find things are not all that you had imagined. In fact there could be one or two things which will surprise you very much!'

Myra blanched. Never had Olwen spoken to her like this before. If this was the way things were in the North Island perhaps she did not want to stay.

'You can start by making yourself a bed upstairs and then keep out of my way,' Olwen said bitterly.

'If it hadn't been for him I wouldn't have come here!' Myra hurled back as she stepped into the hall. 'I liked him!'

'Do you think we should dismember his body and get rid of it in bits?' Olwen asked, leaning on Happi who was washing fruit.

'That man no good for anything except to be cooked and fed to dogs.' Happi laughed. She seemed totally undisturbed by the nightmare going on around her. Brigham's body was of no more significance than a turnip to her.

'I don't think you realize how serious this is. This is not the *pa* or the *kainga*. This is a public place. Part of the land under Queen Victoria with her police force and law. It's not a matter of doing what your neighbours agree with: it's obeying certain laws and one of them is not to be caught with a dead body.'

Happi went on smiling.

'She'll understand when the police come around,' Myra informed them coolly from the door.

Still Happi kept her radiant smile. 'I'll start walking right now,' she said, drying her hands. 'You know where I'm going,'

Back to the *marae* Olwen realized with relief. 'Leave it to you, Happi,' she nodded.

'Where's she going?' Myra demanded as Happi blundered off into the darkness.

'Don't worry about her.'

'It's very dark out there. Someone might attack her.'

'I don't think so.'

Myra stared awkwardly at Olwen.

308

'While she's gone, Myra, I think you and I could have a little talk.'

Feeling she was about to come in for a ribbing Myra nodded meekly.

'I may have to leave here,' Olwen began.

'Don't leave me alone in the house with a body!'

'No one is going to leave you alone,' Olwen said, reaching for her hand. Suddenly she felt ashamed. 'I'm sorry, Myra. I can see you looked forward to coming here. It's just there is so much you don't know . . . that none of you know. I'll tell you later but you must promise me one thing.'

'What?'

'Never, never to tell anyone what has happened to this man. Never tell anyone you found him here! You must promise me this, Myra, whatever should happen between us; if we should become the worst of enemies in the future you must never divulge this.'

Myra nodded solemnly.

'That's not enough, Myra,' Olwen said, racking her brains to think of some final way of putting the seal on it. They were not the sort to cut their thumbs and mix blood. 'Do you believe in the Bible? Will you swear on it?'

'Do you have one?' Myra asked coolly.

'No, but Happi does.' Olwen went to fetch it, hoping Myra would not notice the missing pages which Happi used to roll her cigarettes in.

'I want you to swear, not only on the Bible but on the heads of your sisters and brothers and on your own head, the head of your father, my mother, this dead man, your nieces and nephews from your sister Lizabeth and all that you hold sacred . . .'

Myra paused. She wouldn't get far in Wellington if she

didn't swear and, truthfully, what did it matter to her? The man was dead. There would be others. 'Very well – I swear.'

'Do you realize the solemnity of this?' Olwen asked. Myra nodded. 'Not to put it too finely – there's more where that came from,' Olwen said, nodding towards the stiff body.

'For goodness' sake, Olwen,' Myra scolded. 'For the love that you and I bear each other and always have done – despite your rude reception of me this time – *I swear . . .*'

The following evening as darkness fell Khandallah was greeted with a loud noise as a party of rowdy, clearly drunken Maoris staggered up the hill towards the house the neighbours had come to regard as the troublemaker's house, Miss Laird's! Curtains went back, people grumbled, a volley of remarks followed their progress. 'Do you hear that? There they go again! Shouldn't be allowed!' It surprised no one when the party passed Olwen's house, ('Too drunk to remember!') hesitated, turned back and ploughed up the three steps on to her verandah and began hammering on her door. 'Hope they break it!'

There was the sound of a bottle crashing.

'Brought their own drink with them! She's not coming to the door though! Much good it will do her. You watch!'

Sure enough the door gave way under their pushing and soon the curtains were down and the singing and swaying had begun, occasional glasses were heard falling into the gully and a scene which Myra had never associated with the high life of Wellington was once again taking place before their eyes.

Up and down the street people told each other they couldn't stand much more of this; wives asked husbands to put on slippers and go out on to the balcony and glare; husbands decided to walk past the house and frown; one was in fact on the point of doing so when they heard Olwen's high voice shouting: 'I've had enough! Now get out of here all of you and don't come any more!' Quickly curtains were pulled back again in time to see the Maoris tumbling and falling down the steps, trying to scramble back up again, leaning on each other for support, tripping and stumbling – one of them so drunk he was virtually being hauled along – his feet scraping the ground yet surrounded and held up by his *haka* dancing mates as if he were a hero. They saw Olwen silhouetted on the top of the steps, a younger girl standing behind her as if for protection: 'Just stay away!' she was shouting.

Thus exited Brigham ungraciously from this world with the feeling in Khandallah that the episode had served the young lady right!

With relief Olwen sank down on the couch rubbing her head. 'I shall have to go away, Myra, you realize that.'

'Why?'

'For a short while. In case anyone misses him.'

'What will I say if anyone comes here?'

'You've never met the man. You don't know what they're talking about. Why should you say anything?'

Myra nodded dumbly. 'Will she cook for me?'

'Happi? I hardly think so!'

'I don't want her in the house.'

'I can't leave you here alone: you know that.'

'When I came to Wellington I didn't want – '

'Another thing, don't lend Happi money. Give it to her.'

'Why?'

'They don't understand individual ownership any more than it would occur to you or I that your cape was simply a cape that either of us could wear depending on who got there first.'

'But surely they can see that money – '

'They haven't always had it,' Olwen sighed, suddenly realizing why the *kainga* had been unable to understand blackmail. It was not because they lacked the concept of manipulation but because they had not grasped the role of money in her society. 'It's just magic buttons to them to be quickly spent. It has no ongoing value.'

'Well, I'm not giving her money,' Myra said angrily. 'And I don't want her in the house, or her friends. No one will want to come here.'

'I think you'd better keep quiet for a while, Myra, and try fitting in,' Olwen pointed out grimly. 'This house isn't mine. I'm –'

'And I suppose the boutique was a pack of lies too!' Myra railed.

' – merely caretaking it. If people, especially the neighbours, were aware of this I would have been put out long ago.'

'This is not my idea of Wellington,' Myra growled.

'I can't tell you how to live,' Olwen concluded. 'But Happi is always welcome here and if she asks you to do something – because she was here first – you should fit in.'

With these final words of advice Olwen sent a written message via Happi informing Marshall that owing to a sudden emergency she had been obliged to return briefly to Hexham. She read the note through twice before sending it and, confident that Marshall would be convinced by its sincerity, threw a change of clothes into her portmanteau and headed hurriedly for the unexpected steamer south.

Chapter 22

The days passed and no policeman came. Perhaps owing to his natural furtiveness or the inherent immorality of his business, Brigham had not been in the habit of advertising his manoeuvres and this, plus the lateness of the hour, meant he had aroused no attention when visiting Olwen. At first even Marshall did not miss him until gradually, like a draught from an open door, he sensed something awry. He had, however, been so exercised by postponing the wedding yet a second time that the disappearance of Brigham was small beer indeed. The man had not even had the courtesy to inform him when he had previously departed for the South Island, he recalled. It was conceivable that, having returned, he had gone north or found a sponsor for one of his financial schemes. At the least he might have sent an apology with regard to the guest list.

In Hexham Olwen waited. Time ticked by. Ceci noticed that nobody wrote to her and she wrote to no one. Possibly, she concluded, her circle of friends was so small that her detailed letters had represented the exaggeration of loneliness. There had, however, been three curious postcards, all addressed to Olwen in her own hand, yet bearing nothing other than a childishly executed tick mark of the sort given for good work in school. These cards, she noticed, Olwen snatched quickly from the mat and hid in her bosom. What she did not know was that what Olwen dreaded receiving was a card marked with a cross.

Despite the nonchalance she tried to enact, in her own heart Olwen was afraid. She had lied and deceived and become enmeshed in dishonesty. Nonetheless, now that the obstacle of Brigham had been removed, she intended to persist in the pretence that she was a single woman. There was nothing for it now but to bite the bullet and wait it out. The actual date of her wedding had passed while she was wandering among the spoiled roses of Hexham and, although she frequently reminded herself she was her father's daughter and he must have been up to a fair bit of skulduggery in his time and got away with it, still that sense of personal disgust at her own dishonesty remained.

On the other hand she regretted Brigham's passing not at all. When she returned she would be free of him and that thought was so wonderful she felt like screaming with fear, for the sense of relief that was creeping up on her as the days passed was so immense she could not grasp it. At times she felt moved to hug Ceci and confide in her, tell her she had gotten away with it, had tilted at fate and won! But still she must wait for those last two postcards to come in from Happi. If they were again marked with a tick she would know that she had not been found out; that in the six weeks since she had left Khandallah no one had come asking questions.

When the time came to leave, Olwen felt sufficiently elated to embrace Ceci and say; 'I may be having some good news for you soon.'

'I'm glad to hear it,' Ceci replied, pleased at her joy but at a loss to understand it.

I could almost tell her now, Olwen thought. The divorce may have come by now and if not I shall certainly proceed without it. That matter is very small beer after what I have been through. As she climbed into the Moke trap which would take her down to the trunk route relief soared in Olwen's heart. She was beyond danger. She could give herself to Marshall. Repeating this over and again, she felt her love and desire for him rising, reaching towards its highest limits.

'Did she tell you she was to be married?' Marshall asked.

Myra eased a sliver of ice cream on to her spoon and raised her eyes in a refreshing smile. 'Who?'

'Olwen.'

Returning the spoon to the plate Myra frowned as if confused: 'But I thought you knew she had gone back to the South Island – '

'To her home. I know. I know,' Marshall interrupted.

Myra put her head on one side: 'Well,' she said carefully, 'To *my* home really.'

Marshall frowned.

'I like it up here,' Myra informed him. 'How long has this kiosk been built? It commands such an incredible view and is quite the place to come.'

Marshall explained that Kelburne Heights was in fact so popular that there was even talk of constructing a funicular.

'A funicular?'

'A cable car, you know – like San Francisco.'

'Oh yes!' Myra cried excitedly.

Marshall smiled. What a delightful child she was. Well – her body was that of a woman of course but her enthusiasm, her innocence, was childlike, full of trust.

Myra placed another piece of ice cream in her mouth. If her friends could see her now!

'We will have a real botanic garden and zoo one day too,' Marshall continued, half sensing that Myra would like to put her head on his shoulder. 'So we can exhibit the plants and creatures of other places as curiosities.' He glanced at her. 'I'm sorry, my child. Would you like to

315

meet youngsters rather than listen to my boring ramblings? Shall I introduce you to Gwen and other "grand people" who can be company for you? There is much to do in Wellington,' he said sadly. 'If one has only a companion to do it with.'

Though he felt it his duty to show Myra around in Olwen's absence, as time passed without her return, Marshall fell gently to questioning Myra and found her refreshingly forthcoming. She was not at a loss to point out that Hexham belonged to *her* father but he had been very pleased when he had married Olwen's mother because he had long liked her. Gradually the story of the 'step' situation unfolded, Myra not stinting details of unsavoury West Coast alehouse implications but hinting at brawling miners, a pit disaster, people trying to sue a reputable company and upsetting the shareholders and a distinct lack of interest in going to church. Olwen's mother, she informed him, had married a coal miner but, she suggested, Olwen's father was not 'actually' a coal miner. Though he was careful to let no expression play on his face Marshall was surprised. The girl did not seem to realize she was describing his intended's background in the most unfavourable light.

'Why did she go home?' he asked suddenly.

'Her mother was ill,' Myra stated flatly. What did it matter if he believed her or not? She had promised not to tell about the dead man and she hadn't done. 'Why do you look sad?' she asked.

In reply Marshall shook his head and patted her hand.

To take his mind off Olwen, Marshall took Myra on the weekend boat to Days Bay. It was a favourite turn-out for Wellington's picnickers, the decks of the steamer which cut across the bay being crowded with merrymakers, distinctively dressed Jewish folk, Italian families playing musical instruments and taking the hat around.

'What are they?' Myra asked, clinging to Marshall's arm as a man in a large straw hat passed close to her. Already she had been badly frightened by a Syrian hawker who had knocked on the door at Khandallah shortly after Olwen's departure to know if she wanted any finnibrums. Never having met a real foreigner close up she had gawped while the man knelt on the verandah, opened a large case divided into sections and spread before her a selection of goods which would have put any Christchurch department store to shame. Were it not for the fact that she did not want to look like a country girl from the backlots, she would gladly have got on her hands and knees to paddle amongst them.

'Oh, Jewish people, part of the community, Italians . . .' Marshall's voice trailed off as he saw James heading towards them.

'My dear,' said James somewhat effeminately. 'And who is your charming partner?'

Myra blushed with pleasure. Not twenty-four hours ago Marshall had been helping her on to the hurdy gurdy, lifting her up into a chair as if she were a small child, yet already she was being mistaken for his lady.

'Hetty is with me,' James went on. 'I insist you bring your hamper when we arrive and sit with us.'

'We didn't bring a hamper,' Marshall mumbled.

'Then share ours, my good man, share ours of course,' James insisted.

'I'm sorry,' Marshall said, gently touching Myra's elbow as James moved away. 'I hope this won't be too dull for you.'

But nothing bored Myra. She was not bored by the London magazines which Hetty lent her; nor by the

317

exciting conversations she overheard between Venables, Marshall and other Notables some of whom were even shipping coffins of dead Chinese men back to China!

'Are we boring you, dearest?' Marshall would lightly ask, crossing to bend over her as she sat. Myra would beam up at him. 'I haven't seen a smile like that in a long time,' he would say, laying a hand on her shoulder.

'What a sweet child,' Hetty told Gwen. 'So much more – amenable – than her sister.'

'Be careful, the child will hear you.'

'Look at them now,' Gwen said. All heads turned. 'I'm not so sure "child" is the word to describe her.'

As he took Myra home that night it occurred to Marshall that he had done a good job of looking after her: Olwen had that to thank him for. He had enjoyed her company, particularly in the little things – the way she had been scandalized when at the theatre a man had leaned forward and used his stick to tilt at a woman's large hat which was blocking his view of the stage. It occurred to him that he had not told her it was he whom Olwen had been about to marry.

'Shall we walk through here?' he asked gently, indicating the poorer district of the city which Olwen had found so moving.

Myra hesitated and reached for Marshall's hand: she did not want to go in. As she stood there, her eyes big as a doe's with fear, the exhaust hole of a buried sewer pipe let off a loud gasp. 'Ahh!' cried Myra rushing into Marshall's arms.

'It's nothing, nothing,' he said, stroking her hair. 'Just the sewers. They do that all the time.'

'I thought the devil was behind, blowing on me,' Myra breathed. At that point she wondered if it were worth crying, for she did so enjoy standing in Marshall's arms.

'My poor, dear child,' he murmured and she felt his lips lightly brush her hair. 'Did you know whom Olwen was to marry?' Myra waited for it. 'Me,' he sighed.

A small smile tugged at Myra's mouth. 'Was to?' she asked innocently.

Again Marshall sighed. And again he kissed her.

Returning to Khandallah Olwen sensed a cool insolence in Myra. The girl swore she had told no one about Brigham so clearly there was no problem there. Nor was there sign of Happi but again – this was quite usual.

'Did you keep an eye on the shop?'

'Yes.'

'Have there been any messages from Marshall?'

'From who?'

'A man called Marshall.'

'No one called Marshall left a specific message for you,' Myra replied truthfully.

'I'm going to invite him around to dinner, Myra. You must have friends. Do you think you could arrange to be out tonight?'

'Why, certainly,' Myra smiled. 'I shall make a point of arranging a trip to Lyall Bay. We can be discussing it.'

'We?' Olwen looked queryingly at Myra. There was a racecourse at Lyall Bay with trotting meets and hunt meetings. 'Who will you plan this trip with?' she asked curiously.

'With Gwen,' Myra replied.

Olwen frowned. Gwen was not the sort of person you bumped into and visited casually.

'What time would you like me to be out from?' Myra asked.

'I think maybe you'd better stay here after all.'

319

Myra went to the cabinet and poured herself a drink. 'You didn't tell me you were marrying Marshall.'

Olwen swallowed. 'Did you say anything?'

Myra shook her head. 'I did not tell him you were already married. Nor did I mention you'd dispatched Brigham.'

'Thank you.'

'But I don't think it's a particularly moral idea, do you? Bigamy?'

'Don't play God with me, Myra,' Olwen said bitterly. 'I didn't invite you here.'

Myra shrugged insolently.

'In fact, now that I'm back, I wouldn't mind having my house to myself. I think I will make alternative arrangements for you. Clearly you've made friends.'

Myra began to smirk. 'I'm sure I shall be able to manage, Olwen,' she said mock sweetly. 'Don't worry about me.'

With considerable tension Olwen prepared for the evening. It was a long time since she had seen Marshall and the mixture of joy and apprehension was quite painful. When the doorbell sounded she heard Myra run forward but as Marshall's voice broke the stillness, found she was too nervous to put her head out of the kitchen where she was preparing food.

'I'll be with you in a minute, Marshall,' she called.

'Very well, Olwen.'

'Myra, please take Marshall into the front room.'

Glancing quickly into the corridor she almost thought Marshall was greeting Myra with a kiss. A trick of the light, she told herself, as the two darkened shapes moved apart and Marshall stepped round Myra into the hall.

In the front room they linked hands and kissed passionately against the door's back.

320

'I wish you had told me sooner,' Myra whispered. 'The pain of it.' She placed a hand on her heart.

'I apologize my one.'

'Quickly! Sit down!'

'Marshall!' cried Olwen, appearing in the doorway.

He got quickly to his feet as if an undertaker had entered.

Sensing it, Olwen hesitated. 'I'm sorry I was so long – I mean away so long,' she began. 'My mother – '

'How are things at your – home?' Marshall asked pointedly. Myra looked at her nails.

'Hexham? Fine! Why wouldn't they be? My mother recovered but my – my father . . .' she began again. But Marshall was already nodding as if he did not believe a word she was saying.

'Mr Cavanaugh has been most kind to me while you were away,' Myra said, putting, Olwen felt, the slightest emphasis on the words 'most kind'.

'It was nothing,' Marshall said stiffly.

'Hardly nothing, dear,' Myra said, placing her hand momentarily on his knee then withdrawing it. 'I do declare we have seen all the sights. Not only that but Marshall took me on a most interesting tour of the, how shall I say, poorer parts of town which I found quite – touching.'

The ground began to move under Olwen. 'What is this, Marshall?' she asked. 'I'm glad you have looked after Myra but – '

'But what?' Myra asked sharply.

Now it was Marshall's turn to look uncomfortable. 'The thing is – the thing, you know,' he stammered.

And in that instant with a sinking feeling Olwen realized that in the space of a few short weeks, Marshall and Myra had 'become sincere'.

* * *

'How dare you humiliate me like this in front of her!' Olwen screamed at Marshall. 'I thought you wanted to marry!'

'Yes! I want a wife and a decent situation!' Marshall fired back at her.

'With a mere child?'

'With my guidance she will do very well.'

'Your ridiculous male vanity!'

'She is young, pure – '

'Paint a picture!'

' – trusting and above all honest.'

'Everything I'm not.'

'You think you can start a marriage on lies and deceit?'

Olwen backed off. She had now traced the turning-point in Marshall's pursuit of her to the time shortly after Brigham had come back from the South Island.

'I knew you were not entirely free to marry me,' Marshall stated. 'That I did not mind. Don't you think Brigham attempted to blackmail me too?'

'Did you pay him?'

'No!'

Olwen felt her face crumbling.

'What I minded about you,' Marshall went on, 'was that you did not tell me about him, did not confide in me. That was why I urged you to hasten the wedding. In order to force the issue.'

Olwen stared at him in disbelief.

'But,' said Marshall pacing, 'it became very clear you would persist in your deceit.'

'Independence you mean,' Olwen corrected. 'You were originally attracted to me by my indifference to you, remember? You suddenly expect me to be unable to resolve my own problems?'

'I would have looked after you.'

Olwen crossed the room and stood by the window. 'It was my business,' she said.

'There we have it!'

Turning, Olwen sensed that Marshall was relieved for this way out. Yes, he had been made to wait week upon week. Yes, the wedding had been delayed and he had lost face. Yes, the wedding could now go ahead – but with a different bride. At eighteen Myra was four years younger than her, a mere four years. Supple, for the time being obedient, as easy to fit into one's life as a pocket handkerchief. No wonder Marshall was pleased. She gave him a belittling look.

'So where is Brigham now?' he fired at her.

'Look for yourself,' she replied with disdain.

Olwen closed up the house at Khandallah. As she pulled down the shutters and bolted the back door, she wondered about Happi. There was no point in pinning a note to the verandah, for Happi was no scholar. Nor would the girl expect her to leave any message. In case of trouble she knew Olwen would come to the *marae*. That she did not see her would be no cause for alarm for Happi had no particular sense of time. Having returned the key of the Khandallah house Olwen left instructions at her workshop that, after work in hand was finished, no further orders should be taken. She paid up her workforce and made arrangements with an agent to have the premises rented in her absence. Her decision made, she stored her trunk once again in a warehouse and prepared to abandon it for a considerable period. She would return to England, confront Edmund and wring from him and his family who had rejected her the final freedom of a divorce. Like Faith, she would endure what was necessary to extract her freedom and, despite any disgrace attached, embark on the future to which she as an independent woman had a right. Not for her any moping in Wellington. And she certainly didn't intend to stay around for Myra's marriage to Marshall! At least the girl was still sworn to secrecy about Brigham and this she could trust. She would get a divorce. She would agree any grounds. She would free herself.

Having obtained the receipt for her trunk, in the time left before the steamer would sail, she took a last walk through those parts of Wellington where she had been happiest with Marshall. Past the pawnshop of Taranaki Street she wandered, through Tory Place and Sage's Lane, by Francis Place, Tui Street and Alma Lane . . . This way and that she went till finally she found herself in the vacant lots behind Cuba Street where the poor kept their animals and grew vegetables. Suddenly she paused. What was that smell in her nostrils? It was the sickly sweet smell of the late autumn fennel drifting towards her. That smell she had first smelt the day she set out to plan her deception of Marshall.

Part Two

Chapter 23

The man Stebbins stood on the ridge. Below him through the last line of trees he thought he could make out a thin man bending to the ground, touching it in puzzlement. Stebbins froze. The man was pushing the hat back on his head, scratching it more in alarm than anger. Now he was standing up and looking about him. Stebbins concealed himself and moved in closer. Dirty and hungry, having worn out his welcome in many lowland farms he had not expected good luck — namely the rabbit — to have got here ahead of him. Possibly the clearing now opening up might be more than just a place for a bite to eat: perhaps a home for a few months till he moved on to his regular winter patch. From a distance he tailed Reg through his fields noting the man pause to turn over leaves, kick at hummocks in the ground or angrily fling stones into burrows. Stebbins bent to pick up some rabbit droppings which he put in his pocket: it was always a good idea to leave some and spread the others around. In the first place the smell of it encouraged rabbits to move farther afield and ruin more land and secondly, seeing pellets convinced the landowners that rabbits were already there.

Reg moved on towards his cabin. There was no doubt about it: their crops were getting smaller. Even the plants in Annie's window boxes had been eaten and close neighbours — a few hills away — had begun complaining. Reg half suspected they knew where the rabbits were coming from for on going into the hamlet he had been embarrassed by remarks. The religious people didn't have much to say

327

but those who had come later as the hamlet grew, the storekeeper with his home-brewed ale and the cartwright and blacksmith, though not affected themselves by his rabbits, must have overheard the remarks they repeated with such glee as Reg passed by. For all that, they were glad to buy from him yet the fact of it was, he was beginning to grow frightened. As he stood pondering Reg heard shots in the hills behind him and felt doubly ashamed. Part of him felt, given that they were his rabbits, people had no right to be taking them yet on the other hand the beasts were trespassing. He moved on through Annie's vegetable garden without bothering to look at the damage and stepped into the cabin.

'Them rabbits'll have to go, Annie,' he said firmly.

Annie kept quiet. She knew for a fact they were spreading yet every morning she and Little Annie loved to go to the remnants of the hutch and feed cabbage stalks and left-over leaves to them. 'Now you don't mean that, Reg,' she cajoled.

Reg said nothing. Didn't need to. This time tomorrow he'd've shot the lot.

Annie put his meal before him thinking that it would be nice if he washed his hands, yet, given his mood, better to say nothing. Little Annie came up and saw her father eating his food, frowning.

'I know we've had a hard year,' her mother began. 'Winter wasn't – '

'Nothing to do with winter,' Reg interrupted. 'Think ahead, girl.' He nodded towards Little Annie. 'The fact of the matter is – '

'You got a few pennies saved! I know it!' Annie burst out. 'That child is as fond of them rabbits as – '

'We can't make improvements on the land with rabbits, woman!' Reg shouted. 'We got to make improvements.'

Annie was silent. It was true all the improvements they had to show was their fence, some felled trees, their cabin and the broken waterpump but still . . .

'Ain't nothing here a season wouldn't grow over and where're your improvements then?' Reg asked righteously.

'Reg,' Annie murmured, running to him. 'There's a man in the clearing!'

Reg turned to face the door. 'Get in the back. Take the child.'

As Annie moved to the corner of the room Reg kicked the box away and grabbed his gun.

'Rabbit-hoh!' came a muffled voice. In an instant Reg and Annie were at the door.

'You keep 'em! We got our own!' Reg shouted.

The man came over, eyeing their dwelling as he did so. With pride Reg read the look to mean 'nice place you got here'. Stebbins pulled a string of rabbits from behind his back. 'Know where I got these?' he asked.

'Heard you.'

'You want to be careful,' Annie warned him. 'People around here'll more than box your ears if you're caught.'

'Well, come in,' Reg said, remembering the hospitality for which the backblocks were famous, daft though the idea may have been. 'Sit down and eat,' he went on.

Well, well, thought Annie. Am I seeing the house owner here? Nonetheless she produced an enamelled plate and tipped some of the evening food on to it. It was a pity to get into it at lunch time but she could throw another potato in the pot . . .

As Reg and Stebbins slurped up their food and wiped their fingers across the plates, each one waiting to see if the other would raise it to his face to lick, Annie took in that the man was a professional rabbiter who moved about the country seeking and trapping rabbits.

329

'Don't see why we'd want to share our rabbits with you,' Reg said somewhat sharply.

Stebbins grinned. 'Let us finish this good food,' He nodded towards Annie. 'Then let us walk. Let me show you how many months – I mean weeks – your clearing will support you.'

'Clearing!' Annie said indignantly. 'We got fields beyond.'

'Have you?' asked Stebbins in seemingly genuine amazement. 'Well I'll be jiggered!' He scratched his head as if he hadn't meant to be rude.

Reg picked his plate up and licked it.

'Not as if they look like fields now, is it?' Stebbins asked slyly as his face vanished behind his own plate.

Annie felt like screaming. It was bad enough to have the man in the house yet for Reg to lick his plate in front of him as if it were their custom, for the man to lick his plate, and all this in front of Little Annie.

'Are you sayin',' Reg was asking with annoying naïvety, 'that by your experience of places we're in a bad way here?'

Stebbins wiped his mouth on the back of his hand. 'I seen worse. I won't lie. Myself I don't take on small places like this. Folk can't afford me.' He got to his feet.

Instantly Reg jumped up.

'Know what they say,' Stebbins said, pausing in their doorway. 'A stitch in time . . .'

In seconds Reg was after him, hurrying across the clearing.

'Don't touch them plates,' Annie said sharply as Little Annie climbed on Reg's box to trace her finger in the dip of his dish.

As the men walked on, Reg began to appreciate the gravity of their situation as pointed out to him by Stebbins.

'Ain't you never heard of the Rabbit Nuisance Act?' Stebbins asked.

Reg shook his head, feeling once more his ignorance and inability to read properly had caught him out. As usual he did not like to ask.

'Rabbit Nuisance Acts y'know,' Stebbins went on as the men walked. 'It's about puttin' the land into rabbit districts. All comin' up from the south, rabbits.'

Reg nodded his head.

'I remember me one place.' Stebbins paused. 'Musta shot 608 hares that day.'

'You?'

'Gun club. See they mix their huntin' and boozin'. Gets 'em out in the fresh air.'

'Ain't no rabbits up there,' Reg said as Stebbins stepped out towards the ridge.

'Ain't they?' Stebbins asked.

Reg walked blindly after him.

'See, I seen great long wires with millions of rabbit skins drying on them.'

'Millions?'

Stebbins nodded. 'Export 'em, don't you know? Big export trade. Next time you're in your club in Christchurch you ask.'

Reg looked down.

'Now see here, this is what I was sayin',' Stebbins said gravely, pointing to a handful of rabbit droppings he had left in a most unlikely place.

A gasp involuntarily escaped Reg. 'I had no idea they was up here,' he said sadly.

'Reminds me of one time I tried to get a ride on the back of a train only to find all eight wagons chocker with rabbit carcasses. Couldn't get in. I was balanced between wagons waiting for the thing to stop. Finally I got in with the guard. You know how many rabbit carcasses they had on that train?'

Reg shook his head.

'Twenty thousand,' Stebbins said sternly. 'You know where they was coming from? Just south of here and down a bit.'

As they walked on Stebbins began to whistle. 'Look here,' he said gripping Reg's shoulder, 'I 'ope I haven't 'urt your feelings.'

Reg frowned quizzically.

'You wasn't thinking of farmin' rabbits was you?' Standing on the spot Stebbins turned around to survey Reg's less than immaculate holding. 'Because my advice to you,' Stebbins went on, 'is that the return on rabbits, flesh and fur and all, is about one-fifth of what you'll get off of ewes. Or was it grain you was into up here?'

Reg took off his hat and wiped at his eyes. He did not like the way the man kept saying 'was'. He hadn't finished by a long chalk yet. 'Why don't you walk back with us and stop awhile,' Reg said gruffly.

Stebbins shook his head. 'You tell your missus thanks for the grub. Seein' as things are gettin' a bit lively up here I might season over. Find a place that needs clearin' and clear it out.' Again he spun in an irritating manner as if any direction he chose would welcome him.

'You reckon we've had it up here?' asked Reg.

Stebbins shrugged. 'Good luck mate,' he said.

'Now wait on,' Reg called, hurrying after him. 'I can't afford to pay you much – you could put up with us, split the catch right down the middle.'

'I'd have to 'ave all the pelts,' Stebbins said quietly.

'Suit yerself,' Reg shrugged. 'Don't want them stinking things drying near the house anyway!'

As she stood on the edge of the clearing watching the

two men gesticulating, Annie saw with dread that Reg had turned Stebbins towards her and was now leading him back towards their settlement. Deep within her she knew the man meant trouble, that he was unclean and unworthy of their hospitality and of their home. That he would share it she had no doubt. Unless he had money on him he would rely on them to provide him with bullets and, one way and another, though Reg might urge her to look on the bright side she watched with dread as they stepped towards her clearing.

'Afternoon again, Missus,' Stebbins said brightly.

Annie glared.

Reg knew she was angry and couldn't look her in the eye. 'I'll see about getting you a bed made,' he called gruffly, vanishing behind the cabin.

'If you're so keen on getting rid of the rabbits why don't you do it yourself?' Annie asked, hurrying after him.

'With respecks, Ma'am,' came the annoying whine of Stebbins from behind her, 'it's a professional job – rabbit clearin'.'

'Take ahold of this,' Reg said, frowning up at Stebbins and indicating a large flat slab of wood. Together the men carried it inside, propped it on sawn-off tree trunks which had lain waiting to be chopped, and installed it under the window – directly across from Reg and Annie's bed.

'I can't sleep with you with him in here!' Annie spoke urgently to Reg.

'Don't be silly, woman,' Reg growled. 'Won't be for long.'

'Well, I'm still not sleeping on the same bed with you in front of him,' Annie insisted.

'Suit yourself,' said Reg, walking from the cabin, not making it clear which of them would retain their original slab bed.

Annie glanced at Stebbins now sitting on his slab, boots off, pulling his filthy blue woollen stockings off right in front of their table.

'Don't mind me,' he said.

Furious, Annie swung from the cabin.

As the weeks went by she adjusted to Stebbins' presence. Every time she wakened he seemed to be looking at her and the fact of his being there meant she no longer removed her underthings before retiring and had rarely the chance for a decent wash. More water had to be carried up by Reg, it becoming more precious than their food and although she could not stand the man, Annie tolerated him. It would, after all, only be for the one season, then they could return to normal, make good their losses and be more careful in future. She had not forgiven Reg for shooting her pet rabbits in cold blood, even if he had done it to impress Stebbins. Sitting in the cabin with her hands over Little Annie's ears she had listened to the shots ringing in the clearing and when she peeped over the sill had seen Reg casually pulling their rabbits from the hutch by a foot or ear, whatever came to hand – and flinging them on the floor like so much rubbish.

Recalling the painful scene, she stooped by the tin bath to wash her chest. If she had it right Stebbins should be out combing the hills on one of his final 'professional' inspection runs prior to quitting them. Little Annie was asleep on their bed and Reg away down in the hamlet settling up their credit at the store. At least that was one thing to be said for Stebbins. They had made *some* money off the rabbits even though their vegetable stock had been severely depleted both by the rabbits and Stebbins! Carefully she scooped deliciously cool water in her hands and let it run between her breasts. How good it felt! How good it would be to actually sink into a deep pool in a country river, the sort she used to frequent on the West Coast between wanderings. Of course here she dare not remove her blouse, she thought, reaching for the soap and rubbing vigorously. On the West Coast between mining towns chances of discovery had been so unlikely a quick glance around was all that it took before slipping off one's clothes and dropping into a pool. Sighing, she cocked her head to listen to a bird moving from tree to tree whistling a warning. You did not need a dog in the backblocks: the birds told it all – a bird from a different species, a bigger bird, a trespassing bird . . . She threw the soap at the dish and missed. Watching it skidding into the woodshavings she realized they had reached a peak with their rabbit sales: the hamlet had been saturated with rabbit pie. Stebbins would need to hire a cart to take down his bundles of dried pelts. In any case, the rabbits seemed well and truly to have run out. Scooping up some more cool water she tipped it down her chest.

'Give us a look, then,' Stebbins' voice said from behind her.

Instantly Annie sought to drag her blouse together across her chest, conscious of the soap in her armpits sticking to it.

Stebbins stepped forward. He raised his dirty boot towards the large kerosine can of water Reg had carried up from the brook, which would have to last them all day. 'Kick it over, shall I?' he asked.

Annie hung on to her blouse. Stebbins started to tap at the can with his foot, tap! tap! tap! His foot rested on it, slowly moving it off balance as the twigs shifted beneath it. For an infinitesimal second the can balanced.

'Look!' said Stebbins again.

In a second Annie was on her feet, her blouse flapping open as she leaped at the can and saved it.

'Beautiful marbles,' Stebbins grinned appeasingly.

Annie straightened up, furious.

'You ever heard of the Elgin Marbles?' Stebbins asked.

Annie slapped him hard across the face.

'Makes 'em jaggle about, does that,' Stebbins advised her.

At that moment Reg entered the clearing.

Stebbins turned guiltily. 'I was just telling your wife them rabbits is good as taken care of.'

Reg nodded and went on into the house.

'Kin call me Jack if ye like,' Stebbins said to Annie, before walking after him.

Inside Reg was putting some money on the table. 'What I got left,' he said.

Stebbins looked at it. It wasn't a great deal – certainly not any use to him. He'd achieved his purpose of establishing a 'safe house' on the run between two of his regular bigger jobs. The place hadn't been up to much, barely tolerable, but good enough as a stop-over while the young rabbits he'd left to mature on a previous place came of age.

'I hope that man will be out of here soon,' Annie told Reg as he wandered back out into the sunshine.

'Why?'

'Never mind!'

'He done us a favour and never charged nothing,' Reg pointed out in that infuriating way men have of defending each other simply because both are men.

'I can't wait to see the back of him!' Annie almost swore.

At that moment Stebbins emerged from their cabin. 'Did I ever tell you where these rabbits originated from?' he asked in his 'professional' manner. 'They was let off in sand hills near Bluff, down in the South Land. Thirty years ago.'

'The wife and I have just been saying,' Reg began awkwardly. 'Reckon as how we can get along nicely now . . .'

'You showin' me the door?'

Reg tried to ease his way out of the situation. 'Just thinkin' as how you bein' professional like . . .'

'Tell him to never show his face again here,' Annie hissed in Reg's ear.

'Just go and say goodbye to your little girl,' Stebbins said, a malicious edge to his voice. Although he had already decided to leave, he hated people to ask him to.

'You don't touch her!' Annie shouted, running forward.

Stebbins shrugged, shouldered his swag and headed off across the clearing in the direction of the For Hire sheds where he had left his bales of dried pelts.

'I'm glad to see the back of him,' Annie repeated, slipping her hand through Reg's elbow. 'Thought we'd never get the smell of drying skin out of our nostrils!'

Reg agreed. 'Never knew nothing stunk as bad as that.'

Stebbins stepped off with a light foot. He wouldn't make a lot off the pelts. Rabbits were best collected mid-winter when their coats were good and thick, not summery and scratched up from fighting. But let them think it was the pelts he was after. Although they might not find an adult rabbit on their wanderings, he had been careful to leave a small healthy stock of young ones to allow the population to renew. Without any doubt, give or take a couple of seasons, he could be sure of a welcome there. What he had said about the trainloads of rabbit carcasses, the wire lines stretching from hill to hill on which pelts dried, had been totally true even if the woman Annie had chosen not to believe him. The way things were in the south where he had come from gave him every reason to believe he had an excellent future before him. And what's more, if the man Reg had any sense – he would down tools and do the same himself.

Chapter 24

'I envy Reg and Annie – out there starting over,' Ceci told Faith. 'The challenge of it.'

Faith looked up: 'Are you bored with Hexham?'

Ceci paused. If it was Hexham they were to talk about – she was not bored with Hexham: rather, Hexham did not seem right without Calvin. Certainly she 'loved' Ginger: certainly he was good to her – and it was not a matter of the occasional crooked mat or a name scratched on a banister – but Ginger did not fit in Hexham. He was not part of the country or the tradition that the house Hexham and the man Calvin belonged to. She had fitted, despite her background and, difficult and unnatural as he had been, Calvin had made Hexham. Without him it was a collection of rooms, artefacts and possessions. 'Piece-meal,' she thought. That was the word she would use to describe the way Ginger went about things. 'London was a grand place,' she said, turning to Faith. 'You should go there.'

Faith smiled. Since returning to Hexham she had become fond of Ceci, almost like a sister. 'Were you born in London?' she asked.

'I grew up in the Cheshire Dales. We came to London when I was eight because my father had died and we couldn't continue on.' Ceci shrugged. 'We stayed with my mother's sister in Clapham. Aunty May. She was a solitary woman. When I was fourteen my elder sister died, then the eldest married. That just left me and I came over here. My mother and aunt stayed on together. They're both dead now but my sister has family. Olwen had all her schooling in England, living with my sister's family.'

Faith leaned forward, her interest quickening at the thought of a fifteen-year-old girl striking out alone for New Zealand. It was a great deal braver than moving to Dunedin.

'Do you know it was in this very room that I was first asked about my origins?' Ceci smiled, remembering Mrs Laird's cross-questioning of her. 'I found it so difficult to talk about then, yet now it's a lifetime away.'

Faith nodded.

'I can tell you my life in three sentences, you see,' Ceci smiled. 'You should go to London, Faith. I couldn't possibly explain it to you and there's nothing here that would help you understand.'

'Here?'

'In Christchurch or Dunedin . . .' She let her voice trail off.

'Why don't you take a holiday?' Faith asked gently. 'With my father.'

Ceci frowned. She had never met or heard of anyone who had taken a holiday. 'Where on earth would we go?' she asked.

'You could go south.'

'South of what?'

'South of here! *Our* country,' Faith said almost irritably. 'The Southland. Fiordland. I've been reading about it in the travelling library. It's the last undiscovered frontier of our country and they've made a track through from one of the great lakes along some ravines and canyons to a place of amazing beauty.'

'I wouldn't want to get lost – '

'One woman has already walked the track. I read about

339

her,' Faith informed her. 'It rains a lot there. You have to go at the right time of year.'

'I don't see your father wanting to do that,' Ceci said, though in truth she was depressed by the realization that she did not want to spend three or four days wandering through silent fjords with Ginger, however mystical the scenery was. 'I don't think we could afford it. In fact I know we can't,' she added.

Faith looked at her steadily. 'It's a pity to be a prisoner of this house.'

So surprised was she to hear this Ceci could find no answer.

'Many of the rooms are not used. Make something of the accoutrements. Sell them.'

'And the memories?'

'Do you need the accoutrements to retain the memories? If the boys' racehorse was sufficiently important for you to sacrifice all that porcelain, surely you could part with a couple of rugs and take a holiday with my father.'

'This is very ironic,' Ceci told her. 'You weren't always so keen on me and your father.'

'I am now,' Faith said in that gentle yet firm voice she had developed since regaining peace of mind. 'You enjoyed the last auction. We all did. Lets go again and sell off the rugs.'

The two women moved out into the garden and wandered across the lawn where the first yellow and purple crocuses were beginning to sprout. Typical of Ginger to have thrown them there and let them root.

'This is a bit sudden . . .' Ceci hesitated.

'We'll take the rugs down and get them valued,' Faith suggested. 'Go to Christchurch for a weekend with my father. I can look after the house, the little there is to do here . . .'

* * *

'She doesn't feel like doing anything,' Faith told Ginger. 'She seems to think frequently of London.'

'Can't compete with London.' Ginger shrugged. 'Never been there. In any case it's natural to think about your childhood now and then.'

'I'm folding up some of the smaller rugs and packing them for you,' Faith insisted. 'I'm going to arrange for the Moke trap to take you down to the main trunk route tomorrow. I won't hear any argument.'

'Hold fire! The boys aren't back in Christchurch. Where will we stay?'

'I'm very tired of your excuses.' Faith frowned. 'Have you heard of hotels?'

From the doorstep she watched them leave, the bundle of rugs wrapped in brown paper behind them.

'Think it's a silly idea myself,' Ginger grumbled. 'Didn't want to be away at this time.'

'I didn't either, not that I had anything to do here.'

'Ought to get those crocuses out of the lawn now that I can see where they are,' he yawned as the trap squirted gravel towards them.

Swinging through the gates of Hexham Ceci thought she had never been on such a ridiculous journey in her life. She glanced at Ginger, wrapped in his scarf and realized they knew each other too well, that in fact a point of boredom had come.

'I suppose you're thinking about us not having children again?' Ginger asked.

'I wasn't.' But if we had, Ceci told herself, at least there would be some distraction. Gradually as the land evened out, they saw before them the trunk route and beyond it the great plain spreading away north towards Christchurch. 'I'm glad we're going,' Ceci said. 'Once you get out of Hexham things seem different.'

Ginger stared ahead.

'I'm glad Faith decided,' Ceci repeated, turning to smile at him.

'Christchurch isn't my favourite place,' Ginger crabbed.

Exactly, thought Ceci. That was the whole trouble: there was nowhere in New Zealand that was their favourite place! There was something missing in the social life, in the people, in the land itself. With shock she realized she was wishing she had never come. 'What am I doing here with you, an Irishman, bumping down the slopes towards this plain?'

'I don't know,' Ginger replied truthfully. 'What are any of us doing? Just waiting – and what for I don't know either.'

'I'm sorry. I'm feeling discontent. Calvin would never talk to me and I was so busy being martyred I longed for companionship, but now I've got it, I don't appreciate it!' She tried to laugh at herself.

'You're just going through a patch,' Ginger said kindly, taking her hands and rubbing them. 'Here, put my gloves on.'

Unable to shake the sense of disinterest they entered the Christchurch hotel, Ginger hoisting the bundle of rugs on to his shoulder and looking so like a country farm hand as they passed through the lobby Ceci found herself feeling irritated. She pushed open the door to their room, confident they would not enjoy their stay one bit and sat on the bed. 'Which rugs did she pack?'

'No idea. Didn't miss any.'

With the door closed she felt better. 'You don't have to undo the bundle. We can just leave it like that and take it home after.'

In response Ginger knelt on the floor and began tugging at the string. 'Won't get much for this bit of rubbish,' he said, pulling out, shaking and spreading a small rug before the window.

Ceci ambled over. It was a pale yellow rug she had quite forgotten, now almost paper thin, which had lain in Calvin's study. It had never been one of her favourites but to hear Ginger call it rubbish incensed her.

'Nor this,' he murmured, pulling out another.

In an instant Ceci's determination to keep Calvin's rugs turned to an intense desire to prove their worth by selling them.

'Huh! Calvin's old junk,' Ginger chortled, unfolding a blood-red rug with medallion shapes which Ceci vaguely remembered having seen in Calvin's summerhouse. It had kept his feet warm in winter. 'Not much point going any further, is there? Nobody'll want this junk!'

'Oh yes they will,' Ceci said softly.

Ginger looked up surprised.

'These are good rugs,' Ceci informed him, angry that he dared to criticize Calvin's taste. 'Though I can well appreciate you wouldn't be aware of it.'

'When have you ever seen a carpet of that sort in this country?' he demanded.

'It's a rug!'

'You see? We don't know the difference.'

Ceci hesitated. Maybe he was right. In the days when extremely wealthy people like the Lairds had come out there were people who would know a good rug when they saw one. But the big estates had been carved up and those days had gone: their descendants had been watered down and from what she had heard things had changed so much in England that the type of person coming out belonged to no class in particular. 'I'm sure someone in Wellington would appreciate their worth,' she said carefully. 'As an investment.'

Ginger shrugged. He wasn't going to argue with her. The rugs were completely unimportant. 'I'll tell you what,' he said good-naturedly. 'Tomorrow we'll go to a couple of shops with the rugs and give it a go. If they aren't interested, no harm done. We can always take them home and use them in the stables. Now, at least let's have dinner.'

Still bristling at the idea of Calvin's best rugs being used as horse blankets Ceci followed Ginger to the dining room. During the meal, which was greasy, she began to feel she disliked being in New Zealand. The conversations around were unbearably provincial and, though doubtless the people were happy enough in their lives, of a sudden she felt that she did not belong.

'What's the matter? Don't you like it?' Ginger asked, stuffing half a potato in to his mouth.

'I'm crazy about lamb chops, potatoes, boiled cabbage and pumpkin,' she said somewhat sharply. A few tables away a man turned to glance at the raised voice.

'I wouldn't dream of criticizing anything in this island paradise,' Ceci went on.

The man began to smile.

'I think the people are wonderful, the food is marvellous and scenery breathtaking!' she said loudly.

Two more tables turned to stare.

'I'm absolutely thrilled that we've come to Christchurch and I don't doubt we shall have a perfectly stunning day tomorrow mixing with the cream of the nation, all of whom will be intimately well informed about any matter we care to address them on.' Becoming aware of the faces turned towards her Ceci stopped abruptly. 'You can get on eating, you know,' she told the room, 'I'm just trying out my voice.'

Faces hurriedly bent towards bowls. Only the man two tables away saw Ceci burst out laughing.

The following day as Ceci and Ginger moved around Christchurch, they very soon discovered there was no one with specialist knowledge of carpets, though at Ceci's insistence that the rugs were of value, the occasional shopkeeper was moved to observe in embarrassed tones that they were 'very nice'. In desperation they finally turned into a junk shop.

'They often know a thing or two, pawnbrokers and hand-me-down dealers,' Ginger said cheerfully.

'You go in. I'll stay out here,' Ceci said, by now so tired and dusty she wanted nothing more than to sit down with a cup of tea. What a ridiculous day it had been, traipsing about with the bundle! In and out of shops, asking and being rejected: after a while they had begun to feel like beggars.

Finally Ginger came from the shop with a smile on his face: 'He's offered us five shillings the job lot.'

'Job lot?'

'He'll take the whole lot off our hands for five bob,' said Ginger.

Quickly Ceci rushed past him into the shop and without speaking to the surprised man knelt and hastily bundled the rugs together, the blood pounding in her head.

'No need to be like that, Ceci,' Ginger admonished as they moved back towards the hotel. 'And don't run! The man was only trying to be helpful. You can't expect people to be all fired with interest in a few bits of worn-out cloth.'

Ceci stopped in the street. 'I could cry,' she said softly.

'Come back to the hotel and lie down. You're tired out.'

'What about you?'

'I'll walk about a bit and meet you at dinner time outside the dining room.'

'When we get there,' Ceci asked, 'will you ask the man if he'll bring a cup of tea to my room?'

Feeling distinctly rested Ceci awoke to realize it was dark, well-nigh dinner time. By the door she saw the silhouette of the rugs where Ginger had thrown them and felt vaguely ashamed of her behaviour. She remembered the hotel proprietor's wife tapping gently, bringing her a cup of tea and expressing concern on her behalf. 'Your husband says you're fair wore out,' the good woman had said. Dipping her face in the water Ceci felt hunger quickening within her and with a rush remembered the rude remarks she had made the previous evening about the food and how she had scandalized the tables around theirs. She sincerely hoped none would remember this. It was odd that Faith had chosen Calvin's rugs to be the first to go, rather than those from the general living area. The girl had also packed for her. Selecting a smarter dress Ceci made her way to the hall outside the dining room.

Already couples were moving in, none whom she recognized. It was perfectly possible in a place like this that the diners changed every night, she realized with relief. She glanced into the dining room. Only three of the tables had filled up and although people were descending the stairs, loitering in the lobby and towards the bar area, there would still be time when Ginger arrived for him to freshen up and change before they went in. Enjoying the sight of so many new people Ceci sat on a chaise-longue partly secluded by an aspidistra and waited. Time passed. Diners came and went, left the dining room joking with each other and promising to meet again. Even from where she was sitting it was plain that some of the tables that had been used were being prepared for breakfast, others being readied for dessert and, one way and other, if Ginger did not arrive soon she would miss out on dinner altogether.

'My dear,' said the proprietor's wife, crossing to her. 'Whatever are you doing there? You'd better hurry in.'

'I'll just wait a little.' Ceci shifted awkwardly behind the aspidistra. A single man approached the dining room only to be told that tables were reserved and to walk away muttering.

'My dear,' said the proprietor's wife, beckoning. 'If you don't go in now, I'll have to give your table away.'

Ceci bit her lip. 'Better give it away then.'

'You won't get anywhere else to eat at this time of night. At least, not anywhere as you could go alone,' the woman said considerately. 'Aren't you hungry, then?'

At that moment the man whom Ceci had glimpsed two tables away the previous evening descended the staircase as if he had recently awakened. 'What's the matter?' he asked the proprietor's wife, seeing her bent over Ceci.

'Well sir,' she explained. 'I'm needing a table . . .'

'Perhaps this lady would care to eat with me? Perhaps you would ask her?'

Rising, Ceci smiled gratefully. Ginger could hardly expect her to miss her dinner on his account when he was doubtless tucking into his own in a pub somewhere. 'Thank you,' she said. 'I would have felt conspicuous at a table on my own.'

'Allow me,' said the young man, holding open the door.

Although she had not intended it, Ceci found herself becoming very interested in Claude Bonham. His manners and clothing indicated he was not a resident, his speech that he was a gentleman, yet his complexion – berry brown in places – that he was used to an outdoor life.

'I would say that you received far too much for the porcelain,' Claude informed her. 'Though the difficulty of obtaining delicate items here must be taken into account. Many a crate of fine china and box of watches lies at the bottom of the sea. It's an insurance man's game shipping anything of value here.'

'The people were in a hurry for the porcelain but not the rugs,' Ceci said questioningly.

'Aha! That's the British for you. Know all about bone china, their Doulton, Wedgwood, what have you because of the potteries. Confront them with a good rug and they're lost.'

'We'll probably take them back with us,' Ceci mused.

'I wouldn't mind taking a look at them myself,' Bonham smiled. 'I see your husband hasn't arrived yet. Would it damage your standing if I inspected them in your room?'

Ceci threw back her head and laughed: 'You could ride a horse into a woman's room here and no one would notice!'

Nodding, Bonham lent forward to refill Ceci's glass. She was the most interesting person he had met since coming to New Zealand. In fact he would like to see a great deal more of her.

'How did you get here?' she was demanding.

Bonham explained that he had a yacht which he travelled about on providing free passage in exchange for labour and picking up items of worth and information as he went. He told her he had been the 'awkward' son who had made good when sent overseas by periodically returning heavily laden on steamers or army boats and gradually winning the acceptance and envy of those who had once rejected him. 'Perhaps there is something wrong with me,' he flashed a smile as they moved up the staircase, 'but I can't say I have yet fancied settling anywhere.'

Do you ever have women? Ceci longed to ask, for surely such a man must! European men, artists and painters had always moved through tropical islands, taken the native girls and been enjoyed by them . . . She stared at a scar on his hand.

'The rope slipped coming round the Cape,' he grinned. 'That set of porcelain. Was it complete?'

'Yes.'

'No breakages? Nothing missing?'

'Nothing at all. It was perfect.'

'In that case,' said Bonham, about to open the door to Ceci's room, 'it may well have been worth the price out here.'

Suddenly Ceci felt shy: she did not want to step into the room with him or, more correctly, while she wanted to very much was afraid she might somehow betray the nervousness which was overcoming her. What is the matter with me, she asked herself, feeling the most ridiculous flutterings. How embarrassing, how treacherous one's body could be when the slightest change in surroundings threatened to disrupt its routine.

'May I?' Claude asked, indicating the door.

'Do,' Ceci nodded. 'It isn't locked.'

Bonham entered the room and turned, as if to see where Ceci had got to. She stepped in.

'Aha!' he said, crossing to the bundled rugs. 'Are these they?'

Strangely indifferent to the mess she had left on her bed, Ceci stood behind him as he crouched, pulled aside the dusty brown paper and unrolled the first, the faded yellow from Calvin's study.

'My God,' he murmured, his fingers touching it in reverence.

'What? What is it?'

'My dear,' he said, reaching for her hand and drawing her down next to him. 'This is a pure silk *hereke* prayer rug!' His voice softening, his fingers traced almost invisible lines in the old rug. 'See, here is the Vase of Cleanliness – the Tree of Life here. Look! The birds of paradise. Look at the *mirab*.'

Even as he spoke Ceci could make out a vase towards the base of the rug with a finely wrought symbolic tree coming from it and perched in the top branches two birds. 'Pure silk you say?'

'The entire warp and weft is silk,' said Bonham, turning the rug over. 'Look at the knotting.'

Now on her knees, Ceci leaned forward and traced with her fingers the underside of the rug. Truly the knotting was beyond belief.

As they sat on the bed Bonham explained that the *mirab* indicated the direction in which the mat should be lain; it should point towards Mecca. The Muslim used such a mat in prayer, he said, and apart from everything else the *mirab* helped you to tell which was the right way up for a rug. He thought this particular rug had come from Isfahan in Persia, and puzzled for some while over the signature on it. As his fingers rubbed at the much stained surface with its multiplicity of designs faded beyond recognition, he murmured: 'I think it is. I think it is him, the master weaver.'

For Ceci to see Calvin's rug so appreciated was enthralling. 'What are all those squiggles in the margin?' she asked.

'These?' He crouched quickly. 'These are inscriptions from the *Rubaiyat*. In Arabic.'

Unable to keep pace with him Ceci sat on the bed. The next rug, the blood-red one Calvin had used during winter in the summerhouse, she learned was a superb nomadic rug, a genuine Dowlatabad: 'Red the colour of benignity.' As Bonham pointed at the medallions on the rug now spread on the boards, before Ceci's eyes it came to speak of the inner secrets of life; of thunderstorms, of the inevitability of death and the constant regeneration of hope. It was a masterpiece! And Ginger had wanted to use it for a horse blanket.

'I must confess,' said Bonham, 'that I have always had a particular fondness for Afghan rugs. You can keep your Yayalis.' He pulled the next rug from the bundle. 'Ha! A Mori Bokhara! Quite common but very valuable.'

Ceci began to smile at the back of the youthful man bent before her, busy telling her that the colours were the colours of earth, that it was made of *kirk* wool, the finest wool from the throat of the lamb – virtually worsted.

'We have full-size carpets at Hexham,' she said quite loudly. 'We have one enormous carpet filling the main drawing room.'

'What colour?'

'It would be impossible to say. There are reds and blues in it . . .'

'Probably an Agra,' said Bonham, dusting off his thighs and coming to sit next to Ceci on the bed. 'Mind you, it could be a Jaipur, though I doubt it. Tell me,' he said, turning to look her in the eyes, 'does it have circles in each of the four corners with a, sort of a, smaller circle here – then rays shining off it?'

'Yes! Yes, I believe it does!' Ceci gasped.

'Ah! The miri bote design representing conception in a woman. That's her womb. The rays coming off it – '

Feeling her colour heighten Ceci looked away.

Bonham got to his feet and pulled out another rug. 'This design was once the standard idea of how a book cover should look in Persia.'

'Despite what you say,' Ceci asserted herself, 'we were quite unable to sell any of these rugs. In fact we were offered five shillings for the lot.'

'I would certainly take them off you if it were appropriate.' Bonham shrugged. 'Though I doubt I could approach anything near their true value. The problem is, you see, the older these rugs become, the more their value increases.'

Ceci could not help laughing. The man wanted to pay an incredible sum for something so old it could barely be seen. Without doubt he knew what he was doing; without doubt he was right. What was there to say?

'What are you laughing at, my dear?' Bonham asked.

'Why do you call me that?' Ceci asked, fearing it was a double-edged question.

'Because I do not know how to address you.'

'I – I'm – Mrs O'Sullivan.' She saw confusion settle on Bonham's face. It sounded terrible. It was true Ginger's name was O'Sullivan yet never had she felt it applied to her. 'Most people call me Ceci,' she explained. 'What should I call you?'

'Bonny.'

She went redder.

'My name is Bonham. My friends call me Bonny,' Claude continued. 'If you wish, in return, you may call me "my dear".'

Suddenly each was aware that an atmosphere had arisen.

'I am going to Akaroa tomorrow,' Bonham informed Ceci. 'I would very much like you and your husband to accompany me – '

Ceci looked down.

'I will have you back by nightfall. I can assure you it's very beautiful – one of my reasons for visiting here.'

Ceci squirmed, for she dearly wanted to go 'Thank you for inviting us,' she replied, wishing he had asked her alone.

'When your husband is back,' Claude persisted, 'please

extend the invitation and unless there is some problem, may I see you both in the lobby at five A.M. tomorrow? So that we may make a good start.'

Ceci nodded. With or without Ginger she would not miss a day with Bonham for the world!

As he left the room, Ceci worried over her reaction to being called Mrs O'Sullivan. She had not, she realized, liked the way it sounded Irish. And she had felt like denying the 'Mrs'; had been defensive about it. In confronting Claude Bonham she had discovered in herself the disturbing feeling that she had betrayed her origins. The man was everything Ginger was not and never would be. That she was married and had no right to be entertaining sentiments towards Claude she knew, yet, given that Ginger had not returned, was there any harm in letting the idea of 'Bonny' play in her mind a little longer? It was, in fact, uniquely, unbearably exciting.

As she got into bed, consciousness of the nearness of Claude Bonham stayed with her till she knew beyond doubt that she wished he were in bed with her. She wanted to lie next to and be held by him, to listen to his tales and, the most impossible wish of all, be invited to accompany him on his journeys. At that moment, the thought of getting on a yacht and simply abandoning, sailing away from, everything that constituted her life was vitally attractive. Together they would breach foreign shores, drop anchor and stumble through clear water and white sand towards coconut palms; would stay in nipa thatched lean-to's. Claude would spear fish for them. She would wear flowers, perhaps a grass skirt. All these things went on: why shouldn't they happen to her? They would hold immense shells to their ears and listen to the sea, and as the sun went down they would stare at the huge sky above and be aware they owed nothing to life, that life asked nothing of them.

Chapter 25

Even as Ceci fell asleep — aware she should be worrying about Ginger's whereabouts yet comforted with the sensation of Claude — Ginger lingered in a street near The Commercial. Earlier that day, having left Ceci at their hotel but untired himself, he had looked at shops, walked by the banks of the Avon and fallen into conversation with an old tramp cooling his feet in the water. He did not mind Christchurch but could not imagine living there. As it fell dark he'd begun making his diagonal journey back towards their hotel for dinner with Ceci and, on an impulse, had gone by way of The Commercial — not looking in the door but continuing on past and turning at the corner to stare back. It was at that moment he'd seen Frank. Stunned into inaction he stared. Frank swayed from The Commercial, headed straight into the street, was narrowly missed by a cart, and vanished between two buildings. Ginger began to run, ducking in front of a carriage, with a countryman's confidence giving the lead horse a smack on the nose to turn it away.

'You watch that!' shouted the driver, curling his whip about Ginger's neck. 'Yokel!'

Freeing himself, Ginger ran between the two buildings into a short alley, broken gardens giving off to the left and right. No Frank. The man could have gone through any of the gaps, Ginger thought, inspecting the fences, but he would find him. He was more likely to have made for the street at the far end, he realized, running for it to stand in the centre and stare both ways. 'Move!' cart drivers

354

shouted as he ducked and bobbed, trying to see past a horse tram to get a view of the length of the street. As the tram slowed at an angle towards the Square Ginger saw Frank being thrown off, as if for not having his fare. Ginger took off running

Unaware he was being followed, Frank turned into the square, wandered to the centre of it, scattering pigeons, and sat briefly on a bench by the horse trough. He stretched his hands along the bench's back and looked up at the sky as the first drop of rain started. Slowly he got to his feet and continued to the far side of the Square to try the cathedral for shelter but its great doors were closed and the rain, now slanting at an angle, would soon find him out. As he glanced back across the Square he saw in the centre of it a poor fool turning on the spot, accosting passers-by, grabbing their elbows, pointing around and asking questions. Frank froze. He saw people shake their heads and hurry on. To his relief, Ginger turned and headed back the way he had come. Carefully Frank sidled out of the cathedral porch and slid around the back of the building.

Wet as he was, Ginger had no intention of returning to the hotel after such an extraordinary find. Though he may have lost Frank, he was convinced it had been he for with his mind's eye he had been seeking him in every crevice of Moke and Hexham since the day of their fight. Was there something he should do that another person would have done? What? A more sane and less impetuous man would surely have gone into The Commercial, he realized, and made enquiries there in the first place. If only it had not been The Commercial! If it had been any other hotel he would have felt no compunction in entering, yet this was the place where he had slipped from grace with the barmaid and though he would not be tempted again, the fact that he had behaved like that was downright embarrassing. The management would have known too. Probably they'd laughed about the 'yokel' from the country who'd pointed his cap at the first Christchurch barmaid he'd seen. Well, the hell with it. He pushed the door open.

As before, it contained a handful of men with no one to cook for them eating just enough to prevent them getting drunk on the ale. The barmaid was there. Crossing directly to her, he said what he had to say: 'Was there a man called Frank in here earlier?'

'How would I know if a man was called Frank by looking at him?' she asked, a pleasing smile in her eye. 'My word! Who's a bit wet then?'

Ginger half turned, for the young woman's attention was embarrassing. 'This man Frank was about my age,' he said, 'but dark haired.'

'I think you're nice as you are,' the girl said.

'He went out walking crooked like he'd had too many,' Ginger persisted. 'I lost him at the Square.'

'You want to leave a message?'

'I want to know where he stays. I want to know where he's likely to be.'

'I might see my way to helping you if you was prepared to be a bit nice to me.'

'For God's sake, woman, the man ran off with my daughter!' Ginger shouted, thumping the bar.

'Listen everyone!' the bargirl called out. 'Some feller called Frank ran off with this lad's daughter!'

Flushing from the roots of his hair upwards Ginger listened to cries of, 'Shame! Shame!' and 'So that bloke's married is he?'

'So who knows where this man can see our Frank?' the barmaid called.

'He got any more daughters for us to run off with?' came a rough voice from the back.

'Don't take any notice.' The girl smiled. 'They're none of them any good in that corner. Can't even afford a potato apiece. They sleep down around Addington railroad yards. They're derelicts.'

Ginger glared around the room which by now had forgotten his existence.

'Frank coulda bin in here mind you,' the girl went on. 'You ask him over there.' She pointed at a short, stout man who by his ruddy soot-flecked face looked as if he worked a brazier.

'Frank?' Ginger whispered to him. The man nodded his head. 'You know a man called Frank?' The man nodded again. 'He was in here this afternoon?' The man nodded again. 'Does he live down by Addington Yards?' The man nodded. 'You can get him a drink now!' the girl shouted over. 'He's deaf as a post.'

Ginger ran from The Commerical and retraced his steps through the passage to the Square then thoroughly combed the area behind the cathedral. He passed up and down streets staring into alleys and crevices convinced he would find the man, or if not him – Lizabeth. It was now clear that God meant him to find Frank: why otherwise would he have timed it so precisely for Ginger to turn around at that moment and see Frank leaving the Commerical? Perhaps that was even why God had allowed him to sin there in the first place, for in Ginger's experience all things had a reason . . .

Frank must be hanging on in Christchurch until he could simply shuck off his past by going to the North Island. All who had burned their boats in the South Island headed north! Why hadn't he thought of it? His hunger to catch up with Frank deadening physical hunger Ginger pressed on. Perhaps he would find Lizabeth crouched in the doorway of some hovel awaiting Frank's return. As the mean streets fell away behind him and he crossed the occasional shanty on open land, Ginger became more sure of his success. There was not a dosser or layabout he did not approach and address directly.

'Got any money?' one asked him.

'You tell me where the man I'm looking for is – you lead me to him – and you'll get all the money you want.' Ginger replied.

The hobo listened for a few minutes, then: 'That's him over there,' he said, nodding towards the rails.

On the instant Ginger spun, barely glimpsing the empty tracks, the dosser struck him over the back of the head with a brick.

'That wasn't very gentlemanly,' a fellow hobo advised, coming to stand behind him with a length of iron piping in his hand. 'I think I'll be helping you with some of his pocket servings.'

Together they counted out Ginger's money and valuables, giving him another quick crack to the head as he began to stir.

'You got more than me!'

'Bags I the watch!'

'Take the damn thing,' replied the first man, flinging it a good fifty yards away and running with his cash helping.

His head paining, Ginger sat up, fully aware of what had happened to him. He did not regret the money although he was sorry about the watch. He had been extremely foolish to flaunt himself and speak about money. It was all he deserved. Now at least he could continue his enquiries without fear of further attack. Indeed, he sensed a kind of sympathy towards him as he moved from one sleeping body to another, to little groups crouched around fires they had built from stolen cinders and split sleepers. They gave him billy tea to drink yet, even if they knew Frank, kept silent about him. Sadly Ginger realized the community would hold together and however terrible the thing Frank had done, not one of them, trapped in their own suffering, would peach on him.

Tired and aching, he made his way towards the station. The North Island boats left from Lyttelton. That he knew. Being penniless he'd have to find a Lyttelton-bound train and stow away before it came into service. He was soon apprehended.

'What do you think you're doing?'

After a few mumbled excuses Ginger backed out of the railyard and made quickly for the road. Though he had never been to Lyttelton he knew it lay over the Port Hills and that there were settlements on the way. Possibly a kind traveller would offer to share a cart with him. If stowing away on the train was so hard, doubtless Frank would have been walking anyway and it stood to reason that the railway authorities were fully aware of the desires of the tramping fraternity in regard to their direct link with Lyttelton.

Dawn was already in the sky as Ginger set out on the road. He knew that Ceci would have missed him yet felt she would understand he had to do what he was doing. Stealing himself against hunger and a throbbing head he put one foot in front of the other, ever listening for the sound of a cart from behind.

At about that moment Claude, who had been unable to sleep left the hotel window and crossed to his bed, aware that Ceci's husband had not come home, for his room looked directly down on the hotel's entrance and he had been wondering what time the man would return.

No doubt he would crawl in in the early hours, he

concluded, and be annoyed to learn that his wife had arranged for them to leave the hotel before breakfast was served. He might even be so worn out after a night on the town that he would be about as much use on the yacht as he seemed to be as a husband. As for himself, Claude had never felt better. Sleep would not come nor did he invite it. As a man who was not usually drawn to specific women, he looked forward to the morrow with the enthusiasm of a child.

Chapter 26

Awakening of a sudden, Ceci realized Ginger was not there and that though she should have minded she felt a distinct lightness in her body. Crossing to the window she could see it had been raining. Had she been so enchanted the previous day as to not notice? Quickly she scribbled a note: 'And where were you last night?', placed it on their dressing table and hurried downstairs, hoping Ginger would not return before she and Claude could leave. It was wrong to be so happy, she told herself. Further, it was foolish to show it.

'I'm sorry, Claude,' she began, 'my husband is – indisposed.'

'I take it he didn't return last night,' Claude said firmly.

Ceci hung her head. Despite everything, she did not want to be seen as a woman whose husband was so bored that he played around. Had Ginger's lack of interest in her during their dinner been so obvious that a complete stranger would assume he had stayed out all night? 'He – he – has indigestion,' she stammered.

Claude looked away.

'I hope you will be able to manage the yacht without him?'

'Will it damage your reputation, my dear,' Claude asked gently, placing his hand over hers as he spoke, 'if we go together?'

For answer Ceci glanced around the empty lobby.

'Very well,' said Claude. 'Let us go at once.'

The street was empty as they stepped out into the

incredibly bright morning, the only sign of life being a horse at the corner tossing its head, sending steam from its nostrils towards the tethered conveyance in which doubtless its driver slept.

'The rain has dampened the wind down,' Claude frowned. 'Would you prefer to go to Lyttelton by road or train?'

'Is that where your yacht is?'

Claude nodded.

'I know the road – I'd like to try the train.'

'Either way we'll need a conveyance.' Turning, Claude snapped his fingers towards the drowsing horse which trotted towards them even before its owner awakened.

Once inside the carriage Ceci was ill at ease.

'So your name is O'Sullivan?' Claude asked. 'You certainly are not Irish.'

'No.'

'May I enquire why you are selling your carpets?'

'Oh!' said Ceci, with embarrassment. 'It was the suggestion of Faith, my husband's daughter. She felt Hexham was turning into a folly.'

'Hexham?'

Carefully Ceci explained her past, aware as she did so that the names of too many men were accumulating in it: Old Bowen, Reg, Calvin, Billy and now Ginger.

'Yet when all is said and done,' Claude said solemnly, 'you do not strike one entirely as an immigrant. There is a certain refinement there.'

Listening to him she was reminded of Lord K who had so impressed and enchanted her with his tales when she was a scrawny mite of six, sitting beside him in his study with little twigs in her hair.

'I'm deceiving you,' she smiled. 'I received my education at the best possible hands given our circumstances . . .'

Lapsing into the past she told of her family's life on the estate where her father had been head groom to Lord K before suffering serious injury from one of his horses. 'No doubt that is where I developed a love of fine things,' she said wistfully. 'He showed me everything from seashells to lacquerware.' She blushed furiously.

At the station, conscious that Claude was 'observing' her, Ceci moved from foot to foot. 'If we sell the rugs,' she told Claude, 'we'll probably take a trip south.'

As the first train of the day drew them across the empty landscape, Ceci became deeply conscious of her smallness, of her ignorance compared with Claude, of the great silence around them.

'Look out!' Claude suddenly shouted. 'The tunnel's coming now!'

Never had she been in a tunnel before and as the noise burst on her, Ceci's ears stung, her eyes hurt. Sitting opposite her in the dark was the man who had life given her a chance, she would have chosen. So aware was she of him she could almost see him peering at her through the dark – though of course that was not possible. With pounding heart she feared that at any moment she would feel his hand reaching for hers, drawing her to him.

Claude heard himself swallow and hoped she had not heard. He knew what he wanted to do. The noise of the train was so loud yet if he kissed her passionately, could not each pretend, even to each other as the train burst into the daylight, that it had not happened? Suddenly the light was upon them, leaving him red-faced.

Ceci felt vaguely cheated. The tunnel had seemed to go on for ever making her feel alternately subdued then exhilarated. Yet now in its brilliance Lyttelton burst on them; its berthed ships moving gently on sea water which flashed and sparkled against dry hills. 'It's twenty-three years since I've been here,' she breathed softly.

'I expect you will see some changes,' Claude advised, taking her hand and helping her from the train. 'I inspected the place as is my custom,' he went on. 'They have a gaol and the usual conveniences. Quite a bustling little port.' They moved to the water's edge. 'There she is,' he said, pointing at a yacht which sat magnificently on the water. 'The *Golden Harvest*. Are you sure you wouldn't prefer to take the bridle path across the hills to Akaroa? I imagine there would be one.'

Was he inviting her to walk across hills with him? Unsure of his meaning, Ceci frowned.

'That is,' Claude elaborated, 'are you prepared to help on board – to unfurl the jib and so forth?'

'I can do as you ask me.'

'Can you fasten up your skirts and walk out on a pontoon?'

Leaving her for a moment Claude strode up and down the front calling: 'Akaroa! Anyone for Akaroa today? Free passage!'

Marvelling at his nerve, Ceci watched him become smaller in the distance till finally he returned with a middle-aged couple hurrying behind unable to believe their good luck. It seemed no one had ever offered them anything for nothing before.

The woman sat gratefully next to her as Claude directed the husband. 'I don't know if he can do any of this,' she whispered to Ceci.

'Right then. Like this, eh?' the man said good naturedly.

'I do 'ope he don't fall in!' the woman murmured. 'Good and all as the savings is . . .'

'I'll tell you one thing,' Ceci confided. 'I don't see how we shall get started at all without any wind.'

'I'm just getting ready, girl,' Claude called over. 'I shall have some boys row us out.'

When it was clear the man understood what his role was to be, Claude got four youths to tow *The Golden Harvest* out into the stream, to where the wind could reach in between the hills and help them. Then: 'Let her go!' he shouted, and to Ceci's and her companions' joy the sails boomed out and filled and the *Golden Harvest* started to quest out to the freedom of the open seas, to turn sharply and follow the shoreline of Banks Peninsula at the end of which in an inlet nestled Akaroa.

'Your husband's very good,' said the woman, patting Ceci's hand.

'Hey ho, lads!' Claude shouted after the departing rowers.

Throughout the journey Claude paid no attention to Ceci: presumably it would have been dangerous to do so. As she watched him, so complete in himself, Ceci sensed how much she had run to seed since the day she had first set foot in New Zealand. She looked down at the wet spray dashing her cheek and the dry hills beyond, bald but for the merest scatter of shrubs. From the sea Lyttelton had not changed. Now was a time when sensible people would be having breakfast, when the sky was bright and clear and hunger stirred in their stomachs.

'Not long now,' the woman whispered as they slid past the peninsula's end and came on an immense opening hooded by cliffs, concealed by massive headlands. Taking it by the middle Claude negotiated entry and in an instant Ceci found herself peering down a long channel which ran some way inland and provided what must surely have been one of the safest harbours in the world.

'Exquisite!' she breathed, as the headlands closed up behind them.

'See! There's the town,' the woman pointed excitedly and, peering ahead, Ceci saw at the far end of the inlet a small settlement. Already the sea journey had given her the sensation of having left New Zealand, having parted from all she had known and agreed to. She would arrive at the hidden village of Akaroa as if stepping out on a foreign shore.

'It was settled by the French, this place,' the woman informed her. 'They came out not knowing we'd got this country and arrived about the same time as the British. The company that sent them had made all kinds of promises but when they arrived we'd got here and that was that so they just had to join in and make the best of it. You'll see the street names here are French and the houses are' — she hesitated — 'dainty, and pretty. There used to be Maoris here but they got finished off. A lot of the poor souls, the French that is, came without a franc because they'd sold up and they didn't have no draught animals. Some of the original ones are still living here who'd been children on the ships. They're doing all right except their Catholics went over to the Church of England because they didn't get on with the Irish nuns.'

'In a place like this you would be cut off from everything,' Ceci breathed.

'You are that,' agreed the woman. 'We really belong in Pigeon Bay, me and him, but we'll visit here first then go over the hill. Look!' She pointed.

Following her hand Ceci saw on the rocky shore penguins and colonies of shags.

'It's so lonely here you get God knows what in these waters,' she murmured. 'Not just your average muttonbird either!'

As they neared the wooden jetty the woman anxiously watched her husband doing as he was told. 'I sincerely 'ope he don't knock us into that jetty with everyone watching,' she said softly. But *The Golden Harvest* tied up safely.

'Come in here,' Claude said to Ceci as the couple stepped gratefully off. 'You see this map?' Before her on the wall of his cabin hung a detailed navigation map, showing with minute care every rock and curvature on the coastline. 'We're here now you see,' said Claude, indicating the far end of the Akaroa Bay inlet. 'Down here,' he pointed towards the tail end of New Zealand, 'this is the Southland and over here you see, my dear, the fjords. Milford Sound. I expect that is where you will be going. Do you think so?'

'I didn't pay much attention.' Indeed standing so close to him in the cramped confines of the cabin where he slept and did his note writing Ceci could barely concentrate on what the man was saying. 'It's a shame my husband is missing such a beautiful day,' she said, knowing that if Claude looked at her, he would realize she had not meant it. His hand moved towards the door of the cabin as if he might close it on them. If he does, thought Ceci, I will not have the ability to protest. After a second, which became interminable, she knew she must break the spell: 'Claude, we must breakfast.'

As the day unfolded they worked their way up the cliffs to a vantage point, a look-out which commanded a magnificent view of the ocean on either side of the peninsula. Below them jagged bays and inlets that had chiselled their way into rock hurled crude towers of foam to rise and slap against crevices and float away fronds of seaweed in rubbery, swirling eddies. Dreaming, they sat gazing over the bright ocean.

Claude moved his hand lest he reach for Ceci's. 'Tell me about your life in England,' he began.

'Before coming to New Zealand? I was training in a hotel as a chambermaid. I used to get up at quarter past

367

five, snatch up the shoes and boots that had been left outside the rooms – trying to remember the room numbers – and drop them in the lobby to be cleaned. You see I was really quite a common working girl!'

'I doubt that,' Claude said earnestly.

'Then I'd take the list of who wanted which paper, light the flame under the big kettle in the pantry and run downstairs and hurry past the footmen. They always looked at you with "Don't run" on their faces!' Pausing in her narrative, Ceci turned to Claude and caught an expression of desire on his face. Swallowing, she continued, 'I liked going out into the street in the early morning. The crisp air made me feel wonderful and I was proud of my pinny. The frills were all starched. I had a different one every day and some of them didn't fit well.'

'Can you remember the name of the hotel?'

Ceci shook her head. 'It had thick glass doors. I'd go upstairs and tap on Mrs Newly's door to awaken her – '

'Mrs Newly?'

'She trained me. She said, "You keep your head down when you go into a room as if you know the guests are in bed, but at the same time you keep your head up as if they aren't. Do you see?" This gave me a feeling of great importance, as you can imagine!' Ceci laughed.

Claude raised his knees and put his chin on them. 'You grew up in London?'

'As a child I wandered there. I stood outside a grand house – perhaps similar to the one you live in – listening to a song on the piano. I recall I had stopped, as children do, to watch a carthorse relieving itself. An old rag cart with just one broken chair on the back. While its master made enquiries it moved on its own from house to house – clop, clop, clop – then waited jangling its bells and making a pawing sound on the cobbles till it heard the

368

metallic clank of his boots approaching, and moved on. But he hadn't come and it was standing with its head drooping lower and lower and a great line of froth running from its mouth and falling sideways on the cobbles.

'I was watching him and wondering about life when the piano started up in the house I was standing outside, with a thin voice singing:

> "They played in a beautiful garden
> Those children of high degree
> And outside the beggar maiden
> Looked on in her misery
> But one of the little children
> Who could not join the play
> And the little beggar maiden
> She watched for him day by day."

'I moved closer to the railing to listen.

> "One day he gave her a flower
> And oh it was sad to see
> Her thin white hand through the railings
> Stretched out so eagerly
> She came again to the garden – "

'Then suddenly a cart crashed by and I missed the most important bit! All I heard was the last two lines:

> "For the ways of men are narrow
> And the gates of Heaven are wide."'

The memory still alive in her, Ceci turned moist eyes to look at Claude. 'And I never knew how the song ended – whether the little invalid boy or the beggar maiden had died.'

'My dear sweet child,' Claude gasped, pulling her to him.

Suddenly she started to cry.

As he held her Ceci knew he was using the act of comforting as an excuse to enfold her. 'We'd better walk,' she said, getting to her feet. 'This isn't doing either of us any good.'

Heavily, Claude stood. There was a feeling of something oppressive: something unspoken that was not quite guilt between them, something that should have happened.

How well now could Ceci understand Ginger's temptation to forget his wife and turn to her when she had owned Hexham and Maureen had been ill upstairs. Though she had wanted him, it had been her high principles that had buoyed her up and made her inaccessible to Ginger. Now they seemed ludicrous.

As she listened to Claude talking about his life, saying he lived if not from day to day then from month to month, she knew she wanted him. He was ready to finish anywhere, he claimed, and had never considered exchanging his free life for a hearth and home. Though he did not boast he had clearly been in situations of great personal danger, not least with the elements; yet he was at ease with all and a stranger to none.

'You are really beyond the class system, I suppose?' Ceci enquired.

'When you have depended on naked tribesmen to survive and have been grateful to them for sharing with you, for teaching you to forage – you tend to be. One day I shall probably run into a rock and that will be the end of it. A small cup which is full rather than a large cup half empty is my choice any day.'

Ceci turned away. Almost every word he spoke made her feel she had chosen the wrong options.

'When you get older you will be lonely,' she said, hearing how thwarted it sounded.

'Better than unwilling company. We will have to get back or your husband will be worried,' Claude sighed. 'If I can find no help, can you assist with the rigging?' With his experience of women Claude knew Ceci did not want to get on the *Golden Harvest*, or return to Lyttelton or Christchurch. He doubted her feelings were as intense as his for it was he who had had to exercise control. Nor did he look forward to getting the *Golden Harvest* out into the stream with only a woman to help; most particularly because he did not want to make a fool of himself in front of her.

They spoke little on the journey but made an efficient entry into Lyttelton, dropping sail and sliding gracefully into a berth. Already the sun was sinking and as they had missed the last train, they were obliged to wait for one of the carts, now filling up, to take to the road.

Start in a carriage, end in a cart, Ceci told herself, sensing that despite Claude's exquisite taste he traded only enough to support himself, not to accumulate wealth or to live in comfort.

'Sorry about this,' he grinned as she scrambled up alongside a woman clutching a large hamper of dripping fish to her legs. 'Have to be careful with the local pennies!'

As the cart climbed over the hills towards Christchurch the passengers fell to talking amongst themselves. With the sense of reading an obituary Ceci tiredly answered Claude's questions about her original journey to New Zealand as a steerage passenger, feeling he was asking to pad the silence but as she talked his eyes clouded over, not with pity for the fifteen-year-old girl who had not seen the sea once during the entire voyage, but with an awareness of the exciting person she must have been and still – in his eyes – was. As she relived her journey before him she saw him enjoying it.

'Oh, Hawpin,' she explained. 'He was the man assigned to cook our mess. All we agency girls were in eating groups called 'messes' and Hawpin cooked for us because he had damaged a rib and was not much use above decks. I think he stole better food for us. At any rate it tasted better because the rest of steerage tended to eat food either soaked in grease, half raw or burnt to a cinder.'

'More likely he knew how to cook on a ship,' Claude smiled.

'Oh he'd tell us they were dancing on deck above our heads, or out there looking at the stars. We couldn't tell if it was day or night. "They'll be watching the sunrise now or looking at the sunset," he'd say. Or "I expect they're leaning over the rail holding out letters for a passing ship to take home."'

'Highly unlikely!'

'You think so? He said the people in private cabins had eggs and oranges to eat, plants under glass, songbirds, writing desks . . . even a piano the size of Noah's Ark!'

'Possibly.'

'Oh! And "coffin ships" where everybody died of scarlet fever and they kept burying each other at sea —'

'Trying to frighten you.'

'Yes,' agreed Ceci, 'and he always insisted the women and children went first. If you were lucky enough to reach New Zealand in a coffin ship you'd be shut up on some island until the disease had run its course, he said, and that would be more terrible than death.'

Claude grinned, imagining the old salt revelling in the attention of young girls.

'One time he told us the seas had broken on board carrying away part of the bulwarks and washing the coops off the poops. We had no idea what any of that was but we all said, "Oh dear".'

'The coops would be where they kept the hens,' Claude grinned. 'And the poop deck would be where the hen coops were standing. All quite sensible.'

'He used to talk about "renting the stanchions and mizzen channels fore and aft." Have I got those words right?'

'It would take a hefty gale to do that!'

'Well,' Ceci said sadly, 'we loved his stories and as long as he didn't swear "on his mother" we weren't too worried.'

In the darkness Claude could no longer see her face but had heard a certain softening in her voice.

Arriving back in Christchurch, whenever people called 'Whoa!' the cart slowed and let them off.

'I don't think we'd better go up to the hotel in this,' Ceci whispered to Claude.

'Why not?'

'We can get off here.'

With every step bringing them closer to the hotel, Ceci felt she was saying goodbye. Doubtless Ginger would be back and she would have to explain where she had been. He, too, would have some story for her which frankly, at this moment, she was not particularly interested in hearing. She would probably never see Claude again.

As they stepped into the hotel, guests passing on their way to the dining room looked at them, and behind the aspidistra she saw Ginger waiting, much as she had done the previous night. 'Goodbye,' she whispered before running up the stairs. Although she felt like throwing herself on the bed and beating the pillow she put on the dress she had worn the previous night – an eternity away – and went down to the dining room. Seeing her, Ginger got instantly to his feet.

'Where were you last night?' Ceci demanded.

'When I was passing The Commercial – ' Ginger began.

'Oh!' said Ceci, her voice rising. 'And I suppose you went in?'

'As a matter of fact I did,' Ginger nodded in a hurry to tell his story.

'And did you sleep with her?' Ceci asked.

At the far side of the lobby Claude paused to watch.

'No I didn't,' Ginger said angrily. 'For that matter, where were you today?'

'I expect you'd like to know!'

'What?'

'I said – if you'd been here last night – you could have come too.'

'Oh.'

'Because I had a *very nice day*.'

In the dining room Claude watched Ceci fork some fish into her mouth as if to hide an emotion. He sensed the woman and man were not happy together and was convinced he knew where the blame lay. Although the woman kept her head down, the man was busy explaining, waving with his fork and using it to show some direction across the table cloth, involving a short-cut from the cruet to the water-pitcher, over to the corner of the table, around one side and back to the cruet. It must have been some story! But the woman did not seem particularly keen on hearing it.

Ceci pushed back her chair and rose. In the past twenty-four hours she had been subjected to a tumult of unexpected feelings. From boredom she had been roused by the presence of Claude; disturbed by the discovery of new emotions in herself and shaken by the change of scenery. As to Ginger's deceit – whether real or imagined – with a sense of staleness she realized she did not care if he had slept with every last barmaid in Christchurch.

374

'We'll have to sell the damn rugs now.' Ginger grumbled, geting into his nightshirt. Despite feeling cheered to have seen Frank, the subject of the rugs irked him.

'Claude will buy them – '

'Claude can use someone else's old bits of sacking in his galley!'

'You realize how much he is prepared to pay for those rugs?'

'Enough to impress you.'

'As you've lost – excuse me – been robbed of all our money, can you suggest another way of paying our hotel bill?'

'He's buying them because he's soft on you!'

On the return to Hexham Ceci began to feel sheepish: 'We were bickering like children.'

'I still think that was Frank,' Ginger shrugged. 'I know you think I see Frank coming out of cracks in the floor.'

'Faith will be surprised to hear what we got for the carpets.'

'Be that as it may,' Ginger said after a while, 'I don't think the trip to Christchurch had quite the result she intended.'

Ceci looked away. 'We'd better straighten out now. We're nearly home.'

As they became dwarfed by tussock and moutain, the sense of being two people in a lonely place needing each other returned, so that by the time they climbed from the trap outside Hexham, Faith thought she discerned the trip had done them good. At least she noticed a new sprightliness in Ceci's step and a certain resoluteness in that of her father . . .

Chapter 27

Slowly Reg had seen his land recover and get on its feet again. They were now having larger portions of food and though even Annie had got down to eating fern roots on occasion, the starch had done her no harm and Little Annie had wanted for nothing. They were still being careful but from where he stood, things were beginning to look good.

'I got high hopes of us havin' made them improvements in time,' he confided to Annie. 'Fact, I'm down to the hamlet today to see about a proper metal pipe to take care of our well.'

Annie nodded and wiped Little Annie's mouth. 'You get down and go outside and play,' she told her.

The child stayed on her wooden swing seat which hung from a strap to the corner of their block table, her eyes following something under the roof. 'Look!' she chortled.

Reg and Annie looked up.

'Bird!'

Suddenly in the light from the door they caught sight of a small fantail darting about catching insects.

Reg leaned forward: 'You listen,' he told Little Annie. 'You'll hear his bill snap every time he gets one.'

In the silence of their hillside clearing the three held their breath till the snap! snap! of the bill could be distinctly heard.

'Must have got a beak full by now,' Annie said.

'Won't stop him,' Reg replied.

Suddenly the fantail made for the door and shot out into

376

the clearing, Little Annie scrambling down to run after him.

'You mind you don't tread on a nail!' Annie called after her.

'A nail?' Reg repeated. 'After the way I bin around pulling out every last one and wasting nothing!'

Annie leaned across the table and took Reg's hand. 'It's nice up here, ain't it, Reg? We're lucky, you and me.'

The emotion was too much for Reg. 'Look at this pudding,' he commented. 'Looks like you shot the currants in from the top of a hill.'

'It's early days to be wild with money, Reg,' Annie reminded him.

Reg got up from the table and crossed to the open door. 'Mind you,' he yawned, 'that bird was in early. Expect 'em more into summer.'

Annie cleared the dishes. She didn't know too much about the seasons birds kept but Reg was probably right. He and Little Annie never missed a movement in the bush and seemed naturally drawn to birds. While she appreciated them catching insects and taking care of the odd spider – a nice bit of linoleum would have gone a long way towards her idea of the right order of things.

'All in good time, girl. All in good time,' Reg said, knowing she was thinking about linoleum.

Stepping towards the hamlet to check his credit and see about a proper metal pipe, Reg realized what a narrow escape they'd had with the rabbits – all on account of his wife being so soft on them. Dreadful as the man Stebbins had been, much as it had hurt to have him in the house, he had probably saved their bacon. As he went Reg picked up the few remaining bits of wire he had woven into a fence to protect their first crop of vegetables after the rabbits had gone. 'Just in case,' he had told Annie, caution for the

377

first time overcoming his natural reluctance to perform unnecessary labour. As he stepped on down the path towards the track he was amazed at how thorough his preparations had been: and after all that not a bunny around! Still, the wire could be put to good use. It only took the getting of a couple of hens . . .

On a hill not far away Stebbins stopped his horse, looked around, got down and lifted a crate from its side. Carefully he slid up the latch and watched while three creatures scuttled out. He sat and had a smoke. Then he got back on his horse and moved on. By the time the sun was high he had completely encircled the hamlet and his hutches were empty. He made his way further inland to a small cave he had hollowed out where he kept hutches and traps between seasons. He was hungry but knew it would not be long before he was sitting pretty. The only unforeseen consequence of his activities was the fact that rabbits were now so widespread in areas where his offers had previously been attractive to clients it was not worth the trouble of taking the flesh or pelts. Competition had dropped the price and any child over the age of ten could trap rabbits so plentiful were they. So he'd turned to money – lighter to carry, less smelly and not needing to be skinned. 'Skin the clients instead' had become his motto. What he would do come the day nobody wanted his services he did not know. Go north and dig Kauri gum he supposed. Oh, for a hearth and fire, a warm place to stretch his feet and a nice woman to look at! Oh for a good pudding and a cup of warm milk! He took off his cracked boots and rubbed his filthy feet. What was the point of washing them? The creek was bitterly cold: the dirt was probably an insulation. It could be a Monday, a Tuesday, a Wednesday or a Friday for all he knew. There was no longer ice in the creek and just the merest dusting of snow remained on the distant peaks. Already earthworms were poking about, which meant it was at least late spring. Not much longer to wait.

As Annie wandered along the track with Little Annie she began to suspect that things with the rabbits hadn't been so bad as the man Stebbins had made out. From the safety of their new crops she contented herself with the idea that he had probably been bringing dead rabbits on to their property from somewhere else then walking around blowing off with his shotgun to frighten them. With a shudder she remembered him saying 'Let's get a look at your bosom then.'

She watched Little Annie chasing after a wax-eye, a pretty yellowish-green bird with a pale chest and white rings like tiny spectacles round its eyes, which she had heard trilling and warbling within a tree but could not see. Suddenly the song changed to a sharp click as if an enemy bird had approached. In the next minute it became a staccato burst as, to Little Annie's, delight the wax-eye shot from the bush.

'Look!' she cried, running after it. Even the songs of the birds changed with the seasons, Reg had told her, depending on whether they were mating or building, defending or showing off. 'Just like us,' he had explained it.

Up ahead, Little Annie stood motionless on the path, two fantails playing about her. Whenever they walked down the track fantails would fly from the branches, hover before their faces, even swoop between their legs if they stood with them apart. It's as if they're trying to tell us something, Annie had thought, to ask us a question or lead us somewhere. It was the strangest sensation to be stopped in the middle of a forest and held eye to eye by a tiny bird not ten inches from the face. Sometimes they would hop out of her way, droop their wings and spread their tails in a great fan as if bowing to her. 'Very complimentary is that,' Reg told her.

Coming out of the forest Annie caught up with Little Annie.

'Look!' the child cried.

'What?'

'Bunny!'

'There aren't no bunnies here now,' Annie told her.

Little Annie ran a few paces and pointed. Idly Annie followed after her. 'Bunny!' the child insisted, smiling at the bare swathe of land beyond their line of trees.

Annie frowned. There was nothing wrong with her eyesight but it was not as sharp as the child's. 'Where?'

'Two bunny!'

Frowning, Annie picked the child up and turned around. 'We're going home now and see about tea,' she told her.

'Bunny,' Little Annie complained, looking sadly over her mother's shoulder.

Sensing that it was not a game Annie spun and there, clear as the day, were not one or two but *three* rabbits sitting up washing their paws and boxing with each other.

Reg returned from the hamlet with his metal pipe, so full of himself and his ideas that Annie did not like to mention the rabbits. By tea time she was worrying. 'I've been thinking, Reg. Maybe we was a bit premature in taking them wire fences down – '

'Fences?'

'Rabbit fences.'

'Forget about that.'

'I think I've seen a rabbit – '

'Yeah, well we been professionally cleaned out.'

To pacify her Reg took a walk past the band of trees and over the hill but did not find the kind of evidence he would expect with rabbit infestation. If Annie had seen two, maybe three rabbits, there should have been burrows somewhere. He did not find them.

As the season went on to his mystification rabbits began to appear in great waves, coming from no one knew where. It was not long before Stebbins showed his noxious face at Block 442.

'I thought you done cleared us out,' Annie said grudgingly.

'They spreading, Ma'am. They spreading. This year should take care of it.'

'You just keep going,' Annie told him. 'I'll have a word with my husband when he comes home.'

Stebbins held her in a malicious glare. 'Ain't you even going to invite me in?'

Annie came out, stood on the step and shut the door behind her.

'That ain't no way to treat a travelling man,' Stebbins advised her.

'You just keep moving.'

'We *can't* have him here! I can't stand the man! Its bad for Little Annie to have a person like that in the house.'

'See if we can manage for a bit on our own,' agreed Reg, reaching for his shotgun.

'Well, you tell that man not to come here.' Annie frowned.

'He don't have to stay here,' Reg explained. 'He wants money.'

'Money?'

'Seems he takes money for his services these days but if you let him stay, it comes off the bill.' Reg looked at Annie biting her fingers by the fire. 'I don't like him no more than you do but it's him or the land. I can shoot the odd rabbit but I'm no professional – '

'Professional! Why are we in this situation again?'

'Be fair, Annie,' Reg said, coming to stand by her. 'No man can catch *every* rabbit. Ain't humanly possible. You know as well as me we started with just two rabbits here.'

'All right. It was my fault.'

'Nobody's saying it was your fault,' Reg reminded her. 'But we'll have to have help and I mean to pay Stebbins.'

'With what?'

'I'll take that metal pipe back down and get credit on it.'

'And then? Sell the tools, the jam, the clothes off our backs?'

'Wouldn't get much for none of that!' Reg grinned.

Annie began to twist at the hem of her skirt.

'I'm going down to Christchurch,' Reg informed her.

'And what'll you do there?'

'Never you mind, girl.'

Though he had not asked her to have faith in him Annie knew he would do the best he could and that no amount of faith would help them in the event a solution were not possible. He would probably get the money by taking a second mortgage on the land or whatever they called it. So even as they attempted to 'make improvements,' they would have new debt to struggle with. To survive the rabbits they'd have to rely on Stebbins. She would be forced to put the man up while Reg was away, for they had no money to start him off working with.

'Whatever you say, Reg,' she said tiredly. 'We'll do what we have to.'

'I promise you one thing, Annie,' Reg frowned. 'If Stebbins doesn't clear us this season I'll break every bone in his body.'

Reg sat in the antechamber at the bank waiting to be shown in. Though deeply conscious of his dirty nails, the cracks in his boots and dried mud on his trousers he was not concerned for his appearance. He had come with a job to do.

'Next!' called the clerk.

Getting to his feet, Reg ambled towards the open door, his hat held behind his back. The bank manager took a good long look at him as he waited in the doorway before asking him in.

'It's about my land, see,' Reg began. 'I got me some land up in the backblocks. Nice piece. Wife and a kid. We was wondering if you could see your way to lendin' us some money on it while this time next year – '

The bank manager decided to say nothing but let the man talk himself out.

' – stands to be a good place.'

Apparently the man had finished. 'Do you have title to the land?'

'Beg your pardon?'

'Where are your bits of paper, man?' the bank manager asked with laboured patience.

'I ain't got none,' Reg explained.

'I see. You're on the Improvement Scheme. Is that it?'

The niceties of the situation eluded Reg. All he knew was that he had a hold of a piece of land and meant to keep it.

'Where are you in relation to the Waitaki-Mackenzie fence?' the bank manager asked, referring to a hundred-and-thirty-kilometre-long wire fence which the government had built to hold back the southern rabbit infestation.

Reg scratched his head. 'To tell the truth, I ain't never heard of it!' he exclaimed.

The manager swallowed. Because of the rabbits, land to the north of the Waitaki-Mackenzie fence was now worth ten times what land to the south was. Then there was the eighty-kilometre-long fence starting at Hurunui and the two-hundred-and-seventy-kilometre fence to run south of Orari to be considered.

'You know Orari Gorge?'

Reg shook his head.

By now the manager was genuinely interested. 'Do you have livestock?' he demanded. 'What sort?'

Before thinking, the word was out: 'Rabbits.'

'I'm sorry to have taken your time,' said the manager, rising. 'There seems to have been a slight misunderstanding.'

Before he could say Jack Robinson Reg found himself out in the street. He turned and looked up at the bank's name. Wouldn't go there again. As the day wore on he tried other banks but met with no success. For some reason, possibly because he didn't have his bits of paper, none were interested. In a last desperate effort he turned in at a pawnbroker's.

'Now you look like a man as understands money,' Reg began as roughly as he could. 'What would you lend me now if I was to give you title to me land on it?'

The pawnbroker looked at him steadily. 'What kind of livestock you got?' came the familiar question.

By now aware the less he said the better, Reg parried the question. 'Livestock? I'm into grain. I'm a grain farmer.'

'And how is your grain growing? It growing good?'

'Course it's growing good!' Reg exclaimed. 'Why else would I come swanning down here?'

'So what do you want money for?'

'More machinery. I reckon on making improvements. Seems a shame to see large crops going to waste for want of speedier harvesting.'

Ten minutes later Reg had left the pawnshop in company with its owner who had locked the door. A few short strides to the Land Registry, then to his lawyer's and the deed was done. As he felt the money in his pocket Reg swore one thing. Whatever happened, nobody would get their seed stock off them. Let the house go, the tools, the clothes off their backs — as long as they kept their seed stock, if Stebbins did his job right they could survive.

Up in the hills Stebbins had a few 'professional observations' to make. For his extermination to be effective, he said, it had to take place during winter when the population was stable. During the breeding season and through summer there wasn't much point in shooting rabbits, he insisted. A man might as well go to work on the railways.

'Don't you give us that!' Annie snorted. 'You're just looking for somewhere warm to winter over!'

'She means we don't appreciate,' Reg said a bit more circumspectly, 'why you should let them continue on through the breeding season and into summer.'

'Any fool could see,' Stebbins insisted. 'A rabbit's summer coat ain't worth nothing!'

'Be that as it may,' Annie pointed out, 'we ain't keen on having you spend the winter in our home.'

'Don't you worry, Missus,' Stebbins assured her. 'This time I'll take care of it. I got me some poisonous phosphorus.'

'We don't want nothing poisonous lying around with the child here.'

'Either you have me for winter,' Stebbins replied, a hint of something nasty in his voice, 'or you take the consequences.'

After a short discussion behind their cabin Annie agreed. Stebbins could stay. 'Are you sure we aren't missing a trick here?' she whispered anxiously. 'Something he said don't tie up but it's slipped me.'

'We'll make an all out go of it this summer Annie,' Reg promised. 'And have Stebbins for winter. We can pay him now.'

'And come spring there'll be no looking back?'

'God willing,' Reg replied.

Chapter 28

Since returning from Christchurch convinced he'd seen Frank, Ginger was obsessed with the idea that in a matter of time he would smoke him out. Steamers to the North Island didn't come cheap and clearly the man had been thrown off the tram for having no money . . . 'I got as far as Lyttelton that day,' he'd told Ceci. 'No sign of him.' On the ride he'd begged back, despite his aching head, he'd been aware there was something he should do: some meaningful act he could undertake before leaving Christchurch that would stand him in good stead, an act anyone else would think to perform but which for the moment escaped him.

The sense of invigoration remained, however, making him feel he must do something, be active somehow. It was as if by walking the southern track through the canyons to the great fjord he would prove something: perhaps that he was physically capable of tackling Frank. And he wanted Ceci to walk it with him to prove something too – though what he had forgotten. She seemed so far away these days. She seemed almost beyond reach.

'I want to us to get close again, Ceci,' he began. 'That's why I want us to take that trip Faith mentioned.' With a shrug Ceci gave in. The routine of getting up and going to bed so bored her that the change could not be worse and, after all, she could as well dream about Claude under the open skies as at Hexham.

* * *

Resting his feet on the bundled rugs in his galley, Claude ran a finger down the coastline and decided to allow himself seven days to reach Milford Sound, the great fjord lying at the end of the track the woman Ceci and her husband would walk. He could not free his mind of her and had taken the trouble to enquire about the famous route. If he arrived first — he would wait. Carefully he studied the contours of the coast, the rivers he should pass, their entrances which might be concealed by fog. It was a desolate stretch, the eastern seaboard; a sparsely inhabited place of black sand with a chill wind blowing from the Antarctic; a lonely shore where muttonbirds skimmed rough waves and vanished in rain. He picked out possible harbours; marked where mountains would be visible running close to the sea or where he might hope to see the sun glinting off buildings. It was essential to take care, for he had not been able to interest any in accompanying him and did not want to founder or, once having rounded the southern tip of the island, enter the wrong fjord and forfeit this last opportunity of meeting Ceci. In his life so far he had had an impeccable sense of timing. He knew she would go: indeed felt she was already going. Stirred by romantic thoughts he wiped at a brass rail with his sleeve. He was like one of those young men he had studied in the classics who threw themselves on the seas, fought monsters and had brave adventures. Often they'd left women weeping as they'd sailed away. He wanted this woman very much but he *would* sail away. It was enough that she should cause him to make such a detour.

A few paces from Ceci, Ginger stood on a bluff overlooking the Eastern Ocean. There was a small yacht on it. Two days into their journey and already he felt powerful. From now on it would be mountains all the way to the fabled

Lake Te Anau which was in the shape of a sea-horse stretching. And the mountains would be real ranges, not like the High Country hills.

Ceci glanced about her at the dry land crumpled like rough paper. The sea was behind them now and the comforting sight of the yacht she had seen had vanished. Suddenly she felt an urgency. 'We must hurry, Ginger,' she urged.

'Why?'

'I feel we should.'

'The coach won't leave any sooner because we get there first!'

Though Ceci knew this to be true, she fretted.

'And we're in good time,' Ginger pointed out. 'So long as we join up with the road. This afternoon's free.'

'Why do we have to stay the night at a pass? Can't we keep travelling?'

'We'd be too tired to walk the track at the other end.'

As they continued on, Ceci asked herself: Who was she? The wife of the son of Irish immigrants, himself as cut off from his history as she from hers. They owned a stately home built by one languishing Englishman and sold to another who had died ... Where was the child who had stood on the pavement in London and made the decision to emigrate? All was cut off and inaccessible as if it had never been! Her mother, her sister — faded away like images breathed on glass. She had still one sister alive but she'd never see her again. Oh, how she longed to return! But if she did, she would not fit. She had sold herself for a dream and there was no way back.

'We're lost people in an empty land,' she told Ginger.

'Beautiful land though.'

'If I could have the years back — '

'There's no point you wanting the crowds of London

here,' Ginger said almost roughly. 'Better get stuck into the mountains!'

Steaming south, threatened by clouds, Claude decided to put in. He could sense Ceci near him, separated by only a hazy coastline. By his compass reading he was close to Dunedin. He did not, he told himself letting down the dinghy, relish the idea of struggling with yards of sodden canvas in a gale. There was much to be said for the South Seas where the rain was warmer and the natives more forthcoming. Indeed, as he sank his feet into the deserted black mud of the shore and trod past the dead birds on the beach, he felt that, after he had seen Ceci, this was not a land the gods would have to bid him leave.

'Don't let's go any farther today,' Ceci urged. 'Ginger, let's rest.'

'I thought you were in a hurry.'

'The weather's coming up nasty.'

Mystified, Ginger gave in. On this trip he had seen mood changes he could not understand. She was right though. From the direction of the sea dark clouds had appeared and were rolling towards them with ferocity. 'With a bit of luck we'll get to an accommodation house before – '

'We *must* break the journey!' Ceci said urgently.

Frowning, Ginger leaned forward to ask the driver who, though he heard every word they and the other travellers spoke, chose never to join in. 'Not long now,' he told Ceci. 'We join another track and there's a hostel there.'

By now big cold drops were raining down on them but the man kept to the same slow trot, leaving the travellers to huddle together under tarpaulins. He did not even bother to don his hat but persisted in a monotonous whistle as rain ran down his neck.

'I once felt dissatisfied with my life and situation,' Ginger said, looking at Ceci crouched under the tarpaulin.

'And did it pass?'

For a moment Ginger was silent. 'I lived through it,' he said, wondering Ceci had not known the answer was: 'You would not have me.'

'How long will it take us to get to Lake Te Anau after the hostel?' Ceci asked irritably.

'Three, four days depending on the weather. I thought you wanted to rest – '

'Rain or not,' she said, suddenly seized with a panic, 'perhaps we had better press on.'

Panic pricked Claude. His first attempt to get out on the tide had been a failure and the small population was no help. He could scarcely get up sail and had lost the tide time and again to, he sensed, the amusement of the onlookers. When next the wind came he ran at it only to be turned around and driven back in. Determined to remain on board he had awaited the next tide and, before the silent watchers, had rushed from one side of his yacht to the other, struggling to entrap the wind and failing. As the second tide went out and evening came he had dropped anchor. He would have to delay.

Cursing the god of wind who had deserted him, hungry and irritated, he watched the tide recede slowly, slowly – making it plain the wind had driven him further inland than he had imagined. Soon he felt bottom catching mud, implanting itself, his barque leaning closer towards the water, the chain stretched at full length, the anchor dragging mud . . . As the boat tilted things began to roll, his glass telescope – before he could reach it – plunging overboard to sink in mud, followed by a tin cup. Farther and farther *The Golden Harvest* leaned till she was lying on her side, the contents of his cabin in disarray and the mattress from his bunk bed upended on the porthole. With a last glance at the hostile onlookers across the sea of mud he decided to make the best of it by uncorking some brandy. Let them stare! Their lives were pitiful and deprived. They were bound to this cold windy shoreline where muttonbirds died and bad weather came in great draughts. Oh, for the South Seas where the girls had come running to him half naked, weighed him down, while still in the water, with garlands, repaired his ship with twine! He had been given food and gifts in exchange for nails. Muscular women had swum after his craft, hauled themselves aboard and walked round laughing, feeling the cloth of his sails, his silk handkerchief, the leather binding of his books . . . Six miles from the shore they had dived into the sea and begun the long swim home, chatting as if on a shopping trip. Women with spirit. Women who would swim from one island to another with a child strapped on their backs. Not like those miserable European remnants across the mud! A man certainly knew who his friends were at a time like this and how little Christian man truly cared for his neighbour! Even a common savage would have helped. In South America when his craft had run into trouble in the mouth of a tidal river the people had been sufficently concerned to paddle out to him, standing upright on hewn planks a trader had left. With perfect balance they had approached, poling their way and shouting at him in high-pitched voices, the sounds of which had turned him about and stopped him drifting broadside on into a forest of flooded trunks.

With morning came the next tide. If he did not get off this time he would be obliged to row in, offer money and ask for help. He could not sit day after day while the woman Ceci arrived at Milford Sound, turned around and went back. As he saw the wind begin to play with his sails, pushing and punching, his excitement mounted. There was still time. But the wind looked tricky. What he needed was a southbound steamer that would come by and lash him to its starboard. Once at sea, away from this shore, he would not come in again until he could see the end of the land, Stewart Island and the Straits between them. If he got as far as Invercargill he would be halfway, with another two hundred miles of coastline to cover. Ceci had wanted him that day at Akaroa. He had been sure. She had wanted him in a way she had been unable to conceal that had struck in him a chord of inevitability. Although he would leave her – more than anything he wanted to depart the victor.

In the mountains as they had moved south Ceci had almost felt Claude shadowing her just beyond the peaks, but arriving at Lake Te Anau the sensation ceased. Gradually as their steamer moved up the lake she found herself beginning to relish the idea of the trip with Ginger. Their skipper, an American, talked loudly about the marvels awaiting them, insisting he had seen nothing like it in his own country or anywhere, unless maybe the Canadian Rockies. The Milford Track, he said, had been described by the London *Spectator* as 'the finest walk in the world', and during the eight years since it had opened it had been his pleasure to see one lady walk it in, he thought, 1890. Their journey up the lake would last a good ten to twelve hours, he said, and then they would start walking from the head of the lake to a high pass and then on down to Milford Sound, the fjord which led out to the open sea. It was the only fjord, he solemnly explained, that a sailor could come inland from. All the others were dead ends, as this one had been before the track was cut and the pass over the mountains discovered. The fjords around them, he said, had given shelter to questionable types, to adventurers, whalers and seal hunters. They had names like Dusky Sound, Preservation Inlet, Chalky Inlet, Breaksea, Dagg and Doubtful Sounds. To a bird, he told them, the land around would look like deeply clawed rock, slashed into pockets which had filled up with water. They would never be far from the sound of water, he promised. It thundered from mountains, emptied into rivers, lakes and fjords and could always be heard playing distances away. 'The fact is' he concluded, 'very little of Fiordland has been explored. You should be careful to stay on the Track.'

Ceci noted her fellow travellers nodding their heads gratefully for the morsel of advice, as if they were privileged to be exploring their own country, and obliged to the American for having the goodnes to show it to them.

'You'll have a good time,' he assured them. 'There's a couple of huts and a tent – even a chair to get the ladies across a river, and a guide.'

'Do we have to go with him?' Ceci asked loudly.

Everyone turned to stare.

'I would expect you would *want* to,' the American said in a surprised voice.

Ginger grinned at Ceci now trailing her hand in the water. Much as he would have loved to go without a guide, they had brought neither tent, food, bedding, an axe to chop wood or a billy to boil water so would be dependent on assistance. 'We'll have to join the group,' he told Ceci.

'Some of you, I expect,' said the American pointedly, 'will have brought your own candles so you won't be asking for food. If they're made of mutton fat you can chew 'em and be as independent of provisions for your welfare as you like.' Ceci yawned as he went on to talk about how his boat had been brought up in pieces by bullock team and horse and put together at Lake Te Anau. She moved to the front of the craft, at that moment wanting only to be alone with Ginger and away from them all. The mountains had had an oppressive effect on her and now, out in the open, she felt vaguely ashamed.

As the day grew hotter and people began to doze, peering down into the water she thought she could make out the skeletons of giant long-dead trees, possibly fossilized, catching the light and throwing it back up again. She felt she had forgotten Claude. In the distance grey pebbles reached into the lake and birds leaving overhanging branches darted for cover. A man produced a water canteen and passed it around.

'Some people find it frightening, all this silence,' the American said loudly.

As Claude nosed his way up the granite coast the entrances to the fjords began to look frighteningly alike. From the sea they rose, giant stone walls like city gates. Once inside, a man must choose between branching chasms and face the prospect of being driven against a rock face or thrown into water hundreds of metres deep. Black and very still the fjords offered scant possibility of getting up sail and the difficulty of clawing a handhold on those steep walls impressed him by its unlikelihood. Peering at the rain-obscured coastline he asked himself how many entrances he had counted, how many he had already missed.

Alone in the situation he craved a voice to help make the decision whether to abandon the venture, to put out to sea and await a steamer which might identify Milford Sound by turning into it, or take a chance. It was several days since he had spoken to another human being and his confidence was beginning to wane. Where before he had convinced himself that the mud-grounding incident off the coast at Dunedin had been nothing more than a hiccup, he began to have doubts. For a day and a half he hesitated in the open seas, afraid to turn into a fjord. Either he must enter a fjord now, seek out this woman and confront what lay between them, or turn prow and head north across the Tasman Sea to Australia.

Suddenly Ceci did not want to be with Ginger. She could not put a finger on it but she felt irritated with him, with the Beggs, their travelling companions, and their guide, Tavistock. The woman Begg kept saying 'If you like', 'If you say so', 'I'm easy', 'I don't mind', 'Suit yourself', 'As you like', until Ceci began to feel that if she'd been asked to blast a tunnel through solid rock she'd have been quite agreeable. Though she was being badly bitten by sandflies she seemed undecided whether they should expect this sort of thing in the wilderness or try to evade them.

'Don't scratch,' Tavistock told her in his dour Scots way. 'It'll swell up and itch the more.'

As the walk progressed through beech forest, canyon and mountain, it came to represent to Ceci everything that most annoyed her about her present situation. There was Ginger, enjoying the countryside, drawn by the sound of the river below, pausing to look at butterflies and follow birds – not, of course, having been bitten by a single sandfly. The alpine meadow they were passing through was being ruined by Mrs Begg's talk of her sister Mercy, her sister Loncy, her brother Maurice, her brother Maurice's wife Marjorie, her brother Maurice's wife Marjorie's cousin Aloysius ... As her voice fell on the fleshy white-gold flowers Tavistock called mountain buttercups and landed like fine dust on the red *rata* in the gorge below, Ceci felt herself being called to. Barely did she notice Mrs

Begg's words skimming across the wild onion, accosting the fuchsias, vulgarising and destroying all it touched. She rose above Tavistock telling the legend of the Maori god Tu who had chiselled out the landscape and the Maori goddess of the underworld, Hine-nui-te-po, who'd put the sandfly there to keep man away. Her mind rose above Ginger with his good-natured tolerance of the Beggs that so infuriated her – and flew towards Claude Bonham.

As they passed through ribbonwood scrub, she remembered him kneeling on the floor of her room in Christchurch, moving his hands over the faded patterns of Calvin's rugs. As Tavistock led them from high tussock and rocky outcrop to dark forests of giant tree ferns, her mind's eye was on *The Golden Harvest* as it had hesitated before entering Akaroa Inlet. Tavistock was telling them the women must share one tent and the men another but she heard only the voice of Claude ringing out, telling her to loose sail. She saw diamonds of light sparkling off the sea, the sun flashing from *The Golden Harvest*'s rails, heard Claude laugh behind her, then saw him become serious as he brought his craft safely through a headland. What headland she did not know. Probably by now he would be up around Auckland, possibly even headed for Fiji . . .

With regret she turned her attention to the group and to Tavistock's raised voice telling them that the following day would be their longest: a day rich in bird life and natural beauty. More trees and rocks, Ceci sighed. They could expect to see paradise ducks, forests of *remu*, petrified trees, boulders of every imaginable shade and colour, Tavistock went on, the names of mountains, rivers and waterfalls rolling from his lips. Mrs Begg conceded she was relieved this would be the last night of their four-day hike; the last night of putting up with rats the size of kittens knowing exactly where they would camp and anxious to share their lodgings and provender with them. Ceci sat on a rock. Their last night and then a return to what? The unbearable provinciality of life in a country to which she did not belong.

'I want us to make an early start, ahead of the mist tomorrow,' Tavistock was intoning. 'We'll descend through it – '

'Does that mean we're missing out on the Sutherland Falls?' Ginger asked.

'I've taken the decision – '

'I fully intend to go the falls,' he assured Tavistock.

'Some people don't appreciate that there are other people to be thought of,' Mrs Begg said quietly.

'What about you, Ceci?' Ginger asked, coming over.

'I couldn't care less,' she replied truthfully.

Ginger returned to the group. 'I'm definitely going to those falls in the morning,' he told Tavistock.

'In that case, in all probability we shall leave without you,' Mr Begg muttered.

'I'm not going to the Sutherland Falls,' Ceci informed Ginger over supper, 'I want to finish this walk as quickly as possible. I feel we should hurry – '

'What's all this hurry? When we get there we only have to go back to Hexham.'

'You had better stay with us,' Tavistock warned, coming over. 'You might get lost.'

'This track is wide enough for an elephant to get through!' Ginger shouted. 'A whole series of Beggs have been brushing its sides with their rumps!'

'Please be courteous!'

'Tin-pot emperor,' Ginger muttered as Tavistock withdrew.

'I've never heard anything so rude,' came the wounded voice of Mrs Begg.

398

When Ceci awoke in the morning Ginger was not there. She wandered from the hut and halloo'd but he didn't come. During breakfast Tavistock became increasingly angry while the Beggs fidgeted and kept asking the time. Finally they pressured Tavistock into leaving without him.

'I'll wait,' Ceci said.

'I can't permit that.'

'Oh hurry along,' she snapped, without bothering to look at him.

Having seen the falls Ginger descended to the river and stood gazing into a deep, clear pool. Streams up around Moke were only shallow rockbeds and, never having been in the sea or a large pond, he could not swim. He had seen pictures of people cutting through waves though and read about the thrill of water rushing past a body as it dived down. Taking his clothes off he climbed on a rock and looked up at the mountains closing in above, thick with native beech, their leaves shimmering like water. He bent his knees, put his arms out and tried to dive. Meanwhile, at a different waterfall Ceci shouted, her voice lost in the spumes of thundering foam. The louder the water roared, the more she felt the need to be gone, even if it meant leaving Ginger. 'Ginger! Ginger!' she called, then turned and scrambled quickly along the track after Tavistock and the Beggs.

Kneeling on a rock, Ginger began tapping at the water's edge eyeing the shadows of dapples and stones for movements. Gradually a pale fish came to him, then two brown ones that rubbed at his thumb with wiry lips but as he plunged his other hand in they flashed away. What had Maureen's father, Old Nolan, said about tickling trout? The man hadn't been put to the test for the rivers around Moke were fishless, dried fish being the only sort that came their way. Trying again Ginger started with one hand lying

399

on the river bed and the other breaking the surface above it. His hand began to get very cold . . .

Ceci hurried on. Now that she was alone her sense of urgency became one of elation. It was as if her mind had been waiting to leap to Claude. How often must he experience freedom, leaving the irritations of society behind! Freedom was beautiful, she thought, hurrying on through the ferny forest. To enjoy such, even at the cost of loneliness, was surely worth more than the pain of a fixed domestic situation? If such could be had together with love, she dreamed, what an impossibly desirable combination it would be . . .

As the day got older and the shadows came Ginger woke. He had caught two trout in his bare hands and whatever the music to be faced, it had been worth it. The beauty and feel of those glistening creatures would stay with him always. It was just a pity that Ceci had not seen fit to share the experience, he thought, climbing back up to the path. In the old days a refusal on her part would have been unthinkable. Moving through the trees he thought about Ceci and tried to catch up with her, but sensed she was far away, even farther than the kilometres that separated them as dusk fell. He knew from experience that only the thought of one who is loved more could provoke such distaste for a previous love. She was still thinking about the Englishman, Bonham.

Finally he caught up with her and as the moon rose they walked on in silence, at times Ginger leading, at times Ceci. Although she was tired she would not rest, would not lie down on the track beside him and sleep. On and on they went, the sound of night birds scuffling away, the flash of ghostly waterfalls in the distance, the reflections of white clouds in lakes below.

'I'm so tired, Ceci, I must rest,' Ginger urged, aware that his naked nap in the sun had fatigued him.

Ceci glanced at him and felt strangely free. He could rest. She would carry on.

As dawn broke ahead of her and she saw the Tasman Sea she felt a quickening in her pulse and began to run. To her amazement Tavistock was waiting below, having taken the Beggs across the water by launch to the Milford settlement and returned dutifully to Sandfly Point to await the last travellers when they should see fit to arrive. Hastily Ceci scrambled aboard, knowing something was about to happen.

Even as dawn rose the sight of Mitre Peak soaring from the black waters took her breath away. Drawn by its splendour her eyes moved involuntarily till, in the faint light of the beginning day, they came to rest on what must surely have been a cruel illusion. There before her, eloquent and commanding, rose the masts of *The Golden Harvest*.

At that moment Tavistock heard the faint cry of Ginger on the shore behind and hesitated. 'Why didn't you say he was following you?' he asked brusquely, turning the launch.

Ceci's mind went blank. Claude Bonham was within arm's reach. Whether it was an accident or what fate intended, a course of madness or the behaviour of one rushing into a fire, she must go to him. Aching from the journey from Christchurch back to Hexham, from Hexham to Lake Te Anau, the ordeal over the mountains with the Beggs and everything that went to make up the life she was now so tired of, like a fish swimming up for air she must get on that yacht. Let it cost what it may; without thought for the future, she would go.

Chapter 29

From the moment he saw Ceci coming towards him across the water Claude Bonham knew he wanted her more than any of the priceless belongings he had collected on his travels. Of course she would not leave with him but what a monumental farewell it would be, on a level with the partings of great lovers he had read about in the verse and literature that had filled his life and become more to him than reality. As the images of passionate fables crowded his mind he had a feeling that for the first time he was going to be hurt. But the woman before him was a masterpiece who could make sense of his wanderings by combining them with her spirit. He *had to have her.*

From the shore Ginger watched Ceci going. Her act stung his mind. 'I forbid you,' he had shouted, but she had stepped forward. Raising his voice even louder he had called after her: 'Go then!'

Though Ginger's words drummed in Ceci's ears she would not give them audience. For once in her life she was following blind passion, following it blindly. Ginger objected to her saying goodbye: he was unreasonable. Soon Claude would be gone. Others lived their lives with a total disregard for their neighbours' susceptibility so why not she? People were so used to her bending like a wet rag to accommodate them that they were surprised. The fact of the matter was that most people behaved in a way to suit themselves all the time.

From the shore Ginger made out the sight of Claude Bonham standing on deck and longed to throttle him. If the damn woman had had a child, if he had given her one she would have been too busy, would have had more to think of. Not that it profited him now!

Claude watched Ceci approach, her face in a cautious smile whose freshness belied her lack of sleep. Like morning, she was radiant, each pore of her skin proclaiming that something he had never had. *If she would only leave with him!*

'I came to say goodbye,' she began, standing in the small row boat, steadying herself with a hand against his yacht, eyes shining up at him. Behind her an oar slipped its rowlock and floated away.

Claude reached towards her: 'Careful.'

On the shore Ginger imagined their fingers touching, saw Claude lean, grasp Ceci under the armpits and haul her aboard.

'You're going, aren't you?' Ceci smiled.

'I would happily stay,' Claude said softly. He picked up one of her hands and kissed it.

> 'I have an orchard that hath store of plums,
> Brown almonds, services, ripe figs, and dates,
> Dewberries, apples, yellow oranges;
> A garden where are bee-hives full of honey,
> Musk-roses, and a thousand sort of flowers;
> And in the midst doth run a silver stream,
> Where thou shalt see the red-gill'd fishes leap,
> White swans, and many lovely water-fowls:
> Now speak, Sweet Ceci – wilt come with me or no?'

Moved by him, Ceci's eyes filled with tears.

'*Come,*' he repeated.

Ginger would forgive her: Ginger was a sport. Why, if he loved her – surely he would not mind? And if he did? Already she was indifferent to the small group on the shore watching them, the owner of the row boat angrily seeking another in which to pursue the original – now floating out into the Sound.

'Kiss me,' Claude pleaded.

To her amazement Ceci felt calm.

Claude knelt and held her waist. 'If I leave thee, death be my punishment!'

Though she knew he was quoting, his words disarmed her. 'Claude, you're going too far,' she said softly. 'I'm sorry if I've misled you.'

Tricked by his eloquence Claude frowned. Where were the arms he had expected to coil about him, the words of promise if he would only stay? He had imagined himself withdrawing from her, pointing to her beleaguered husband on the shore. Suddenly it occurred to him that it was *she* who was leaving him. She had come to say goodbye simply because she had seen *The Golden Harvest* sitting on the waters. What was more it did not look as if, after he had put about, she would stand on the shore calling 'Come back!'

Oblivious of the group outside the accommodation house, of Mr Begg running up and down the shore pointing towards where her row boat had drifted, of Tavistock going after it in the launch, Ceci stared towards the giant rock gate through which Claude would shortly sail with or without her. She would not need to look back. Claude could turn them about and once past Mitre Peak there would be no sound of humans, nor even the cry of their voices. Two, three minutes, all would be gone forever.

'It won't take long to get out of this fjord,' Claude whispered. 'Then the open seas.' Quickly turning she looked up at him and he saw her eyes fill. His heart leapt. She would come.

'I cannot come with you, Claude,' she said softly. 'I am a married woman.'

'What do you think your husband thinks having seen you like this?' Claude reasoned. 'Will he thank you for going back now?'

'Whether he thanks me or not I must go,' Ceci said, shaking the tears from her eyes and turning to look back at the shore.

'I will be gone in a minute', Claude choked. 'You'll never see me again.'

'I realize that.'

'*Come!*'

'I want to come more than anything in the world but I am a married woman!' Ceci shouted, her voice carrying across the water towards the shore. 'It may be a tired habit of no meaning to anyone but I cannot break it!'

'Are you thinking of your husband now?'

She shook her head.

'I see.'

On the shore, though Tavistock offered to convey him to *The Golden Harvest* in his launch, Ginger declined. 'Just get her if she jumps in,' he murmured. 'I doubt she can swim.'

Nodding, Tavistock put forth in the launch. This incident certainly explained a lot of the peculiar behaviour, the atmosphere and tensions on the trip. It would make good telling and was not something he had actually experienced before – a woman whose lover would sail right up a fjord. The incident seemed to have been planned more carefully than a prison break.

'So you won't come with me?'

Ceci shut her eyes and tried to imagine Claude gone. Quickly she opened them again for reassurance. Soon when she opened them he would not be there, yet while this moment was so precious, somehow she could not profit by it. On an impulse she ran into his arms.

'You'll come?'

If she could only keep him there for two days, if they could only lie together and exhaust their feelings before he left – it would be enough.

'I wish you could have stayed,' she said quietly. 'I wish we could have disagreed, come to hate each other.'

Devoid of expression Claude remained facing her. He was like a child who had come upon his parents' house burned to the ground. There was nothing he wanted to eat or to drink, nowhere to go. For the first time in his life he wanted a woman he could not have and she wanted him. He saw her glance towards him then move quickly to the back of the boat. 'Please,' he said, knowing she would not hear.

Seeing her waving Tavistock brought the launch alongside. When he arrived, to his surprise the woman was dry-eyed, business-like, much as if she had been saying farewell to a cousin.

'How kind of you, Mr Tavistock,' she said, lowering herself into the launch.

In a hurry to be gone from this place of suffering Claude longed to sail yet could not unglue his hands from the wooden railing. His body shook and tears coursed down his face as he listened to the squeak of the rowlocks receding across the water. Though his mood prepared him to smash the *Golden Harvest* into the first rock wall it encountered, a sense of preservation would guide him through. He must sink his thoughts, bury them deep where they could lie for many years before being brought into the light and examined. He had crossed a treacherous ocean containing creatures of the deep he had not known existed. Yet, like all waters, it was a reflection of himself . . .

As the launch beached Ceci walked past Ginger towards the accommodation house. No conventional phrase would serve between them. Aware of the Beggs' and Tavistock's eyes on him, watching for his reaction, Ginger merely sat and began whittling a stick. Not a literary man himself, he knew Cupid was reckoned to be an irresponsible child who shot arrows about creating havoc. He did not feel anger or resentment towards Ceci, just sadness that she was suffering. He could remember very few details about the Englishman, other than that he was educated and probably, like everyone else, a decent enough sort in his own place.

'I'm sorry, Ginger, I don't know what came over me.'

'It doesn't matter.'

'I must have been weighed down by the sheer mediocrity of the Beggs,' Ceci apologized.

'It doesn't matter.'

'I can't stand to be simply forgiven like this.'

'Maybe that's your cross,' Ginger shrugged. 'To always know there was something there you wanted and didn't have.'

'He would never have stayed with me. I don't think he would have valued me, even.'

'Maybe he would have.'

'I ran after him like a child for candy floss,' Ceci said, her eyes filling up again.

Ginger put his arm round her and she let it rest. 'You once told me,' he began, 'to let thoughts like that fly around your mind but not settle.' He began to stroke her head.

'When I think how I – I preached at you!' she sniffed.

407

'That stirring moral gospel when you came to me in Grevillton!'

'Never mind. It's all right.'

'I wrote you letters,' Ceci sobbed, 'Telling you how you were supposed to be married to Maureen.'

'Sssh.'

'It's only now I realize how brave you were when you left me. You were unselfish. And then all that time you struggled to get Hexham for me – just in case.'

'I'm sorry he left you,' Ginger murmured.

'I don't suppose he would have kept me for ever.'

As he watched the sadness of the truth sink into Ceci's eyes Ginger felt he loved her even more. He had certainly been there himself and had reason to know how she felt. The sense of desolation would take some time to go. 'You know us Catholics,' he said, trying to sound cheerful. 'We like to think there's a purpose in everything. Could be Claude Bonham was meant to happen to us. Maybe we'll appreciate each other more now.'

As she dried her eyes and looked across at him Ceci realized with a shock that Ginger was right. Yet at the same time she sensed that from now on there would always be that hankering . . .

'Don't worry about it,' Ginger urged, seeing fright cross her face. 'You may be too numb to feel anything for me now other than that I'm your best friend, but carry on as we are and it'll come back again – I promise you.'

Wearily Ceci slipped her hand into Ginger's. She was tireder than she knew possible, yet neither the thought of bed nor a cup of tea could revive her. 'I don't know how we're going to get out of here,' she murmured. 'Will you see about a steamer?'

'There's a choice. Either up the West Coast towards Hokitika and Greymouth or back around via Dunedin.'

Ceci nodded.

'Failing that, if we wait, we may pick up a steamer going clear up to Lyttelton.'

Lyttelton, Greymouth, Hokitika. It seemed all place names had some memory for her.

'I intend to pull myself together, Ginger,' Ceci assured him. 'You didn't deserve to be treated like that.'

'I was hurt,' Ginger said. 'Actually.'

In the dining room that evening the Beggs glanced across at them as they ate quietly. They could not make head nor tail of the relationship, yet Tavistock noticed that when the man raised his eyes to the woman there was gratitude in them and when the woman looked directly at the man there was respect.

'If we can get a direct steamer to Lyttelton,' Ceci began. 'Let us rest some days in Christchurch and – and – try to make new memories. Perhaps the boys will be back with their racehorse.'

Ginger leaned forward: 'Faith will certainly flatter herself that despite the – er – sandfly incident, this trip has done us good.'

Almost afraid to be alone, Ceci decided she would lie very close with Ginger that night.

Chapter 30

Lizabeth crouched behind the bandstand and waited for Michael or Kevin to come by. Surely it would be soon, for the horses were already parading prior to the start of the next race.

'Sit still,' she said to Little Frank. 'Don't go out there!'

Usually she could control Little Frank and the twins at meetings, could stop them running into the crowds after colourful sights and sounds. Just as she was wishing she'd brought something for them to eat, Michael appeared. Lizabeth got to her feet: 'Michael!' she called, cautioning the twins to 'Stay there!' as she stepped from behind the bandstand. Quickly she pulled back. Had she actually seen her father out there? Leaning further out, against all odds, there was Ceci! With such an entourage around him Michael would be difficult to 'touch' and this time she did not need just money. With mounting frustration she held Little Frank and the twins to her while Ginger, Ceci and Michael receded into the crowd. There was no sign of Kevin.

Already she could hear the names of horses being shouted, numbers going up and arguments about divvies as the crowd surged away from the enclosure and towards the bird cage where the horses were parading. Suddenly she saw Kevin turning in the crowd, looking for the others. 'Kevin! Kevin!' she shouted. He did not hear. In the next minute she saw Michael steering Ceci and Ginger towards him, and turning in her direction. She shrank back. As their faces passed – her father's older and more lined than

410

she remembered, Ceci's with a wistfulness to it — she held still. If Ginger had turned he could have touched her. Little Frank started to cry. 'Quiet!'

'Make him turn around, make him turn around,' Lizabeth prayed, her eyes on Kevin's back.

As if by magic Kevin turned.

'Kevin! Over here.'

'What is it?' he asked, ducking under the bandstand. 'You've seen Dad's here.'

Lizabeth nodded: 'I need somewhere to stay.'

Kevin reached in his pocket for his keys. 'You know where the house is.'

Lizabeth nodded gratefully. 'If I go — will you promise not to tell anyone I'm there? Not even Frank?'

'All right,' Kevin said without thinking.

'Especially don't tell Father.'

In the club house Ceci saw with amusement that doors sprang open at Michael's approach. Nobody could do enough for them: clearly he was a person of some consequence in these circles, was aware of it and enjoyed the fact. 'Where's Kevin?' she asked.

'Sloped off again, has he?' Michael asked. 'May I get you a drink, sir?'

'Sir?' Ginger returned. 'Is that what chaps call their fathers down here?' Michael grinned. 'Double brandy, gin, there's a good lad! What about you, Ceci?'

Sinking in a large leather armchair Ceci watched Ginger being introduced to the club secretary, the club president and various other high-ups in the Christchurch establishment.

'Actually it was Melville's reserved place we parked in,' Michael was saying. 'Good sport, old Melville.' He took a cigar from a box on the table and expertly cut the end.

'Mind you don't choke,' Ginger warned.

'I would have thought you'd need a pass to get in here,' Ceci observed.

'You do, you do,' Michael assured her.

'But *you* don't. Maybe Kevin's round at the stables?' Ceci suggested.

'More likely caught up in the action,' Ginger grinned. 'Listen to that!' From beyond the windows came a great rising cheer as some lucky horse made it home.

'Going to show us something, are you, Michael?'

'I don't think you'll be disappointed, sir,' Michael replied, leading them from the club house.

As they approached the stables everyone jumped to attention, touching caps and standing out of their way.

'That's ours up ahead,' Michael said, nodding towards a stall outside which a youth was standing guard. 'Where's Ritter?' he demanded.

'I'll fetch him directly, sir,' the boy stammered, running from the spot.

'Ritter is my trainer,' Michael explained. 'I'd like him to show you the horse.'

'Everything all right, sir?' a small man asked, hurrying up.

'Ritter. Show the filly, will you?'

Although Ceci took a back seat it was obvious from the noises Ginger was making that the filly had been a good choice and showed great promise.

'Not much longer, sir, and she'll be taking every cup that's going,' Ritter assured Ginger.

'Are you racing her today?' Ceci asked.

'We want her to *win* her first race,' Michael explained. 'And from then on, every race. She's already established a track record that will beat anything you'll see today. Just want to give her a bit more stamina first.'

'I think she should race now,' came the softer voice of Kevin from behind.

Michael frowned. 'You don't appreciate, Kevin,' he began.

As at an agreed signal the argument stopped, but not before Ceci sensed how far apart the boys had drifted.

'Nice horse,' said Ginger approvingly. 'Very nice horse.'

Even watching them Ceci felt Michael's disapproval of his father's lack of sophistication. She went to stand by Ginger.

'Michael,' Kevin whispered as they passed down the walkway together, 'I have to tell you something. Keep it to yourself?'

'Depends what it is.'

'I've given Lizabeth the key to our place. You're not to say she's there.'

Out in the paddock Lizabeth ran in and out of the crowd hunting for Clarrie. The child was impossible! While Hope would sit quietly, Clarrie only had to see someone offer a child a toffee and she would be off over there, holding her hand out saying, 'Diz me one! Diz me one!' 'Clarrie!' Lizabeth shouted, turning to glance towards Hope sitting quietly under the bandstand holding Little Frank by the wrist like a good girl, and, despite his crying and thumping, not allowing him to run after their mother. It didn't take much to make Hope sit still, poor thing. Even when their father had been angry the previous night she had simply sat there holding on to Little Frank as she had been told to, while in the next room all hell had broken loose, largely because of little Clarrie. If only her father had not been there! How very much Lizabeth would like to have talked to Ceci.

Climbing to their reserved seats on that portion of the grandstand which was covered, Ceci listened to Michael,

413

Kevin and Ginger talking. From where she sat she could see not only a large section of the track but a space in the paddocks where people were milling, children running in and out and casual vendors selling refreshments. For a moment a shape in the crowd struck her as familiar – a woman bending over a child – shaking it, but in a second it was gone. Even casually listening to the conversation behind her concerning totalisators, Ceci could sense the extent to which the boys disagreed on that subject. As far as she could make out, the totalisator itself was both an idea and a machine; the idea being that punters who won should share equally the total of all money put on the race, a certain amount being taken off for costs and government taxes. The machine, apparently, was the apparatus that did the addition.

'It'll take care of the bookmakers,' Kevin pointed out. 'Stop them manipulating the odds.'

'And *us*!' Michael insisted angrily. 'If people want to bet, let them!'

Quickly Ceci concluded it was Michael who had substantially gained from advising people where and when to place bets.

'We're not short of a bob or two,' Kevin said firmly.

'Look,' said Michael, as if the last word lay with him, 'already a lot of clubs have totalisators. The on-course bookmakers have no power to ban them. A lot of clubs won't allow bookmakers! I doubt the poor sods have ten years left before bookmaking becomes illegal. So there's no need for you to take such a moral tone.'

Gradually Ginger realized the boys were arguing. 'Steady on,' he cautioned.

'It's Kevin,' Michael complained. 'Always afraid to stick his neck out.'

'More like Michael wanting to control other people's lives,' Kevin offered.

'We'll talk about something else,' said Michael. 'How's the family?'

'Fine,' Ginger nodded.

'Myra?'

'She's good.'

'Faith?'

'Faith is all right.'

'Lizabeth?' Michael said pointedly. 'You ever hear from Lizabeth?'

As Kevin looked down Ceci sensed that Michael was taunting him with this question yet it was Ginger who took it like a body blow. As at a shadow crossing his mind he withdrew his eyes from the track and turned them inwards. The purpose of his trip to Milford Sound had been to get in condition to tackle Frank. What was it he should have done before leaving Christchurch that time? He did not hear Michael gasp 'Look at that!' as the three-year-old colt he was interested in took off with a spurt. 'Supposed to be second favourite!' Michael told Ceci, leaning forward pointing at the track where by now the bunched horses were beginning to string out. Around them the tension became unbearable as in utter silence binoculars were snatched, hearts beat faster, breaths were indrawn with sharp exclamations as the first two horses came into the straight, each trying to displace the other. As the crowd below thrust forward and fifty yards from the finish line the whips came out, the jockeys standing, almost lifting their mounts, Ginger was not watching but thinking.

And suddenly he remembered! He looked up. Although he could see no conclusion, apparently the colt had won.

'Damn!' Michael exclaimed, climbing on to his seat to

observe the triumphant horse being led towards its owners who were receiving congratulations.

'Looks a fine horse to me,' Ginger grinned.

'They're all horses to you!' Michael snapped with marked disrespect. 'Doubt you know the difference between a thoroughbred and a hat!'

As they left the enclosure Ginger's spirits lifted. He knew what he had omitted to do in Christchurch and, knowing it, willingly returned his mind to Michael who was talking about the threat the young colt posed.

Behind them walked Ceci with Kevin, noticing him glance from left to right, his eyes straying, hesitating by a deserted bandstand en route to their carriage. Never had the difference in the two boys' characters been so obvious. Whether it was that Kevin had stopped allowing Michael to speak for both or that they had always disagreed but not about things Kevin cared enough to speak up about, she did not know. Now it was as if the horse they had brought from Australia had marked an end to their 'oneness'.

'What's the matter with you two?' Ginger asked, sensing an underlying tension between them.

'My whippet got his kittens,' Michael drawled. 'He brought back this mangey stray from under the grandstand because its kittens were falling out of it and Sadie went into the kitchen and ate them up.'

'Ate them up?'

'Warm and fresh as they came out.'

Revolted, Ceci looked away. She had heard of this sort of thing but that was no excuse for Michael's cavalier attitude towards it. 'I'm so sorry, Kevin,' she said, leaning forward.

Kevin blinked.

'He's being a chump,' Michael teased.

'Leave him alone and respect his feelings,' Ginger suddenly shouted.

As they entered the boys' house Ceci sensed the evening would be uncomfortable and during tea conversation dragged so badly they heard a door bang upstairs.

'What was that?' Ginger asked.

Kevin went crimson. 'I – I – there may be a window open.'

A wry look crossed Michael's face.

At a faint sound like the cry of a child, Kevin began struggling to make conversation but, lacking Michael's social graces and unsuited to simple chatter his efforts to fill the silence rendered it more embarrassing.

'Why don't you two stay the night?' Michael asked when Kevin finally desisted.

'I think we'll stay in a hotel,' Ceci instinctively replied. 'It would be more convenient.'

'There's plenty of room here,' Michael continued.

'Next time perhaps,' Ginger said, rising. 'If you should come on Lizabeth though – I believe she's down here – let me know her whereabouts.'

'We'll tell her you want to get in touch,' Kevin said quickly.

'A man can't do better than that,' Michael smiled, adding, 'can he?'

'Kevin has changed so much,' Ceci observed as they left the house.

'A bit.'

'Apart from disagreeing with Michael he's – how shall I say – considerate of others.'

'Speaking his mind. That's all.'

'More than that. He's become thoughtful.' Ceci paused. 'And more withdrawn.'

'Don't know where he gets that from!'

Turning, Ceci looked back at the house they had just left and noticed a light going out in an upper room. 'The atmosphere in there – I couldn't understand it.'

'They're growing lads.'

Once Ceci was in bed, with the help of the hotel proprietor Ginger did what he had set his mind on. He located and talked to a private detective. Nor did it take the man long to determine that he was the father of the 'racehorse boys' – as Michael and Kevin were known. He listened just long enough to gain sufficient information to appear knowledgeable. 'It'll cost you dear,' he began.

'I've money,' Ginger replied.

'I'd have to put a man in to gain the confidence of the down-and-outs. If this Frank is living as a tramp, one of my men will have to pose as one. He'd have to be in a position to stand the tramps a billy of tea now and then, you appreciate ... the odd beer.' He stared at Ginger wondering how much he was worth. 'Not a pretty sight ...'

'What?'

'A young woman with twins begging in public.'

Ginger whitened. 'That's a vicious lie!'

'A woman with twins and a toddler stands out. Seen her myself.'

'I warn you – '

'Twins and a toddler. The toddler musta been about – what?'

'The boy'll be three, the twin girls four and a half.'

'That'll be her, then,' the man nodded.

'You get me the man first.'

'The woman's easier.'

'Follow her to the man.'

'So it's the man you're after – not the woman?'

'As long as the man is at large – the woman will run to

418

him,' Ginger shouted angrily. 'I should have thought that was obvious! I – I want to – take care of him first.'

'Against the law,' the man said, trying to rile Ginger and knowing the more angry he became the more he would talk. 'Seems to me, you're more concerned to punish this man than to get your daughter back.'

Ginger got to his feet. There was more than a little truth in that but once he had found out where the couple lived he would either arrange for Frank's wife and children to arrive there, or would somehow get Frank down to Dunedin and contrive that Lizabeth should follow and come on them all together. If all parties were destitute as he imagined, a large sum of money could propel Frank or his original wife in any direction. Failing that he always had the photographs. 'I just don't want the girl frightened away,' he said firmly from the door.

Returning to the hotel he found Ceci asleep.

'The Commercial Hotel again, was it?' she teased the following morning.

'I was walking off my feelings.'

'It's unlikely you'll ever see Frank again,' Ceci said, guessing. 'And less likely that it was Frank you saw previously.'

Ginger changed the subject. 'I shan't be sorry to get home,' he said.

'Nor me. It's as if we've been around the world! Do you think,' she added, trying to demonstrate her renewed interest in Hexham, 'we should have Hexham insured?'

'Insured?'

'Like they insure shipping cargo – '

'Can't insure against rabbits,' Ginger shrugged.

'There's a lot in the paper,' Ceci pointed out. 'People trying to re-let ruins. The back pages are full of notices of auction. I think land prices are dropping.'

Ginger shrugged again. At that moment he was more

interested in the contents of Hexham than its land value because he intended to sell off whatever was necessary to raise sufficient capital to put out so many detectives and agents that within the space of a very short time, were Frank and Lizabeth indeed in Christchurch, they would be in his pocket. There would not be one place from the poorest shanty to the wealthiest hotel that would be safe for them. Lizabeth would only have to appear on the street with the children to be picked up. In fact, any young woman stepping out with twin girls and a toddler would not get far. As the detective had said, it was unlikely that any sighting would be false.

'Christchurch always seems to restore your sense of purpose,' Ceci observed, watching him pack.

'I'm ready to leave, Ceci. I assure you.'

Allowing him to help her up Ceci climbed into the carriage. She too was ready for the High Country. She needed its quietness and open spaces to adjust to the changed awareness of Ginger which had come to her since the incident on the *Golden Harvest*. 'I can't believe what I did in Milford Sound,' she said softly. 'Did I really do that?'

'You rowed after him in a boat.'

'I can't believe it.'

Grateful for his support of her she recalled again how she had been unable to offer sympathy to Ginger at his time of rejection – yet he had been compassionate towards her. She had much to make up to him. The *Golden Harvest* had unleashed in her a stronger, perhaps the real, love they had been waiting for. Because she had 'fallen' she could appreciate his nobility in the face of her earlier sanctimoniousness. Intimacy now would be different in that he knew her so much better, at a much deeper level, that it would be difficult to hide. Indeed as the coach wound back towards Hexham she felt slightly in awe of him and less confident of herself. As he glanced at her then away she detected in herself a new shyness. The fact was, she realized with a sense of relief, she was linked to Ginger forever.

Chapter 31

'Now I don't want to be mucked about,' Reg warned
Stebbins on his return to the backblocks. He had been
made to do a lot of to'ing and fro'ing in Christchurch,
even visit the Land Registry with the pawnbroker's lawyer
friend and by the time he'd done signing this and signing
that he was not sure what his position was, other than that
he had enough money in his pocket to pay Stebbins clear
through to the other side of winter. On the way up he had
had the intelligence to hide most of it in a biscuit tin dug
into the ground in a sheltered spot of woodland which was
unlikely to be cleared. It would not have done for Stebbins
to know exactly how much he had or to be given the
opportunity of stealing the lot and vanishing. This way he
felt fairly safe.

'Way I look at it,' Stebbins went on, 'you pays me a
particular sum a week.'

'How much?'

Stebbins elaborated.

Reg did his sums. 'Too much.'

'A man's got to be paid.'

'I'll make you an offer and if you don't like it, that's it.'

Stebbins listened. 'Can't do you the whole season for
that. Could stay up to — say two weeks from the end.'

Reg realized he had made a mistake in being honest. He
should have started lower, leaving himself room to bargain. Not much point in trying to appeal to the man's
honour. 'If you want to fling in a whole season's money
for two weeks' work — that's your affair,' Reg shrugged,

turning away as if the matter was of complete indifference to him.

Stebbins picked at his chin. 'Well – seein' as I'm getting full board . . . go on with you then.'

With a sense of relief Reg went in to break the news to Annie, warning her to make sure he got plenty to eat as they were getting him on the cheap. 'I cleared it up with him that he wouldn't leave us halfway with our money spent,' Reg explained. What he did not add was that they'd reached the mid-point of their trust period on the land. If they did not survive the season and get in a position to make improvements – never mind all the bits of paper: the land would go right back to the government.

'Now don't you hang around here staring at me dressing the child,' Annie scolded. 'You get out there and get Stebbins organized.'

Reg moved to the door.

'And pull your shoulders back!' she called after him. She did not like the way in the past few weeks he'd developed a kind of stoop.

Reg stepped out into the sunlight. Maybe he was getting a little soft in the head: that's what came of living with a woman and child. Often when he should have been working he'd found himself remembering moments like when Little Annie had first discovered an ear on the side of her head, how her hand had kept returning to it and he could see her thinking, What's this thing stuck here? Or the time she had suddenly become aware of her feet. It was amazing to see the child growing, to be privy to almost everything she knew as her awareness of her own body, and her parents, and the dimensions and possibilities of their home opened up before her. He remembered with delight how she had learnt to crackle dead leaves in her hands, how the new sounds had frightened then attracted her, her fascination at the way water splashed up and hit her in the face when she beat at it with a stick. Realizing he was smiling again Reg looked up to see Stebbins observing him.

'Now you're to keep out of the men's way today,' Annie told Little Annie, 'because they're doin' something very important.' She always talked to the child when she dressed her, often of their future together – the three of them; the things she would do, wild promises about the dresses she would make for her. She'd even found herself chattering on about events quite close to her daughter's wedding day! But Little Annie wasn't listening.

'Put your arm through here.'

Nor did she want to get buttoned into her top when there were voices outside in the clearing. 'Go out*side*,' she said, backing away from Annie.

Annie let her go. The child had even brought her closer to the hamlet, for sooner or later she would need some form of schooling and though they did not belong to the community, she was confident her little girl would not be kept out. Indeed when she went to the hamlet people sent their children over to talk to Little Annie as an act of charity. Shyly the children came forward to look at the little girl who lived beyond the hamlet but was not afraid of them. Watching, Annie felt that as the children became friends she too would get to know their mothers. Perhaps one day even Reg would see fit to be neighbourly. Maybe even one day they would have people from the hamlet up to dinner!

Out in the hills Stebbins put a proposal to Reg. 'Seems a pity to just kill 'em,' he said, pointing at a small group of rabbits he recognized, having reared the mother and father by hand before releasing them together and now seeing the mother's floppy ear and the father's fight marks.

424

'Kill 'em!' Reg ordered.

'I'll sell some live down the hamlet and split with you, shall I?' Stebbins offered.

'You'll get rid of the lot.'

'Someone'd be glad to buy a breeding pair. It's more money for you too. Said yourself things weren't out of hand yet.'

'Ain't interested in more money at this stage.'

'Well, I got to look out for myself.'

'You're getting your full whack.'

'You're the boss,' Stebbins said wisely.

'You dig a hole over there and into it goes every rabbit,' Reg stated flatly. 'That's what I'm paying you for.'

'Right ho.'

'Go on. Get started. What are you waiting for? Shoot those bleeding rabbits.'

Reg pointed at the small group looking with affection towards Stebbins. 'I mean this to be the last season we're eating rabbit pie.'

Stebbins shouldered his gun. He was a mite tired of rabbit himself. Maybe he could see some way to talk Reg into slaughtering beef cattle. 'Well I'll bring us a couple of rabbits then, shall I, for lunch?' he asked civilly. 'You know any different ways of cooking 'em.'

Reg shook his head. They would have to be very careful with their winter vegetables as it was difficult to make things go three ways. Maybe Annie could do something with the parsnips and eggs to brighten up their diet. Stebbins had to be kept under control but in a good humour. 'I'll see about it,' he murmured, moving off.

Having bitten the bullet Annie continued to sleep with Reg despite the fact of Stebbins being in the room. While they were quiet about it they shared the same bed, usually with Little Annie coming in between them for warmth. In

425

the darkness which was never complete Annie felt Stebbins' eyes on her and resented his presence. Every time Reg breathed trustfully out or Little Annie made a wakeful noise she resented this stranger being privy to them. Because he insisted on being treated as one of the family he ate with them and though Annie had asked Reg if she and the child could eat alone first, Reg thought it unwise. She never let distaste cross her face at Stebbins' presence in the room and following her mother's lead, Little Annie seemed not to notice him. Nor did she ask Reg to have him mend his ways. There was not a hair's worth of difference between the two men to a casual stranger, she supposed, yet Reg was a man with a sense of purpose and dignity. Stebbins was perhaps what Reg might have become if she had not taken him under her wing.

Knowing how he had longed for a home, at times Reg found himself feeling sorry for the man. The fact that he washed off round the back of the house, slopped great quantities of ice-cold water over his sallow white body and made loud shuddering noises calculated to attract women and children as he did so, Reg put down to ignorance. Probably the man thought that on his twice a year wash, people who had houses with conveniences like water butts chose to wash by the house. Didn't seem to occur to him that it would have been the decent thing to do down to the creek with a piece of soap.

As winter went on it looked almost as if they'd be able to give him his cards, for fewer rabbits were to be seen and evidence of them too was declining. Nonetheless Stebbins was up and out early every morning 'on his rounds' as he put it.

'What does he do out there?' Annie asked Reg, moving closer to him. Secretly she feared he was simply beyond the window, or with his ear pressed to the planks just near to their bed trying to hear if they were being intimate.

'Don't know,' Reg murmured.

Out in the hills Stebbins bent down and took a little brush from his pocket. Carefully he swept up the rabbit droppings he could find, pocketed them, and moved on to the next lot. Nobody would think anything of a burrow unless there were droppings by it and if he made enough noise as he and Reg approached on their inspection, the man would assume the burrow was deserted and be pleased. The situation could be allowed to ride for a few weeks then gradually, place by place, he would stop sweeping up the droppings. At that time he could definitely negotiate for an increase in his wages. Tipping the rabbits' droppings into a hole he had dug near the creek, Stebbins rinsed off his hands and turned to head back towards the clearing.

'Here's your breakfast,' Annie said abruptly, placing it on the table as he entered. She did not meet his eyes – a fact which irritated him. The eggs were fried the way he liked them, she had made a sort of sausage from some ground-up rabbit spiced with pepper pod seeds and bush clover, and alongside that were two potato patties made from the potatoes saved from the night before. Instantly he realized that neither she nor Reg had had potatoes.

'At least it ain't parsnips again,' he teased.

'You know very well you never have parsnips for breakfast!' Annie snapped.

Stebbins smiled up at her, pleased to have drawn her out. He gave her a slow wink. In a minute he would call her 'Annie'. See how she liked that. He watched her cross the room and noticed her bottom wobbling. As she bent before the hearth her dress rose so that he could see her

427

ankles and lower calves. What a fine thing a woman was, he thought sadly.

'What are you staring at?' Annie cried, spinning.

'Nice bum.'

Quickly Annie snatched the pan of scalding water from the hearth and crossed to him with it. 'Would you like this over your head right now?' she demanded.

He looked at her heaving breasts, knowing she would not dare. 'I seen them before, remember?' he said, nodding towards her bosom.

'You're right I wouldn't waste this boiling water on you,' Annie said calmly. 'It's not worth my husband's trouble fetching it.'

Stebbins watched her return to the hearth. He'd like to put that woman across his knee and that was a fact. He wiped his mouth on the back of his hand and leaned from the table. He had never run his hands through a woman's hair or stroked her head. What would it feel like to hold a woman next to you in the night? If Reg were out and he didn't need a place for winter, he could've gone the whole hog . . . Again he glanced covertly at Annie, now singing by the open doorway, oblivious of his existence. How unfair it was that a man like Reg, no better than him in any way, should land on his feet with a woman like this and be in a position to give him money. To have a wife and a child made a man respected even if he were poor. Decency was a land too far away for him to reach. Now if this couple would take him on permanent and give him a salary, perhaps he could find someone in the hamlet to marry him? Oh, it was pointless. He had nothing to offer anyone and must get what he could by his wits.

'You need any help around the house, Missus?' he asked dolefully.

'No,' Annie assured him. 'In fact if you've finished clearing up our rabbits, you can leave right now!'

Huh! Nobody even cared where he wintered over. Even the sheep were better provided for.

As they drew deeper into winter Stebbins' resentment at his status increased. The nights were bitterly cold, the creek had frozen over and although he was still being paid by Reg there was no food to be bought in the hamlet. Annie's winter supply of fresh root vegetables, plus those that had been stored, was carefully marked and measured out, the foliage having been eaten off the tops before they were dug – at which time it had been discovered that a plague of mites beneath the soil had riddled their way into carrots and turnips alike. Those leeks which had withstood the first snow were spindly by comparison with previous years' and although there was no question of starvation, it was a winter that would be remembered as being 'difficult'. Even the rabbit supplies had dwindled, making folk wish they'd purchased a breeding pair. Unwilling to sacrifice their hens or cocks, men took to hunting wild fowl.

'I think we could get rid of Stebbins right now,' Annie pointed out to Reg. 'He doesn't catch rabbits. We're clear of them. You can't tell me there are any out there because if there were, a selfish man like that would get one. He's as hungry as we are and you know that.'

'Best let him finish us up,' Reg said after consideration.

'Well what does he do all day? He gets up, eats a big breakfast – at least bigger than we do – then he's off out there!'

'I don't know,' Reg said truthfully. 'Must be some left or he wouldn't stay. When Ju-Ju's sorted, I'll follow him and find out.'

'Ju-Ju? What's wrong with Ju-Ju?' Annie said alarmed,

for the young cow Ju-Ju – like all the others, named by Little Annie – was the child's favourite.

'Won't get on her feet. Won't eat.'

'Let me have a look,' Annie cried, hurrying from the house. As she reached the shelter, she found the poor beast lying on the ground rolling her eyes.

'Oh my Lord,' she murmured, grasping her mouth. 'What shall we do?'

Reg went down to the hamlet and returned with the man Pieter and a brother who stood shaking their heads. 'We don't know so much about a cow,' they explained. 'Maybe if she sick, better you keep her away from the others.'

'But there's no other shelter,' Annie protested. 'Poor Ju-Ju will be terribly cold outside.'

With Stebbins' help the men constructed a shanty half-way up the hill to which Ju-Ju was half dragged, half carried. She moaned hideously when touched, her cries being almost human.

That night in bed Annie could not bear the thought of Ju-Ju.

'I'll go and see her, shall I, if you like?' Reg asked.

'You'll never find your way up there in the dark.'

'Can hear her from here.' Quietly he slipped into his boots and crossed the floor, pushed open the door and stepped into the clearing.

Lying opposite Annie, Stebbins gave him a good five minutes. The cow would not get better: he was quite sure of it because he had pushed a length of wire into her behind and twisted it around. This usually ruptured them and when their pain got sufficiently bad, a man would slaughter them, providing a good bite of meat. The thought of the roast beef was so tasty he forgot for a moment that Annie was within reach.

Suddenly Annie felt his hand on her shoulder.

'Move over,' he whispered urgently, trying to roll her forwards with his hands.

Instinctively Annie braced herself against the bed to protect Little Annie, who lay in her arms, from the movement. Mercifully the child slept on.

'My word you're warm!' Stebbins gasped, getting his knee in the small of her back, pushing and struggling to pull off the full set of clothes he slept in. With horror Annie felt his sharp toenails scrabbling at her ankles, his rough knee behind her thighs, his arms reaching around her as his panting wild breath urgently blew in her hair. With resolve she held on to Little Annie so that her body, like an iron cradle, did not move. If anything woke the child it would be the heart-rending moans of Ju-Ju getting louder by the minute — against which Stebbins' efforts were pathetic and mediocre.

'Just let me slip the head of it in where it's nice and warm,' he wheedled, rubbing at her.

Annie did not move.

'I won't clear out the rest of your rabbits then,' he said in a voice giving away the fact of his mounting excitement.

Gently she held Little Annie steady. She would not get pregnant from a man like this: she had only just finished her period. Securing herself to the bed's frame she opened her legs very slightly, just enough with a deal of squeezing and squirming to let Stebbins in from behind her.

'That's a good girl,' Stebbins breathed. 'I'll get rid of your rabbits for you now.'

As he sawed against her in agitation, Annie thought of the timber saws dragging against the hardwood on the West Coast, their whine, the smell of sawdust ... Above it rose the agonized screams of Ju-Ju, suddenly cut short

431

by a gun shot. Stebbins pulled out and sat up. In a second he was scuttling across the room to his own bed.

'It's all right,' Annie murmured to Little Annie who had awakened, 'Daddy's coming.' Casually she rose, went outside and tipped cold water between her legs in the moonlight. Returning inside the house she got the fire going. As she put water on to make some tea, Annie realized that the time it took Reg to come down was an indication of his sorrow. When he appeared his eyes were red from crying.

'I had to shoot her, Annie,' he apologized. 'I couldn't bear the sound of it.'

Annie squeezed his shoulder.

'Poor little thing — she was so trusting.'

'She died suffering,' Annie nodded. 'There's nothing I can say will change that. Sometimes I don't understand God.'

Reg blew his nose. How any God could let a little animal suffer like that he did not know. If it had been him that had to suffer, well, fair enough. He'd done plenty to deserve it and, no doubt, given time, would do plenty more.

Annie glanced at Stebbins who was making a show of pretending to come awake. 'My husband has had to shoot that cow,' she told him.

Stebbins sat up. 'Never mind, Missus. Seein' as it's upset him and rightly so, I'll give a hand with the slaughtering.'

Reg turned on him angrily: 'We're not eating Ju-Ju.'

Stebbins frowned. He hadn't counted on sentimentality.

'Could've had anything. Could've eaten some of your poison for one thing.'

'I ain't never used no rabbit poison this side o' that band of trees,' Stebbins shouted. 'And that's a fact.'

'I'm burning her.'

432

'Oh Reg! Couldn't we bury her instead?'

'Annie,' he replied, his voice rising, 'we've got to think of the community, the other people here. Suppose she's got some real bad plague that will get to their cows. Never mind us! It'd wipe everyone out and they've done nothing to deserve that.'

Annie looked down.

'You're a bloody fool,' Stebbins shouted angrily. 'That's a nice piece of beef and you don't have to eat the cow's stomach!'

'Give me a cup of tea, Annie,' Reg murmured, ignoring Stebbins. Maybe the poison would have stayed in the animal's innards and not got into its muscles but he dare not take the chance. Stebbins was right that the beef would have fetched a fair price in the hamlet. Truth was, he'd like to have been in a position to give it away as the folk there had always been kind to him. If he buried the cow to satisfy Annie, chances were a dog, or even Stebbins, would dig it up.

On an empty stomach and cursing inwardly, Stebbins set off towards the hills. If he'd had an ounce of sense he would have broken the cow's leg, not ruptured its innards. Problem was with people that poor, they'd go to any lengths to mend the leg rather than slaughter. A big farm, a place with hired hands, would shoot a damaged animal straight out rather than carry a tale of it home by which time they would have forgotten where the beast was or it would have dragged itself off somewhere else. Problem was you could pull that one too often. If a farmer found too many cows or sheep were breaking their legs, questions got asked.

Reaching his destination, breathless from the climb, Stebbins looked down into the gully where his breeding

433

stock were kept. On second thoughts it was not worth pulling the one about a sudden resurgence in rabbits and asking for more money. With a man like Reg it wouldn't work and he could turn very nasty given their original agreement. On second thoughts, better to just let nature take its course. He would continue sweeping up what pellets he found, encouraging them in the feeling that all was well until the weather turned and he could be on his way. In the meanwhile there might be a little sport left with the woman but nothing else to look forward to in this hungry winter. This was positively the last time he would go rabbiting at such an altitude. Lucky rabbits with their fur coats! In fact seeing the way he had been treated over the cow, he had a good mind to breed them faster and set forth a veritable plague on his departure. Yes! he decided angrily. That is exactly what he would do.

A couple of days later when the weather lifted he made a second approach to Annie. This time she was alone behind the house, her child sleeping within. Creeping up behind her, he pinched her hard on the bottom but to his surprise, instead of submitting as before, she swung and hit him with such force that he reeled against the house and cracked a board. Then she spat in his hair and walked off.

'You're not treating me right,' he called breathlessly after her.

For a while after Stebbins left, things were so good between Reg and Annie that she was tempted to tell him about Stebbins – but good sense held her back. It would serve no purpose to give substance to a totally insignificant piece of behaviour on the part of a wandering man. Although she had disliked and done her best to avoid him she could understand what he had done and why. What difference was there really between Stebbins' trespass on her and her stealing coal in the old days? The man was a wretch but now he had gone she could feel sorry for him.

Though it had cost them dear. They had survived winter and Stebbins and the rabbits and what with the damaged crops they hadn't bothered gathering, their land had lain fallow, which could only do it good. Despite hardship they had taken their medicine yet succeeded in saving their seed stock.

Congratulating himself that the winter had only cost them the one cow, as time passed, so excited was Reg by the fact of their survival, he could not sleep. 'It's no good, Annie,' he said turning over. 'Think I'll get up and take a walk.'

'You can do as you like now he's gone!' Annie laughed.

With a sense of pride and satisfaction Reg stepped from their home into the moonlight and crossed the clearing. Already they had broken the ground up after winter, their seeds were planted and with a bit of luck their loan would be paid off by autumn. Carefully he stepped around their vegetable plot and set off towards the hills. Chances were the hamlet people would take even more of his cocksfoot harvest this year. Maybe he could even up the price – given they had so many cows down there. He felt like standing on top of a hill and shouting.

As he rose above the trees and paused to take in the sleeping landscape silver beneath the moon, he noticed how silent it was, how changed from the days when he had stood in this very spot and by dint of following scavenging birds had been drawn to the carcasses of rabbits Stebbins had poisoned. Those days were over and thank God for it! Reg got to his knees and prayed. Rising, he turned to go back down the hill but in the moonlight something moved in the corner of his vision. Spinning quickly he scanned the horizon. Nothing. Cautiously Reg crouched then lay on his stomach. From this position what he had seen became quite clear: it was the silhouette of a fully grown buck male rabbit observing him.

Chapter 32

Hardly had Ginger and Ceci returned to Hexham than Faith broke the news that while they were away Ginger's father had died. Having stayed with her grandparents – in fact it was there she had met Dougall – Faith had known the old man's chest was weak and that the indifferent sea air of Dunedin had done little to justify their original move down from the High Country – yet still the death was a shock. Without consulting Ginger, she had invited her gran to come and live at Hexham and, never having met her, Ceci hoped things would go smoothly. The inclusion of a newcomer in a household often led to friction and lately both she and Ginger had come to appreciate that if they did not settle down to the task of creating a child – in fairness to both themselves and the child, they should stop trying.

'I'll say one thing,' Faith observed. 'She got over the death very quickly.'

When she arrived, the old lady came in like a lion, quickly arranging her crucifix on the cupboard top and her medals and rosaries around her room which soon resembled a shrine. No one was allowed to enter without knocking and on both sides of the door she made her presence felt.

'We can hardly stop her cooking if she wants to,' Ceci reasoned with Ginger, as his mother bumbled about their kitchen economizing with a sheep's head. However, when the old girl wanted to be called 'Mother' by Ceci too, Ceci felt she had to draw the line, for it was clear that the old girl wanted the title for the authority that went with it and nothing else.

'If you want me to call you something personal, I'll call you Gran, Mrs O'Sullivan, if you prefer – or how about Adelaide?'

When she did not get her way with the 'Mother' title she began knowingly to call Ceci 'Maureen', which in its own way did quite some damage between Ceci and Ginger.

'You know she's not Maureen,' Faith scolded gently.

'Sure, but it serves her right,' the old girl replied. 'Your mother was a poor thing . . .'

Ceci watched Adelaide moving about the house, falling over, cracking her shin, acerbic – spending a lot of time talking to Faith or twisting her wiry hair around curling tongs.

'I don't mind her,' Faith said. 'I think she's amusing actually.'

Gradually the old girl decided where the battle line should be drawn up: Ceci and Ginger should not have a child. How she knew they were trying Ceci hated to think but having settled on it, from that moment on it became her cause and duty.

'You don't want any more children,' she told Ginger firmly.

'I do,' Ginger at first replied.

'Why else would I come to live with you but that me other children haven't the room and you, with that child-less woman – '

Ceci saw Ginger's face drop. He could not look her in the eye; could not challenge his mother's authority. Already Adelaide had discovered, perhaps always known, that Lizabeth was his soft spot.

'It's me livin' grandchildren I'm wanting to see. Not more children,' Adelaide insisted.

438

Ceci waited for Ginger to say something.

'You should be ashamed of yourself,' the old girl went on, 'a man of your age, flying in the face of nature!'

While she did not exactly refer to Ceci as 'that Protestant bitch' it was clear she was not enchanted by her. A formidable opponent – looking into drawers, re-arranging things, lifting lids off pots on the stove and keeping up a continual mutter about who was poisoning whom and who was no better than they ought to be, the old girl's presence saturated the house.

'You know Ginger is sensitive on the subject of Lizabeth,' Ceci put to her. 'Why don't you leave it alone?'

'That's not the half of it!' Adelaide replied, cracking open the cake tin and sending its lid spinning to the floor.

Quickly Ceci picked it up and handed it to her.

'I can manage! I can manage!'

Ceci folded her hands and waited.

'You don't know much about your husband,' Adelaide said knowingly.

Realizing the remark was meant to send her from the room, Ceci sat at the table.

'It wasn't like this at No. 5,' the old girl grumbled.

'Is something not to your satisfaction?'

'I don't expect to be useful here.'

'We're happy to have you.'

'You won't be having a child, so you can take that silly look off your face.'

'Do you think I want to get up early every morning?' Ceci enquired. 'My time with Ginger is far too precious!'

'Still think of him as a boyfriend?' the old girl retorted.

'Childless couples are each other's children,' Ceci smiled. 'A cup can be full regardless of size. Children magnify the joys but also the sorrows. And don't think that standing in our way can harm us.'

At this the old girl fell silent. 'You're a selfish piece,' she told Ceci.

'Be that as it may we have to get along.'

'I'm sorry she's making life difficult,' Ginger began, placing his hand on Ceci's shoulder.

'You wouldn't do that if she was in the room, would you?' Ceci asked.

Ginger's eyes dipped. It was true that since his mother had re-asserted her power over him he'd been unable to stand up to her.

'I know she's charming at times – '

'She just seems to have some hold over me.'

'Start calling her Adelaide,' Ceci suggested, 'not Ma. It's ridiculous from a man your age.'

'Couldn't bring myself to do it.'

'Do you like calling her Ma?'

Ginger shook his head.

'Certainly she was your Ma when you were eleven years old. You're a grown man now! Be with her as one adult to another. It's because you behave as her child she's forcing this trespass on you. She's the child out of control! Stand up to her!'

'I can't do that.'

'But at times you'd like to wring her neck.'

'Ceci's right,' Faith agreed. 'Someone has to be in charge in this house and it shouldn't be her – much as I like her.'

Within two months of the old lady moving in with them Ginger had become almost impotent. His lovemaking, such as it was, was confined entirely to Ceci's safe periods, possibly because the old girl, who clearly knew when Ceci was fertile, managed to engineer disagreements between them at those times. How she knew that Ceci hated to think. Theresa had put it to her that it was the period she had gotten wise to: those little changes in behaviour and complexion, the number of times a person returned to their room or the times at which water could be heard running or certain 'items' were seen drying in careful corners behind screens. Burying the unpleasant thought Ceci accepted that the old girl probably did know. Perhaps she was waiting for them to cease altogether so that she could say she had seen no children of Ginger's enter the world other than by her approved choice, Maureen.

'I'm going to fight her on this,' Ceci decided. 'I'm going to fight her on this, Theresa.

'Because of the child?'

'Because the decision to have one was something Ginger and I had reached together.'

Theresa looked at her solemnly:

'Have you forgotten everything you've ever learned?' she asked sadly.

'Ginger,' Ceci began in bed that night, 'about you and Maureen. Who arranged the marriage? Your mother or your father?'

Ginger didn't remember. 'She was pregnant anyway,' he said. 'You knew that. I suppose they thought it was a good deal as her father's land went along with it. I didn't mind – seeing as you wouldn't look at me . . .'

'She was pregnant with Lizabeth?'

Ginger nodded.

'It was your father, not your mother who used to call me "Maureen",' Ceci mused.

'His mind was wandering.'

'Whereas she's being mischievous?'

He nodded again.

'Why is she always praising Maureen in front of me?'

'To irritate you.'

'It's more than that,' Ceci said, seeking to put her finger on it. 'It's almost as if she has a debt to Maureen.'

'The other way round.' Ginger shook his head. 'No one else would have married Maureen. Not meaning any disrespect.'

Ceci looked hard at Ginger.

'Why are you staring at me?'

'I was just thinking,' she sighed, 'how amazing it is the way adopted children pick up their parents' likenesses by looking at them.'

'You're fooled by the fact that Lizabeth's like the others. It's Maureen's likeness.' Ginger drew Ceci closer and put his arms around her. 'And my mannerisms.'

'Even though I respect Lizabeth's independence, I wish more than anything for your sake that she would come back here,' Ceci sighed. 'For Adelaide's sake too. I wish it even more than that we could have a child.'

'Ceci,' Ginger whispered, 'if you only knew how much I wanted her back.'

As gradually Ceci sought to comfort him she found him becoming excited. And six weeks to the day she was sure she was pregnant.

'If I were you,' Theresa advised, 'I'd go on hanging out little items once a month to confuse the old girl. Otherwise she'll try and make you miscarry.'

Ceci grinned. She had never felt happier.

'Have you told Ginger?'

'I wanted to be sure and decide on a line towards the old lady first.'

One by one, Ceci told herself, she had been loyal to Ginger's children yet fought off encroachment from them. She had refused to let the old lady put the damper on and, although she had not damaged the bond Ginger seemed unwilling to break with her, at least she had managed to squeeze past her power over him. 'I feel like celebrating but I wouldn't know how,' she told Theresa as they walked through Moke together. 'I want to tell everyone. To write to Annie, to my daughter – '

'Sssh!' Theresa cautioned as they passed Moribund's store and he half raised his head from a box of vegetables he was arranging.

'Olwen says that the thing she likes best about England is that they have snow at Christmas,' Ceci laughed for Moribund's benefit. 'You'd think being born here she'd accept Christmas coming in mid-summer but apparently to be in a place that looks like the Christmas cards we used to receive appeals to her!'

'That girl's a romantic.'

'Hardly.'

'Is she working over there?'

'She doesn't say.'

'Well, you'll have to tell all of them sooner or later,' Theresa said, Moribund safely behind them. 'Even young Myra and how *she'll* take it! Probably think you're trying to race her to the baptismal font! Is there any action on that front?'

Ceci smiled. She felt prepared to be generous and loving to all the world, even Adelaide. 'I've been quite beastly to the old girl,' she confessed. 'All that must change.'

'If it does, she'll find you out. Be warned.'

'Then maybe I'll carry on hanging out the odd cloth now and then . . .' Ceci grinned.

Unaware that Ceci was pregnant Ginger merely noticed the atmosphere in his home improving. While his mother seemed suddenly more alert, it bothered Ceci not at all and she moved from room to room, smiling serenely.

'We ought to invite the boys up to see their grand-mother,' she'd even suggested.

'I'll go down and get them.'

'You stay here. Going to Christchurch depresses you.'

Ginger frowned. He was due for his monthly trip to Christchurch and wanted to go.

'We'll have a party here,' Ceci suggested. It would, after all, be a good time to break the news.

Ginger shook his head and frowned. 'It's the races, you see. Want to know how the horse is making out,' he said, avoiding her eyes.

'Very well,' Ceci said cheerfully. 'I'll come with you.'

'You think it's all right for me to travel?' Ceci asked Theresa.

'Good heavens, girl,' Theresa replied. 'Two months pregnant? Of course it is! Now if you'd been one of those girls who'd got pregnant when she was very young and been silly enough to get rid of it – well maybe – having a first baby at your age but . . .'

'All right, all right.'

When they reached Christchurch she would tell Ginger, she decided. That way they could really celebrate at a safe distance from the old girl and could come home together with a united front.

'What are you smiling at?' Ginger asked as she climbed from Moke's local trap to await the main coach on the Christchurch route.

Ceci looked at the open hills around them. Could there ever be a better time? 'Because I'm pregnant, Ginger,' she replied. 'We've finally done it. Despite everything, we're going to have a child.'

With a great whoop Ginger swept her in his arms.

By their reckoning the baby should be due the following summer.

'A Christmas baby,' Ginger murmured.

'We have to tell your mother.'

'Not just yet,' Ginger pleaded.

444

Entering the grounds of the boys' house Ginger reminded himself that despite the good news and Ceci's presence, he had a job to do. 'You go on in,' he told Ceci. 'I've left something under the seat.' As Ceci followed Kevin upstairs, Ginger quickly pulled a package from his travelling bag and handed it to Michael.

'What is it this time?'

'Keep your voice down!'

'Why are you selling off all this stuff? Doesn't she miss it?'

'She thinks it goes into Adelaide's room,' Ginger whispered. 'Just hide it before she sees.'

Michael shoved the package behind some boots in the lobby. 'Selling off a lot of things,' he grumbled.

'All right,' Ginger almost apologized. 'I've put a detective on Lizabeth.'

'Wait till Kevin hears!' Michael grinned in the full knowledge that Kevin had just done re-housing Lizabeth and her children in a small hotel for the duration of Ginger's visit.

'Don't repeat it.'

'I already heard,' said Kevin, coming back to close the front door.

'Well remember you heard it in confidence,' Ginger advised.

When the three men joined her Ceci sensed they had been speaking about something personal. 'Don't say you've told them already?' she asked Ginger. His face went quite blank. 'Told them – you know . . .' Ceci prompted.

'Oh.' He suddenly remembered. 'No. Not that.'

Ceci smiled.

'My wife and I have some good news for you,' Ginger said, putting an arm around Ceci with exaggerated fondness. 'She's pregnant!'

445

Though they had not expected a particular reaction, the silence was deafening.

'You look thoughtful, Kevin,' Ginger observed.

'It's partly the combination of . . .' Kevin flushed trying to think of a word.

'Sharing and deceit?' Michael helped out.

'Michael!'

'Excuse my sense of humour,' Michael quipped, reaching for a cigar. 'Any excuse to celebrate. Where's the whisky?'

'Why don't we take you both out tonight?' Ceci asked brightly.

Ginger's face fell. 'To tell the truth Ceci – ' he began.

' – the journey has tired him,' Michael continued. 'And he thinks he might prefer a solitary turn about the park.'

'I usually go for a walk when I'm in Christchurch,' Ginger agreed weakly.

After he had gone, Ceci turned to Kevin. 'Have you seen Lizabeth?'

Kevin hesitated. 'It appears she doesn't want to get in touch,' he finally said.

'So you have seen her?'

'I didn't say I had.'

'Why didn't you tell?'

'My agreement was to ask her to contact you. I have to respect the privacy of – the confidentiality of – ' he fumbled.

'Where is she now?'

'At this exact moment?'

'Would you tell me if you knew?'

Kevin paused. Ceci could almost see him squirming. 'I'm afraid I would be unable to.'

Ceci sighed. 'I would love to see her again.'

'She'd like to see you,' Kevin said quickly.

'Then why?'

'Dad. He treated her like an equal till she married. Now he wants her to be a daughter.'

'You're very perceptive, Kevin.'

'I was there.'

'Is there anything you can do to help her?'

'You're fishing.'

'How's Frank?'

Silence.

'I mean – are they still together?'

'I'm not clever enough to make polite conversation and fend off your questions as if I was answering them, Ceci,' Kevin smiled. 'I said I could be trusted.'

With much to think of Ceci went up to bed but could not sleep. During the night she arose and, wanting a handkerchief, reached into Ginger's jacket pocket where, to her amazement, she found a much larger sum of money than they needed to have brought to Christchurch. For a while she puzzled about it but after a bite to eat, went back to sleep.

Two days after they had gone Lizabeth and the children returned to Kevin and Michael's house.

'There's a man been following me,' Lizabeth said. Kevin looked down. 'He hasn't seen me come in here though.'

'In this house you are protected.'

'I know there are perverse men in Christchurch but – do you think Father has set a detective on me?'

'Do you think he would tell me if he had?' Kevin asked carefully.

'He might.'

'If he gave me any message for you I would give it to you,' Kevin hedged.

'Has he?'

Kevin hung his head.

'I see he has,' said Lizabeth sadly. 'I'll leave tomorrow.'

Arriving back at Hexham still filled with the joy of their child within her, Ceci wandered the grounds thinking of Lizabeth and decided to pick some delphiniums to arrange in the Chinese vase. She loved the delphiniums, blue and bold, growing in the path where Lizabeth had planted them. Snapping the stalks she thought of the girl, of the day she must first have met Frank, of how she had returned to live with them and reconciled with Ginger, and the day when Ginger and Lizabeth, the boys, Faith and Myra had all been together – had all gone out while she had remained at home and let in the stranger who turned out to be Frank. As she returned carrying the tall flowers she recalled the two men brawling on the lawn, she and Lizabeth watching from the window above. Still thinking of Lizabeth she sought the Chinese vase but it was nowhere to be found. When she asked Faith she shrugged and Ginger looked away. By the time she had done searching she realized there was not a tall vase left in the house to arrange flowers. Not only had the vases gone missing but several other items she had expected to encounter in searching for them. Aware this should have been one of the happiest days of her life, with a sense of deepening mystery, Ceci stood holding the delphiniums.

Chapter 33

When the old girl perceived she had been tricked she was furious. 'How dare you go on hanging out bits of cloth!' she said, giving herself away.

'I can hang out bits of cloth if I like, can't I?' Ceci retorted. Her swelling stomach, she was aware, a claim to power, a fence between Adelaide and her son. 'In any case, why should you mind? It'll be Ginger's son.'

'But not Maureen's!' the old girl replied sharply.

'Maureen is dead and buried,' Ceci protested. 'Let the poor woman rest in peace.'

'And all this will go to your brat?'

'However distasteful you may find it, this place was once mine.'

'Well I shall leave at once. You may depend on that.'

'Come on, come on, Granny,' Faith said, seeing how upset the old girl was. 'You don't know the half of what you're saying when you're angry.'

'But the other half I do!'

'Why shouldn't you have another grandchild to go along with your great-grandchildren?'

'And where are the great-grandchildren I already have hiding?' Adelaide demanded, turning on Ceci.

'You can't think I drove them out, surely?'

'Granny,' Faith whispered. 'Lizabeth went away. It was nothing to do with any of us.'

'This house should go to Maureen's children,' Adelaide stated. 'Not a child by another woman.'

'I'm sorry, Ceci,' said Faith, slipping her arm around her. 'It's as if my mother had been her own daughter.'

'I'm sure of one thing,' Ceci frowned. 'She's not confused.'

'I'm delighted for you. I'm looking forward to it.'

'I'll try and make up with Adelaide for Ginger's sake,' Ceci told Faith.

'I don't know why she's against you. She's nice to me.'

'*You're* Maureen's daughter!'

From Adelaide's closed door, for Ceci's benefit, came the sound of her raised voice intoning scriptures:

'Those who sprawl and those who bawl will be exiled! Woe to those ensconced snugly and to those who feel safe lying on ivory beds and sprawling on divans, dining on lambs and stall-fattened veal.'

'I hope she's not talking about us,' Faith murmured.

'They bawl to the sound of the harp. They invent new instruments of music and drink wine by the bowlful and use the finest oil for anointing themselves but about the ruin of Joseph they do not care.'

The voice paused. 'That is why they will be the first to be exiled,' it continued expansively. 'The sprawlers' revelry is over.'

'She's impossible!' Ceci gasped, going forward and knocking on her door.

'Who is it?'

'Ceci.'

'Leave!'

'We can't have you sitting in there comparing yourself to Joseph. It's ridiculous!'

'This is the word of the Lord!' the voice of the old woman rang out.

Ceci retreated down the stairs. 'Your mother is impossible,' she told Ginger.

'It's all right for you to be nice to her now because you've won,' Ginger observed.

'I'm not going to be ashamed of being pregnant by my own husband in my own house if that's what you mean.'

'She's just a poor old woman. Let her have her own way more of the time.'

'If she would just talk to us normally – '

'Normally? In this house?' shrilled Adelaide from the top of the stairs.

'Is there anything I can do to make you happier?' Ceci asked.

The old girl paused. 'To tell you the truth,' she began slowly, 'there's a great number of things you could do. But I doubt you would contemplate them . . .'

If she had thought the direct speech was the beginning of a thaw between them Ceci was wrong: there was something gnawing at the insides of the old girl which she would share with no one. While she would accept affection and support from Faith, she could not relax with Ceci and became increasingly difficult with Ginger. Consequently they took to walking in the garden when they wished to converse privately, carefully passing behind the screen of trees to share even the most primitive of joys.

'Look how big you're getting!' Ginger grinned.

'I know.' Ceci cupped her arms around her stomach.

'I reckon a girl. I always wanted a girl to get Hexham.'

And that girl, Ceci told herself, was Lizabeth.

'Myra won't be back – or the boys, Faith'll go . . .'

'You're relieved, aren't you, to have someone to leave it to?'

'Pardon?'

'Weren't you listening?' Ceci asked.

'Sorry. I had some news in the mail,' he began brightly. 'About Lizabeth.'

451

Ceci's heart dropped. She had accredited his joy that morning to her condition.

'I put a detective on her,' Ginger admitted, 'She's been seen.' He hesitated. 'Don't you want to know where?'

'Where has she been seen?'

'You're not really interested, are you?'

'Of course I am! You took me by surprise and I – I'm not sure you did right in putting a detective on her.'

'It worked,' Ginger defended himself. 'She's been seen in Hagley Park.'

'So you'll be going down there?'

'As soon as I can.'

They walked for a while in silence.

'What was she doing there? Were the children with her?'

'She was talking to a man. When she walked off the detective followed her towards some trees but she turned and headed diagonally back across the open space, sort of doubled back on herself. He couldn't cut around the green in time or walk directly across it after her. Seems he wasn't long-sighted enough to see where she was going so he cut back and questioned the man she'd been talking to – '

'I think it's an awful cheek.'

'He wasn't willing to talk.'

'Could have been any flower seller the man was with! It probably wasn't Lizabeth at all!'

'You're supposed to be happy for me!'

The truth is, Ceci thought as they returned to the house, for Ginger's sake she hoped he would find her, yet for Lizabeth's she hoped he would not. In fact for Ginger's sake it might even be better that he did not find her: that way he could live in hope. But if he did and her circumstances were such as would cause pain – they stood a fair chance of ruining their forthcoming event.

452

'I just feel that if she wanted to be with us, Ginger, she would,' Ceci concluded lamely.

'Well, Granny,' Ceci told Adelaide the next day, 'here's some news you'll like. Your son has gone down to Christchurch to bring back your legitimate great-grandchildren.'

The old girl frowned. She had decided that this was one of the days she was not going to talk.

Ginger hurried. The detective, expensive though he was, had been true to his word. There had been other sightings he'd said, but they were not conclusive: not worth bringing a man down from the High Country for. Briefly he thought of Ceci as the carriage swung on to the main route. It was a fact that every time something that should have been beautiful happened between them events concerning one of his children rose to mar it. A thought nagged at him: the previous night she had asked him to massage her back but he had been too busy writing instructions for the detective. It seemed he could not grasp the reality of their forthcoming child or that it would change their lives. When Ceci bubbled over and could not contain her happiness, in his current state of anxiety about Lizabeth the sight actually irritated him. It's wrong of me to have no patience, he thought briefly, but in the next moment was planning what he would do on his arrival in Christchurch. When Lizabeth came home, he decided, she would have her old room back. No, she would have the large room overlooking the lawn. The fact the girl was reduced to talking to strange men and had been seen without Frank surely indicated she was destitute. Was she possibly hoping, praying even, that someone would find her and bring her back? Perhaps only her pride and self-respect were keeping her away. As the coach descended, within the safety of its confines Ginger permitted himself to imagine the emotional reunion between them, Lizabeth rushing into his arms crying: 'Oh, Father!' He saw himself fumbling for a handkerchief, brushing tears, telling her it was all over . . . It would be nice with Little Frank and the twins up at Hexham. They would make good playmates for his child to come. It was not good for a toddler to be without companions, he reasoned. All in all, he told himself, things had turned out remarkably well.

'I think I can get us a passage,' Frank told Lizabeth.

'Where?'

'The North Island.'

Since she had reconciled with him and they had gone into hiding she had aged a great deal. 'I'm not in a particular hurry to go north,' she said tiredly.

'We can go a long way north and start again.'

Lizabeth looked away. 'I want to talk to a priest.'

'What this time?'

'You said when you married me you didn't admit to the priest you were divorced.'

'To protect you. As long as you didn't know you were all right.'

'I don't like living in sin. I'd like to be able to go to Communion again.'

'Any priest will tell you our marriage is legal.'

'You told me there were no children!' Lizabeth shouted. 'When you finally admitted you'd left a wife that was all you said. If it weren't for that court order for maintenance, if it weren't for that poor woman going through the Church Board to find you and them firing you I would never have known!'

'I admit,' Frank said sadly, 'it kills me, but I admit I left a wife and four children. For you.'

'Why are we *living* like this?' Lizabeth said despairingly, glancing across at her children sleeping on bare boards under a stairway.

Frank covered his face.

'Why didn't you tell me before I had them?'

'Don't leave me.'

'It was a weak, wicked thing to do,' Lizabeth sighed, putting her arms around him. 'But no – I won't.'

Lizabeth did not cry. She felt stronger for the knowledge of Frank's need of her. She knew a lot about men's weakness – how they lied to themselves about women. 'Of course I love you,' she said.

'Listen,' Frank began, 'I can get the money for one passage now. But you and the bairns'll have to follow on.'

Lizabeth nodded. 'You go.'

Frank frowned around the shack which had been their home, feeling almost sorry to leave.

'How would you send the fare to us?' Lizabeth asked.

'I could send it here.'

'This place has no address.'

'I'd give it to a man boarding the steamer and tell him to find you here.'

'Suppose "here" isn't here when he arrives? Suppose "here" burns down?'

'I'll get it to you.'

'I'll get the money myself,' Lizabeth sighed. A second passed. 'How did you get yours?'

Frank looked away. 'When we get north,' he promised, 'we'll be able to be honest about things again.'

Since he had gone Lizabeth had determined how to get the money. She would ask her father. The matter of luring him had been exceptionally easy, given the relationship she had worked out with the man who was following her. She knew he was short-sighted for she had followed him too;

455

even knew where he lived and that, by the look of the place, he was dependent upon keeping her in view for a living. Thus she had been obvious to him yet always careful to choose her moment to vanish. The scenario she had staged in Hagley Park had been designed purely with the intention of luring Ginger. Doubtless he would now come and be informed of the two or three 'sighting' places he would be most likely to find her. Securing the twins and Little Frank with a neighbour, Lizabeth set out to wait. Without Frank she was lonely and in a hurry to join him.

Courage, she told herself, walking into the railway engine shed. It'll be worse than this arriving in Wellington and looking for Frank.

Ginger followed the rails into the shed and looked about. The place was dank and musty and he was sure the man must have been mistaken. If Lizabeth was indeed here she'd be very glad to come back to Hexham! She could be pregnant as a result of mixing with strangers but one more child would make no difference. 'Lizabeth?' he called carefully.

From the roof of the train shed Lizabeth watched him walking, turning about below. 'I'm up here,' she called.

Ginger's eyes turned up. 'What are you doing on the roof?'

'Waiting for you.'

Ginger began to feel uncomfortable. 'Do you love me?' he heard her ask from her vantage point above. Anger, not love, stirred in his heart. 'Come down!'

'I can't trust you enough.'

'Everything I've done is for your sake.'

Lizabeth's silence accused him.

'I want money.'

'I'm not giving you money for that man.'

'For *me*! I want it for me.'

'You can have everything you want. Only come home.'

456

'You have money to pay that detective behind you on the tracks! He gets your money.'

'Lizabeth! Listen to me – '

'How can you refuse when I ask?'

'Doesn't Frank refuse you money?'

'I need it!'

'I hear you've been begging in parks – '

'You aren't going to give me money, are you?'

'Back at Hexham – '

'I can talk myself dry but you won't help, will you? *You won't help*!'

'Lizabeth – '

'You don't love me at all,' Lizabeth began in a low voice. 'You want obedience! Not love! I hate, hate, *hate* you!' Before the tears could come – shocked by the truth of what she had shouted – Lizabeth turned and ran to the apex of the roof. On the tracks below she saw the detective who had led Ginger there, idling, hands in pockets, disinterested.

'Quick!' Ginger shouted to him. 'Where's the way down?'

Now the object of pursuit Lizabeth made her way over the low rooves, a quickly moving figure stumbling on skirts.

'For God's sake, man,' Ginger demanded. 'Where is she?'

The man turned on the spot. He could not see more than fifty yards at the best of times. 'There,' he stabbed blindly.

Turning, Ginger glimpsed the slightest movement as a figure, running across the track, vanished between the wagons. It could even have been a vagrant.

'Shall I take you back to her last known whereabouts?' the man asked lamely.

'What kind of a fool are you?'

Returning to Hexham Ginger agonized over his rash act. With the detective fired, the fact of Lizabeth's refusal to see him because she did not want to had finally sunk in. It was nothing to do with Frank. It was her choice. She had said he wanted to own her; made it clear she had no further use for him in the role of father. He was a thing of the past; like an old shoe thrown aside. As the coach climbed higher towards the hills a passenger who had also been on the outward journey recognized him and concluded he had been to see his bank manager, for the smile Ginger had carried into Christchurch with him had been replaced by a look of bitterness and anger.

Beyond Hexham in the stubble Annie noticed their crops getting smaller and smaller. Reg had not told her about the rabbit sightings – almost as if by not mentioning them they would go away – but Annie was aware their numbers were increasing, for they ate everything in their way. Wandering now beyond their clearing with Little Annie she looked with fear at the ground, once soft to sit on, now a barren playground across which pellets blew, carrying with them the smell of urine. 'Don't touch them, Annie,' she said as the child bent down to pick one up. Since the grass cover had gone, frosts and rain had done their work in denuding the ground till in places exposed pockets of rock showed how truly poor it had always been.

'That one full!' Little Annie cried, pointing in delight to a dip in the earth's crust, filled with pellets as a jar might be with sweets.

When they returned home the stink of the rabbits would be on her shoes, between Little Annie's toes. As her eyes filled with tears at the pungent smell she remembered Stebbins insisting he ought to stop longer but her making him go. She bit her tongue. There weren't none left, she reasoned with herself. He was just trying to stay on. Even Reg had said there weren't none till he came back from that walk looking so black. Two seasons with the dreadful

Stebbins, his smell and obscenity, his shooting and poisoning activities . . . Well, there would be no next season for they could not afford to pay him again.

'I knew they'd be back,' Annie told Little Annie as they crossed the clearing again. 'Knew it in my heart.'

Once she had fed Little Annie and tucked her in her hammock she sat down to cry. The dream had been too beautiful to last: they had a small child but their land was wasted.

'I tell you what I'll do,' Reg said, crossing to her. 'I'll become a professional rabbiter meself.'

'I won't let you do that!' Annie retorted. 'We're not profiting off other people's miseries.'

Reg scratched his neck. They couldn't go on as they were much longer. He was taking charity from the hamlet which he didn't entirely like.

'If we have to finish up, we'll finish up together here,' Annie insisted.

'Feel ashamed,' Reg murmured.

Annie stood and put her arms around him. The fact of the matter was that the hamlet folk had been less affected because, being genuine cow cockies and careful to store their fodder, they had not been at risk in the same way as Reg and Annie who had turned to crops for a balance and depended on supplying their extra vegetables to the hamlet.

'I curse the day Ceci brought those two rabbits here,' Reg murmured.

Annie looked afraid. Cursing would do them no good. 'We bin taken in, that's all,' she replied.

Unable to put the puzzle together, Reg drew some coins from the few remaining in the buried biscuit tin and went to the hamlet for a beer. Sometimes there was solace in the company of men, and the hamlet men, being kind and generous, were of a type he had not experienced before.

They renewed his faith in human nature. However, he hesitated to enter the grog shop. The good men didn't drink there. It was really no more than an awning, a continuation of the store where people could sit without getting wet when it rained. His real reason for hesitation was that he had only enough money for one drink and must therefore figure out whether somebody was in there who would buy him a drink and put him in the awkward position of having to return the favour. Could he get in quickly and make off to the corner with a quick bottle before anyone saw him, he wondered? By the sound of it there were at least two or three people within, so, caution having the upper hand, Reg approached the lean-to from the rear, pressed his ear briefly to the planks and listened.

'Oh, I just come back for one or two o' me bits and pieces,' he heard a voice saying.

'Not working around here any longer then?' Malachy, the store owner, enquired.

'You wasn't here before,' said the first voice.

'But I think I heard of you,' Malachy went on.

'Stebbins the name.'

'Aha.'

'Stebbins the name. Rabbits is the business.'

'Wasn't you stopping with some couple up here?' Malachy asked.

Stebbins reply was drowned in a massive slurping of ale. 'But I always left a few to see me good for the next season,' Stebbins concluded.

'Trick of the trade, eh?'

Reg heard Stebbins wiping his mouth.

'The laugh was on them for throwing me out.'

Too ashamed to come out from behind the store, Reg stood holding his coin. He had been taken in. He was a fool to have trusted a man like Stebbins, a man who was

460

exactly what he had once been – a cheat and a thief. Becoming honest himself he had expected others to be honest. How wrong he had been!

Stepping from the store Stebbins turned on to the track. At the last minute he could not resist going up and taking a look at the Bowens' homestead, just to see it had served them right. Leaving his horse on the track and finding the place, he turned in. There ahead of him it was, the clearing – exactly as he remembered it. The house looked the same too, except for the addition of the small homemade hammock. From behind it came the sound of water splashing. Was the woman bathing herself?

Having taken careful stock of their situation and decided what they might get for selling their cows Annie dusted off the table and crossed to the back window to see if Little Annie was managing all right in the tin bath. Her splashing noises had stopped, as if she was watching a butterfly. But the child was watching Stebbins, standing amidst the ruins of their once flourishing farm, staring at her.

'Nice place you got here,' Stebbins taunted Annie as she ran out. 'What you looking bitter about?'

'May God forgive you your wickedness!'

'Me? It's you what wouldn't treat me right!'

Trembling in anger Annie stared back at him. 'Well you wait a minute and I'll treat you right,' she assured him, turning into the shed.

My, my, thought Stebbins. Maybe things are finally looking up, given she finds herself in a pinch. Almost ready to drop his trousers he turned around at a sound in the doorway. The woman was levelling a shotgun at him. In the next moment she had shot him between the eyes.

Chapter 34

'It looks like a Christmas baby for you,' Faith said, patting Ceci's stomach. 'Why don't we have midnight mass at Hexham this year?'

'What a lovely idea,' Ceci replied. Since becoming pregnant she had felt even more part of their community, the help and consideration she had received from the other women truly warming her.

'Half of those women would give the rags off their backs if they'd thought you needed them,' Ginger observed as gifts for the new baby flowed in. Having 'got over' Lizabeth his longing for their child had strengthened him to the extent he had finally asserted himself over his mother, even on occasion telling her to 'be quiet' or leave his wife alone. It was clear to Moke his hopes were pinned on this child, behind his back known as 'Baby Hexham'. Word was that, be it male or female, it would be heir to the estate and local feeling had it this was right.

'There'll be nothing from Faith,' people murmured. 'Never see nor hair nor hide of the boys. Lizabeth's gone, and as for Myra, who ever heard of a body returning from the North Island?'

'Be nice if it were twins.'

'Me, I'm praying for a girl.'

'A girl?! What Hexham needs is a boy with his mother's good sense and his father's bullheadedness!'

'You know they're all talking about you, don't you?' Faith asked Ceci.

Ceci nodded. 'This time I don't mind. When I was

carrying Olwen, it mattered more than anything in the world.'

As Ginger settled into becoming the perfect future father he was able, as far as Faith and Ceci could determine, to see his own grown children as adults free to pursue their lives, to even call him 'Ginger' or 'Vincent' if they pleased. His new attitude also encompassed his mother whom he took to addressing as 'Adelaide' – shortened to 'Adela'. It seemed to Ceci that the breaking of this last taboo had come as a blow in the stomach to the old girl whom she already felt sorry for now that Ginger was keeping her rigidly in line. Somehow, spoken to by name rather than title made it impossible for her to do anything other than acknowledge Ceci as head of the household and speak politely to her. In this new light Ceci began to feel even more sorry for the old girl now the fight had been kicked out of her. Though it had not been easy before and perhaps she was hanging on to a false dignity, it was something Adelaide had needed. Watching from the sidelines it occurred to Faith that Ceci did not realize it was the fact of the new child that had given Ginger the confidence to assert himself. Ceci seemed only thankful to be at last one with him.

Upstairs Ginger strode into the waiting nursery, the quilts and toys, the dolls' house that no new-born infant could possibly have use for, the spinning top, the skipping rope, the wooden dog and other little gifts the community had given to show their great joy at the coming event. Not so long ago he had not been on speaking terms with any of them yet the birth of this child was an occasion to which Protestants and Catholics alike had responded and it warmed him. All, however, had been careful to avoid giving bibles or prayer books.

'Bound to be baptised a Catholic,' people whispered.

'You never know,' others replied.

In fact Ginger and Ceci had not discussed the issue.

'I'd always assumed the child would be a Catholic,' Ceci began. 'I have no real tradition to offer.'

Ginger looked moved. 'She can be Church of England if you like,' he said in a husky voice.

'She?' Ceci smiled. 'You're a Catholic. I married you. The child will be Catholic.'

'You don't realize what you are saying goodbye to,' Ginger said softly.

'Not everybody looks down on Catholics,' Faith reminded him. 'And I'm sure this is one child nobody will look down on.'

As the day came closer it reduced itself to a race between whether Midnight Mass or the baby would come first. In the end, the ceremony won by a hair's breadth.

'Faith, you had better be godmother,' Ceci urged as together they entered the large room specially arranged for the service, the first one Ceci had openly attended.

'First things first,' Faith smiled.

Never had Hexham looked more beautiful – the old building glowing in the light from the hundred candles, the dining table covered with white sheets and set up as an altar, the rugs removed, their places taken by kneelers and benches brought up from the barn. The fact of a summer Christmas meant that unlike the northern hemisphere, there was a plenitude of flowers and an exceptional feeling of the birth of a child coming in a season of security and richness. Instinctively Ceci had not picked delphiniums. She had been happy to arrange the altar flowers and had deliberately chosen a theme of cream and yellow, with large bowls of fabled Mount Cook lilies, the glorious yellow and white wild flowers which Tavistock had referred to as mountain buttercups and which Ginger had daringly dug up, and succeeded in transplanting at Hexham. Now, looking at their fleshy white petals cupping golden centres, their thick buds and lush leaves, she was reminded of the centre of all life, of Christmas, of her baby, even of the fertility design on the corners of the Agra carpet.

Before her, faces she knew, some she half knew, entered the grand doorway, greeting each other; other pregnant women looked shyly down, while their older brats escaped up the wide staircase to explore the rooms of Hexham, and exchanged news about adventures and presents: the house throbbed with love. Never had it glowed like this. Replete with joy, feeling close to tears, Ceci turned and caught Ginger looking at her.

'You don't know how much I love you,' he whispered, squeezing her hand. 'Quick, we'd better go in.'

In a rush of happiness Ceci imagined herself lifting the child above her head, laughing, drawing it back down and kissing it.

'Thank you,' she prayed. 'Thank you for letting my life have come to this. It was hard to be grateful in the times things went wrong but now . . .' She raised her face. All around her the heads were bowed in utter silence and reverence before the glimmering white host, the light from the candles flashing off the monstrance, the golden vessel housing the host.

'Dear Lord,' she prayed, 'please bless Reg. And thank you for sending Little Annie to civilize him.'

Aware that another bell was tinkling she dipped her head. This was the chalice being raised, the wine which the Catholics believed was being metaphysically changed into the living substance of their Redeemer for them. Ceci did not like to think too deeply on these subjects. Irreverence was always so close when she thought of religion it

465

was better not to think. Yet at times like this she felt a presence advising her that words and physical facts, the bread and chairs and flowers, were no more than embodiments which a listening person might understand; she sensed there *was* a God who loved each of them and came repeatedly to their hearts in the form of a child, or a hobo, or a thief to meet them.

'*Ite missa est*,' she heard the priest say. '*Deo gratias.*'

In the next minute the chairs were being scraped back, the people rousing as from a dream.

'It is very beautiful, your mass,' she said to Ginger afterwards. 'Though I don't understand it.'

'It's not to be understood with the mind,' Ginger smiled, 'but felt in the heart.'

For some reason Ceci wanted to cry.

'What is it?' Ginger asked.

'I feel overcome – with joy,' Ceci replied.

Ginger's heart swelled. Surely this was a sign that she would follow him into the Church? He had put no pressure on her, had refused to comply with the priest's demand at the time of their marriage that she take instruction, yet against all odds she was coming in. Why this meant so much to him he could not explain.

'It's true the place was like a cathedral tonight,' he smiled. 'Candles give it a sense of dignity and tradition.'

'It isn't that,' Ceci whispered. 'I just sensed a great beauty at the heart of your service, like a moth fluttering to get into my soul. I was almost tempted!'

'My dear,' Ginger said, grasping her.

'You had better get into the kitchen and give the father a glass of sherry,' Ceci reminded him, pulling gently away.

'He'll fall off his horse!'

'The poor man should stay the night here.'

'And do the next place out of their Christmas morning mass?'

'You're a hard man, Ginger,' Ceci teased, moving heavily up the stairs. Now that the excitement was over she felt full and bloated.

Faith came out and looked at her as she paused halfway up, her hand in the small of her back. 'Be careful on the stairs,' she called.

Ceci turned. At Hexham's grandest moment, the old lady had been forgotten.

'How is Grandmother? Is she all right?'

Faith went to check. The old girl had not come down to mass, saying it was too late and decent souls went in the morning.

Reaching their bedroom before Ginger, Ceci lay and dozed. She felt that her time was close, yet as she sought to remember how labour with Olwen had begun, the facts eluded her.

'Are you in pain?' Ginger asked, appearing in the doorway.

'Not at all,' Ceci smiled.

Ginger got into bed with her. 'This bed's wet! Your waters have broken.' In an instant he was struggling into his trousers, calling for Faith. 'Quick! Run after Theresa,' he ordered her.

'The midwife?'

'On the West Coast with her sisters for Christmas.'

'You run, Father. I'll stay here.'

'Don't you think I've done this before?' Ginger asked impatiently. 'All right, Ceci?'

In a haze Ceci heard doors banging and feet running; she saw the face of Adelaide peering in at the door, part curiosity, part disdain. 'I feel fine,' she murmured. 'In fact I was almost asleep until you all started.'

Faith banged on Theresa's door.

'It's no emergency,' she assured her, 'but it looks like being tonight.'

'And I suppose your father's panicking?' Theresa asked. 'Typical man.'

'She broke her waters.'

'You can break 'em two days in advance – a week even. It's not as if she swished the whole lot out, is it?'

Faith shook her head.

'As I thought,' Theresa said, locking the door behind her. 'A mere cupful and that man of hers is making a fuss.'

'You shouldn't have sent for Theresa yet,' Ceci declared. 'I just sat down too suddenly. I've been leaking on and off – '

'Fuss and nonsense!' they heard from the door as Adelaide went back to her room.

'You'd better make up a bed for Theresa. I can assure you it won't be tonight and we can't keep her to'ing and fro'ing. You'll have to get Theresa's keys off her, give them to Faith and have her hold the fort there until we're clear.'

Ginger relaxed. There had always been an element of panic with Maureen, loud, noisy births in which the roof could have caved in without being noticed. He had heard women could have babies naturally but had never seen it. 'That's it, then, it's got to be a girl,' he told himself.

When her time came Ceci found the going rougher than she had expected.

'It's worth it,' Theresa said. 'Keep pushing.'

'It's too early! You're wrong!' Ceci protested.

Theresa frowned. It was a fact that the child was hardly co-operating. 'Are you over sensitive to pain?' she asked.

'What do you think?' snapped Ginger angrily, pointing at flecks of blood in Ceci's hands where her own nails had bitten in.

'We'll help then, lamb,' Theresa said in a quieter voice. 'Ginger, go downstairs and fetch us all a nice Scotch.' Under any other circumstances he would have argued, but Ginger went.

'Now listen, Ceci,' Theresa said, helping her to sit up. 'Here's a drink to strengthen you, then Ginger and I will push the baby out. We'll push on your stomach and get it moving down.'

Ceci gulped at the Scotch. They would certainly have to do something for she could not push, the child would not come and it was the same old story about the pig won't jump over the stile to get to market.

'With me,' Theresa said, 'I usually got them stuck at the other end – coming out. I'd reach a pitch where I couldn't push any harder, yet they wouldn't come. Then me husband would slit me with a knife and out they'd pop. What a relief!'

'Do what you have to,' Ceci murmured. 'I'm exhausted.'

Fleetingly afraid that he might lose her in childbed Ginger hurried to stand opposite Theresa and began pushing.

'Not like that, dear,' she said gently. 'You get behind her and put your hands on the crown of her head. Don't grip so hard, dear,' she told Ceci. 'You'll be over the top of the bed.' With the Scotch and exhaustion struggling within her, Ceci lapsed into unconsciousness.

'Now!' Theresa urged.

Standing opposite her Ginger did as he was bid.

'Umph!' Theresa gasped, bringing all her weight down on Ceci's belly just below the breasts. 'Move, damn you!' Tears of sweat and confusion were gathering on her face. 'Ginger! Push harder!' she urged.

'Is Ceci all right?' he asked, trembling so badly he exerted no pressure.

'She's only fainted. This is our big chance, man! Push!'

Vaguely swimming up as from a great depth Ceci heard a voice '. . . baptize thee – John – in the name of the Father and of the Son and of the . . .' A son! Still groggy she lifted herself on to her elbow. There in the corner was Theresa, bent over the child, the water dripping from its head on to the floor. Theresa turned: 'I caught him in time.' Her voice faltered. 'I hope the name John was all right.'

'Ginger?'

But at the sight of the dead child Ginger had stepped outside and fainted. In time? Time did not exist with God, God was beyond time – yet Theresa believed that the fact they had baptized the child as soon as they had got their hands on it would count for something. It was assured of eternal life. Sometimes it happened that way.

'Bring him here,' Ceci said weakly. 'It's been dead for at least a month!' she screamed. 'Look at it!'

Theresa passed her hand over the shrivelled, partly consumed body.

'My own body was devouring it,' Ceci said wretchedly. 'Will I never learn?'

Theresa, however, took the child and knelt with it in her arms: 'Out of the depths we cry to thee O Lord, Lord hear our voice,' Ceci heard her say. 'Let thine ears be attentive to the voice of our supplication,' the voice went on. Ceci looked at the bent shoulders shaking above it. 'From the morning watch even unto night my soul hath relied on thy word . . .'

Outside the room Ginger became conscious of Theresa's voice keening brokenly the words of the *De profundis*. The tears streamed down his face. How had he ever dared to hope so much? In his soul a great bell rang and rang and rang, each echo hurting his ears. Looking up as he felt a bony hand on his shoulder, he saw his mother.

* * *

It was days before Ginger could speak of the death to Ceci. He did not mention it. Though Faith was supportive of her the fact it had hurt him so deeply moved Ceci to tears. Nothing at all was said: he acted as if she had never been pregnant. Although the old girl tried to take a back seat Ginger sensed a certain 'Told you so' which made him want to hit her. In response she tried to become more independent, preparing her food on a tray herself, taking it to her room and consuming it there. Seeing how sad she was, despite her own grief, Ceci longed to put her arms around Adelaide and comfort her.

'I want to talk to you, Ceci. May we walk?' Faith asked. 'I know you have a lot of sadness but there is something I would like to discuss with you.'

Vaguely concerned for Faith, given the girl was so serenely unselfish, Ceci allowed her to take her arm and steer her into the garden. As they crossed the lawn, the dry leaves blew towards them – sign of an early autumn. 'What is it, Faith? What do you have to tell me?' Ceci asked.

'Since Olwen was here and talked to me about the Maoris, I have thought more and more about them,' Faith began. 'I would like to – protect them from our worst excesses but cannot think how to begin.'

'Don't you ever want a life for yourself, Faith?' Ceci asked carefully.

'I want to *do* something with my life, yes,' Faith explained. 'But there are plenty of people around to raise families. I don't feel the need to do that.'

Ceci looked down. Now that she had got over the baby, the idea of it was merely a sharp stab in the side.

'I don't want to be – part of another person's picture. You know?'

'An appendage?'

471

'I want to make my own picture with my own life. I have waited and prayed and thought about it. I haven't moved out of the way of anything that came to me – yet still the answer hasn't come. Can you suggest anything I might be doing wrong?'

Ceci smiled. 'You are the soul of goodness and kindness, Faith. As for your life so far – I don't know what your father and I would have done without you, me in particular,' she cried, hugging her.

'That hadn't occurred to me,' Faith replied.

'Nor Adelaide. At first you were the only one she would talk to. You have been very important to her.'

Slowly the women returned to the house. It was uncannily quiet.

'I'll see if she's all right,' Faith offered, starting up the stairs as Ceci turned into the drawing room.

'Granny?' she called, knocking on the old woman's door. There was no reply. 'Granny?' she called again.

Though she would not normally do it, Faith opened Adelaide's door and peered in. She was not there. Calling her name, Faith searched the upstairs rooms then with a sense of urgency ran downstairs and made straight for the kitchen. There on the stone flags in the half light lay Adelaide, the smallness of her frame belying the strength she had projected, now seen for what she was: a frail old lady.

'Ceci,' Faith called. 'Quick! Granny's fallen!'

Together they turned the crumpled body over.

'At least she's alive.'

'Her head must have struck that wooden block,' Faith gasped, gently touching the swollen lips and nose.

'We must revive her.'

Thankful that the old lady had not lost all her body warmth to the stone floor Ceci set about heating water to bathe her while in the dining room before a huge fire – the first of autumn – with smelling salts and brandy Faith reassured the old lady.

'What were you trying to do, Gran? Fly?'

Wrapped in blankets, the wind knocked from her sails the old girl tried to smile. She had had a nasty shock. When the bath was ready she submitted meekly, allowing them to undress her, sponge her bruises, gently ease the caked blood from her hair and carefully pat her dry. By the time they had finished, the night was chill and the water in the tub stone cold from the window's draught.

'You'd better boil some more for her bed warmer,' Faith urged.

Without a word of complaint Adelaide allowed them to put her to bed, motioning to Faith with her eyes that she wanted her rosary. Having both kissed her, the girls left.

'I'll go back in the night and cover her up, just make sure her quilts haven't slid off,' Faith promised. 'I don't think Father will take this news very well. He's hardly been gentle with her of late.'

'She'll be up and about in no time,' Ginger barked roughly on hearing the news.

'She's hurt worse than you think,' Ceci assured him. 'That was quite some fall.'

'But nothing's broken?'

'No.'

Though Adelaide recovered from the fall it was the pneumonia that got her; that final touch of irony when, because she had briefly abandoned her independent stance and permitted her erstwhile antagonist to bathe her, with both her resistance and spirit lowered, the cold had entered in.

'Ceci,' she croaked. 'I have something to tell you. Come in here and shut the door.'

473

'I'm so sorry, Granny,' Ceci cried, squeezing her hand.

'Don't be,' the old girl said. 'Some good has come out of it.'

Humbled by her magnanimity Ceci listened.

'I need to see a priest. Don't tell your husband. Just get one up here.'

'Where do I get a priest?'

'Don't tell Faith either. Just get me one.'

'May I ask Theresa's help?'

'Nobody from Moke.'

Surprised by the old girl's secrecy yet not considering her in any way disturbed, Ceci sought the advice in confidence of a visiting doctor. In no time a priest had arrived, ostensibly asking directions, yet agreeing to see the old girl when asked. He was not Moke's regular priest and Adelaide seemed grateful for this. For her part Ceci managed to get Faith and Ginger from the house.

As they sat outside the summerhouse at the far end of the lawn, Faith's eyes strayed periodically to Adelaide's window. 'When the priest has finished with her, I think I might like a word with him.'

'About what?' Ginger demanded abruptly.

'About me,' Faith replied.

'May I have a word with you, Father,' she called, running towards the priest as he appeared.

Ceci noted the phrase as if an alarm bell were ringing in her head.

After the priest had gone Adelaide became quite thoughtful. During the week that followed she struggled both with high temperatures and a pressing problem she was trying to come to terms with, something her indomitable will insisted she settle before giving in.

'I want to tell you something,' she finally confessed to Ceci.

'Don't overtire yourself. Say it in as few words as possible,' Ceci advised, reaching for her hand. Gradually the story came out.

'Get ready because this is Moke's best-kept secret,' the old girl croaked in a last attempt at humour. 'Nobody knows this.'

Ceci leaned forward.

'You'll have noticed, despite her being illegitimate, Lizabeth's likeness to her father? Reason is, my husband sired her.'

Ceci gaped. In her wildest moment it had occurred to her that Maureen, apparently the last child at home, could have been gotten into by her own father but that Ginger's father ... No wonder these particular grandparents had never visited! 'Does Ginger know?' she asked.

The old girl shook her head.

'It must have been hard for you to accept,' Ceci added sympathetically.

'The priest wouldn't give me the forgiveness,' Adelaide went on, 'unless I – '

'Forgive *you*?'

'For concealing this from Ginger. He has to know.'

'Don't worry,' Ceci said. 'When the time is right – he will know.' But she did not intend to tell him. Ever. 'He wouldn't forgive you unless you what?'

'Unless I promised I intended to tell. I promised – so – I got conditional forgiveness.'

'You promised to see he knew?'

The old girl nodded. Nonetheless she looked frightened. 'But how can I? It was me who arranged the marriage – kept him away from you all those years – caused them to bring these – unfortunate children into the world.'

'Maureen and Ginger's children have done very well,' Ceci contradicted.

'Except Lizabeth.'

'I'll tell him for you,' she lied again. She owed nothing to the Catholic Church. Let God come after her if he chose.

'I would tell him myself but – '

'I know. The time isn't right.'

Trying to come to terms with the fact that Ginger and Lizabeth were as good as brother and sister, Ceci listened to the tired voice crackling urgently on. 'You could have told, though, looking at Lizabeth's nose,' Adelaide insisted. 'But nobody thought. The priest knew my husband had committed adultery and that Maureen was in the family way but he didn't put two and two together: he wouldn't have been allowed to by his profession even if he'd seen them holding hands behind the church shed.'

'Surely each of them confessed?'

'But not who with.'

'Surely he would have known?'

'Outside the confessional he's not to think at all of what he's heard. He's not to put faces to voices or names. I forgave him. I had to,' Adelaide explained. 'But you can be sure we moved out of Moke before the baby appeared. That's why I didn't go downstairs to Midnight Mass. Didn't want anyone seeing me.

Ceci watched her hands worrying at the bedspread. 'I still blame myself. Maureen's father came over and put it to us that he was looking for a husband for the girl but I didn't get the drift of what the men were saying. They were careful I didn't. I think it was Maureen's father put it to Ginger, casual like, that his daughter was in the family way and he was casting about for a son-in-law. When Ginger told me all I could think of was, well, her being last, probably they'll get the old boy's land. I encouraged him.'

'I think in her heart Lizabeth knew Ginger was more equal to her than a father,' Ceci said slowly. She watched the old lady pull the quilt around her shoulders. Dearly she regretted having given her the bath that had caused her pneumonia.

'If I had insisted my husband take his medicine at the time,' Adelaide fretted –

'He would have denied it and the blame would have gone to Maureen's father. And as for keeping Ginger from me – I'd turned him down before you gave him a way out, Adelaide, I assure you.'

The old woman's eyes opened wide with relief.

'So you haven't managed to ruin anyone's life you see.'

'But think what that poor girl suffered at the hands of my family,' Adelaide urged, wiping at her eyes with the heel of her hand.

'Marrying Ginger?'

'There are two worlds for a girl who gets into trouble. The world before and the world after.'

'So now you're holding yourself responsible for her suicide too?' Ceci asked, wondering if it had been an underlying sense of guilt which had motivated her defence of the dead woman.

'Without our family it would never have happened,' Adelaide said sharply. 'She would have had a home of her own away from that father of hers. Depend upon it, he teased her. No wonder she strangled him and ended up in the asylum! Yes, I blame my family.'

Ceci hesitated. The situation was tricky. 'But you are sorry! You've confessed to the priest and been forgiven.'

'On the condition that I tell Ginger so that he can tell Lizabeth at a time of his choosing. I have to make restitution for those years of silence.'

Ceci began to worry. More than anything she wanted a

happy death for the old girl. 'I think you should see the local priest,' she said quickly.

'I've confessed meself to pieces already! What have I left to confess?'

'To help you accept forgiveness. It seems a bit ungracious to – to keep insisting you are guilty – to blame yourself for something God's forgiven you for. We're all human. This is the way we learn. God knows why these things happen to us – but don't we come to see the difference between bad and good and come to prefer good, to choose it over the bad? That's why you're able to be sorry. If we were punished for bad deeds and rewarded for good, we'd all be good out of an instinct for survival! Because it often pays to be bad there's merit in choosing good. But without these freedoms to make mistakes . . .'

The old girl nodded.

'Did your husband ever regret it?'

After staring at the wall for a while Adelaide cocked her head like a bird: 'His body didn't but his ears did! I took care of that!'

'Yes, we did wrong. Yes, we were guilty. Yes, we are sorry. But yes – we are forgiven!' Ceci insisted.

'Forgiven, yes,' the old girl murmured.

'Then have the good grace to accept it,' Ceci urged.

Adelaide thought for a while. 'Do you think Maureen ever told Ginger?' she asked.

'I don't see how she could have,' Ceci replied.

'If we had brought out the truth at the time of Maureen's committal, explained the strain she'd lived under – '

'They would still have put her away,' Ceci insisted. 'I'm sure of it.'

'Get me the local priest then,' Adelaide agreed, sinking back on her pillow. 'I'll confess to ingratitude in not accepting forgiveness. Taking God to be meaner than I am.'

'You see. He's not like us at all,' Ceci teased.

'You're a fine one,' Adelaide smiled. 'You Protestant you!'

Feeling the relief in the room Ceci got to her feet.

'Send Faith to me,' the old girl sighed. 'We'll say an Act of Contrition together.'

'Let me kiss you first,' Ceci said, bending as Adelaide turned towards her. She saw the thin hands reach to grasp at her arms, felt the delicate hair of the old lady press against her skull as her lips touched down. Taking an extra minute she sat down and cradled her in her arms. 'I'm so sorry you're not well, Adelaide,' she said softly.

'We all have to die sometime,' the old woman replied.

After Faith had been in to say an Act of Contrition with the old girl, she noticed her manner changing.

'I think she's leaving soon,' she murmured. 'Better go in.'

Ginger got to his feet. 'I don't know what to say to her . . .'

'You may not need to say anything. Leave it much longer and you won't have to.'

'Make it up to Lizabeth for me. Take care of that unfortunate child,' Adelaide murmured. Ceci sincerely hoped these would not be her last words. 'You will remember, won't you,' she said, turning to Ceci.

Ceci squeezed her hand and moved her face closer to the unfocused eyes. 'She can hear us, Ginger,' she said. 'Say whatever you have to say.'

Ginger bit his lip. The words did not come. Adelaide lay back, her eyes crossing the ceiling as if searching for something.

'Go in peace,' Ceci whispered, nudging Ginger violently.

'Goodbye Mother,' he said in a broken voice. 'And thank you.'

With that Adelaide's breathing slowed. Noticing her hands were twitching, Faith quickly placed her rosary in them and, putting her mouth close to the old lady's ear, slid the beads through her fingers for her while whispering the Hail Marys. With the force of a lifetime of habit Adelaide's lips touched and parted, touched and parted at the familiar feel of her beads, the sound of the words brushing her consciousness like leaves falling, fluttering, blown away as the Grand Silence descended.

'She's gone,' Faith murmured, 'into Everlasting Light.'

Unwilling to let go of her hand, Ceci turned to look for Ginger. She saw him beyond the door in the corridor, on his knees, crying like a baby.

Chapter 35

On the denuded hills of the backblocks, the land laid waste – its very bones showing through – Pieter stood behind Reg, his hand on his shoulder. 'Courage.'

Local sentiment that Stebbins had it coming to him – that rabbiters were on to a good thing and it served them right when they got their come-uppance – had done little to save Annie.

'It was no one here, you know,' Pieter said.

Reg nodded. Word of Annie's brave act, the sheer honesty of it, the desperation of her circumstances and the morality of her beliefs, had fired the tail of the story till it had spread like wildfire. Soon the law had come looking.

Inconsolable, Reg sat hugging their toddler, Little Annie, aware that for the first time in his life he had known happiness with a good woman, one who in her own way – despite being of fierce and independent mind – had been subject to him. Though the local population was behind him there seemed little doubt that now his Annie had been taken away – she would be hanged.

'I'll get back down,' Pieter murmured. 'Come eat with us, Reg.'

Reg shook his head. He was sorry for the hamlet folk too. The spread of his rabbits had wreaked havoc on their pasture and their cows, already scrawny, would be feeling it this winter . . . and the next – if there was one.

When Annie had been taken from him no extra horse had been brought, no arrangement made for his transportation to the towns below. Suddenly it was as if they were not man and wife, as if each of them now existed separately and the law had interest in one but not the other. Reg picked up Little Annie and hurried after Pieter. The people in the hamlet kept a respectful distance as the shattered man passed between them, pushed open the gate and hurried to Pieter's house. Heads shook.

Leaving Little Annie with Pieter and his wife, Reg set off on a borrowed horse for the lowlands. That the story of Annie had become a nine-day wonder did not occur to him coming, as he did, from the backblocks which were beyond the reach of newspapers. The world of trains and express trains, court houses, judges, prisons, two-storey stone buildings and high churches he had forgotten.

'Do you have money on you, Reg?' Pieter's wife had called after him and, as he paused, had come running forth with a small leather pouch and thrust it into his hands.

'I can't take this,' Reg had said with awkward indignation.

'Take it and welcome,' the good woman insisted, tears in her eyes. 'Just mind you don't get Pieter's horse stolen.'

Reg rode on down, the hills falling away behind him and the land evening out into the flat sour scrub he remembered crossing with Annie those years ago when they had climbed with hope in their hearts; when the profits from her nugget had translated themselves into an accessible dream they had believed, with nothing more than hard work and honesty, they could achieve. Fools! he told himself. On the horizon he saw a rabbit looking at him. 'Whoa!'

Standing by the horse Reg stared at the rabbit and the rabbit stared back. Soon another was looking at him and then another, their rounded heads the colour of the stones they crouched between. 'Gerrar!' Reg shouted, his voice echoing across the landscape as he quickly snatched up a handful of stones and pounded them with them.

In the first town Reg came to he learned where Annie was: she had been sent to Dunedin gaol. 'Because of overcrowding in Addington, the women's place,' the storekeeper hastily informed him.

'Some disease broke out there,' the wife put in. 'Wouldn't do to have that woman die of fever and not stand trial, would it? she demanded earnestly. 'People have their rights.'

Nosy cow, Reg thought. Had she realized the 'woman' was his wife, would she have spoken different?

'For all as she was provoked,' the woman went on, 'can't have that sort of thing in a colony.'

'I remember being in Lyttelton when there was a hanging,' her husband said chirpily. 'The bell started to toll. We was in school. They always toll the bell when they bring 'em out from the cell to the gallows. Toll it all the way. It was a right racket!'

'Me mates used to hide when they heard it tolling but I never. Remember me mother saying, "Now you go straight to school and stay out of the way. There's a man to be hanged today."'

'You all right?' the woman asked, seeing Reg wavering in the doorway. 'Look Fred! You're upsetting him.'

'Got a ticklish stomach, have you?' the man grinned, flinging a block of wood at a rat. With a squeal the rat fell into the onion pit. 'Get him when he comes out,' the man murmured.

'I remember the hangings too,' the woman said dreamily. 'The whole town would go quiet. Sometimes we'd put flowers on their graves after . . .'

'Girlish sense of romance,' the husband said, reaching for the block as the rat's head peeped cautiously over the onion pit's planking. 'Sssh!' As the rat came out, the storeman's fingers crawled towards the iron five-pound weight of his scales, cradled then slung it expertly through the air, crushing the creature's neck as it reached the floor.

'Good shot,' murmured his wife.

Looking up they saw their visitor had gone.

All the way to the coast it continued: hangings and talk of hangings.

Annie could sense Reg was coming. He had not been at the trial but she supposed he would have been as overtaken by events as she; so disoriented by the group of strangers walking into their midst, and dragging her away. The sensation of being stared and pointed at, run from by children, talked down to by sergeants and locked in a cell had taken her back to her West Coast days and revived in her a sense of fight. Now she sensed Reg was getting nearer she hoped he would not be too broken on his arrival.

'Chèer up!' she told him. 'They can't find anyone to hang me. Not in the entire colony. *And* they've advertised!'

Reg dipped his head to conceal the tears filling his eyes. 'I'm going in there and tell them I did it,' he insisted.

'I love you, Reg,' Annie replied. 'But that won't do it.'

All around Reg were sounds of misery and madness, the only defiant streak in the goal being Annie's gentleness and acceptance.

'It'll be a while yet,' she told Reg. 'Don't hang around here. Go back and give Little Annie my love, then come again and tell me how she is.'

That terrible phrase, hang around! Reg got to his feet trembling.

He is so rounded, so full of love for me and our child, so – whole, Annie told herself. As he stepped to the door, in her heart she knew she had succeeded. Pain? She'd been there before.

Reg stood outside the gaol wondering which way to go. He was fairly sure there would not be time to go to the backblocks and return . . . yet with Annie inside the gaol and he being separated from her, he felt incomplete; neither his stomach nor head nor even his limbs would work right. People stared at him and passed by seeing only a confused hobo. He had not the sense or organization to look for a boarding house, to even cross to a hotel and eat a meal. Soon the day of the hanging would come. Should he stay away or go to it? Would it be done in an open field with a big crowd like a crucifixion? Suppose he went and could not get to the front? Would she want to see him in the mob as they hanged her, her skirts blown about, an object like a piece of meat on the end of a string? The idea of strangers seeing his Annie die, timid and soiled with a purple tongue, choked him. What were these humans he lived with who could do such a thing? Standing in the centre of the busy town Reg saw only panic. He would go to the hanging he decided. He would get to the front and shout his defiance, shout her name!

'You can look a bit sharp today, love,' said the gaoler. 'We're moving you.'

'Upwards, downwards or sideways?' Annie asked.

'Invercargill. Be a riot if we hanged you here.'

Annie put her head on one side.

'That poor wretch of a husband of yours, hanging outside the door, has caused such an upset I doubt they'd let the hangman through,' he said indifferently.

'So you got one then?'

'Long journey and we had to pay his train fare.'

485

Annie nodded. 'So you're sneaking me off to Invercargill? Going to tell my husband?'

'You want us to tell him?'

'Don't you have to?'

'Not unless he goes through the right procedures, identifies himself legally and comes to the office and asks.'

Although Reg did not grasp what was happening, the rest of Dunedin read the papers so he quickly heard it: the woman Bowen was being taken to Invercargill right down the tip of the Southland to be hanged.

'That's 'cause none of us can afford the fares and folk down there won't know nothing,' people grumbled, angry to have been done out of a free circus.

'Has she gone yet?' Reg demanded at the gaol door.

'Who?'

'You know.'

Reg turned his mount towards Invercargill.

Because she was a realist Annie knew that she would hang. Although she had meant it and would do the same again she had broken a fundamental law of the land and was not surprised at the outcome. The only reason they had not got rid of her already was that she was a woman. They would hang a dozen men like Reg and think nothing of it. Reg. That was where her worries lay. What would happen to him and Little Annie up there in the backblocks? She could be of no help to him now. The backblocks! Briefly the vision of the bright sun slashing through the glimmering leaves of their clearing as she stepped out of their lean-to in the early days came to her. How far away, like another life, was the sound of movement in the bushes, the cheeky fantail darting before her path, the wax-eye arguing by its nest! She saw Reg trying to drill the well bore, the first season the bright green cocksfoot had poked through their dark earth, rich with the ash of burnt timber;

486

saw the early morning mists rising above the blackened stumps beyond their crude picket fence and heard the cry of the wild birds.

'I don't want my body cemented into the walls of that there gaol,' she'd told the warder with whom, in the routine of the gaol, she had fallen into an easy camaraderie. 'Nor do I want it dissolved in quick-lime and buried in the compound.'

'Ah well,' the man replied, 'then it'll be up to your husband to identify himself and go through the right channels and put in a request for the body.'

'You see he does it, will you, for me?' Annie urged, seeking in her pockets for some little item, not a bribe but a reminder of her words.

'Not allowed,' the man murmured.

'Surely if you see him you could say something?'

'What does he look like?'

'Truth is he doesn't look any different from anyone else,' Annie said sadly, sitting on the bed. 'I suppose it's silly but I would have liked to be buried outdoors somewhere – somewhere with the birds and the sunshine.'

The warder stared at Annie.

'If he doesn't know where my body is he won't be able to visit it. That will be bad for him, not having a place to go to when he wants to think with me,' she pleaded. 'I don't mind dying. It's only a couple of seconds – but I don't want my husband to be left without my body afterwards. At this moment, that is the only thing I require.'

On the day of the hanging Reg found himself in the strange town of Invercargill. Although the event was to take place there for privacy's sake, the height of the buildings surrounding the gaol made it easy for folk of every description to gain a good vantage point and thwart the intentions of the privileged six or eight *men* the state had agreed should be privy to the act. Reg pushed through the crowds and arrived at the gaol door only to find it closed.

'I'm her husband. Let me in!' he demanded.

'Get away.'

Urgently Reg circumnavigated the building, staring up at the high walls. Already the bells were beginning to toll, a dreadful sound of mourning washing from the sea over the town and towards the hills. As the dreaded ringing spread carriages stopped in their tracks, faces turned, people nudged each other, opened their mouths and waited.

In her cell Annie heard the bells begin. 'I'm all right, padre,' she began. 'You don't need to read any of that.'

But the minister went on reading from the burial service.

'I'm not dead yet,' Annie told him. Sensing that she had just made her last joke she saw two men come into the cell and instinctively got to her feet.

'Put your arms in front. Cross your hands over.' As Annie did so, they bent her elbows and quickly strapped her arms to her sides.

My God, Annie thought, if my skirt blows above my head I can't help it now.

'Is my hair all right?' she asked.

Ignoring her the minister went on reading the ridiculous ungrammatical words: '. . . in the midst of life we are in death . . .'

Annie felt like telling him to be quiet, that she was thinking, but the awareness of the preciousness of her last few seconds, the need to draw her energy in impressed itself upon her. Glancing up she saw the head gaoler appear in the doorway and motion the two men out. Behind him was the medical officer of the gaol, two newspaper men and a gaol official. The minister glanced nervously at them.

'Look, he's coming,' one of them whispered and all faces turned.

'I demand from you the body of Annie Bowen for execution!' Annie heard the sheriff's voice ring out. They had not asked for Annie Bowen. They had asked for the body of Annie Bowen. In that, too, they were premature. At this moment the gaol bell itself commenced tolling and with a quick nudge in the back, Annie realized the procession was about to start.

From his vantage point on the roof of a building opposite Reg saw first a gaol official, then a doctor, then a priest of some kind reading from a book, one behind the other, come out into the sunlight. Suddenly Annie appeared with a prison guard on either side. Instantly the hangman stepped in behind her, to be followed by the sheriff.

Annie glanced up. How many faces on the buildings and rooves around! How very public this hanging! These buildings, built long after the old gaol, were so crammed that not another face would have fitted at their windows. Because of the minister directly in front of her, Annie did not see the steps of the scaffold till almost the last minute. Stumbling forward, yet instinctively reaching to lift up her skirts before the steps, she found her arms bound but with a quick lurch regained balance. Neither gaoler reached for her elbow. Now on the platform the men moved themselves to assigned positions, Annie in the middle – close to the gallows – took a deep breath and gave a lingering search of the faces turned towards her, at the tops of the heads of those in the courtyard below and the hands of the hangman, now struggling to ease the opening of the white calico bag he would place over her head.

He nodded with his head towards the trap door. Annie stepped on to it. Behind her he began adjusting the rope to her height, fastening a length of string around her thighs to keep them from thrashing.

Reg leaned forward. A man was speaking to her. 'Annie!' he croaked, his voice lost in the crowd.

'He's asking her if she has anything to say,' a woman whispered loudly.

It seemed Annie had. She nodded vigorously and shouted at the top of her lungs: 'I love you Reg!'

It was the last sound proudly shouted in the still afternoon before the drop.

In a haze Reg descended from the building, the image of the hangman's ugly body struggling to get the cloth over Annie's face, the noose over her unresisting head as she stood proud and defiant, having shouted her last message.

In the turmoil Pieter's horse had either been stolen or wandered away. Where had he left it? People were talking, congratulating each other, moved by an exceptional event which they felt might serve as a warning to them. No one looked at the man, blind with grief, hurrying from the scene.

By the time he reached the foothills Reg felt he had some direction. Little Annie was there and he must look after her. He had wanted to sell their cows to raise money to somehow help Annie in her trial, but the folk in the hamlet could not afford to buy so had passed the hat around instead. Much good it had done them seeing as he hadn't known where to go! After a while he sat down to rest and fell to kicking stones. At a sound from behind he turned and saw the pawnbroker descending from the hills, driving his cows towards him, his gun on his shoulder.

'I went to shoot them for the meat but your neighbours say they won't buy even a leg of it,' the man said disagreeably. No doubt he'd read about their case in the paper and realized he wouldn't get anything back on his loan, Reg thought, watching the poor beasts passing, their thin tails swinging like bits of rope from their bony hips, occasionally tossing off a piece of impoverished dung to blow from the track and lose itself amongst the stones and rocks of this soured landscape. Vaguely he remembered kicking bits of scattered dung like that together to make the fire to cook the stolen chicken on the way up at the beginning with Annie. He'd half wondered then where the dung came from. Now some distance away the starved animals' hooves did not even raise dust as they headed to the slaughter house. Not far from the track was the remains of a fire, perhaps theirs. Sitting, he remembered Annie stabbing at the ground with her shoe, digging for water. 'Courage, Reg,' he heard her say. 'The game's not played out yet.'

By now the pawnbroker had vanished into a dip in the land and the other way the hills were lost behind rolling cloud.

'What else you got in store for me?' he asked the sky.

Chapter 36

'Do make an effort, Ginger,' Ceci urged wanly. 'You were not that fond of your mother and the fact we lost a child surely you can accept as – as . . .'

Ginger went and sat by the fire in exactly the same position as the night he'd been tempted to betray Maureen. 'Lately I feel bad about Maureen,' he confessed. 'She was upstairs in bed having a mental breakdown. I was down here wanting you. Remember?'

'Well you didn't have me. Nor did you cause her breakdown.'

'I was hardly a help to her – '

'You gave Maureen a good home.'

'She knew I wanted you. There was always – something – unsaid between us.'

'But you could be wrong about what that was,' said Ceci carefully, remembering her promise to the dying Adelaide to see that one day Ginger knew.

'While we had the hope of a child,' he sighed, 'I forgot. But Mother's death – '

'Has succeeded in bringing it all back to you.' Ceci nodded. It was uncanny!

'Her last words were about Lizabeth – '

'She was Maureen's problem before she was yours.'

'Either way it's my fault.'

'That is the most ridiculous thing I've ever heard,' Ceci said with conviction.

'You think so?' Ginger asked, walking to the door.

'Ginger!' Ceci called after him. 'What would you say if I was to tell you Lizabeth was – was . . .'

'Was what?'

'Your father's child?'

'I'd say you needed a good long holiday!'

Generally frustrated, Ceci picked up a letter from Kevin which was addressed specifically to her. He had asked her to break some extraordinary news to Ginger:

. . . you will realize this is the happiest event in my life. I know Father will be as glad but his first reaction will be shock which he may show as anger. If you can prepare him first – if you can tell him I want to become a priest . . .

Ceci folded the letter. She did not know how Ginger would react to any information but Kevin was probably right that a new disruption would unsettle rather than please him.

I don't know the first thing about priests and he should know that very well, she told herself, slipping the letter into her davenport and deciding to reply that she would tell Ginger, but not just yet. What did one say to a person who had decided to become a priest? Did you say you were very happy for them? Did you offer congratulations? Did you express regret that they would not marry? Did you ask them why they were doing such a peculiar thing?

Down in Christchurch Kevin had never been more certain of anything. When the idea had finally suggested itself to him in a cogent form, he had recognized it with such clarity that it could have been his own reflection he was looking at. Why it had taken him so long to come to it he did not know, yet now the awareness had arrived, he could not wait to begin. He had not told anyone but Ceci. The realization was so important that he almost wanted to keep it secret, to cherish it as a man might carry the picture

493

of a woman before announcing they would marry. As a priest he would open himself to others, be available, share their fears and burgeoning lives. Instead of taking just one life and selfishly gathering material objects and struggling with one woman to experience the Divine, he would open himself thoroughly. The idea of the poverty and denial which lay ahead filled him with such joy he wanted to embrace those nearest him and it was only the knowledge that Michael and his 'young lady' would consider him most peculiar that stopped him. He knew from Ceci's letter that she had not told his father; that his father was shortly due for another Christchurch visit and could do with some cheering up; hence was probably not ready to be told yet. He sensed in Ceci's letter an awkwardness; that she did not know how to congratulate him but was 'delighted on his behalf'. So many phrases: 'glad you have found a direction', 'happy that you have settled on something at last', 'hope it doesn't disappoint you', 'horses for courses' . . . These were the phrases he would have to expect from people from now on. If they only knew the joy he felt!

As Ginger stepped on to the race track, he heard around him the sound of cheering and saw up ahead at the front of a crowd Michael and a certain type of female letting off champagne and celebrating what was obviously a first-class win. The woman, he noticed, was embracing his son with a reckless abandon which those around seemed to find acceptable.

'Darling!' the woman shouted, wrenching at a shoe, pulling it off and holding it out to be filled with champagne.

'Don't be predictable, Miranda,' Michael grunted, but the woman filled both shoes and simply flung them away.

'Here,' she said to Michael, pulling open the front of her

dress. With a slightly drunken giggle, Michael began to pour the bubbling champagne in.

'Ooooh!' the woman shrilled. 'It tickles!'

'He's over there,' Kevin said, taking Ginger's elbow and steering him towards Michael.

'You want to get in there and get yourself a bit of that, son,' Ginger urged, uncharacteristically nudging him.

Kevin smiled good-naturedly. 'Horses for courses,' he grinned.

'You see!' Michael said, pushing his way towards Ginger. 'It paid off! The sheer madness and gamble of bringing a horse all that way! Don't tell me a chap doesn't know how to enjoy himself!'

'Is that your father?' the girl asked, in amazement.

Michael fondled her bottom: 'He knows a thing about horses,' he whispered mock confidentially.

Overcome by the noise and glory Ginger allowed himself to be led to the bar, to be fêted and praised with Michael and his hangers-on. 'Where's your brother?' he asked Michael.

'Oh, snook off somewhere I expect.'

In the bar the drink was flowing. It began to occur to Ginger that this was not a bad place to be, it took a man's mind off things. He might even see Frank hanging around the track or Lizabeth going through the bins for toffee wrappers for her kids.

'What are you laughing at?' Michael's woman asked him loudly.

Ginger's face was pink and he knew it; he would bask in his boys' glory and down as much ale as he could, with one eye on the door . . .

To Michael's surprise he suddenly ambled over, reached up and threw an arm around him: 'You're a good boy to gladden your father's heart in his old age,' he said.

The girl tittered again. The man was not that old and she would have gone with him herself for a consideration.

Back at Hexham Ceci was finding Ginger's increasing absences and intoxication difficult to deal with. She understood Kevin had made plain his intentions to him, only to be met with drunken incredulity and incomprehension. The more befuddled he became the more angry he got with himself. More often than not he would have to stay over in Christchurch till he sobered up or was brought home by Kevin in apologetic state.

'He needs love – like this country,' Kevin had insisted roundly. 'All my life I've seen it – especially here in Moke.'

'Will you be going away to a seminary?' Ceci asked.

'If one will have me.'

'Are you going to work with the Maoris?'

'I'll go wherever I'm sent. I wouldn't mind helping the white man to enjoy God in the same way the Maori is able to. I'd prefer the slums though. It's the rich who need love most.'

'Leave your father there. I'll put him to bed.'

When he finally sobered up Ginger took a long slow look at things. He was ostensibly without heir unless Faith did the trick. Around him most of Hexham's finery had been sold off in the search for Lizabeth, and beyond the fences the land was depreciating both in terms of the amount of work he put into it and the effect of the encroaching rabbits. Neighbouring farms had brought in cats, weasels, ferrets and stoats – specially shipped from Home by the government – but they had been about as much good as the endless wire fences. They had not stopped the rabbits and as new pests had themselves done plenty of damage. Leases on which the pasture was still sound were going unwanted and on top of everything else

– Michael was not about to settle down, Myra showed no intention of ever coming south and Kevin had chosen the priesthood! His sense of bitterness at this last blow was second only to a fear of examining why he should feel this way. There was no doubt about it: these days there was only one place for a man to be and that was at the race track! As soon as his head felt right again, he would get himself together and go back down. Why, they might as well sell up Hexham and move down altogether.

Though Kevin counselled patience, Ceci was puzzled at Ginger's decline into liquor.

'Perhaps he's using drink to adjust to the fact that Lizabeth doesn't want to see him,' Kevin suggested.

'It may not be that he's adjusting to,' Ceci said slowly.

'What then?'

'It's a matter I must conclude with him when the time is right.' She hesitated.

Kevin raised an eyebrow.

'I mean when he's sober,' Ceci smiled.

Once again Ginger had vanished to Christchurch. Left alone at Hexham Ceci flicked through the newspapers which had accumulated during Adelaide's illness and death, at first sight an unreadable mass but on perusal, interesting. She read land prices were still falling, somebody had shot himself in Parliament House, six and a half thousand volunteers had gone off to fight the Boers – the South African War being the first foreign war the colony had engaged in; some enterprising female confidence trickster had represented herself as a man – married a vicar's daughter and made off with all their belongings before chancing discovery on a honeymoon; some woman in the backblocks had shot a passer-by in the forehead and was to be hanged for it. The narrative was sketchy as if the incident had already received much coverage. The man had been standing some feet away in the woman's clearing, Ceci read, his horse down by the track, not touching or molesting her when she had illogically . . . He must have said something pretty ripe, Ceci told herself, opening the newspaper further and coming on the headline 'Annie Bowen To Be Hanged'. Horrified, she searched through the paper seeing the date was long past. In following editions the woman was forgotten in favour of the Boer War but sure enough, there it was again, a hangman had been secured and a date for the hanging set. Her finger hovering over it, Ceci realized her friend Annie was no more. Shaking with shock she got to her feet. There was no one to tell. Ginger was away on a long bender in Christchurch which could last for anything up to three weeks, given that Kevin no longer had time to wheel him back and forth. Faith too was away on 'private business'. As she listened to her breathing in the empty house Ceci realized she must go at once to Reg.

Fumbling to pack her saddle bag, in her mind Ceci put together the words of the note she would leave for Ginger. There was no point him coming after her. She intended to go cross-country, that being a great deal faster. Indeed she would not even need to pass the store she remembered standing at a fork. Since the backblocks had been opened up numerous tracks had criss-crossed the land so that with a full moon and a horse, good time could be made. Remarkably enough there were even no rivers to be forded.

'Dear Ginger,' she began. 'I have gone over to Reg and Annie's because . . .' Quickly she scratched out the word Annie. What to say? For one thing she could not believe that Annie had been hanged. She seemed to be leaving more and more notes for Ginger – half of them not read – for in his present stupor her words went in one ear and out the other. He could agree to anything at night time only to have forgotten it by morning. Finishing the note as best she could she hurriedly propped it on the table, hoping he would not stand a glass on it and walk off with the note stuck to its base, or leave the door open till it blew under the table, or simply roll it up and use it as a quill to light the stove. Taking a last look around, Ceci locked the front door and set out towards the stables.

As the moon rose over the backblocks Reg sat on the hard stony ground listening to the plaintive cry of the morepork: 'More-pork, more-pork, more-pork,' it called. He knew it was the morepork owl from his days in West Coast forests but hadn't heard it up this high before. 'Ru-ru-ru-ru-ru,' it called, hidden from him yet not far away and no doubt observing him as it got about picking up insects and spiders on the ground, the odd lizard or whatever it could find. 'Not much to choose between us,' Reg murmured.

Bereft of Annie's companionship, he looked about for some human agency to blame for his circumstance. The fact that rabbits ate land cover; the fact of Stebbins' dishonesty; the pawnbroker's instinct for self-preservation masquerading as greed; the law's indifference to individual justice – all these were things a grown man could expect. Nor could he honestly say, given how he had tried since joining with Annie, that he had behaved badly, taken advantage of others, or been greedy or lazy. Given he had not defaulted on his responsibilities, wherein lay the explanation or blame for what had happened? Someone, somewhere, had to be responsible. That the events of his life had made him a near-perfect human being he did not grasp. Gradually it came to him. It was Ceci who had set the chain in action by bringing the original two rabbits! That expansive gesture, with the sort of theatricality (if there was such a word) she had brought from England with her those many years ago which had so angered him in the old dwelling. He remembered her getting smart with him for trying to pass on the mouldy sheep, taunting him, saying he couldn't read, saying she imagined they got to see a lot of newspapers up there by the time they'd finished being chewed by everyone from Christchurch to Te Anau! Well he'd taken care of her that time, the cheeky kitchen maid! So she couldn't accept simple hospitality but had to come roaring in with her rabbits and hey presto! You might have known Annie being soft-hearted and full of mother's milk wouldn't let him brain them!

Getting to his feet in the moonlight Reg went to Pieter's to reclaim Little Annie. He could never repay his hospitality nor the loss of his horse. It didn't matter how often the good man squeezed his shoulder and told him to think nothing of it. They must be gone. Already Little Annie was picking up strange words in — was it — Norwegian? Ceci owed them a home and Ceci could provide it. Taking the sleeping child in his arms and permitting both Pieter and his wife to kiss him goodbye, with anger in his heart Reg set off towards Hexham.

Suspecting himself of having become *persona non grata* in Christchurch, Ginger made his own arrangements to return. Already he was a little tired of his own drinking. It created a haze between him and Ceci which he now felt it necessary to penetrate and emerge from. The woman had been very patient with him when, for some reason, he hadn't seemed able to sort out his life any more. How was it, he wondered, that when he could not have the one thing he wanted — Ceci — he had managed so well. Yet now he had her, not only could he do nothing to realize the magic of it, it seemed everything he did went wrong. He had been against the racehorse; she had been for it. He had not even been told about the annulment, his own children preferring to confide in Ceci. Even his mother had turned to her in the end rather than him. Why? What had there been so unsuitable for his ears? Well, the old woman was dead now so he could drink all he liked, he told himself, turning into a wayside hostelry. 'Twas always nice to enter a pub with money in his pocket and he regretted not for one minute disposing of the trivia of Hexham to furnish their needs.

'Will you be wanting to stay the night, sir?' the proprietor asked, noting his condition.

'I might and I might not,' said Ginger, vaguely aware he was on the point of giving up drinking.

'If you are to continue on, I'll ask the next coach to wait,' the man informed him to show he wasn't touting for custom.

Shame, thought Ginger. Nice little pub too.

Thanks to the consideration of the coachman, or maybe his need for an extra fare, Ginger found himself at the end of his pint heading in the brisk air towards Hexham. The price of another pint saw the man bring him right to his door, an improvement on walking the last few miles.

'Ceci!' he called, entering. 'Ceci?'

Annoyed that she wasn't there, frightened to find himself alone in the Gothic-style house, Ginger poured himself a drink. Though the autumn had been early and winter started mild, the nights were now chilly and in the large house, empty of people and belongings, positively cold. Instinctively he gravitated to the great hearth. They had not lit the fire since Adelaide had her fall. Casually putting the memory of it aside along with the embers, Ginger bunched up the newspapers Ceci had left lying and tossed them into the grate. He walked through to the kitchen, thinking how cold and empty the place felt and pushed open the door to the tinder shed, returning with an arm of kindling and several large logs generously laced with spiders' webs, the woodlice jumping to the ground as he entered the house.

As the flames flickered and darted in the once dead grate his eyes strayed to the chopped logs. It was such a log he had brought his hand down on that evening before this hearth with Ceci when she, a young widow, had offered peace and quiet to his deranged wife Maureen upstairs. Gradually the scene arose. He wanting her – she in humility ignorant of it; he – unable to contain himself, lashing out at the log and receiving for his troubles a great splinter. He remembered her gasping, reaching for the heart-shaped pin cushion which had hung in the chimney breast and quickly beginning to work at the splinter with a needle, the tip of her tongue resting on her lip, afraid of hurting him. Unaware of the effect of her touch until the instant she had sensed him relax rather than tense up at the needle's pry – she had glanced up, caught the ecstasy on his face and dropped his hand in shock. How innocent they had been! She had all but fled him and had not stopped running until Hexham had gone and she was safely ensconced in the deep mud of the West Coast.

At a sound Ginger turned his head. There stood Maureen in her white nightdress. 'You're the lucky one,' she'd told Ceci. 'And aren't you clever?' (This to him.) He saw glass flash through the air, miss Ceci's back and shatter; saw the servant Hallam appear; heard Ceci's voice: 'Say goodnight to your wife'; heard her bid him leave and remembered how he had tried to come back.

He put another log on the fire. Chopping the logs. Ceci gone those many months. No help from the bank manager in finding her – just the agreement to forward letters; the waiting; the silence of it; his axe flying through the afternoon sun, his tears glinting – Lizabeth's hand on his shoulder, her words: 'Go to her.'

The first journey to Grevillton, too painful to remember, he quickly brushed from his mind. He poured more Scotch. But Lizabeth had comforted him. The second journey? How had he stood the rebuff? Lizabeth of course. Ceci's early letters – the rejections – Lizabeth's encouragement. She looking after the children while he set off to find the woman he would not live without, to bring her back. As the Scotch pricked at his brains he realized something was wrong: he had wanted to show Ceci to Lizabeth as a young man might show a girlfriend to his mother. Briefly something he had been told lately played on the edge of his mind, something which had been trying to communicate itself to him but which he had been struggling to quench with alcohol. It was – what? No! It was gone. Only Lizabeth remained: Lizabeth running out to meet him on his return from Moke. Lizabeth keeping Maureen's sister Edna in line after the funeral, her firm loving presence and reassurance giving him the confidence to set out on that final journey of rejection to Grevillton . . . let Edna glower as she would. There was that day again. He saw Lizabeth taking little Myra and turning her face away at the sight of the man from the asylum on their doorstep with his news, taking her into the kitchen, knowing in her heart even before he did that Maureen was dead, sensing and being relieved at it. How different they had all been in the days before Ceci! When the man from the asylum had come Kevin and Michael had been hiding in the grass at the end of Old Nolan's track flinging stones at passing horses – including that one – and Faith had been sitting on the gate to their old land, legs wide apart, skirt over her knees, shouting encouragement at them.

For a while Ginger dozed in the kind heat, aware that he was thirsty but the Scotch was nearer than the water-pump so he made do. Might as well make a night of it by the fire he decided, banking it up clumsily. 'Get along my lovelies,' he murmured as the last of the woodlice hurriedly scuttled in a state of deep shock from the rapidly warming wood; jumping recklessly into the flames. Tutting he picked out a log on which one was wavering, flicked it off on to the boards and replaced it.

He crossed lurchingly to the window, crashing into the table on the way. Outside, the night was utterly still. Bereft of leaves Calvin's poplar fence beyond the lawn made a faint clacking sound, something disturbing its broom-like branches, causing them to rub together. No dead leaves blew on the gravel path nor did an owl or night bird shatter the crisp winter silence or fly against the white moon. Sharper than usual, the dark lines of the hills stood out on the sky – not a cloud moving towards them or away. There was no sound, no light to indicate that a small settlement of humans lived and loved a few miles west or that in any given direction a half day's walk would come up with the image of a forge, a homestead, or the view of the trunk route below. From all he could see, Ginger could have been alone on a black rib of land in the middle of the darkest ocean. In a moment of blinding clarity, with the help of the alcohol, it suddenly came to him that it was *he* who was wrong; *he* who owed Lizabeth an apology; *he* who ought to be asking forgiveness of her!

Hardly had the thought settled than he must communicate it to her. If she would not see him, which he now understood, at least she would let a detective pass a letter to her. It had been his determination to get rid of Frank, his lack of interest in any reconciliation which had pushed her to the brink. Under everything had been his unyielding jealousy of another man. He had even allowed it to come between him and Ceci. In haste he banked up the fire and ravaged Ceci's desk for paper and pen.

'My dear Lizabeth,' he began.

Struggling to make the pen keep up with his thoughts, the alcohol made his brain slow, the fire made him sleepy . . .

Resting on the journey, Little Annie still sleeping on his shoulder, Reg recalled that he was homeless; that Ceci whom he had got from the Immigration in order to do her a favour had destroyed everything he had ever set out to do. Because of her he had lost his original homestead which was his birthright. Condemned to a wandering life, he had finally made good – only to be deprived of his loving woman by Ceci's reckless gift. Before Annie he hadn't loved himself enough to care. Now there was Little Annie to think of. Who would employ him, a man approaching sixty? Without a younger wife, did he not look ridiculous carting a toddler around? At fifty-nine he was a conspicuous failure.

Against his shoulder Little Annie stirred: 'Uncle Pieter?' she murmured. '*Har Mamma kommet?*'

'What?' Reg said gruffly.

'Is Mummy back yet?' Little Annie asked.

Unable to believe her eyes Ceci arrived on the devastated landscape of Reg's backblock. Sinking from her horse she bit down on her fingertips. A large buck rabbit washing its ears in Reg's doorway observed her. The door stood open. Clearly the place was derelict. Clearly he had been chased away and somehow the seemingly gentle creatures, the rabbits, had been responsible for it all. Peering around in the moonlight at the bare land she sensed that, without

505

intending it, once again she had sown the seeds of destruction in Reg's life.

Suddenly awakening, unsure of where he was, what he was doing, Ginger felt the many sheets of paper beneath his hands. Cramped with the cold he crossed to the fire with them and tried to focus on the blurred handwriting. Why had he been sitting at Ceci's desk? The collapsed fire had spread its embers to the far sides of the great hearth and good as gone out.

'See that won't happen again,' he murmured, kicking in the rest of the logs and replenishing the supply from the woodpile. As a man building a house he set the logs, one on top of another, like the Great Wall of China. Now he could see what he was writing! Hastily scrawling 'Lizabeth' on an envelope to alert himself to the urgency of his task should he doze off again before dawn came, Ginger leaned back against the side of the hearth and continued writing. It was all coming out. The clarity was blinding! The happiness and peace of mind he had reached, the sense of new life, of hope burgeoning within him had successfully overcome the alcohol-induced tiredness and warmth of the room which had sought to control his limbs. Determined to say it all, though his hand moved slower and slower and his head was heavy, word by word Ginger forced the message on.

Dawn could not be far off, Reg told himself as he headed towards Hexham, tormented with grief at the injustice of life, his child crying though he held her close to him. Through his mind rushed thoughts he dared not put into words yet wished to scream aloud. As his life encapsulated into one emotion he wanted to get his hands around Ceci

506

and strangle her. Never had he felt such concentrated anger in his life.

Though he was fairly sure he was on the right track – the buildings, not the shape of the land having changed – Reg saw a glow on the horizon. It could not be a town or he would have heard of it. In an instant he realized it was fire. Running to the top of the nearest hill to gain a better vantage point he realized with horror – Hexham was burning.

Chapter 37

Using his belt to tie Little Annie to a fence-post Reg rushed at the flames, his earlier wrath at Ceci displaced by an urgent need to save her. Shouting her name he burst into the trembling structure, dodging pockets of flame, and thundered up the great staircase, holding well in the blaze. There was no sound other than the wind playing with the fire, no sign of life. Rushing down again he tried to get into the front room – previously so grand – the room in which he had confronted Calvin so long ago, but on opening the door was met by a gust of flame and the wind blowing in from the garden. The room – the great hearth – all the finery was gone. Reg ran from the house, the door handle stuck to his melting flesh.

Outside by the fence Little Annie screamed in fear at the clouds of smoke rolling towards her, the wicked crackling coming from the old wooden structure as its walls and turrets plunged helplessly into the frightening yellow flower before her. She saw her father run, coughing, his face made up like a bogey man – his breath and eyes wild.

Reg heard her screams but for a moment could not see her. Hexham was different from how he remembered it. Hexham was gone! Quickly unfastening Little Annie he put her on his back and ran towards the hill lest the building, now in its final state of collapse, should topple towards them or send part of the fine roof – on the hot air currents circulating so freely – to land on them as they ran. 'Christ!' he murmured.

* * *

Ceci did not linger in the backblocks but, depressed by what she had seen, turned her horse and headed back for the security of Hexham. As she passed down the road the residents of the hamlet slept in utter stillness, no sound from their cows or even a dog. It could not be three o'clock for the cock had not started to crow. On Reg's side of the hamlet – almost as if reaching out for him – they had started building their church. Slowly, she picked out a word cut into a timber and rubbed with charcoal: Swedenborgians? Continuing on she did not press her horse. They had ridden to the backblocks at such a hard pace that in any other circumstances she would have permitted him to rest, would have changed him for another horse were she continuing on a journey. Diagonally the horse wended its way downwards, lifting its hooves over stones, slowly heading in the direction which meant home.

Fascinated by the fire Reg lingered on the outskirts. 'Can't be. Can't be in there,' he told himself, his early grief now forgotten, his mind filled with the ghastly image of Ceci burning to death while he rode towards Hexham cursing her. A spectre moved through the flames like a human running. Reg moved nearer: only a giant drape twisted around on itself, pulled and sucked by the air until it looked human. Suddenly the drape shot upwards, spreading into the sky, flaming and coming apart to skate away in erratic black patches, their edges dancing with flame. The sound of the burning was so intense, the crackling and thudding as ceilings caved and wooden walls giving up the struggle leant into the flames. Reg clutched Little Annie. The force of the fire was so great it had created a pocket sucking them in. Carefully planting one foot behind another they backed away.

Well before reaching Hexham Ceci had smelt burning.

It was odd in that the time of the year for burning off fields had passed; nor did anyone light bonfires after dark. The precise location of the fire she could not determine except that it was to the east of Moke if Moke was, indeed, in the dip she suspected. As the land turned on itself and she faced directly towards it she realized with horror that Hexham was burning.

'Get on!' she urged her horse but the beast, frightened by the smell of smoke now rolling towards them in great clouds, turned and tried to back off. Though she kicked and hit at it, it would not obey. Finally jumping down, unable to even pull the horse after her, Ceci left it and began to run forward in the direction of the flames. Then she saw it! There stood Reg, and behind him – Hexham burning! As she had destroyed his home, so had he hers! The man had set fire to the place!

Quietly she came up behind him, saw him watching the flames as if fascinated by them. What was there to say? Gradually it occurred to her that his shoulders were shaking, he was crying. 'Reg?' she said softly.

Spinning and determining she was not a ghost Reg rushed forward and wrapped her in his arms. 'I'm so glad you're safe!' he choked.

Confused by the event Ceci stepped back.

'What is it?' Reg asked, seeing her eyes open wide in panic.

'Ginger!' she shouted, rushing at the flames.

'I've been in – there's nothing there,' Reg contradicted. 'Get back!'

'The bedroom?'

'There was no one upstairs.'

Indeed there was no 'upstairs' left, Ceci realized, staring at the remains of the great staircase standing before the sky, the rubble around it already settling into grey dust. 'The front room?'

Reg took her shoulder and turned her around: 'I opened the door to it. You could see clear through to the garden.'

Ceci dropped to her knees and began to weep. Kneeling, Reg rubbed the back of her neck. He knew that nothing he might say could comfort her, that her suffering was now on a level with his own. Nonetheless he continued to rub her neck.

'Oh Reg,' she whispered, turning to him, burying her face in his chest. 'I had been so awful to him of late.'

'I know,' Reg murmured. It seemed the right thing to say. Gently he led her away from the dying fire, its fine ash blowing over what was once their lawn, no smoke even left to send to the sky. 'These old wooden buildings really go when they go,' he said.

Beyond speech, Ceci allowed him to lead her to a sheltered position behind Calvin's poplars where she found Little Annie crouching.

'Thought at first these poplars might catch,' Reg said. 'They didn't.'

Ceci stood looking about.

'Sit down,' Reg invited.

She did not want to sit, drink, eat or sleep. There was no activity which would satisfy her. Caught out of step with time she wanted to be back on her horse, hurrying up the gravel driveway towards the stables; to hear her key turn in the front lock and step into the hall, to look up the great staircase and call, 'Ginger? Faith!' Never more! Above her the stars looked down with utter indifference on the winter landscape. They did not even notice the two human beings and small child huddled by a break of poplars next to a large black smudge on the landscape, not a stone's throw away from their original dwelling.

* * *

The mass of timber Ginger had piled in the hearth had not actually caught by the time he left Hexham. Consequently he was cold. It was one thing to suddenly become aware he had desired to cause pain, to punish even his daughter by confronting her with that poor woman beyond the tracks in Dunedin and stir her guilt by showing the intolerable human suffering she had caused by disobeying him. It was another thing to accept that he had actually wanted to possess Frank's wife in order to even the score with Frank, and yet another to realize he had slept with the barmaid as a mere substitute for his thwarted anger. He had been a prize chump, he realized. He certainly wouldn't ask Lizabeth to come home, yet hoped she would forgive him. Getting to his feet he hurried urgently from the room, slapping his arms for warmth. He ran his hands along the rack selecting his thickest greatcoat, carefully tucked the vital letter in an inner pocket and set out to get it to Lizabeth as fast as possible. When all was said and done, he realized as he swung on to his horse, now that he understood he felt a great deal better about himself.

Leaving Hexham at a good gallop he set out for the trunk route. Behind him the old house rested against the hills, the sky studded with stars which reached on endlessly into the bright cold of night. On a good day a loaded coach could make 123 miles over rough country so a man, even should he fall from his horse, as long as he fell easy, could expect to do a deal better than that.

Coming up on the trunk route and spotting a coach in the distance ahead, he put on a final spurt. The effect of staying upright on the moving beast was proving hard and his hands ached from the cold. Coming abreast he called to the driver, asked the startled man to pull over at the next hotel, then fell to following him. When the building loomed up Ginger loosed his horse with a shout in the direction of the stable boys' quarters and boarded the coach.

Inside, wedged between farmers who'd travelled through the hours of darkness to reach a certain point by dawn, he was soon nodding, soon asleep. Around him their voices swelled, talking about a stock sale they were organizing as a matter of urgency; about stockyards; prices; falling prices; about what they would like to do to the original 'philanthropist' who'd released the first pair of rabbits on sand hills at the southern tip of Invercargill.

'Would you believe the man was actually a doctor? Actually the Superintendent of the Province of Southland?'

'Bloody fool needs his hide thrashing.'

With a lurch the coach stopped.

'Out! Out you get!' the voice of the driver rang. Forcing his eyes open Ginger saw below him the urgent ruddy face peering up, the man's dark coat, his freezing bulk silhouetted against the greying light of dawn.

'Hurry and close the door,' a voice opposite Ginger muttered.

Easily Ginger swung to the ground and paid.

'Over there,' the man said, taking the money. 'Follow the rails.'

'Oh, ah. Thanks.'

In the next minute the coach had gone. Ginger looked around. Dawn was coming and he had made good time. He should be in Christchurch by eight A.M. Stepping on to the track he stared in that direction. The rails were absolutely straight as far as the eye could see – not needing to waver to accommodate woods, hills or even river beds. 'This must be the flattest piece of land in the world,' he grumbled, beginning to walk up the plain towards Christchurch.

Gradually the rails took on a kind of mechanism that

hypnotically drew him on, lifted his feet from one wooden sleeper to the next and carried them over the stones between. Briefly he tried walking on a rail for variety but the balancing was too hard.

As the light cleared and day came in, clouds from the coast rose above land level, slanting the sun, bouncing it at an angle off the rails into his eyes till his head ached and he longed for a good sleep and some breakfast. Still he walked on. He was walking quite automatically when he was struck in the back by the first train of the day, the express thundering from Dunedin to its seven A.M. rendezvous in the great city of the plain – Christchurch. As the train bore down on time, the fireman turning to stoke up the boiler, Ginger continued walking. There was a pounding in his head, a throbbing in his feet as if the whole world was about to explode. In the next minute, it did.

Turning to face front the driver was curious. Had they hit something? Briefly he thought of stopping but the express must never be late. He leaned over the iron half-door and peered out on the train curling along behind him under the great cloud of smoke issuing from above his head and blown back down by their speed. They were going very fast. They were making good time . . .

Walking by the track two children on their way to a remote schoolhouse found the body and went for their parents. They stood back watching a policeman slip his hand into the pockets of the greatcoat and draw out their contents.

'Letter for someone called Lizabeth,' the constable said, trying to keep his voice steady. 'He seems to have had gingerish hair.' Beyond that it would be difficult to say, he concluded, the train having made a right mess of the man.

* * *

514

As the Dunedin express pulled into Christchurch Faith reminded herself that this was the most precious day of her life. The sister who had interviewed her had asked her to explain the phrase: 'Time belongs to God' and although she had never thought about it, in struggling for an answer had obviously said the right thing. It was as if someone had been putting words in her mouth. Never had she spoken so honestly before in her life and it seemed the more openly she replied, the more appropriate her answers were.

'No,' she had said, 'I had certainly never thought of becoming a nun. My reasons could not be more selfish. Father Mulligan said that no one else would send me to work in the Maori areas.'

'You mean no one would clothe and feed you?' the sister asked.

'I'm sure I can manage that,' Faith shrugged. 'If the food runs out, I die. It's while I'm alive I want to put my time to use.'

'You don't consider it sailing under a false flag?'

'Not consciously.'

'What is so wonderful about the Maoris?' the sister asked.

If it cost her the interview, Faith was determined not to skate on the thin ground between civility and fact. 'They are divine creations,' she replied. 'I feel they have a better grasp of it than us.'

'But that is due surely to their social organization being closer to the Christ life than ours – '

'I need them. That is why I want to be with them; perhaps I should have gone and asked them if they would have me. I may not have anything to give.'

'You are welcome to join us,' the older woman said softly, 'if that is where your work lies.'

Her heart spilling over, Faith leaned and grasped the sister's hand. As she walked from the house, phrases from their conversation ran in her mind. They had talked about serious topics, not the useless social patter her days in Christchurch had been filled with, nor the carefully structured 'wadding' she churned out in Moke to make people happier in their circumstances. The woman had said, 'You will work in health and education in primitive conditions. It will mean the North Island.' Though she had warned of resistance to new ways, of revenge raids, of serious illness and a lack of hygiene — Faith had readily agreed — almost with indifference to herself, savouring the freedom to agree to go anywhere. If anything, she felt spoiled and selfish. It was the people who stayed behind and hung on to their obligations that deserved medals.

'Don't expect too much in the way of congratulations from Father,' Kevin warned her as, like co-conspirators they sat sipping coffee at the wrought-iron table which Michael had installed in the garden. 'Did she talk to you about prayer?'

Faith shook her head: 'I'm not ready for that.'

'I'm being sent to Wellington.'

'That's wonderful,' Faith cried, grasping his hand.

'I suppose we can visit — but you can hardly stay at the seminary!'

'I wasn't surprised at you, Kevin,' Faith said.

'Nor me you.'

'This calls for a celebration,' said Michael, lurching towards them across the grass, an open bottle of flat champagne in his hand. 'If you two stuffed shirts know how to celebrate, that is!'

'Don't be so prudish, Michael,' Faith teased. 'I can remember *you* being quite straight-laced at times!'

At that moment a series of shrieks from above made it clear Michael's 'young lady' had chosen to stay over. 'Where is my dress?' she shouted, flinging open an upper window.

Glancing up, Faith saw her wrapped in Michael's bedsheet.

'Tell that beastly brother of yours that if he doesn't return my belongings I shall leave like this!' the girl shrilled.

Michael ignored her. 'Looks like no contest for the old homestead then,' he grinned, pouring the flat champagne. 'Thought I might use the place as a stud farm.'

'What's wrong with down here?'

'Everyone and their uncles raising horses down here. Besides, why lease land when you've got it?'

'It's the house he's thinking about,' Faith said knowingly. 'Nice for parties.'

Michael winked. 'Mind you,' he admitted, 'there's a lot of secrecy up there. No one would know what you were up to.'

'With women or horses?'

'Michael's afraid someone'll loose a filly in his field and get her back in the family way. He doesn't like competition,' Kevin explained. 'Our horse is finally carrying.'

'If it turns out to be a *male* – ' Michael began.

'Who's the father?'

'Wouldn't you like to know,' he grinned.

'It was that colt, wasn't it?' Faith suddenly realized. 'The three-year-old. You "borrowed" him! You sly beggar! Did you pay his owner?'

'He should pay me for giving his lad such a good time!' Michael replied.

'I thought we might convert Hexham into a preparatory school,' Kevin joked. 'What do you think, Faith?'

'Me? How about an – '

'The hell with both of you!' Michael laughed, wandering back to the house with the empty champagne bottle. 'Listen! Let's all go up there this weekend and put it to them?'

By the time Ceci, Reg and Little Annie reached Theresa's house, it was well light.

'Come in, come in,' she said. She did not remember Reg nor even any talk of him so long had he been gone, but whoever the man was, clearly there was something wrong with him. Ceci too looked out of her mind with grief.

'Hexham is burned,' she sobbed. 'I think Ginger was inside.'

Theresa frowned. Now that the front door was open, she could distinctly smell burning on the damp morning air .

'The land is as flat as if it had never been there! Oh, Theresa!' Ceci cried, bursting into tears.

Keeping a hand on Little Annie's shoulder, Reg stood respectfully back, his hat behind him. Their own relationship was far too complicated to explain to the woman but clearly she was a good person, one at least who would take care of Ceci.

'You stop looking at me like that, you, and sit down,' Theresa urged.

Reg sat.

'Come here, little girl,' Theresa said. 'Cathline! Get in here and make some warm milk for this child,' her voice rang out. 'Give them all warm milk.'

Reg heard a mumbling in the kitchen and the raised voice of Theresa: 'Don't argue with me! Go and borrow some!' He saw a tousled-haired girl of about eighteen peep

518

curiously in at him, her large bare feet leaving steam marks on the cold floor, confusion on her face.

Standing up, Reg saw the chair he had sat on was streaked in soot and as he dusted at his hair, fine fragments of charcoal floated down. Behind Ceci the woman was preparing to light her boiler, having the good sense to keep the flames from view. As he watched Ceci leaning on her and felt her pain, he was aware that a new chapter in their lives was beginning; it was as if they had both completed a very long journey which had simply brought them back to each other again.

'Ginger might not have been in that fire, you know,' he heard the woman telling Ceci. In his heart he knew different. She was even more alone now than the day he had first got her from the Immigrant Barracks. What's more, he realized, this time he would have to treat her better. Somehow the woman had become his responsibility; it had been decided by whoever it was Up There that arranged things. Uneasy at being personally confronted with a Great Plan involving himself, Reg shifted slightly on his feet and pulled Little Annie closer to him. He had the feeling that they were not alone in the room, that some great Player with a full deck was watching them and deciding what card to pull next.

Chapter 38

In a burst of generosity characteristic of him since getting on good terms with money, Michael had hired a coach, complete with streamers and fog horns to crest all the way up to Hexham and make a grand entry there. Still the big spender he had ordered from a Christchurch hotel hampers containing turkey, ham, smoked chicken, dressed salmon and a variety of imported goods such as figs and oranges that were hard to come by in the colony.

'They'll like all this,' he said, casting a lingering look into the game hamper before reclosing its lid. 'Funny how we made do with mutton. Don't think I ever tasted turkey till Christchurch.'

'Turkeys are hard to raise,' Kevin pointed out. 'And who's going to knock off a porker once a week so's you can have bacon?'

'Let us go!' shouted Miranda, Michael's female, who had come along to display herself to any who would look as the coach bumped through the clusters of dwellings, not yet townships, marking the route inwards.

'Probably where oxtail soup came from,' Michael continued, ignoring her. 'Easy to snip the tail off the beast and leave it functioning. Better yet a neighbour's beast!'

'Stop being so positively revolting,' Miranda pleaded. 'One could retch!'

With great clamour and noise the coach party set off, Kevin and Faith ensconced in the middle.

'Take this, darling,' Michael called, giving Miranda a screamer. Miranda blew into it. '*Wheee*' came the screech as the screamer unrolled and shot out like a trumpet before her. 'Marvellous! *Wheee, Wheee, Wheee.*'

Sober Christchurch families hurried to their windows, incredulous at the sound, and also the sight of the coach decked with bunting.

'A trumpet!' a child squealed. 'That lady's got a trumpet!'

Hardly a lady, thought her mother, gently drawing her away. Clearly the party had been drinking.

'It's the lad from the track celebrating again,' the husband murmured.

'Oh!' Instantly interested the woman was back at the window. Whatever he did, Michael was seen as becoming increasingly colourful. There was even a rumour he might run for local government.

As they crossed the plain and ascended higher Faith's thoughts ran away with her. In front, the good-natured fun of Michael and Miranda tinkled on the air; inside her, the promise of her own future throbbed.

'Oh let's stop!' called Miranda. 'Anyone in favour of stopping say Aye.'

'What for?'

'For a rest!'

At the next hostelry they pulled in, Miranda anxious to rearrange her hair and get more cover on her shoulders. Nudity was all very well but away from an audience and with the horses whizzing along at a veritable gallop, too cold.

'I say. Look at this. Get over here,' Michael called. Kevin ambled over. 'Looks like Father's horse.'

Kevin shrugged.

'You know more about horses than me but it's his bridle all right.'

'I'm not in the habit of being wrong about horses,' Michael said, looking about. 'Boy!'

'He left it, sir, to join the early coach – couple of days ago.'

'The sly dog,' Michael murmured approvingly. 'Probably said he goes to our place.'

'Should we turn back?' Faith asked, coming over.

'Not with all this loot,' sang Miranda, fiddling with the top of a champagne bottle with her bare toes. 'Enjoy!'

The carnival moved on.

The letter had been carefully opened and resealed. It took only the mention of the name 'Hexham' to guide the officer's thinking in the right direction. There were other names too, but the relationship between the writer of the letter and the place Hexham was enough that a man from Christchurch be immediately despatched to Moke to further the enquiry . . .

Tramping through the cold ashes, since rained upon, the inspector felt something shatter under his feet. 'Look at this,' he said, bending to pick up a couple of framed pictures.

'What is it?'

'Picture of . . .' His jacket elbow wiped at the cracked glass which obligingly fell away. '. . . a couple on their wedding day.' He glanced at the one underneath which had been protected from the fire. 'Here they are again – with their kids this time.'

'Not this lot, is it?'

The inspector shook his head: 'Dunedin. Recognize the skyline.' He threw the pictures back in the ashes.

'You'll have to tell that woman it wasn't suicide. Clear from the tone of his letter the man felt he never had more to live for.'

'Must have been quite a big place,' the inspector said, staring around at the extent of the burned area. 'I'd heard of it of course but never seen it.'

'Wind spread the ash –'

'No. You can see by the perimeter of the ash the size the place must have been.'

Silently the old house gave out its memories of blue curtains fluttering at a child's room above, six-year-old Olwen carefully closing the front door and tiptoeing across the lawn in the summer morning to rouse her friend Jock in the stables; the silent faces of Mrs Laird and Ceci peering at Calvin below as he stooped to pull a weed from the path; Jock's naked buttocks vanishing into the bushes as Mrs Laird hastily swished the curtains to, concealing the sight from embarrassed party guests . . .

Though winter in the southern hemisphere, it was now summer in the north and, leaving England, Olwen considered how she would run the seasons and be back in Wellington by spring. Hot as was the day she bade her English cousins farewell at Plymouth, Olwen knew that in her homeland it was the cusp of winter.

'Goodbye!' she called. On the dock below, Bella, May, Florrie and Tring – the children of her mother's sister Molly with whom she had lived from the age of seven to fourteen, attended school and shared the greatest adventures – now looked up at her as distant strangers. It would be a relief to sink into the anonymity of the ship; to be with people who did not remember her as someone she no longer was, people who, like her, had changed beyond friends' recognition. Yet they had been good to her and she had been grateful for their support.

'Goodbye!' she called again.

In no sense had the trip to England been wasted, she

told herself, returning to her second saloon cabin rather than stand gawping as the last piece of land slipped away. Let others crowd the rails: for her it was the third time. She intended to gather in her strength and on her return to Wellington reclaim it, take it by storm. Setting out to locate Edmund's family, fate had put every conceivable obstacle in her way yet she had not given up. She had commissioned a lawyer to make contact for her and set up an appointment and, during the necessary wait, had, as the English said, 'made the best of it'. 'The best of it' had taken her to Huntingdon for the simple reason that she could remember seeing on Calvin's tomb: 'Born Huntingdon, 1846.'

Arriving at Wisbech in the windblown fens – in a flat land so different from home – she had made the remarkable discovery that Calvin had been kept apart from local children; that folk had not known of his existence till he had been seen at a window. Whether this was because of ill-health, shameful damage to him caused by chastisement or even the fear he might bring others into the house, she could not determine. Suddenly, it seemed, he had begun to reach out and in the next minute the estate had been sold and the family had gone to New Zealand, to one of the loneliest places Olwen knew from experience they could possibly have found. There was no word of how – or where – Calvin's father had died.

Returning to London and finding her lawyer's efforts were still wanting in results, Olwen had continued on to Bath to visit the grave of Granny Bath, as she had called Calvin's mother, though she could not now remember having met her. Here she had made yet another discovery ... On Mrs Laird's return to England following Calvin's marriage to Ceci – which had in effect forced her to leave – the woman had been obsessed by guilt on the subject of her dead husband. In her final delirium, mixed with protestations of deep love for Calvin had been the recurrent theme of her husband's having 'been caused to pass on ...' With the maturity she had acquired, however, Olwen settled for laying a wreath and simply making a note of Bath's fashions and architecture. One day, though, she might share some of this with her mother ...

Back in London, as they said, 'third time lucky', she prepared to meet Edmund's family. Her anger against Edmund had dissipated somewhat yet she had not forgiven him or his parents for ignoring her written pleas for a divorce, nor for not even bothering to inform her that they had received her letters. I would have been married to Marshall by now, she told herself briskly, aware at the same time that she was glad it had not happened. Even on her way to the meeting arranged by the lawyer, her mind was toying with design, not Marshall. In fact she wondered at times what she had ever seen in him. There were far more men in London who had taken her eye. It was the lack of opportunity in New Zealand, the distinct watering down of everything from food to fashion which had made him seem grand. Would he even seem interesting when she got back? It was not Marshall she wanted to meet on her return but Happi she realized! But all that to one side, she had some positively wicked designs and from now on intended to travel regularly between Europe and New Zealand to see that she stayed on top. First, however, the business with Edmund. She would leave England a free woman even if it meant dragging herself through acres of mud in a divorce court.

'This is the house,' the lawyer said, pausing outside a pleasant Regency house.

'Aren't you coming in?'

'I think not. You will receive my bill in the morning.'

As she touched the brass bell-pull Olwen found difficulty

remembering Edmund's face. It would be very awkward if his wife opened the door which, of course, would account for the lawyer's desire to avoid an embarrassing situation. She glanced over her shoulder. Already the cowardly creature was scuttling down the road.

'Miss Laird?'

Looking up Olwen saw an elderly face she hardly recognized.

'Come in.'

The next half an hour had been one of the most painful in Olwen's memory. Edmund's father, now a broken man needing constant attention, bore no resemblance to the harsh military creature she remembered who had been so set against her marriage to his son. The shocking news that followed perhaps went some way to explain his decline. Edmund, their only son, had died of diphtheria shortly after Olwen had left India.

'I'm so sorry!' Olwen gulped. All that time she had been free and hadn't known it! 'You might have told me.'

Edmund's mother's hands moved vaguely about, indicating the extent of their misfortune, the reduced circumstances they were now living in.

'We didn't know if we were coming or going,' she murmured. 'I'm sorry. I suppose I ought to have – '

'But you didn't know where I was.'

The woman shrugged. She was not sure if she had even received any of Olwen's letters. There may have been difficulty with the stamp.

'What did you say your name was?'

Olwen rose to leave. It seemed that the poor woman had the greatest difficulty functioning in the modern world of opening, reading and replying to letters without the active assistance of her husband. 'Do you have anyone to look after you?' she asked from the door.

The woman shook her head.

Water under the bridge, Olwen told herself, crossing the street to sit in a square inside iron railings. Beneath the plane trees she watched children trying to play in their stiff clothes under the stern eyes of nannies. Her glance moved up the trees' speckled brown and yellow trunks to lacy branches dangling ochre balls on a grey sky. She would always remember these trees, leaves stuck to wet pavements, peeling yellow bark silhouetted against the slate-coloured façades of government buildings. She had not even felt bitter about Edmund. 'Nanny, that lady's laughing,' she had heard a child say. The point was, she realized, standing, it had been her own secrecy and lack of trust in Marshall that had brought about her situation. Closing the gate of the square behind her, she resolved that from that moment, she would live straight as well as strong.

Now that he was dead she found herself thinking with affection of Edmund. Had anyone gone to his funeral? Diphtheria was rumoured to be an ugly death, people choking on their own saliva. The image of Edmund under his mosquito netting, the old Indian woman servant, who had packed her trunk for her when Edmund had cast her out, tending him in his last hours lingered. Just a bony brown hand with small command of English patting at his forehead with a wet rag saying, 'Achaa, achaa.' He would not have been prepared. You could meet a person in good spirits on Friday and by Monday they would be dead of diphtheria. Shuddering, Olwen stepped carefully over an open drain.

Feeling the need for fresh air she went out to stand on the deck and breathed deeply. She was lucky to have come away from England with little more than a portfolio of sketches.

'You've missed it!' a young man further up the rail called.

'What?'

'Old Limey!' he smiled tearfully.

Olwen felt a surge of freedom: 'Oh.'

'Are you going to New Zealand?' he asked, somewhat naïvely.

'I live there,' she replied, trying to keep the supercilious ring from her voice.

The young man moved closer, hoping she would know a thing or two about his intended homeland. I'm not getting caught this way twice, Olwen told herself, remembering William.

'You'll have to leave me,' she said not unkindly. 'I'm thinking.'

How were they all now? Ginger and Faith and Kevin and Michael and Hexham? Her mother's friend Annie? Her father Reg? She was returning to a slow, backward place where nothing happened. Myra, of course, would have married Marshall Cavanaugh: that was one change. Gwen, Hetty and Muriel's faces would be worth seeing when she presented her European line for the new century, she supposed.

Sailing home Olwen could not know that the last woman to be hanged in New Zealand had gone to her rest; that Faith and Kevin had chosen the ministry and Michael was even now toying with Miranda's 'idea' that he run for local government. She did not know her stepfather had been killed and Hexham burned down or that the conflicting paths her half brothers and sisters had chosen would, through her friendship with the Maoris, align her with Faith and Kevin and against the politician Michael.

* * *

Although Ginger's funeral had been published in the Christchurch press in the hopes of attracting Lizabeth, she had not appeared. The people of Moke, however, still in deep shock at the bare landscape, crowded the event, their eyes dusting Miranda as she pressed a large handkerchief to Michael's nose and Faith, her mind's eye examining her earlier cruelties to her father. Unremembered by Moke, Reg lingered on the outskirts, wondering at the size of the family Ceci had inherited. Bereft of tears Ceci listened to the priest's words, feeling that now Ginger was dead, she was saying goodbye to her life with the Catholic Church.

'This man stood for human affection and social justice,' the priest said quietly, 'It is the ultimate humanity of such a man that makes him live in our hearts.'

Faith dipped her head. For she and Kevin the shock, coming at a time when each thought they had become immune to suffering of the common type, brought humility.

'Let us thank God,' the priest continued, 'that from his letter we know that when God called him, this man had hope in his heart, forgiveness on his lips and a belief in the future together of those he loved.'

As Moke listened to the priest comparing Ginger to St Peter, the founder of the Catholic Church, with his impetuousness, his willingess to rush into situations, often unwisely, and take on all comers, they asked themselves where was Myra. Humanity made mistakes, the priest said, yet admitted when it was wrong. People nodded. From the day when he'd dared to unhitch Reg's horse to the day he'd galloped after the sheep dealer and forced open the minister's door in the matter of the crumpled wedding banings — Moke agreed Ginger had been impulsive. Remembered, Ceci smiled.

*　*　*

She had not opened his letter to Lizabeth but passed it to the priest, aware of his position as keeper of confidences. From his eulogy, however, she knew it had been a letter of reconciliation and now that it had been returned to her, she must hold on to it until such time as her path crossed with Lizabeth's. The priest told her there was nothing she need know about it, nothing concerning her, but that perhaps, as it had been Ginger's intention, she could give it to her.

Picking up the threads of her life once Ginger had been laid to rest in Moke's tiny cemetery, Ceci realized that her final duty as Myra's surrogate mother required that she visit Wellington and spend time with her talking about her father. Why the girl had not been at the funeral was a mystery. Her husband certainly had the money and travel was no longer difficult. Afraid that Ginger might slip from Myra's mind, Ceci decided to hurry while grief was fresh on her face to share it with her. Otherwise the girl would one day waken to the fact that her father was dead and she had not mourned him.

'Possibly your Olwen will be there by then,' Theresa had offered.

'I wouldn't count on that,' Ceci smiled. 'Do you want to come, Reg?'

'Me and Little Annie'll stay here,' Reg replied. 'Too cold to be on that steamer yet.'

The truth was, Reg knew, that he was a landlubber and afraid to cross the drink!

As Ceci said goodbye to Theresa, Reg and Little Annie she caught a look in Reg's eye which made her aware that her life with Ginger – which began in desire – had not been all that she had expected, whereas his with Annie had exceeded the wildest imaginings his brain could engender. Reg had arrived. He had won. Before her the frightening gap the fire had opened up, that had wiped out all she had ever done and stripped her of the justification of belonging to a husband, made her feel fear and a void opening. For the third time this had happened. And this time not a stone's throw from the hovel where it had all started. Was there some force in those stones which drew her back repeatedly, repeatedly destroyed her? All her life since coming to New Zealand had vanished, leaving her only the obligation to visit others.

'You take care of yourself, girl,' Reg said in a rough voice as she scrambled on to Moke's trap which would take her to the main trunk route north. 'Mind you don't get your feet wet.' He cracked her an uneven smile.

Ceci grinned gratefully. One way and another things were moving very fast these days.

Chapter 39

As Olwen entered Wellington Bay her eyes sought out the caves and rocky inlets, traced the bare hills with their scattering of shrubs where she and Marshall had picnicked. Around her immigrants peered anxiously into the placid waters, frowning at their depth or searched rugged cliffs wondering which obscured the town.

'There it is!'

By now wooden houses could be seen scrambling up green-splashed hillsides; the occasional glint of metal flashing in the sun. Sounds were coming to them: a shouting and cheering.

'What a country!' she heard a man murmur.

Olwen smiled. It would be a different story when gale-force winds ripped through Cook Strait, turned on the harbour and gave them all a belting!

Even as she began recognizing streets and buildings Olwen's pulse quickened. From her vantage point there seemed to have been reclamation going on so that now there was more flat land at the water's edge and various quays she had not remembered having seen. Would the house in Khandallah still stand? She recognized the fire station, picked out the band rotunda. Ahead of them a small West Coast steamer laden with coal patiently waited to enter a wharf where carts for hire and carts bringing goods to be taken back on the steamer jostled. Already excited, as they put about to tie up at Queen's Wharf, the reason for the shouting and cheering became apparent. There, on Jervois Quay Wharf an official ceremony was going on, the wharf being jam-packed with smartly dressed people all facing towards a platform from which various personages were making speeches.

'Looks like the Prime Minister's there,' she heard a man with field glasses say.

'And His Excellency the Governor.'

The woman with him wrenched the glasses off him. 'My word!' she said, putting them to her face. 'Lady Constance Knox and the Countess of Ranfurly! Whatever is it about?'

'Probably a contingent leaving for the South African War,' a traveller guessed.

It was then that Olwen glimpsed the soldiers, massed by their hundreds, in identical uniforms which must have given some workshop a good deal of trade. 'Volunteers,' she heard a voice say. She pressed forward. Clearly Wellington had never seen such a spectacle. The ship awaiting the volunteers was decked with bunting, patriotic songs throbbed from a thousand throats – it being seemingly agreed there was no finer thing a young man could do than rush off to die of a mysterious disease far from his homeland. With their love of fighting, their appreciation of vigour in battle, surely the Maoris would be there! But though she searched, Olwen could find not one. The word 'Empire' floated towards her from a voice enlarger. So New Zealand was trying to get on to the world stage at last, she told herself!

Having put her trunk in storage Olwen fought her way along Lambton Quay through out-of-towners revelling in the military music. Up every turning and alley, walking sticks, handkerchiefs and ribbons were being waved and beyond the massed heads rifles as thick as corn stalks in a field bristled. It was as if the entire population of Wellington had set out to position themselves between her and the woman who held the key to Khandallah. Even as she climbed higher and looked back, though the rigging and masts of the berthed vessels could be seen and the hills beyond, all else was blocked by the surging throng. How likely was it that the lady who held the key to Khandallah would not be amongst them? It was hardly a day to have returned home!

As the afternoon waned she climbed to Khandallah congratulating herself. She had the key! Had it been the levity of the day that had persuaded the woman to put her in charge of the house again or had nobody, indeed, been interested? The feel of the key jingling in her pocket was good. To have her old place back was a distinct feather in her cap – besides which she had plans for that place.

Myra laid her book down. Everything there was to see in Wellington she had seen, all the people had been met, so they were, in fact, no longer colourful or exciting. Some, she concluded, like James, were unforgivably dull.

'Still thinking about your father?' Marshall asked kindly, glancing at her.

Tempted to sit on his knee, Myra shook her head. Though he had worn her on his arm like a hastily plucked flower when she'd arrived in Wellington, she knew her 'refreshing innocence' had palled; in fact needed to be replaced with something else. But what?

Seeing her eyes fill with tears Marshall crossed to her: 'It's a tragic loss but you have me. Your sisters and brothers have no one.'

'I must make an effort, mustn't I?' Myra sniffed. 'What do you suggest I do?'

Marshall frowned. 'You could begin preparing for Ceci's visit,' he concluded.

Perhaps she had better do something, Myra thought, rising, before her idleness irritated Marshall.

* * *

Entering their house Ceci sensed the sadness. 'Is Olwen back yet?' she casually asked.

There was a silence.

'Why I – I don't know,' Marshall stammered.

'I'm thinking she may have returned to Khandallah.' Myra looked pained.

'We could send a runner up to find out,' Marshall offered. 'The least we could do.'

'I expect you'd like to see Olwen again, wouldn't you, Myra?' Ceci asked, seeing how unhappy the girl looked.

'Listen – I'll go,' Marshall declared.

'I'll come with you,' Myra said firmly.

'Wait,' said Ceci, alert to an atmosphere. 'If Olwen had returned I'm sure she would have called here.'

'We'll send a man,' Marshall insisted. 'That's settled. Now if you ladies will excuse me?'

'Myra,' Ceci began as Marshall left. 'I want to talk to you about the last months of your father's life.'

'Why didn't he come up and see me?'

'He thought he had all the time in the world.'

'I couldn't go to his funeral because we didn't get word in time.'

'That's all right.'

'And the steamers don't run to schedule and it can be very difficult living far away in a horrid city.'

'Whatever's the matter, dear?'

For answer Myra's eyes filled with tears. Ceci cradled her in her arms, sensing the child she still was, smoothed her hair and spoke softly. She had not realized the girl was so fond of her father. Indeed it was a good job she had come to stem such an outflow of grief, she thought. Better that Myra get it out of her system and get over it.

* * *

After the runner had left Olwen selected a cruel, almost military style dress which would announce to any who glimpsed her that fashion was not dead: it simply lived in Europe. The dress also signalled her return, its style showing that women were a force to be reckoned with, even given a South African war going on. It was important that a dress like this be worn with dignity however; anything gauche would undo its power. Because this meant holding the head high it could hardly be worn in country areas where one had continually to look where one trod. Carefully checking the distance between her front steps and the carriage, Olwen raised her head, crossed the short space to the conveyance Marshall had sent and climbed in.

The minute Marshall saw Olwen he realized he was seeing a strong, a magnificent and – he knew instinctively – a totally free woman; one unlikely to receive any suit he might even at this late date offer. In his heart he knew he had made a bad mistake – and he was sorry.

'Good day, Marshall,' Olwen murmured, extending her hand. 'Where's my mother?'

In the instant before Ceci ran forward to greet her, she saw Myra pull back as if, despite the fact that she had once hero-worshipped Olwen, at this moment Olwen was the last person in the world Myra wanted to see. She saw Marshall glance longingly at Olwen as if they had once been friends and, though it was ridiculous, sensed Myra felt threatened by this, or that a battle was about to be fought out . . .

'Mother!' urged Olwen. 'I'm so desperately sorry for your news.'

Afraid to burst into tears Ceci turned quickly to Marshall.

'I took the liberty,' he said, 'of including with my runner

a short note to your daughter informing her of recent events.'

Fear crossed Myra's face.

'The preparation was appreciated,' Olwen said flatly.

As Olwen clasped her, Ceci asked herself how she could ever have felt her life was empty? At twenty-six this handsome girl with the strength and purpose of Reg and that deep dignity, coming from God knew where, was with her.

Olwen looked at her mother. The open life she had led in the High Country had assured her, even at forty-two, of a complexion of a woman half her years.

'Let them be together,' Marshall whispered. 'You have the food to prepare.'

When Ceci and Olwen re-emerged the table had been spread in the form of a high tea, Marshall busily disposing of his guests in appropriate seats.

'You here, dear Ceci,' he said with genuine concern, pulling her chair back.

'And I think you – there,' he murmured, indicating a chair to Olwen.

Myra tensed. It was not right that Olwen should sit at the head of the table directly opposite her own husband at the other head. Nonetheless, for the sake of decorum she sat herself opposite Ceci.

'I was telling my daughter,' Ceci said, her hand on Olwen's wrist, 'of my concern for Little Annie.'

'She can come to me,' Olwen offered at once. 'I'll see she attends the best schools in Wellington.'

Admiration fleeted in Marshall's eyes.

'Are you sure she won't – compromise you?' Ceci asked carefully. 'You're quite alike across the eyes.'

'Same father!' Olwen retorted. 'I shall love having her.'

Vaguely Ceci sensed Marshall's irritation that Myra had not offered first. They were, after all, a married couple and nicely situated. Perhaps it would even start them on a family of their own.

'Reg will be grateful to you.'

'If you continue with Reg,' Olwen remarked as if they were alone at table, 'as Annie's stepmother – we're a family again.'

'Reg and I?'

'Why not marry him? You never did.'

'It would be – be . . .' Ceci paused, seeking a word.

'Because you once married his father?'

'Trite,' Ceci decided. 'No set of words could describe Reg's and my relationship.'

Marshall looked attentively from one woman to the other. A conversation like this was not often heard in the upper reaches of Wellington. Indeed he had once thought Olwen's circumstances shocking himself.

'You have chosen an exciting time to return,' he told Olwen. 'This will be the year for the politicians. New century and all that.'

'One can hardly miss the jingoism,' Olwen remarked drily without looking at him.

'So you saw the parade?'

'It was nothing to be proud of.'

'I think it's very exciting,' Myra chirped. 'All those brave men off to fight the Dutch – '

'The Boers,' Marshall corrected. 'And it's hardly bravery. If we do not help protect the British colonists in South Africa we can hardly expect the rest of the Empire to front up and help us. It was less than a sense of total duty that instigated that little display!'

'Help us how?' Ceci asked.

'Internal problems.'

Olwen laid down her fork.

'Are you talking about the Maoris?'

'There is certainly an – attitude towards them,' Marshall hedged. 'James can explain.'

'I had noted there were no Maoris amongst the regiments being farewelled,' Olwen said pointedly.

'That's because James,' put in Myra, 'thinks you can't have black men fighting white – even if the whites are our enemies.'

'Excuse me,' said Ceci. 'I didn't think from what I had heard that Maoris were black?'

'They aren't,' Olwen assured her.

'And I still think it's brave of the individual soldiers to go,' Myra insisted.

'I believe you once had an especial interest in Maoris, Olwen?' Marshall enquired.

'Whatever I have an especial interest in doesn't always come to pass,' Olwen informed him.

'Nonetheless I am sure that you are the creator of your own destiny,' Marshall returned.

'And you yours. I at least,' Olwen said pointedly, 'have every reason to be happy about the way my situation has turned out.' Marshall frowned. 'I learned that my dear husband Edmund – I believe I mentioned to you that I was married?'

Marshall swallowed, determined not to respond to her baiting in public.

'He apparently died of diphtheria a few days after I had left India.'

Although Marshall had expected a shock and had been ready to control his breathing, he could do nothing about the size of his pupils which Ceci now saw widening. 'I'm so very sorry,' he said in a studied voice.

'Yes, it was sad, wasn't it?' Olwen returned. 'I had a

feeling something like that had happened when I didn't hear from him. They were such — responsible people if I might use the word — *here*,' she said icily. 'His father never recovered from the shock — which as you can imagine has quite undone his mother.'

'An only child is often a mistake,' Marshall observed.

'I, fortunately,' said Olwen, getting in the last word, 'have a sister.'

As Myra would not accept any help with the dishes, at Marshall's suggestion Ceci and Olwen took the air outside.

'I don't like to seem nosy,' Ceci began, 'but were you two duelling in there?'

'That's the way people talk in London,' Olwen replied. 'Why?'

'I just saw Myra flinch a couple of times.'

In the kitchen Myra felt uncomfortable. She wished Olwen hadn't come back. She knew she had been very bad to her, and her conscience pained. Yet at the same time, she now felt terrified of her. 'I don't believe we should intrude on Ceci and Olwen at this time,' she told Marshall anxiously.

'You mean you would prefer Ceci to stay up at Khandallah?'

Myra counted to five before replying: 'Yes.'

Returning across Cook Strait Ceci thought of Lizabeth to whom she must one day deliver Ginger's letter. This act remained as an absolute duty. When the steamer docked at Lyttelton, on an impulse she walked into the administration building to check the shipping list and there found that Frank had 'gone north' two years previously, followed three weeks later by Lizabeth and the children. She stood in thought until the clerk asked what was wrong. Lizabeth in a wilderness of burned gums in some far Northland amongst kauri diggers, most of whom were rumoured to be Balkan immigrants: the thought was worrying. She could not cut the girl off as easily as Ginger's departure had slashed through her life as a married woman. The only inheritance he had left her to give his children was his caring . . .

As the plain fell behind her and the familiar shapes of the hills rose in a yellow haze to the sky, Ceci recalled the landscape was as she had seen it that day long ago from the back of Reg's cart when he had got her from the Immigrant Barracks. The emptiness, the lack of sound other than the wheels' crackle had then frightened her as had the man's reserve. Silently he had sat ahead of her, his wild hat rearing up against the sky, taking her into the hills. She recalled the sun had been sinking, slanting into her eyes and her head had throbbed. Surely they had stopped a night? As her mind ran backwards, the image of a dun-coloured tent emerging from the landscape stirred; outside it a four-foot woman with cruelly short hair and a sign 'GOLD BOUGHT MEALS'. Wondering what use she would be to anyone in the future Ceci recalled sharing that tent in a lonely place. The woman had supplied flour to the wanderers who'd passed through and kept secrets for the many. If I could find a place where two roads cross, she told herself, I'd be a tent woman. I know how she felt when she said, 'I do my bit'.

'I've decided,' Reg told her. He had come to meet Moke's trap and was in a hurry for her to get down so he could share his wisdom. 'We're going north.'

'*We*?' She could not believe her ears.

'You 'n' me together.'

'When I've just got back?'

'Rabbits have finished it for the South Island,' Reg went on. 'Not just the backblocks either. I bin readin' the papers.'

'Olwen has offered to take Little Annie.'

'Olwen's all right,' Reg replied, meaning she took after him and left no place for false sensibilities.

'She'll raise her like a lady,' Ceci smiled. 'But we can hardly move in with Olwen, not both of us as well.'

'I shall work,' Reg frowned.

Ceci surveyed his battered hat, his boots with their glorious disregard for laces. 'It was generous of Olwen to offer but she just meant Little Annie.'

'We have to go,' Reg reasoned, his mood dropping. 'No one would buy the bit of land at the dwelling what I gave Olwen, even if she had a mind to sell it. Good 'n' all as it is for an investment.'

'If you're imagining Wellington to be anything like Christchurch it — it's not,' Ceci assured Reg, trying to imagine him in a dinner-jacket, standing beneath a chandelier twiddling a cigar. The vision vanished.

'What's this Khandallah like?'

'Did Theresa suggest this to you?'

'She revived me spirits,' Reg said gratefully. 'Reminded me I got two daughters to support!'

As they turned in at Theresa's gate Little Annie came rushing from the open door but stopped at the sight of Ceci.

'Well, look who it ain't!' Reg said, crouching, extending his arms. Her fear of Ceci forgotten, Little Annie ran forward to be swung in the air and set down on Reg's shoulders. 'There yah go!'

As Ceci smiled at the child she had sung her first nursery rhyme, Little Annie burst into a wild giggle so like her mother Ceci almost turned and called: 'Where are you, Annie?' Reg's eyes filled with tears.

Theresa came with them to Lyttelton to see them off and observed that, with the child between them, they somehow looked 'right'. What lay ahead she dared not think, for Reg, willing though he was, must be nearing sixty. She saw Little Annie stumble on the gangplank and reach for Ceci's skirt; saw Ceci pick the child up and hand her to Reg as he ducked out of the way of tackle swinging from the steamer's derrick. Amongst its crates Ceci and Reg fought to keep a railside view, to keep Theresa in sight. Already the boat was rolling, making Reg feel bilious. He had never seen the land from the point of view of a ship before and felt it was not an experience he'd care to repeat. The noise and uncertainty of the movements around caused him an alarm he dare not show in front of women and children and the sooner they were under way the better.

'Excuse me,' he said to Ceci handing Little Annie back to her. 'Taking a look at the other side.'

Ceci figured he was going to be sick. Over the rail Reg leaned, the swell below sparkling, flicking bright pellets of water up at him. Beyond he could see the hills pressing in on them, protecting them from the ocean. Somewhere there would be a way out to sea he supposed – to the dangerous Cook Strait he'd tried not to hear about. The people on the steamer around him were not the sort he'd mixed with before and he feared, for a moment, he was making a mistake.

As they slid out to sea Reg leaned into the wind using it, Ceci suspected, as an excuse for the water in his eyes. How strange it was that she, who had once arrived alone and eager at this very port was now taking with her the man who had frightened her and he, because of her, was leaving the South Island for the first time in his life. It was as if they still had a journey before them; as if their real story was just beginning; as if Annie and Ginger had been much-loved stepping stones – but they too must finish together what they had started. She glanced across at Reg, his thin face cut against the choppy water, still deeply sad that Annie, the light of his life, had been taken from him. He looked at Ceci. It was as if their lives were parts of a symphony in which the same melodies were repeated, rising, at times distant from each other, but climaxing to subside together in a kind of peace. What had they to offer? They had arrived, Reg realized, at a companionship beyond the exchange of sex, beyond personal considerations. Glancing at him Ceci sensed they would discover some Truth about Life. It would be hard but they knew each other well. In her breast she felt the letter Ginger had written to Lizabeth.

'To the north, my girl,' Reg said, coming to stand beside her as the boat hit the warring waves.

'To the north,' she replied.

Steadying Little Annie's shoulder with one hand, Reg reached his other arm round Ceci to prevent her rolling with the boat's motion. She felt his rough thumb brush the edge of her hand. Already Ginger was part of a life she would remember with fondness but Little Annie and Olwen were their true children. Turning from Reg she looked piercingly around at the open seas . . . But the kind clouds came down obscuring their new horizon . . .